# Ruin & Redemption
## K. J. Fury

Copyright © 2024 by K.J.Fury

All rights reserved.

No portion of this publication may be reproduced or transmitted in any form or by any means, electronic or mechanical, including photocopying, recording, or any information storage or retrieval system, without prior written permission from the author, except as permitted by U.S. copyright law.

**Dedicated to:**

Every broken little girl, lonely teenager, and daring woman deserving of love and a happily ever after. I see you.

# Character Index

**Main Characters:**

Lilith - Sister to Ronan & Artemis. Best friend to Katie & Larissa.

Blaine - College roommate and best friend to Ronan & Artemis.

Ronan - Brother to Lily and Artemis' fraternal twin.

Artemis - Brother to Lily and Ronan's fraternal twin.

Katie - Lily & Larissa's best friend. Lives with Ronan & Artemis.

Larissa - Lily & Katie's best friend.

Elliott - Artemis' close friend in the inner circle.

**Secondary Characters:**

Kell – Lily's friend growing up.

Robert – Lily, Ronan, and Artemis' uncle.

Rye – Blaine's father's best friend. Blaine's temporary guardian.

Jenny – Blaine's housekeeper, chef, and estate manager.

# Playlist

'Chills – Dark Version' by Mickey Valen, Joey Myron

'Darkness' – FATE Pathways EP

'Streets' Doja Cat

'You Can Do It' – Ice cube Feat. Mack 10 & Ms Toi

'Frozen' by Madonna, Sickick

'Let's Go' by Trick Daddy, Bigg D, Twista

'See Me Fall – Y2K Remix' by Ro Ransom, Y2K

'VooDoo Child' by Brick + Mortar

'Lovely' by Billie Eilish, Khalid

'Keeping Your Head Up' by Birdy

'I Found' by Amber Run

'Princesses Don't Cry' by CARYS

'Pony' by Gynuine

'Get Low' by Lil Jon & The East Side Boyz

'Middle of the Night' by Elley Duhe

'Forever' by Labrinth

'Snow on the Beach' by Taylor Swift, Lana Del Rey

'Where Are You?' by Elvis Drew, Avivian

'Bow – Slowed' by Reyn Hartley

'Go Fuck Yourself' by Two Feet

'Play with Fire' by Sam Tinnesz feat. Yacht Money

'Lo Vas A Olvidar' by Billie Eilish, Rosalia

'Turning Page' by Sleeping at Last

'Stand By Me' by Skylar Grey

'A Thousand Years' by Christina Perri

### An Important Note To The Reader:

Your mental health, well-being, and comfort take precedence over anything. I kindly ask that you review the trigger warnings and other notable topics here before reading.

This is a contemporary romance with some darker aspects at times. I in no way encourage or condone the behavior of the men in this book. It is fiction and should never inhibit realistic judgment in your daily life.

### Trigger Warnings/Notable Topics:

Sexual assault, gun and knife violence, unaliving, exhibitionism, gang mentions, kidnapping, reference to foster care facilities, CPTSD, and others that may not be mentioned here.

"You have
walked through fire
survived floods
and have triumphed
over demons
remember this
the next time you doubt
your own power"


-Yung Pueblo

# 1

# LILITH

## *Before:*

You would think that the sudden death of a girl's father would be cause enough to set aside elitist condemnations. You'd apparently be wrong.

Even in grief, I am the outsider.

I watch from my hiding place in the next room, sitting with my back against the wall as everyone weeps and hugs my brothers. Quiet, sorrowful murmurings and muffled sobs reach my ears. Every person in the room damn near wrapping my brothers in the warmth of condolences and promises of support. Things I imagine are pillars in such situations for most. Affection has always been their birthright, a sharp contrast to me.

One of the older men I've seen before notices me as he walks by, the row of chairs between us acting as a poor barrier as our eyes meet. A simple nod and a tight smile should feel like a gift compared to the other interactions up to this moment. As he passes, I'm left with the sense I'm somehow in the wrong, caught in a shameful act by hiding away.

Something cold has settled in me now, though, and I cling to it. A ghostly shroud of lidocaine has found its home in my mind, draping itself over every thought and feeling. I find I don't have the capacity to really care anymore. Not like before. Most days, there's just... numbness in the area of my heart that should be reserved for feeling. What's left of me just feels hollow.

The thing with tragedy is that life moves on and keeps going around you while you no longer feel like a part of the flow and movement of the world and its people.

Everything slows and speeds up simultaneously, like a bad dream that won't end. When nothing is comfortable, not the silence, the noise, the chaos, the calm —none of it. Nothing feels okay anymore like your skin is just a little tighter than it used to be, smothering the breath right out of your lungs.

Every moment feels like crippling loneliness, and yet everything becomes... more, swelling and intensifying until you feel so full and so empty you know you'll explode. How can the human body possibly contain this much feeling?

Watching through the tangle of wooden chairs, I see the pain on my brothers' faces. The guilt that they have to endure this devastates me. They were close to our father. I gave up on that relationship long ago. I was never the daughter he wanted.

It's only then I feel the cracks form, fissures deepening inside me, trying to break through that layer of numbness. Clenching my fists,

I dig my nails into my palms, desperate to put an end to any thought that could lead to too much feeling.

"What the fuck are you doing down there? Show some goddamn respect, girl. God, what is wrong with you? Useless waste of space you are." My uncle's voice shatters the bubble I've built around myself, his words echoing against the fragile barrier. I feel the familiar tightening in my chest, the instinct to curl inward, to hide from the force of his presence.

Images, pain, and phantom touches flood my mind, seizing me. Something else flares —hot and sharp. The feeling overwhelming and too sudden. The image of plunging a knife into his chest blazes across my mind from deep in me —a buried fury. The heat of it spreads through me, igniting every nerve in my body.

Some days, I feel weightless, light as the galaxies of stars reflecting their strength against the ocean. Other days, I feel like the sand beneath the shallow waves brushing the shore, drowning, unsure which way is up.

But there are the rarest days when the veins in my body host the power of the sun, and I dare anyone to come too close. The silent screams in my head vibrate past the surface of my skin, waging war beneath as his voice echoes in my mind.

I open my eyes to look up at him, letting every ounce of hatred burn through my gaze, pure threat in my stare.

Tilting my head, I bare my teeth like an animal. There's no mistaking my contempt as anything other than a warning —a dare.

No, his days of reign and wreckage are done.

He will hold no power over me.
No man ever will again.

# 2

# LILITH

The infamous fuzzy, pink cowgirl hat is out in full force. From across the club, it bounces and sways, bright and unapologetic as its owner. Kathleen yells indecipherable nonsense, half laughing from the dance floor. When you look like an honest-to-goodness goddess, I guess you can get away with just about anything and pull it off. Alternatively, that monstrosity sitting atop another, less appealing face, this would look to be the outcome of the undesired end of a dare starring a Florida gas station souvenir.

I sit back and take a breath, letting my eyes wander over the crowd in front of me. 'Torched' is the newest club to hit downtown, and both open levels are packed. Everywhere I look, glossy lights flash and wave through various abstract designs from floor to ceiling, and speakers blaring upbeat dance music. Private tables take up partial space, where I'm choosing to currently hide.

The place is packed with people dressed to be seen, their outfits practically peacocking under the lights, exuding a silent need to be noticed. Bodies move together in pairs and groups, but each person seems wrapped in their own spotlight, craving to stand out just a little more than the next person. I'm thankful the guys got us a private table.

And then there's Blaine, Artemis and Ronan's best friend— the two of which are currently on the dance floor with the remainder of our group. Sitting alone with me, he's not someone the eye simply passes over without noticing. He sits just a handful of feet away, quietly observing the crowd with his usual distant, unreadable expression. Colored lights flash across golden-tan skin and short waves of dark brown hair that seem to fall *just so* onto his forehead. But it's his eyes that captivate me: a stormy gray with a hint of green at the center. They have a way of fixating on whoever they fall on, like they can see everything without giving anything away in return. A little secret through? He's kind of a dick. No, actually, not kind of. He is absolutely a dick. Ask anyone, they'll agree. And he never smiles. I'm pretty sure he hates everything and everyone. And yet, a small piece of my heart feels like it's carved out just for him. It always has been. Forcing my eyes away, I find the others. Our birthday girl, Larissa, and Elliott are now close to Katie, Art, and Rone.

I don't really do the clubbing thing anymore. But I love being out with everyone, getting dressed up and ready for the night out, the music. Once we get here? I've never been great at small talk or the interactions that seem unavoidable in crowded settings. People watching though? I live for it, observing everything. There's a young couple just ahead, lights reflecting and bouncing off their faces. It looks as though she's about to start crying, yelling at him, while he sports a desperate expression.

*"WHY? How could you?!"* She pleads to her betrothed.

*"My darling love, I didn't know! Please forgive me!"* She cries into her hands at his determined words.

*"It was my LAST cupcake! I was saving it!"* She pushes the foul beast away, storming into the darkness as he chases after her, begging for her forgiveness.

I can't help but chuckle aloud at the thought.

When you're right, you're right.

I can feel Blaine's eyes on me after my seemingly arbitrary outburst. Sure enough, he's looking my way... nope –*scowling* at me, like I did something to offend his ancestors. Jesus. *See? Dick.* No matter how many times I tell myself to ignore it, there's a part of me that's always acutely aware of him, like a magnet's pull to a deep-freeze.

I shift in my seat, offering a small smile at his attention. How does he respond? He leans back, sets his drink on his knee, and looks away. I tell myself I don't let him get to me, that his dismissive coolness rolls right off my shoulders. But the truth is, something in that icy charm pulls me toward him even when I'm fully aware what I feel will always be one sided.

Blaine's been in the picture since I came back to Denver. Since my brothers saved me all those years ago. He roomed with them in college and they've stayed close over the years.

And now, he apparently owns the building I live in, so there's no escaping him –not at my brother's so-called family dinners, not parties like this, and now, not even at home. The sigh my body releases is surely audible, even over the music.

I'm pulled out of my thoughts by a ripple of laughter, and suddenly, my brothers and our friends surround us, tumbling back from the dance floor. Kathleen claims the booth like she's the queen, tossing the pink cowgirl hat onto the table and grabbing the vodka from the ice bucket under-lit with glowing LED disks.

Our bottle server appears dressed in a skimpy black lingerie piece, quickly taking over Katie's efforts to pour a row of shots. I watch as she throws Blaine a coy glance, her eyelashes fluttering with the precision of a practiced move.

Typical. Blaine's magnetic to women in a way that makes me roll my eyes. I've heard his stories by secretly listening in on my brothers' conversations. Apparently, women fall to their knees for him, leash in hand. He's not the only guy at this table, but to her, he's clearly the only one worth noticing. And I tell myself it doesn't bother me at all. Not. At. All.

"Lilllllyyyy! Come on!" Larissa yells, yanking me to my feet. Blaine rises last, his quiet presence somehow holding its own even in the middle of our loud, chaotic group. The music vibrates through me as we lift our glasses in a birthday toast.

"Happy Birthday, babe!" Katie hollers to Larissa as everyone else chimes in before downing their shots. I can't help but wince. *God, I despise shots.* I turn to hide my cringy face and notice Blaine's eyes meet mine with the slightest smirk on the left side of his pouty lips. I'm sorry, did Grumpy Cat just smile?

My world tilts, and I'm hit with a flicker of curiosity.

But before I can give it too much thought, Kathleen grabs my hands, twirling me to the beat and pulling me into the here-and-now. Call it a placebo effect, but I already feel looser and happier, warmth flowing into my body. I smile back at her and lean forward, singing and moving to the beat thumping through the air.

And, just like that, I start to let go.

The music, the lights, the energy —for now, it's enough.

# 3

# LILITH

Another half of a shot and cocktail later, I need an escape. "Bathroom. Be right back." I mutter weakly. Not that anyone's listening. Making my way out of the booth, security offers me a tight hand and helps me step down from the platform our table is on. I push my way through the crowd, breathing through my mouth to avoid the cloud of about ten different colognes. I'm not looking for the bathroom, though. I head to the dark stairs leading up to the second floor for a quiet area. The energy is a little different up here versus the absolute chaos that is the dancefloor on the main level.

A long bar stretches the entire length of the wall on the right as soon as you enter. Everything is hued in a soft, dim, golden light. Glittering chandeliers hang over booths along the opposite wall, and there's another DJ playing more chill house EDM. Huge pots of tropical plants perfectly spaced, with minor bursts of red and yellow flowers, frame an entire wall of glass to the immediate left, which has been opened to transition seamlessly from the room to a huge balcony.

I step from the top of the stairs into the bar and eye everything over as I cross towards the balcony. I have to admit, this is absolutely beautiful. The terrace is wrapped with clear glass connected with bits of metal and has a few areas of comfortable, upscale outdoor seating to serve several groups. As I approach the glass, I'm mesmerized by the view. The club and bar that comprise 'Torched' sit at the top of a well-known luxury hotel downtown, and the view is breathtaking. You can see the entire span of the city skyline glittering. Ten years ago, Denver didn't feel like this. The city has exploded with transplants from all over the country's major cities and with it, the downtown skyline. I love it. It feels more like an actual big city now, which I appreciate. Looking out at a sea of lights that comprise the city, each office and apartment glowing amidst the night sky, it's oddly comforting to think they may be just as lonely as I am.

The guilt at the very thought nearly consumes me on the spot. How awful I am for feeling so alone when I have my brothers and my best friends. There was a time I didn't use to have the luxury and blessing of family or friends, though.

I think sometimes the ache of isolation for so many years is triggered, even by the most unsuspecting things.

There's a slight breeze that feels amazing on my sweat-sheened skin from the club downstairs, causing my hair to flutter. These are the moments I crave.

The moments away, but still in proximity.

Alone, but not.

I've learned that there can be nothing to smile about, or there can be a thousand moments to smile about. It took me years to understand this and to start to let go of the anger I held onto for the hand I was dealt. I continued to grip the blade of a knife, trying to stop it from penetrating my heart. All it did was end up slicing my hand deeper and deeper along the way, doing more damage than if I'd just let it go.

I held onto the past that continued to hurt and hinder me from moving forward. That version of me needed to die. So, I just... let go of the knife —and felt the death of her. Only sometimes, it feels like she can't seem to stay buried. So... I made it a practice to find and appreciate the little moments like this and *feel* them. I close my eyes, my hands resting on the cool, thick glass of the balcony railing, and smile at the moment's beauty. I imprint the skyline, the beautiful bar, and my friends and family, whom I love more than anything, all into my mind. -The very friends and family that care about me in return. Sometimes, my cross-wired brain lies to me, telling me they don't. But they do.- The gentle breeze, the music... I can't help a sigh of pleasure.

This is chasing happiness.

I slowly open my eyes, still smiling, and jump, surprised to see Blaine just a few feet away. "Blaine, jesus fucking christ, you scared the shit out of me!"

"You're certainly your brothers' sister with that mouth. —Better me than one of the pieces of shit dampening the air downstairs." He joins me in leaning against the glass, looking out at the city. "What are you doing anyway? Why do you always sneak off to be alone?" My immediate response wants to be that I don't always sneak off to be alone. But he's not wrong; I do. But he does, too. A decade or so is long enough to notice these things. I pause for a few moments before answering.

"Taking a mental screenshot." The left side of my lips twitch up, knowing it was an odd thing to say.

"Mmm, I see... hard to do that with your eyes closed, though." It must be the booze because I playfully smack his right arm.

"You know what I mean."

"Not entirely." He looks at me with that easy gaze he always wears, hosting fire and ice behind those eyes. Sometimes it feels like he's just waiting to light the match for the world to burn, too. There's genuine curiosity in his eyes, though.

"Feeling it. All of it. And trying to capture it as a memory. The cool breeze on my skin, the skyline, the music, my friends smiling. All of it. It's a nice moment to remember. I'm —just trying to collect the nice moments." I look away from him, back out to the city. We both stay silent before I ask, "What about you?"

"—Taking a mental screenshot." He straightens to his full height and almost, *almost* smiles at me. I half laugh, half huff out a breath at his comment.

"You're such a jerk," I reply teasingly as I spot a tall, thin, platinum blonde walking over to us, looking like a supermodel. She stalks up to Blaine, sliding her hand over his bicep and stepping between us to capture his attention.

"Blaine." She smiles seductively up at him, placing her hand on his chest. "I had a great time last weekend. You didn't tell me you'd be here tonight." I suddenly feel so uncomfortable, and my arms too heavy.

I say nothing as I lower my eyes, trying not to make eye contact with him as I step away towards the stairs, running away. It's what I'm good at. I run from everything. I turn back to see where blondie's hands have landed now and see him scowling directly at me as if this is somehow *my* fault. Never in my life have I experienced another human as hot and cold as Blaine Vogeleir. As soon as I think he can be normal —nice? He goes back to being a dick.

It's getting late anyway; I should call it a night. I already drank more than I usually do. Any more, and I'd do something foolish, surely. I get downstairs, back towards our booth, and spot Katie in front of my brother, looking rather smiley. Yeah, I'm not even going to pull at that string tonight. Katie is my best friend, always flirty, pulling men to their knees. She's undoubtedly a wicked goddess incarnate with the power she holds over them. One look and they beg for more of her, desperate for her attention. Fuzzy hat and all. She'd never hook up with my brother though. Artemis isn't even her type, thankfully. "Hey! I'm heading home, super tired," I say as I pull out the LED-lit drawers under the booth seating, trying to find my purse and phone. I stand up, both in hand, and nudge it shut with my heeled foot.

"Nooo, you're leaving? It's my birthday!" Larissa slurs. She'll be feeling this tomorrow. Note to self: bring Lissa a smoothie and something greasy tomorrow morning.

"I knowww, I'm sorry! I'll make it up to you, okay, I promise!" I grab her in a hug and kiss her cheek, walking away before she can protest anymore. "Happy Birthday, beautiful; I love you." Waving at my brothers and Katie on my way out of the booth. I mouth, *'I love you!'* in silence. There's a good chance Larissa isn't going to remember my departure, so I don't feel too terrible cutting out early.

Walking toward the exit, I spot Blaine returning to the table, no blondie. That's a little surprising. I head down to the lobby and make my way outside, pulling out my phone to order a car and wait until the white sedan finds me. Just a few blocks away.

As the car pulls through the valet loop, an older woman leans out, her warm smile glowing. "Car for Lilith?"

"Yes, thank you so much. I really appreciate it." I slip into the backseat and glance back at the building. Just as we begin to pull away, I catch a glimpse of Blaine standing there, his gaze sweeping the area. Did he see me? Or was he just leaving at the same time, by chance?

I lean back and close my eyes, exhaling as the car merges into the busy street. There's a soft tug at a corner of my heart, a barely-there thread stretching back toward the man on the sidewalk.

What a strange, wonderful night. A smile rises to my lips as I let the thought settle over me.

# 4

# BLAINE

## *Before:*

Walking up the rickety wooden stairs to Rye's piece of shit trailer, the dirty white door is open, the screen door the only shield to the outside. I don't need to step inside to know he's already piss drunk. Shitty music is blaring through the stereo as I step into the living room, Rye nowhere in sight. The right side of the living room is where I stay. I hung up two dark sheets against the corner walls on the ceiling to give myself some semblance of privacy. Space that feels more like a bedroom. The couch and coffee table sit not even three feet away from the hanging fabric. I stand just staring at it for a second and how fucking ridiculous it looks. God, two sheets for walls. How the fuck did I get here.

I step through the corner where they meet and toss my bookbag down on the floor next to the shitty black futon couch and use the wooden safety pins to keep the sheets together.

Flopping down onto my back, I stare straight ahead at the constellation of stains on the textured ceiling. I don't know how long I lay there before passing out, but the door slamming shut startles me awake. Feminine moans and whimpers fill the air through the music as I hear Rye mumble nonsense and bump into the walls as they make it to his room that shares a wall with one of the two I have. "Fucking great." I toss my arm over my eyes and let the cool numbness take over as the thin wall starts to rattle.

I never really thought about college before my parents died. Now, it's all I think about. I refuse to spend the rest of my life living in places like this shithole, surrounded by deadbeat drug addict bikers. It's my vow to do whatever it takes to make as much money as I can, starting with college in the fall.

My arm swings out and bangs against the fucking wall in my pissy state, listening to him have uneven shitty sex, and I punch a hole in the faux wood paneling without meaning to, covering my face with my hands in frustration.

I'm still numb and angry. But at least now, I'm motivated to get the fuck out.

# 5

# LILITH

This.

This is why I'm not too fond of alcohol. Everything is too bright, loud, hot, or annoying. Ugh. I wait for the blender to stop before uncovering my ears, blocking the sound of my smoothie being blended. "Why? Why are you so loud?" I pad along through my apartment, shades drawn with my smoothie in hand, towards the bathroom to turn on the shower. Somehow, Kat was up this morning and not a bit hungover, organizing a coffee meet-up for her, Larissa, and myself.

I toss my hair in a messy bun and cover it with a clear shower cap adorned with pink hearts while connecting my phone to the speaker in my studio apartment. Healing frequencies start playing through my speaker when I hear a knock. No one ever knocks on my door unless I know they're coming. I'm not expecting any packages or deliveries. I slowly approach the door, wondering if I should grab a knife, then sigh. *This isn't a crime podcast.* I look through the peephole. *Blaine?!* You have got to be kidding. Today, right now, of

ALL the days... he chooses to just drop by when I look like I slept in a dumpster. "Seriously? Not funny, universe." I murmur to Spirit, Goddess, whatever the hell you wanna call it.

Taking in a deep breath, I slowly open the door, just enough to peek out through a sliver of open space. "Blaine... umm hey. Everything okay?" He gives me an odd look, pressing his eyebrows together; I assume wondering why I'm hiding behind my damn door.

"Uh, yeah. Hey... is now... a good time? Do you have company or something?"

"What, no?" I asked, confused.

"Okay. Anyway, I just wanted to... check in on you." He looks skeptical or annoyed.

"Check in on me? Why?" I clear my throat lightly, nerves causing my voice to be less steady than I'd hoped.

"—Lily. What the hell is going on? Why the fuck won't you open th..." He pushes open the door, barging in, revealing my nearly exposed body: shower cap, bunny slippers and all. One of my favorite robes is a beautiful hand-made piece by a local aspiring designer. It's stunning in that it's a work of art in itself, but it doesn't leave much to the imagination. It's more about the piece itself and how it makes me feel versus the practicality of wearing it. The floor-length, sheer, nude fabric is almost entirely see-through; hand-sewn flowers embroidered in select places, hiding some, but not nearly enough at this moment.

"BLAINE!" I gasp and grab at my robe, covering my nipples with one arm and my downstairs region with the other. Blaine freezes, and I swear I can see his eyes scanning my body through the fabric, lingering just a second longer than they should. I grab the umbrella hanging on a hook by the door and toss it at him, hitting his chest. "Turn *around!*" He listens and turns towards my kitchen area to the right of the entryway as I turn the corner left into my bathroom. I quickly grab my thick, fuzzy white robe and toss it over my sheer masterpiece.

"Your brothers told me to check on you; that's what I'm doing. And believe it or not, I've seen a woman's body before," he says, annoyed from the other room. Does he hear himself when he speaks sometimes? Unwanted thoughts of the beautiful blonde from last night come roaring back. *Yeah, I bet you have.*

I pinch the bridge of my nose as I return to the main living area, where Blaine stands, still facing my kitchen. "It's too early, and I feel like shit, Blaine. Do you need something?"

He slowly turns around to make sure it's okay and then gives me another once-over, landing on my feet. I look like a bag lady; I know I do. Hungover with no makeup, shower cap, two layers of bathrobes, and just below, my bunny slippers smile up at us with their obscenely oversized ears flopping around.

"Cute." He smirks before looking away and runs a hand through his hair. "Your brothers wanted me to keep an eye on you and check in after last night. You just disappeared without saying anything.

They just wanted to make sure you were good and got home safe. Here."

"Oh... you got me a coffee?" I notice the logo on the cup immediately as my beloved local cafe. "That's my favorite; did my brothers tell you?"

"Yes." He passes me the large cup, chilly under my fingers. "Anyway, last night?" he pushes, seemingly impatiently. He clearly has other things he'd rather be doing. That's fair.

"Right, yeah. I just got tired and wanted to get home. Everyone was drunk, and Larissa wouldn't've even noticed I was gone if I hadn't said goodbye," I joke. "I'm fine. Thanks for checking, though; that's really kind of you."

"Artemis asked, not a big deal." He runs his hand through his hair again, pausing with that infamous scowl. "What the hell is that sound?"

I huff a bit of a laugh. "It's the 528-hertz healing frequency." He stares at me blankly, blinking slowly once, so I continue. "It's restorative and healing for the body." I bring the cup to my lips, taking a sip of my coffee, and release a little hum of joy before realizing it's a hazelnut latte with oak milk. I can't believe he happened to order my favorite drink from the cafe. He must've asked my brothers what to order. I bite back a smile at the thought. "It's beneficial for you. You should try playing it as background music. It's relaxing and helps me focus." I shrug.

His phone goes off in his hand, causing him to glower at the lit-up screen. "I have to handle this." As he takes a few steps towards the door, he brings the phone to his ear.

"Okay, sure. Than—" The door shuts, and he's gone. "—ks again for the coffee?" I take another sip before heading back toward my bathroom. Why does every interaction I have with that man have to be so damn weird or uncomfortable?

## BLAINE

There could never have been a better time for my phone to go off, forcing me to distance myself from Lily. "I have to handle this," I say, bringing my phone to my ear and stepping into the hallway. "What?" I snap out, pressing my hand to my face, my palm onto my forehead. I barely listen as Evan goes into our current business endeavor, making my way to the elevator at the end of the softly lit hall.

*"... is countering our proposal..."* I'm positive time stopped when I saw Lily's lithe body under that robe. She has the most beautiful long legs, deadly hips, and little pert nipples, perfect for licking and nipping. Entirely impractical attire, but I'm undoubtedly a fan.

*"...claiming he spoke to Sheila on the modified mutual..."* I lean my weight into my other hand propped against the elevator wall, eyes closed, heading back up to my place. I let the image of Lily on her knees under me play out behind my eyes.

*Her arms stretched out in front of her, gripping the pillow... the curve of her waist and hips as I hold her in place, pushing into her from behind. Moans and begging fill my bedroom, as the walls of her cunt tighten around my co....*

*"Sir?...Mr. Vogeleir?"*

Fucking hell. What is wrong with me?

"Yeah. I got it. I'll take care of it," I grit out at Evan, grinding my teeth. I hang up before he can say anything further. What the fuck am I thinking. If I'm resorting to imagining my best friends' little sister taking my cock, maybe I should have taken Francesca up on her offer last night. I'll text her later to make arrangements for this week. I sigh audibly, making my way back to my place upstairs.

# 6

# LILITH

"What the hell, you already have a coffee? You should have told me!" Katie has a small tray of iced coffee in her hand as I walk over to her on the trail.

"Long story, I'm sorry. Forgive me? I bring greasy burritos."

*"Oh... you got me a coffee? That's my favorite. Did my brothers tell you?"*

*"Yes."* Blaine's words and sweet gesture replay in my mind, glancing at the tray in her manicured hand.

"Eh, it's all good. Lissa might want it. She could probably use two coffees." She smiles teasingly. "Morning, though! You look cute!" Katie leans in to hug me, fixing her black hat back in place, from behind her head. Kathleen is absolutely beautiful. In some ways, I've been envious of her over the years of our friendship. She has gorgeous, thick, long blonde hair, is just slightly shorter than me, around five-eight, and has big green eyes that make her look innocent despite the fact she's a little crazy sometimes. Well... maybe crazy is a little harsh. She is just totally and completely herself, unapologetically. And a little wild on occasion. Her motto is 'regrets over what-ifs'... or something like that.

She's also staying in my childhood home with my brothers right now. She broke things off with her awful ex that she was living with and didn't exactly have the funds to afford a place on her own at the time. There are eleven rooms if you count the two 'offices' in my brothers' estate, so they were happy to help. Hell, Ronan is gone half the time, and Artemis works too much. They probably don't even cross paths with her all that much, to be honest. She seems really happy there, too. And it's helping her save a little cushion money for savings and to get on her feet. It's the perfect setup for her.

"Where is Lissa?" I ask, looking around for her car. We decided to meet at the park at our usual spot and walk off our hangovers versus stuffing our faces and re-drowning our sorrows at brunch. There are a few main parks in the city: Washington Park, City Park, Cheeseman, and Sloan's Lake. Wash Park is closer to me. But, still technically in the middle of Katie and I, and is the best one in my opinion. It's huge: two lakes, rows upon rows of volleyball nets in the warmer months, walking and biking trails, plus basketball and tennis courts for eye candy—the perfect inner-city getaway.

"Yeahhh, she's running a little... late." She lowers her sunglasses to wink at me with a huge smile, obviously wanting to tell me more.

"Oh my god, what... what did I miss?"

"Wellllll.... let's just say she didn't go home alone. Wink Wink. OH! Speak of the devil! LARISSA! Over here." *Oh my god*, poor Larissa. I can't help but stifle a laugh. She has on huge black sunglasses, leggings, an oversized sweatshirt and is the poster child for miserable and hungover. She makes her way over to us quickly, making grabby hands for one of the extra coffees in Kat's hands.

"Please tell me this is for me?" She groans. I hand her a burrito cure-all to go with it.

"All yours, babe. How ya feelin'?" Katie asks, bringing Lissa in for a half hug before I do the same.

"I could literally throw up on that bush right now. Or that baby." She looks at the stroller passing by us as we start to walk the gravel trail by the lake. "I don't even remember drinking that much! Ugh... at least it was fun and worth it, though. I seriously had such a great time. Thanks for coming; I appreciate it. Did you guys have fun?"

"First, what did that baby do to you? Let's keep our vomit to ourselves and hands at our sides. And, uh huh, I bet you did have fun. I'm just going to say it and move past the elephant in the room. You went home with *Elliott!*"

I can't help the genuine surprise that crosses my face, pausing on the trail in disbelief. "Oh my god, did you really? How did that even happen?"

"Okay, no... I did not go *home* with Elliott. It wasn't like that at all, actually. Part of me is embarrassed he saw me so drunk —that *anyone* would see me that drunk— but another part of me is a little happy he was there. Like... he took care of me; helped me remove my makeup, took off my heels, and get this —left my ibuprofen, water, and a note on my nightstand. I didn't even know men like that existed. Especially not someone as sexy as Elliott."

Katie and I both exchange a look of shock. "Wait, so you didn't hook up?"

"No, Kat. Sorry to burst your bubble. No sex was had. And no, before you ask, he didn't kiss me either."

I take a drink of my remaining coffee before responding and step to start walking again. "Wow. I mean, there's a lot to unpack there. But I can't believe he was so sweet like that. He doesn't come across as a dick by any means, but that's still a little surprising. I'm impressed more than anything. Wow, go, Elliott." I huff a laugh.

"Trust me, I really don't want to get into it today. My brain isn't even functioning at half capacity right now." She groans painfully. "Anyway, did I miss anything last night?"

"Oh yeah, Lil, by the way, thanks for letting me know you got home safe. I got your text and told the boys you were good before we left Torched to go home. They just wanted to make sure." I completely forgot I had texted her.

"Wait, they knew I got home safe? That's so weird. Blaine said they told him to check in on me this morning?"

"Blaine?" Lissa and Katie say simultaneously. "Please, oh please, tell me there's a story here, Lil." Katie lowers her sunglasses to look at me.

"I mean, I don't know if I'd say a story per se..." Katie gasps before I even get my complete thought out.

"Oh my god! But there is *something*. I KNEW it!"

"How could you *know* anything, Kat? The man's hardly spoken to me over the years. I don't know... I mean, last night, we had a weird but nice... moment, I think... on the balcony upstairs. And then, this morning, he stopped by to give me this." I lift my iced coffee. "But what's weird now is that he specifically said that my brothers told him to stop by. I was surprised he happened to have this for me, too. I asked if that's how he knew my favorite coffee to order, because of my brothers, and he said yeah. Is that weird, or am I just hungover?" I grab the bridge of my nose. "I don't think my brain is working either, Larissa, good god. —OH!... Ohhh my god. Oh my god, I didn't even tell you the best part of this morning." I cringe, putting my hand over my eyes. "He basically saw me naked." I can't help but gasp as Katie spits out her coffee and starts choking, bent over on the gravel trail.

"Jesus, Katie, are you okay!" Larissa puts her hand on Katie's back until she stops coughing, and they both look back at me.

"He what......?" Kat asks incredulously, wiping her mouth.

I tell the girls every detail of last night and our unfortunate exchange this morning. Including my wardrobe malfunction, him leaving without so much as a goodbye, and the stunning blonde with her hands all over his too-perfect bisceps. All of it.

"Lily, I love you to pieces. But the fact you're walking around blind when a twenty-foot, neon flashing sign, with an arrow, is directly in front of you is killing me."

"I literally have no idea what you're talking about, Katie; please be more specific."

"Exactly, Lily. Blaine is *IN to you*. I've been telling you this for over a year."

"Are you kidding me? *Mr. I-can-have-any-woman-I-want? Mr. Magazine-cover, too-hot-for-my-own-good?*" I mock. "I know you're having fun with this, Katie, but... let's not be delusional. No offense." Crossing my arms, I give her a bit of a pointed look.

"Look, I'll leave it alone if you really want me to. But I know I'm right on this one, babe. I know men. Call it intuition if you want."

# 7

# Blaine

### *Before:*

At some point, everything around me stops being real. I feel like I'm living in a dream and waiting for the moment I wake up panting in bed, relieved it's over. But here I am—living this nightmare of a life.

Some nights the heartache consumes me, pressing in on me until I can't even breathe, begging a god I don't believe in for the pain to just fucking stop. Until so much tension and pressure comprise my body, it all starts to fade to black, and I hope it's the end for me, too. I never believed you could really die of a broken heart until now.

Those nights, I cry, screaming inside as I keep the noise to myself so I don't wake Rye. If anyone ever wondered if you can physically feel a heart breaking, you can. It feels like tiny pieces of it are physically falling apart inside your chest, strings fighting to hold on until they can't anymore, and it all crumbles. That's what physical heartbreak feels like. If I could rip my own out, I would at this point.

Other nights, I'm numb. It's like my ability to feel anything is flipped like a switch, and I wonder if something's wrong with me, but I don't have the ability to even give a fuck if there is.

But most nights... most nights I feel so fucking consumed with anger that I can't hold it in my body. A burning rage builds in silence under my skin until the idea of strangling the next person I see feels like a sweet relief. The fantasy of watching the light leave their eyes, the blood rushing to their face as they go slack with my hands around their neck and become nothing. It's what ninety-nine percent of people deserve. It's what I deserve. I fucking hate people, and I hate myself.

That's what death and tragedy do to a person, I guess. Or maybe I really am fucked in the head now.

I didn't use to be like this.

Trapped in my own tornado of thought, I snap back to reality and realize my knuckles are covered in blood. There's so much fire in my veins that I barely feel it. I just watch as my fists slam into the worn-out padded circle against the tree over and over, pieces of bark falling, and the white fabric wrapped around my hands slowly turns a captivating shade of red. If I were capable of smiling, the sight of the new stains would do it.

But numbness swallows me whole, keeping pace with the rage, my mouth twisting into a silent snarl as my hands and arms thrum with static from the repeated impact. The now familiar ache is sharp and grounding—and I know it's what I deserve.

# 8

# Lilith

I excuse myself from the formal table covered in various breakfast foods and juices as I stand up and push my chair in.

"Absolutely. Look, I have a few minor business items that require my attention, so I have to run to the office. But I'll be back very shortly. It won't take much of my time if you'd like to hang out more when I'm back. I hope you'll stay." Artemis, charming and posh as ever, sets his cloth napkin down on the huge table, finishing the last of the coffee in his mug as he stands, too.

"Sure, I can stay for a while today. I'm just going to head to the library for a bit. Text me or find me later when you're home." This house holds a lot of hellish visuals for me. But I try to make my way here for their sake every so often. They've done so much for me, it's the least I can do. Artemis crosses the short distance between us, pulling my shoulder in and pressing a kiss to the top of my head.

"Wonderful, I'm glad to hear it. I'll return soon. And, Ronan should be staying in today so long as nothing has pulled his attention for the afternoon?" He looks over to Ronan who's shoveling pancakes into his mouth as he confirms with a thumbs up.

"My bad, yeah. I'm here all day! The game's on if you wanna watch it with me in the family room, Lil."

"As tempting as watching grown men chase a ball for three hours is, I think I'll pass this time." Ronan throws his head back laughing, and gets up, chugging his orange juice.

"It's hockey, baby sis, no balls. Just ice and fists. If you change your mind, you know where to find me." He yanks me in and starts rubbing the top of my head in a noogie, laughing as he holds his arm around my neck.

"*Stop!* Seriously, Ronan? How old are you! You're so annoying! And go put a shirt on. No one wants to see that, jerk." I use all my strength to push him off me, setting my hair back in place. God... man-child.

"I think your friend Kathleen would sure disagree, huh, Artie?" He looks over my shoulder to Artemis with a devilish smirk before taking off down the hall before we can respond. I can feel Artemis' glare at him, though.

"Umm, what? What the hell does that mean?"

"Nothing, he's full of shit. He's an idiot; that hasn't changed. Be good, I won't be long." And then he's out the door, too, leaving me alone in the dining room. Pretty sure they're both idiots.

Their housekeeper comes around the corner smiling.

"May I get you anything else, Miss Stemmens?"

"Oh, no, thank you. This was perfect. Thank you for preparing all of this; it was delicious. I will just top off my coffee before I go, if you don't mind." I grab the glass container before Matilda gives me a teasing, chastising look, taking it and filling my cup for me.

"It is my duty and honor to provide such things. Here you are, Miss. It's always a delight to have you back in the manor." She hands my warm cup back to me, smiling. She really is so sweet. I bow my head shyly in thanks before turning to make a quiet exit.

I head to the east wing of the estate, to a closed room on the right of the hall, guarded by large wooden doors. I came to my brothers' place to have brunch and catch up with them, but I am so glad I get some time in the library. It's my favorite room in the house. The only one I can bear, really. The estate is rather old, but constant renovations have kept it quite contemporary in most areas other than the library. I'm the only one who has ever used it a lot, and I asked Artemis to leave it as it is. Libraries like this are meant to carry old charm and magic, to act as Narnias to other worlds.

As I push open the old doors, the study unfolds before me, a vast, two-story haven wrapped in warmth, rich wood, and soft leather. Just inside, a beautiful grand piano sits untouched, polished and pristine. At the far end, a spiral staircase of black metal winds upward beside a cozy seating area —an oversized leather couch and two matching chairs facing the large bay windows. Floor-to-ceiling curtains, a deep red with ornate gold details, frame the windows, their sheer inner layers drawn to let sunlight filter in, casting soft, golden shadows across the room. Warm sconces and lamps are scattered thoughtfully along the walls and above rows of bookcases while a low-lit chandelier glimmers faintly from the ceiling's center, bathing everything in its own gentle glow.

When I lived here, much younger, this was my escape. The room I would hide in when I desperately needed to leave but couldn't. A lot of my prior best friends live in this room, tucked between the pages on the shelves. I can't help but feel a little twinge of sadness at that.

I approach the chair closest to the window, overlooking the open space. The back of the leather chair is cool, contrasting the end of the seat, warmed from the mild sunlight. I reach back grabbing a small, knitted throw blanket behind me, and toss it over my legs, resting them on the ottoman. Sitting, I pull my book out of my purse. I've spent weeks reading a series of ten books, crafting a world of romance, magic, war, and politics. It's the best, most spellbinding series I've stumbled upon in years, which says quite a bit about the world-building and talent of the author. I've nearly completed the final book that rests in my hands. I desperately want to travel back into my new world. But I know as soon as I finish the series, I'll just be heartbroken it's complete.

I settle in, opening the book where I left off, and fade into the world where I've spent much of my time living. I forget everything. I forget time, my life, my job, and that storm just under the surface and let myself fall away.

# 9

# LILITH

A couple of hours later, I turn the last page, closing the book and with it, my life inside. I knew this feeling was coming, and yet, it's still overwhelming. It's like a final goodbye to a dear friend or lover who's brought you nothing but happiness and beautiful, treasured memories and moments. I close my eyes, allowing myself to feel the slight heartache, knowing it won't be the same even if I reread the series. I know it's silly, but I just don't care. I'd prefer many worlds and lives over the one I'm in.

Looking around the study, I take in the magic in the walls before closing my eyes, holding my book to my chest, and silently allowing myself to mourn the people I've spent all my time with. Images of the moments, places, and romantic embraces flow through me as I remember to smile.

I raise my head and open my eyes, lifting the blanket atop my lap before a shadow to my left by the door causes me to gasp and jump halfway out of the chair. "Jesus christ, Blaine! You scared me. Stop doing that!" I put my hand over my heart, momentarily closing my eyes, willing my body to calm down and convince it we're not being attacked. "What are you doing here?"

"I didn't mean to scare you; I just stepped into the room." His eyes study the room before stepping towards me another fifteen feet or so. The moment bleeds with a sense of bittersweet deja vu. The first time I laid eyes on Blaine, he was standing in nearly the exact spot, years ago. Not a word was spoken, yet I'll never be able to scrub it from memory. "Am I interrupting?"

"No, you're fine." I wipe a couple of stray tears that must've fallen from my eyes, removing the blanket and grabbing my now long-cold coffee.

I watch as he makes his way to the right side of the room, slowly looking over the books. "Are you crying?" I huff a quiet laugh that seems far too loud in the silent room. *No.*

"Why are you in here?"

" —This is my favorite room in the house. It always has been." He glances over at me briefly, and I can't help the tiny patter of my heart, hoping that same memory might be why. Immediately, I feel foolish even thinking it. The chances of him even remembering are slim.

"You read?" I ask, honestly a bit shocked.

"Try to contain your astonishment; I did learn to read as you did, yes. Although, I may come across as illiterate at times." That's not what I meant, really. With how successful he is, the actual thought never crossed my mind. I watch the pads of his fingers trace across a row of books, before stepping slightly closer to where I sit in the back of the room.

I can't help but chuckle a little. "That's not what I meant. I just didn't imagine you as a big reader, I guess. Mr. Cool and all." He raises an eyebrow before scowling slightly, looking at me momentarily.

"Mr. Cool... interesting name. Although, I'm not sure how entirely fitting it is."

"Oh, *come on*. The car, the penthouse, the clothes, the looks. You're the epitome of cool. Everyone wants to know you. Women practically throw themselves at you, and men would do anything to be seen with you." I swear his lips curve into the tightest of smiles, and I roll my eyes and scoff at his arrogance.

"Mmm... the looks, huh? You think I'm attractive then." It wasn't a question as much as a statement. I feel my cheeks heat, but I manage to huff with indifference.

"Please."

"Begging —already, Lily?" He says it so smoothly that I nearly choke.

My chest and cheeks are blazing. Thank god he can't see me in the shadows of the room. Even my brain can't process a response to that. I think I must've glitched, sitting with my lips parted. An actual laugh escapes him as he glances at me, pushing a book back on the shelf. "Another time then, maybe." He stalks over and sits across from me in the second chair, face chiseled and carved to immortal perfection in the soft, golden light. *Unfair.* He gestures down at my book. "What are you reading? Is that why you were crying?" I can't deny I was, I guess.

*"It was only a couple of tears,"* I mumble. That earns me another smirk. *Jerk.*

I look down at the cover, thumbing through the pages on its free edge. "Well... this is the final book of a long series I've been reading for quite some time. I'm just sad that it's over, I guess." I shrug.

"I can understand the sentiment." He looks away towards the books behind me, mind wandering momentarily before readjusting, crossing his ankle over his knee, and looking back at me.

I manage to keep his gaze for a few long seconds, studying his face —the man that I've known for so long, so many years. Today, though, he's... different. I shake my head at the thought, continuing.

"I just get lost in it all, I guess. I've spent so long searching for an escape. This gives me that. When it's over, I can't help but feel a little heartbroken. I've been chasing something as long as I can remember, and still, after all these years, I don't know what it is. Running from some heavy darkness. Just feels like a relief for a while." I hold up the book slightly as a display of my sentiment, nerves hitting me. I feel ridiculous and suddenly flush, regretting saying anything at all.

It's all true, though. Every minute I could let go and open my eyes to wake up in a new world, fall in love with the characters and how I felt there. It feels like I'm saying goodbye and don't know where to go next, the helplessness rushing back, real life pushing back as everything that finally made me feel whole evaporates at the edges. While I am grateful for what I have and the people close to me, there is always something missing. When I read, I feel more complete. More of who I was supposed to be, or at least who I wish I was. Like I just somehow ended up here, by mistake, instead of another world in the stars surrounded by magic.

I look back up to meet his unreadable eyes and laugh half-heartedly, trying to hide the pinch of fingernails digging into my palms to distract myself from the embarrassment. "I know how ridiculous that sounds, trust me, don't worry." His brows seem to bunch at the comment.

"I think I understand more than you may expect. I may not read nearly as much anymore due to my business and social obligations. But when I was younger, after my parents died, I needed that too. My life became a mess I couldn't make sense of." His eyes grow distant and nearly full of sorrow as if replaying memories in his mind. "Just like you, I would escape into books, video games, fighting, sex, music— as often as I could, every waking moment, really. Anything to drown out the noise. The clubhouse made it pretty easy when it was all at my disposal." He sighs, and I realize the frequency with which he makes the sound. "Anyway, don't feel bad. It's natural to want to feel something more. The author probably felt that way too when they wrote it."

He pauses, his expression somehow deepening. "That darkness you feel? It might not ever go away. But you... you've got more light than you think. Enough to hold both shadow and sunshine. That's its own kind of strength."

I knew his parents had passed, but he's always kept his past tightly guarded, never really revealing anything about his childhood. This is the first time I've heard him open up about any of it, and I'm stunned by his kindness and depth. There's a rare, raw honesty in his words, a vulnerability that takes me by surprise. I feel something soften inside, wondering if perhaps I could be a safe space for him —maybe even the first person he's felt comfortable enough with to truly open up. "Blaine..." I pause, swallowing, and find I can barely find words. Any words. Nothing feels like enough in response. "—that was really beautiful. Thank you. I'm so sorry you lost them so young. I know what that loss feels like, to grow up with that emptiness. It never really leaves you."

He slowly looks away again at the bookshelves, both of us sitting in silence. Studying him now, I can see it: the angry mask of a hurt boy. "If you ever want to talk more abo—"

"I noticed the paintings you had set up in the corner of your place." He cuts me off from going further with my offer. I realize what he's doing and nod, letting him lead the conversation. "You have talent. They were good."

A sense of embarrassment washes over me at the idea he saw my artwork, though. "Oh... thank you. I've been painting for a while since I was able to start doing it. It's difficult being in a smaller space. I don't create nearly as much as my brain wants me to. It's just a pain to constantly set everything up, take it down, and worry about paint spills and the smell. But thank you, I appreciate you saying that." I offer a shy smile in return, face heated.

"Hmm... well, if you're interested, I have plenty of space at my place, since it's the same building you'd have easy, quick access. I could find a room you could claim for the time being. Until you annoy me."

What... "Wait... are you serious?"

"Why not? I have too much space as it is. I don't give a shit." He shrugs nonchalantly.

"That would be amazing! Thank you!" I grin.

"I'll set a code for you to have access to my place at your leisure. Just tell my housekeeper if you need assistance moving anything. She's my right hand with anything regarding the place. Think of her as my estate manager. I'll give her a heads-up. But, she'll be happy to assist. And Lily...don't go snooping if you get curious or bored. I have cameras, and I will always know. That's my one rule."

This is amazing, oh wow. I smile over at him. "Of course, anything you want. Thank you."

He grunts in acknowledgment, turning to gaze out the window, his profile softened by the gauzy light streaming in. He looks so... serious. Something tells me there's a lot more going on in his head other than his ongoing task of how to be a bigger dick today than yesterday. "I feel like all you need is a tobacco pipe and a glass of bourbon, and you'd fit right into this room." I joke smiling at him, earning a raised eyebrow.

"Didn't realize I'd stepped into a board game. Next time, I'll be prepared to play Colonel Mustard, who did it in the study with the candlestick." His eyes light up enough to make my heart skip a beat as he meets my gaze with an unexpected warmth that's almost disarming.

"So, what are you doing here? Ronan's in the family room if you're looking for him."

"He knows I'm here. He invited me to watch the hockey game. Although, at this point, I've most likely missed it. I left him to go to the bathroom quite a while ago, surprised he hasn't come looking. Then again, it is Ronan." We both stand and head for the door.

"Oh, sorry you missed the game... mayb—"

"I really don't give a damn about sports," he interrupts. "Besides, I'd much rather spend my time having a real conversation with someone who thinks I'm attractive. We'll talk about your begging later." I nearly run into him, wide-eyed, as he suddenly stops to turn around and smirk down at me before opening the door for me to pass through. I make sure to give him my own best scowl —his signature move.

"You left out the part where I call you a jerk," I say, glaring, but my cheeks are on fire. I hear his deep, inconspicuous laugh behind me as we walk down the hall toward the family room, where Ronan has another loud game on the giant TV.

"Easy, Ms. Stemmens. You wouldn't want to lose your new privileges so soon."

"And you wouldn't want to end up with a paintbrush up your ass." I bark back and can't hide my smile when his genuine laugh echoes down the hall behind me.

"Indeed."

# 10

# LILITH

I close my laptop and let out a huge sigh, finishing my workday. My insufferable boss is out of town traveling, which is my favorite time. So, I worked from home today. Friday night and no plans. I get off my couch and stretch my legs and arms above my head, yawning before going to the kitchen to grab a sparkling water. I guess I can see what the girls are up to tonight. A chill night sounds perfect, though. This entire week has been stressful —one where nothing can go smoothly.

> Hey loves, any plans for the night? I'm thinking wine and movies. Order a pizza?

Katie
> Sorry babe, sounds amazing, but I can't tonight :(

Larissa
> Same, I'm sorry! My fam from the East Coast are visiting. We can only get together tonight while they're in town. Send good vibes, plz.

> No worries *heart emoji* Have a good night, girls. Be safe. Good luck!

Katie

> *Kissing smooch emoji*

Mmm. Well, I guess not, then. I lean on the counter with my chin in my hand, thinking. Screw it, I want wine. And if I'm going to be bad, I'm going all out and having cupcakes for dinner. Wine, cupcakes, and a smutty book? Hell yes.

I head to my room and change, putting on fuzzy socks and comfortable boots, tossing a hat on.

Rounding the corner towards the front door, I make quick work with my coat and head out.

There is a cupcake and dessert shop just a few blocks down, with a liquor store just a few blocks past that where I can pick up a bottle of wine around the corner. The biggest perk of city living? Cupcake access.

Stepping into the tiny shop, I almost moan at how wonderful it smells —cake, vanilla, icing, and everything perfect and delicious. Behind the counter, the young girl in her late teens greets me with a smile. "Hi there! Let me know whenever you're ready to order." I smile in thanks and approach the glass, looking over all the cupcakes, cookies, and other alluring treats. I have always been a whore for sweets; I can't help it. I have no self-control if there's anything remotely sweet near me. Entire sheet cake? I'll eat until I'm sick. 'Family size' candy bag? Same. I've learned not to keep anything too tempting in my apartment.

There are various cupcake flavors, all with their own homemade and famous icing. This shop may not look like anything special from the outside, but the number of awards and news articles hanging on the wall behind the counter will tell you otherwise. They're a little on the pricey side, but it's worth every cent. I end up ordering a half dozen because, again, no self-control: a variety of chocolate, vanilla, and rainbow with various icing flavors and toppings of glitter sprinkles, cookie crumbles, and a few just icing. It takes everything in me not to dip a finger through a whirl of icing right now. I grab the box after paying and make my way to the door.

"Thank you again. Have a good night."

"Absolutely, you too. Enjoy!"

I make a pit stop a little further at the liquor store for a bottle of red. Leaving, I turn left to make my way back home. I'm too busy holding the cupcakes practically to my nose to realize that a black car rumbles up next to me, window rolled down.

"Lily." Blaine. Of course, it's Blaine when I look like shit yet again. Mother Mary. I stop on the sidewalk a few feet from him, pulling the brim of my hat down a bit.

"Hey, Blaine. Didn't anyone tell you Batman already has this same model?" Even in the shadow of his interior, I notice his lips tilt up. Blaine has a few vehicles I've seen, but he mainly drives his blacked-out, new McLaren.

"Need a ride?" I don't really, I guess. I'm not walking far.

"Um, no, I think I'm—"

"Get in the car, Lilith. It's dark, and you're alone leaving a liquor store that belongs in East Saint Louis." He rests his left hand just outside the window, his arm and watch reflecting the lamps lighting the sidewalk. He's wearing a black, fitted short-sleeved shirt, which is incredibly unusual for him. I think maybe a handful of times I've seen him so casual. I roll my eyes, but he has a decent point, I guess. I make my way to the passenger side in front of the car, climbing in with my wine and cupcakes on my lap.

"Half a dozen cupcakes?" He pulls over, back into traffic.

"Don't judge me. It's my dinner." I tuck my hands in my sleeves over my box.

"I'm not sure that's helping your case. And you need protein."

"Congrats. That might be the most bro-ish thing you've ever said." He adjusts his hand on the wheel, but I see him smile even if he tries to hide it. "What are you up to tonight? I never see you look so... normal. Attire wise."

"It's been... a week. I just want to relax in peace and quiet. And that didn't really align with my suit collection." He rubs his hand down his face and through his hair. "You? Girl's night or something?" He glances down at the box and wine in my lap.

"Uh, no, not exactly. The girls are busy tonight. But I'm exhausted from the week, too, and just wanted a night in. So... cupcakes and wine it is." I shrug. He doesn't say anything other than slowly nodding in response. "Do you... want company? I'll share, and I'll be quiet. I don't really feel like talking much tonight. Up to you, but it might be nice." He pauses in what I can sense is hesitation. "Also, I'm surprised you don't sleep in silk suits or something, too." That breaks the tension a little as we pull into the back of the garage to his private entrance.

"Who said I don't?" He pulls into one of his open spots and turns the car off, everything going silent —slats of lighting splayed over the interior of the car in the darkness. "But... I guess you can come up for a movie or something. If you're annoying, I'm making you leave, though. I'm not in the mood. —And you're eating more than that for dinner. Jenny should be preparing steak and asparagus tonight as long as her menu hasn't changed." He sighs loudly, opening his door.

"Don't sound so excited."

"I don't beg, like some people." He gets out and shuts his door, walking around the car. I exit as well, and I mock him behind his back. *JERK.* I glare at him as he holds the door open for me to walk into the building. He presses a code into the elevator keypad, followed by his thumbprint, opening the doors to take us to his penthouse.

# 11

# BLAINE

I fight the smile waring to take over my face as we get into the elevator. She's cute when she's frustrated like this. Like an angry kitten.

When we reach the top and the doors open, I hold my arm out for Lily to go first. Walking through the double black doors, she doesn't say anything, and neither do I. That's one thing I appreciate about Lilith; she hardly ever tries to fill the silence. She's just as content with it as I am. I think that's partially why we tend to end up alone together when the group gets together to go out. It's refreshing. As soon as we enter, I know Jenny is already preparing dinner on my estimated arrival, hit with a symphony of smells. I haven't had time to eat today, and it's been the same every day this week. I set my keys and wallet down on the island, greeting her. "Jenny. Lilith is joining us for dinner. Would it be a bother to adjust to accommodate her?" She looks up at us, smiling warmly.

"Oh no, sir, not at all. Just give me a few more minutes then, please." She looks back to Lily with wine in her hand. "Would you like a couple of wine glasses, Miss?"

"Thank you, no rush on dinner." I look back over to the little flower, who's also set her 'dinner' and wine down.

"That would be wonderful, thank you very much." She tells Jenny.

"Make yourself at home. I'll be right back. Jenny may assist with anything you need." I grab my coat off the island and make my way towards the hall, down to my bedroom. Fuck, I'm exhausted. I toss it over my chair and head to my closet, kicking off my shoes and grabbing a pair of lightweight, dark grey sleep pants to replace my black jeans. I let out a deep breath, taking a minute to look out the floor-to-ceiling windows at the view of the outlying cities just past Denver. It's far too dark to see the mountains, but the further away lights glitter and pulse. I enjoy it. Something about it calms me.

I can't shake the feeling that it isn't a good idea to have Lilith over. We've known each other for years and have had chill nights. Just not alone. She's a bit shy and awkward but in an endearing way. And she's easy to be around, considering almost everyone is insufferable at best. That is an area in which I'm positive we differ. I despise people. Ninety-nine percent of people are just absolute imbeciles. Lilith, on the other hand, I believe she wants to like people and generally does. I don't.

I walk to the adjoining bathroom and turn on the sink, splashing water over my hands and face. I should go ahead and shower now, but honestly, I'm tired to my very core. Jenny is a great overall addition to my small team. She adds personal touches and anticipates a great deal of my needs, so I don't even have to ask anymore. She's been with me for years, and I do recall it taking us a while to get to this point.

She has a small towel warmer on my counter with rolled washcloths in it. Steamed on the bottom row and dry on the top row. It's one of her many small touches that I've come to appreciate significantly. I grab one of the dry, warm towels, pat it against my face, and momentarily put it on the back of my neck. My body seems to be easily betraying me as I age. Just one night of sleeping slightly off, and my neck is stiff for days if not longer. I press my hands to the counter letting my head fall forward, rolling my neck before looking at myself in the mirror. The week's events are certainly reflected on my face.

Stepping back out to the kitchen, I see Lily on one of the stools, already almost done eating, as Jenny places a plate for me next to her. Good, she needed to eat. I'm glad she didn't wait. "Jenny, do you know where that muscle cream is you gave me a couple of months ago?"

She makes a *'tut-tut'* noise at me a couple of times in response before wiping her hands on the towel in her apron. "Of course, one moment. Eat... eat. While it's hot." I sit next to Lily in quiet. The steak is cooked a perfect medium rare and is so tender that I plow through it in what feels like seconds. Although Lily started eating before me, we finished nearly simultaneously. I remember her being a slow eater, come to think of it. Her brothers have given her shit about it in the past. I huff a half laugh at the thought and get up, grabbing the second glass of red wine, assumingly for me. It is now.

"Would you like to share your two cents with the rest of the class, Mr. Vogeleir?"

"Nope." I smile bigger, knowing there's an eye roll behind me. The theater would be good, but I don't feel like it, and the view from this room would be better. I have a considerable beige 'U' shaped cloud couch in the room, wide enough to easily out-stage a twin bed. Guiding us into the living room, I lightly collapse into the corner, remote in hand, as Lily sits nearly to the other end across from me. "Here. Choose something. I don't care what it is." I reach forward and hand her the remote before leaning back to check my phone —text from Ronan and Francesca.

Ronan S.

> Hey man, private get-together in the RR. Couple people planning scenes if you catch my drift and wanna join. Gonna be a big party.

*Pass.*

Ronan occasionally hosts what are essentially secret sex parties for the rich. NDAs and negative tests required, no phones, and virtually no limits. Ronan, being Ronan, of course, exempted himself from the fine print as the owner, putting himself in the perfect position to hold information and blackmail the most influential people in the city —a very dangerous game.

Their carriage house was turned into a legitimate club with more pleasurable areas upstairs and in the basement for privacy; 'The

Red Room.' I know he's implying people plan to act out sex scenes in front of an audience. Any other night, and I'd probably be attending. It's proved itself the best place to meet the women I need: daddy issues, defiled, and a warm hole or two. I never said I was a good man; quite the opposite. I know who I am. I'm far too exhausted to even give a shit about fucking, tonight.

> **Francesca – Red Room**
>
> Feeling lonely tonight… if you want to meet up for a little playtime…

*Pass.*

I toss my phone to the side and look up as she settles on a vampire rom-com. I dim the lights from my phone as Jenny makes her way into the room. "I apologize, Mr. Vogeleir. There isn't any more cream. If you'd like, I am happy to run out and pick some up for you?"

"No. Thank you. Maybe tomorrow if you find the time. You can call it a little early if you want to head out. Have a good night, Jenny."

"Of course, sir. Thank you. Enjoy your evening. Miss Stemmens, good to see you, good evening."

After dimming the lights, I turn on the fireplace and lean onto my elbow, resting my head on my hand as the movie starts. Lily is cuddled up to two pillows against her. "Are you cold?"

"A little?" Right.

I reach forward to the other side of the couch closest to me, grab a faux fur blanket, and toss it to her.

We make it about ten or fifteen minutes into the movie before my neck starts killing me, and I wince a little, trying to sit back up and stretch it out.

"Does your neck hurt?" Lily looks over to me, her face lit by the light of the television.

"It's fine. Not a big deal." I lean forward, my hands pressed on the edge of the couch, hanging my head. I can feel Lily get up and walk over to me. "What?" I grind out, annoyed. She crawls onto the couch behind me, both knees on either side of my hips. What the fuck is she doing? I pause and stiffen, sitting upright. "—What the hell are you doing?" I snap.

"Just hold still. Artemis and Ronan used to pay me to give them massages when they played sports in college, remember? It'll help. Just sit still and relax; you're super stiff." Yeah, no shit. Her knees are straddling my back close enough to feel her body heat. I go to look back at her as I hear her rub her hands together to warm them and just strain my neck even more in doing so, letting out a short stream of curses.

"Lily. Just... it's... it's fine." Her hands press against the middle of my back as she moves them up and over my shoulders, getting familiar with her movements. Her immediate touch feels so foreign and unwelcome I'm practically gritting my teeth. She moves her hands to the sides of the lower area of my neck, pressing her thumbs along my spine. I don't even stop the groan that comes out of me.

Fuck, okay, I'll admit that was good. The chill of her hands only adds to the intensity of the pleasure. She moves both hands to one side and starts slowly but deeply massaging my shoulder and into my neck. I close my eyes and lean into her touch, trying to wrap my head around how those tiny hands have so much strength.

"Actually, can you lift your shirt so I don't have to move over the fabric?" I don't even think before I reach behind me and pull my shirt off onto my lap. I can feel her adjust her position and move slightly behind me, feeling her inner thighs on both sides of my waist as she kneels. She starts over, and it feels even better with her on my bare skin. She slowly rubs and traces her hands over my back, shoulders, and neck, resting on tight spots and kneading them out. I move to the left slightly for her to access better. My voice comes out a little rough when I speak after another short groan, and a curse escapes me.

"Thank you, Lily." She continues working on the side of my neck for a few minutes before adjusting herself behind me. I can feel her spread her legs wider and then up and down, moving against my sides before settling. As she moves, I'm nearly positive I start to scent her arousal and I groan again immediately imagining her in very un-friend-like positions. She works her hands slowly from the base of my spine upward to my neck and onto my biceps and shoulders. I am entirely sure I smell her scent now, and my mind promptly reminds me of how easy it would be to flip her around to the back of the couch and rip her leggings down to fuck her. Seconds; I could be inside of her in a matter of seconds. Buried inside my best friend's sweet, innocent sister. I don't even bother to shut down the visuals flashing through my mind as she sits behind me, torturously rubbing her hands all over me. She finishes by patting my back, and I open my eyes, losing the image of me pushing into her from behind, when I realize my dick is very, very, obviously hard in my thin sleep pants.

"All done... hopefully that helped a little." She says brightly, as if entirely naive to the sinful thoughts clouding my head.

"Uh, yes. That... thank you." I clear my throat to stop speaking so roughly towards her. She moves from out behind me to my side. As she starts to take a few steps, I adjust myself when I'm out of her line of sight and lie down again with a pillow pressed against me. I look over to the TV, and see the movie is still playing, although I have zero fucking clue what it's about. Lily sits a little closer between me and the opposite end of the almost comically large couch, grabbing the blanket I gave her. I close my eyes and hear her adjust a few times. Her hands felt phenomenal, and my neck feels ten times better already, if not a little sore. I slowly realize I can't recall anyone ever touching me like that outside of physical therapists or professional masseuses. I've never cared to date in the ordinary sense of the word or have a partner, and in turn, I haven't experienced intimate exchanges like that. My parents weren't exactly the most loving or stable, and I can recall but a few times my mother embraced me in a hug. My father sure as hell didn't. I don't know how to feel about that revelation. I've spent my life blocking or repressing any feelings outside of indifference or anger. It doesn't sit right that I suddenly feel something in my chest, thinking about her hands on me, caring for me. I can feel I'm scowling, my thoughts reflected on my face as I fight a heavy, exasperated sigh, a sudden thickness filling my throat. Frustration and anger gripping my chest.

I hear her shuffle again. I just don't register that she's gotten off the couch until I feel her rather ungracefully climbing in next to me. My eyes fly open, watching her situate herself like the kitten she is, trying to get comfortable. "What the hell are you doing?" I hate that my voice comes out towards her as sharp and salient as it does. She settles into my side, resting her head and hand on my chest, the blanket now over both our legs. I hold my hands back from instinctually wanting to push her immediately off.

"You looked... like you could use a hug. And I could, too. So... yeah." She whispers against my side. *Fuck.* What do I even do here? Tell her to fuck off and move? I can't do that. It's Lily, not one of the women I use for sex. Lily's never fit into a category other than 'best friends' baby sister'. I don't even know what to do with my fucking hands. Like, do I put them on her? I've never *cuddled* anyone. I have no clue what to do. I rub my hand down my face, still not saying a word or moving otherwise.

It feels so foreign. Godmotherfuckingdamnit.

Seconds pass, and after a few deep breaths, I guess it's not entirely terrible. Moderately vexatious, I suppose. I hate people touching me. I don't feel content or happy or whatever the hell people get out of touch. All it does is aggravate me and make my skin crawl. I audibly sigh. She does smell... fuck, she smells nice, though. I can still scent her arousal slightly, mixed with her perfume. And her hair is soft and smells like sweet honey. She did just do me a favor by helping me... albeit unsolicited. I guess I can return whatever the hell favor this is to her —my best friend's sister. I sigh again, lowering one arm and resting it around her back, touching her arm. I think that's right. She hums and snuggles closer into me, moving her leg on top of mine and extending her hand over my chest.

Five minutes. I'll do this for five goddamn minutes and then get up to use the bathroom or grab a drink to get her off me. Honestly, I could just tell her to leave and go to my bedroom, no discussion.

"What was it like growing up for you? I know you said your parents passed away?" So she wants to do *this*, I guess. I clench my back teeth, using my free hand to clamp down on the bridge of my nose. Jesus fucking christ, it takes everything in me not to push her off onto the floor and tell her to leave. But again, it's Lily, and I can't find it in me to do so. Literally, anyone else would already be shoved towards the door. An odd little category I've placed her in, I'm realizing.

"There's not much to tell. I grew up, my dad was a One Percenter in a notorious motorcycle club, mom was in and out of prison. Both had addictive personalities and never really planned on having a child. When they passed in a motorcycle crash, I moved in with my dad's friend Rye from the club, who certainly didn't want a young teen suddenly under his care—spent a lot of time at the clubhouse. Booze, women, other stupid shit too young. I took off a week after I turned eighteen and crashed with friends until college started that

Fall. That's it." She's silent for a while, and I'm not sure if it makes me feel worse or relieved.

"You deserve love, Blaine. I'm sorry you never received it growing up. Every child, every adult needs love and support to feel... okay. Happy and fulfilled, I guess. I just hope you don't push it away forever; push people away forever. One day, you'll find it, and your heart will start to heal. You deserve it, always."

I grunt in response to close the conversation and wonder if she's talking about me or herself being deserving of love. If she is speaking of me, she couldn't be more wrong. She has no idea the sins I've committed and will continue to. Hell, if she knew the dark parts of me, she would jump off this couch and run out the door. It would be wise. There is something about the ease of her innocence that pulls me into her presence, though.

Five minutes and she needs to go home. The last thing she needs is to be lying curled up next to a wolf.

Those five minutes came and went, but I couldn't bring myself to move or push her away. If anything, something primal and possessive surged within me, a fierce protectiveness that sharpened as I became fully aware of how small, soft, and delicate she felt beside me.

Every part of me seemed to anchor to her warmth, easing the relentless weight on my chest. Her presence, her light —it felt like an invitation to something I'd almost forgotten. Peace? If only for this moment.

We lay there together through the rest of the movie, her steady breaths and warmth grounding me in a way I hadn't anticipated. And as sleep crept in, it took me quickly, almost mercifully, pulling me under into darkness where everything—the worry, the ache, the noise— faded away, including the warm body on mine.

I truly am selfish. If I cared for her at all, I would have made her leave.

# 12

# LILITH

I begin to stir, my eyes still closed against the soft morning light filtering through my lids. Mmm. I'm so warm and comfortable, my body relaxed against a cozy, solid heat. Without thinking, I snuggle in closer, draping myself over it. A drowsy part of me sighs in satisfaction, sinking deeper into the warmth.

I vaguely register the firmness under my hand, the distinctly masculine feel of it beneath my touch. I must be dreaming. Smiling, I let my fingers drift along that warmth, savoring the sensation. Not just warmth, but strength —solid and unyielding beneath the thin fabric. I sigh contentedly, gently rocking my hips, my hand trailing slowly over each inch. I nearly whimper. Hell yes. This kind of dream I can get on board with.

Just as I'm about to let myself fully indulge, I think I hear my name —a whisper, brushing past my awareness. *"Lily..."*

*"Lily..."* A deeper, rougher voice now, pulling me further into consciousness. I shift slightly, still enveloped in warmth, feeling a solid body beside me. I take a deep breath, a gentle, contented groan escaping me as I exhale.

*"Lilith."* I freeze, eyes snapping open, the sleepiness in my mind like a fog. I blink, confusion settling in as I take in the unfamiliar room. *Where am I?* I'm half aware of my hand resting on something very...firm. *Oh god, what did I do last night?*

My gaze travels upward until I meet a pair of intense eyes looking right back at me —Blaine's. His face is calm, but there's a spark of something else in his expression as he takes me in.

"Blaine...?" I stammer, my voice thick with confusion. "What...why...?" I blink a few times, trying to right my vision and wet my dry contact lenses, willing a full-formed thought into my brain.

His voice, low and edged with something dangerous, rumbles through his chest deep enough that I feel it vibrate against me. "Lily..." He draws a slow breath, eyes locked on mine. "Your hand is on my dick and has been for the last minute. Now, you're welcome to continue... but if not, kindly move it." His words sink in slowly, and my eyes drift down to where my hand is resting —right on his erection.

Horrified, I yank my hand back, scrambling to sit up and put distance between us. "Oh my god!" Heat floods my face as I cover it with my hands, mortified. "I... I thought I was dreaming! I thought—" My voice drops to a whisper as I barely manage to say it. "I thought it was *a sex dream*. I'm so sorry."

Still hidden behind my hands, I want nothing more than to disappear. I risk a peek at him, trying to gauge his reaction, only to find his gaze still fixed on me, one eyebrow slightly raised. His lips twitch, and for a second, I think I see him fighting back a smile. Oh, no. Oh, god, no. This is worse than any nightmare.

## BLAINE

Another ten seconds of her little whimpers and hand on my dick, and I would have come in my pants like a pubescent teen. Jesus fucking christ. I sit and then stand up, trying to hide how hard I am. A futile attempt in these damn pants. "Feel free to grab breakfast. Jenny is in the kitchen." I mutter before I walk down the hallway to my bedroom and immediately go into my bathroom locking the door and pull out my cock. Pressing the dispenser for a pump of lotion, I think of Lily's hands on me, her scent still lingering on my skin, and stroke myself several times before focusing on the tip, speeding my touch. I hang my head, letting out a deep groan.

Not even thirty seconds and I explode at the image of her on her knees and the crude and cheap sound of the lotion sliding across my skin. Holding still, I press my hand against the counter while the stars retreat from the edges of my vision and catch my breath before grabbing a wet towel from the warmer to clean myself.

I wash my hands clean of both my seed and sin and splash water on my face before grabbing a shirt to head out to the kitchen and try to hide that twinge of shame. I just jerked off to both my best friends' baby sister.

I make my way down the hall, past the kitchen, and into the dining room to see Jenny has a full spread and coffee ready, with my laptop for me next to my seat at the head of the table. "Mr. Vogeleir, good morning! Would you like something to drink, sir?" She greets me with a warm smile. "Our Ms. Stemmens is here bright and early today." She winks at me as I give her a quick warning glare. She just pats Lily on the shoulder before chuckling to herself and walking back to the kitchen. I look over and notice Lily awkwardly picking at a waffle and a piece of bacon. I clear my throat and take a drink of the orange juice in front of me.

"I have a couple of items that require my attention this morning and then I'm meeting Ronan at the gym at ten o'clock." Lily momentarily pauses at the mention of her brother's name, undoubtedly thinking the same thing I am.

*Hey Ronan. Great Morning. Slept with your baby sister and woke up to her basically fisting my cock moaning for me in her sleep. Ready for leg day?*

Fucking hell.

"Yeah, no, of course. I have... things to do too. A lot of them. So yeah, I need to go right now, actually, now that I think of it." She immediately stands up, throwing back her coffee before grabbing a muffin and turning to leave. "Bye then." I watch her leave, glancing at her ass in leggings until she turns the corner, and I hear Jenny wish her a good day, the door shutting behind her. Her pink box of cupcakes sits untouched on the island, and I frown slightly. I'll have Jenny run them down to her; I know she was excited about them.

The smirking older woman makes her way back towards me, and I purposefully don't make eye contact, staring at my screen to my left. She chuckles to herself and adds, "An overnight visitor, Mr. Blaine. I never thought I'd see the day. I checked the skies for flying pigs, and it's all clear. But maybe check the weather in Hell, hmm?"

"*Jenny...*" I give her a tone that implies no discussion. This is what happens when you have people work for you this long. They start thinking we're friends.

"I'm just saying she is a very beautiful and very sweet, lovely young lady. I won't say anything further." Her shorter frame and curvy hips sway as she walks away, laughing with a spray bottle in one hand and cloth in the other. I can't help the loud, heavy sigh that I let out before cutting into my waffle with a little too much force.

# 13

# LILITH

## *Before:*

The old, splintered wooden floor beneath my knees and arms digs into my skin. I rock back and forth, biting the inside of my cheek hard in an effort to stop my tears, the metallic taste of blood starting to fill my mouth. The memory of my mother's gentle humming and singing plays through my head as an unusual torture. *"You are my sunshine, my only sunshine..."*

I don't understand how I got here. How I went from having my mom and brothers and a mostly normal life going to school and doing homework to this. This terrifying, awful place with too many other kids, not enough food, and adults with heavy palms.

Orphans... that's what they call us, among other names.

That's what I am now. *"You make me happy when skies are gray..."*

The pain overtaking my chest fills every cell in my body until I'm positive I'm going to burst or my heart is going to physically break into pieces. The urge to claw my way into my own chest and rip it out from behind my ribs is overwhelming, and I regret I can't actually do it.

I've only experienced a physically broken heart once before. When my mother died. I thought my world had ended there that night. When numbness started building its walls around what became my reality. Now, both my mother and father are dead, and I've been taken from my brothers to live in this Hell. If there is a higher power, I can't help but wonder if I'm being punished.

My sobs become so overwhelming I can't hold them back, the pain built in my body forcing its way out, out, out. I hide under my metal bedframe in the corner against the wall, away from the others, fisting my hands so tight my fingernails dig and dig into my palms, and it oddly feels like something of a minor release. The pain feels right somehow. *"You'll never know, dear, how much I love you..."*

"God, would you shut up over there! We're all trying to fucking sleep! We're all orphans too, get over it. No one cares." Grumbles follow the outburst directed toward me in the otherwise silent night. All I can do is pull my hair in fistfuls from the root at my scalp and clench my jaw in silent screams.

I thought they'd come to get me, that this couldn't possibly be really happening. My brothers would find a way; they had to. But, they haven't, they didn't. Everything I knew, everything that made me crumble, and I'm left here in a broken pile begging for my own death to just end this pain, this nightmare.

The words *no one cares* echo and repeat in my brain as I realize just how true they are.

## K. J. FURY

*"...Please don't take my sunshine away."*

# 14

# LILITH

The next several weeks pass as normal. Work, go home, read, check in with the girls and my brothers here and there, squeeze in painting at Blaine's, struggle to sleep, repeat. My job is exhausting sometimes. When I got into this company, I thought it was a huge accomplishment. I didn't realize how much of a *prick* the corporate executives would be. I'm introverted and like to keep to myself, and I've learned I am incredibly sensitive to others' energy and my environment. So, the fact my boss and my boss's boss, and my boss's boss's boss are tyrants physically and mentally drains me. They certainly didn't get to their current rankings off of their charm. I can't help but angrily sigh. Actually, no, I guess that's not true. Because when money's involved or there's something they can get out of it, they're as charming as they come. *Vomit.* Honestly, I hate my job most days. Despise it. There may or may not be days when I imagine pushing them all out of the window or lighting the place on fire.

I lock my computer screen, grab my coat and purse, and shut my frosted glass office door. It's already getting too cold for my liking and is dark incredibly early, so the office is in shadows as I head out into the lobby where our receptionist, Demi, is sitting. "Have a lovely evening, Ms. Stemmens." She politely smiles.

"Thanks, Demi, you too. Have a good night." I step on the elevator and head to the first floor.

My therapist taught me to visualize a powerful 'forcefield' going up between myself and the building as I leave work each day to regulate my energy levels and boundaries between work and personal life. Truth be told, it doesn't work. It's utter bullshit. But I find myself still doing it, thinking one day it'll click.

It's surprisingly cold when I step out of the revolving door to the darkened downtown street. I'm meeting Larissa and Katie for a spin class at seven o'clock, which gives me just enough time to get home, make a smoothie, and change before meeting them. As much as I grumble about exercising, the spin classes are enjoyable. The one we go to is like walking into a club. The room is dark with lights and strobes, the music so loud you can't possibly even think. And the instructors have so much positive energy it's contagious, practically vibrating through the room until you're forced to accept it into your soul.

There's a free trolly that accesses a specific area of downtown. Part of my commute is along the route, so I try to jump on when I can. But, for the most part, I walk to and from work every day.

My favorite thing about mountain cities in winter are the lights. Every tree, lamppost, and shop along the way is glittering, making it feel almost surreal. A transition into the calm of the season, a temporary rest before our collective rebirth in the spring. The lights, I suppose, truly are just a glowing costume of despair and darkness... and isn't that just magnificent, too?

It's breathtaking. Not quite as storybook-esque as Vail, Aspen, or Breckenridge, but stunning, nonetheless.

The girls and I head back to the locker room after we finish up the class, drenched in sweat. "Oh my god, my legs are rubber; I can barely stand." Larissa collapses onto the bench in the center of the women's changing area. "That new instructor killed it, though, wow. Her playlist was one of the best I think I can remember." She grabs her water bottle, chugging it.

I try catching my breath and regulating my heart rate. "Yeah.... amazing..."

Katie just leans her hands on the lockers, as if trying not to faint. Between the three of us, we look incredibly out of shape, and I can't help but genuinely laugh at the image. "Can't... talk... one... minute."

"I'm going to hit the shower."

Larissa and Katie both grab a folded towel from the shelf at the end of the wall, following me.

"Same."

"Me too. Jesus christ. If I fall to the floor from a stroke right now, do me a favor and keep my plants alive and empty the bottom drawer of my nightstand if I die." Katie huffs.

We grab showers next to each other, our heads peeking over the tops of the cement barriers, and the curtains pulled closed on our individual stalls behind us. We take our time, as other women leave until it's just the three of us.

Katie moans like a ghost, standing under the hot water. "God, this feels so good. I think my skin is going to melt off." Lissa and I just hum back to her in quiet agreement. "Wanna grab a beer after? Nothing fancy; I look like I was hit by a truck. But a beer sounds good."

"Eh, I don't know. I have stuff I need to do. You girls, go ahead. I'll see you both this weekend, though, right?" I ask.

"I'll be there, definitely. I have a pink, fuzzy leopard print top I wanna break in. Lissa, are you in? Beer-thirty?"

"Screw it. Yeah, I'm in. And yes, I am planning on coming Saturday. The last time I really went out was on my birthday. Which, let's be honest, I needed a while to recover from."

I shut off the steaming water and grab my towel to dry off and wring out my hair. "Okay, cool, let's catch up then. And if anyone can pull off a pink leopard top, it's you, Kat."

I receive a small mock bow in response.

We all make our way back to the changing room, digging through our things and changing. I rub oil through my wet hair before wrapping it into a low bun at the base of my head.

"How's the painting at Blaine's going, Lil?" Katie looks over at me as she pulls her sweater down.

"It's going well, actually. I've been over several times, and Blaine has literally never been there. It's always either just me or me and his housekeeper. She's hilarious and super kind. It's been nice talking to her here and there. It's kind of weird, though; I thought I'd have seen him there by now. It's silly, but I was actually hoping I'd run into him when he's home. It's been weeks since our run-in at my brothers' place." I never told anyone about our movie and cuddle night. Blaine and I never spoke about it afterward, either. The bulk of our sparse interactions are limited to our passing in the lobby. Sometimes I wonder if it actually happened, and then I remember my embarrassment of stroking his dick and think yep, definitely real, definitely happened. I'll bring it up some other time to them.

"Well, he told Ronan he'd be there this weekend."

Why did I just internally sweat at that? I figured he'd be there. Hell, I want him to be there. —Ever since he opened up a little to me in the library, I've had a full-out crush on the man. Cuddling did not make that go away. It only intensified it, which is ridiculous. Not only have I always thought he was an asshole, but he's also both of my brothers' best friend. I know logically nothing could ever happen between us. But just the idea that I'll see him in a few days makes me giddy. "I gotta run, but group text for Saturday, kay? Love you girls, bye!" I didn't even put my coat on before running away. I just didn't feel all that up to talking about Blaine.

I know Katie thinks he may have a thing for me. But she believes everyone wants to fuck everyone else all the time. She's lost her credibility. Until I have reason to spill, my little crush needs to stay under wraps. She doesn't need ammunition. I sigh. Just remembering his playful, devilish smile in the low light of the library... the warmth of him and feeling the rumble of his voice in his chest next to me... the way he always crosses his ankle over his knee cockily, taking up so much space with his presence... it makes my smile spread ear to ear as I try to bite my lips into staying in place.

I throw on my coat and hood in front of the door before walking outside, where it's now lightly snowing, heading to my building. Daydreaming of a particular male eats my time, and I'm home before I even register that I am, as the concierge greets me.

# 15

# LILITH

I place the backing of my earring on as I stand straight to give myself a once-over before heading out. I went with one of my go-to dresses when I want to make a statement or catch someone's attention. It's a red, lightweight, silk spaghetti strap number that has loose fabric hanging over my chest and a slit up my left hip that's *far* too high to be ladylike. But it seems to get the job done. I even got my nails done to match too.

My hair reaches my lower back, and the shimmer spray I use causes every wave to catch the light in such a pretty way. I used to hate how tall I was and the color of my hair, growing up. Especially in school. For years, they were two of my biggest insecurities. But now, I own it. At around five-nine, five-ten, and add in heels, I can anticipate being as tall, if not taller, than at least fifty percent of the men around me. And damn it, if that doesn't make me feel a little wicked. A part of me wants to be the dark queen they bow and cower before—the small, buried part.

My ride-share pulls up to the upscale 'Ice and Oxygen' bar on the lower two levels of a popular boutique hotel. "Thank you. Have a good night." I hop out and make my way towards the entrance, gripping my black coat closed in the front to block the wind.

The front of the bar is seemingly plain. Just a white front with four black fire towers along the wall, and a bay of windows stretching from either side of the building. I show the doorman my ID and walk through a short, open alcove. Directly ahead is the open space of the main bar. The bartop stretches the length of the room and is entirely ice with a blueish lighting underneath causing it to glow. There are blue and golden string lights at various heights across the full ceiling, mimicking the night sky and stars. Past the main room, all the way to the back of the building, I can see the dancefloor and the club area, nearly black with LED lighting and lasers, the DJ right at the border of the two rooms on the right. However, upon walking in, there is a quiet area to the immediate left. Doesn't look closed off, there's just no one there and no bartender on that side. Definitely going to remember that later when I need to recharge. The place is pretty great, honestly. It's upscale and the ice thing is new and unique. Oxygen bars are common in higher-elevation towns in the mountains, but not in Denver. Along the left wall, there is raised booth seating stretching the length of the wall with individual tables and a few stools on the sides. The middle of the room is open. I'm sure, for patrons later in the night once it's even more packed.

I spot Ronan at one of the tables along a seat almost to the dancefloor at the end of the large room and make my way over. "Lily, you made it!" I smile, walking up to the group with two bottles already on the table. Ronan, Artemis, Katie, Larissa, Elliott... no Blaine. A wave of disappointment washes over me that he may not be here.

"Hi, guys." I make my way around to give quick hugs to everyoneealizing I forgot to check my coat at the door. "I'll be right back; I need to check my coat." I make my way back to the front of the bar, careful not to bump into anyone along the way. It's not packed yet, but it's definitely a popular spot if this many people are here at nine o'clock. I reach the small coat check counter and give my name and number to the younger brunette girl working it. I take off my heavy coat, revealing my dress, and a couple of men are already looking my way.

Works Every. Damn. Time.

Handing it to her and accepting my ticket in exchange, I turn back to rejoin the group, tucking the piece of paper safely into my purse.

"Lily..." I freeze, and a wave of excitement shivers through me, palpable as my skin pebbles with goosebumps, my heart jumping a bit. I know that deep, commanding voice anywhere. I can feel his eyes on me.

Turning to face Blaine, he immediately drops his gaze down the length of my body, lingering on my bare thigh showing through the high slit. "Hi." God damn it, he looks fine tonight... *fuck me.* He usually sports all-black, but tonight he's wearing a white button-up, folded at his muscular forearms, emphasizing his broad shoulders, and showing a peek into his tattooed chest. His eyes are practically the same color as the ice bar itself. And he's got just enough stubble on his face to add an additional edge he doesn't normally have. What was I saying? "Glad you could make it out tonight," I say. At least, I think those are the words that come out. Some sort of noise escapes my lips.

He leans forward, placing a warm, heavy hand on my shoulder enough so that his low voice and breath touches my ears and hits my stomach instead. "Lilith... you're going to have every man here tripping over themselves, fighting for your attention with that dress." He pulls away enough to look me in my eyes and study my face as I just stare up at him, lips parted, before lowering his hand to the small of my back and guiding me to the back where our friends are. It feels like he's claiming me by touching me in front of the other men here. *Be like Katie tonight, Lily. I am sexy. I am confident. Blaine is attracted to me, and I am desirable.*

I immediately feel the lack of warmth as he removes his hand when we near our friends, aka: my brothers. I don't miss the subtle caress against my bottom as his hand leaves me, though. A sudden pulse in my lower stomach at the feather-light touch causes me to nearly trip. As everyone settles around the table, the girls and I end up together at one end while the guys all talk and drink next to us.

The DJ starts to play better dance music as the night progresses. A couple of drinks later, Katie and my brothers made their way upstairs to explore the oxygen treatment bar on the second floor. Larissa grabs Elliott and me to the dance floor for a remix of a sensual Madonna hit. It's getting packed in here and we barely have room to move, sweaty bodies bumping into us. I let go into the music a little and sway my hips with my arms up, dancing with Larissa; Elliott to our side, towering a little over us —a cocoon in the blackness of the dancefloor. I glance to the table and see Katie is back and sitting with Blaine while my brothers must be upstairs still. I think she's trying and failing to have a conversation with him, fluctuations of amusement and annoyance flashing across her face. He's never been the most talkative person, though, and always seems grumpy. He certainly doesn't look engaged now. But I think I'm starting to understand him a little more. I definitely see a new side of him that others don't get access to. Or, I assume, very few.

I feel a tap on my shoulder as someone grabs my arm to get my attention. *Oh god... no. Xavier.* He's an old ex from years ago, but he still tries to hit me up now and again on weekends, always after eleven. He's such an asshole, and just looking at his cheetah print shirt unbuttoned way too low, I immediately know he hasn't changed. He used to get high out of his mind and drink too much and then take his anger out on me. I feel sick just thinking of the ways he humiliated and treated me —the things he did behind my back.

His touch feels like a lit brand, a surge of lightning to my nervous system. I'm frozen, working to keep my breath even.

Before blocking him, the rare time I checked social, I could anticipate a post of him trying to show off how much money he blows or how many strippers can fit on his lap. "Hey Lily... it's been so long. I can't believe you're here tonight. You look absolutely amazing. You are definitely wearing that dress, baby." He tries to grab my hand to bring it up to him, licking his lips, but I pull away. "Look, I'd love to get together again sometime. Relive old memories." He tries again, putting his hand on my hip, trying to pull me closer, suffocating me. Any words feel trapped in my throat. "Maybe tonight? You're here; I'm here. I have a new place, no roommates, that's not far." He licks his lips again as he tilts his head, looking me up and down —a predator assessing its prey. Before I can push him away and turn to leave, he grabs my wrist, stopping me and pulling me back into him. He's so close I can feel his body heat and the smell of that same cologne, the whiskey on his breath. "Lily, baby, don't leave. I guess that was a little forward." I feel his hand holding my lower back, anchoring me, and I can feel a spark of panic in my chest. The voice in my head telling me to *run, run, run.* "I just miss you is all, and you look fucking sexy as hell, baby. Come here. Please." The words are on the tip of my tongue, stuck, to tell him to go fuck himself, just as a familiar scent and warmth comes up behind me. Immediately, it's like a comforting blanket surrounding me, nearly muting the sounds around me, enabling deep breaths.

"Who's this, Lily?" Blaine wraps his arm around the front of my waist, pulling me possessively, but gently out of Xavier's grasp and into his own, against his hard chest. Looking him over with that menacing, quiet, confident way he always does, Xavier looks back between us, stiffening and broadening his shoulders.

# 16

# Lilith

"My bad, man. I'm just an old... friend. Lily, if you change your mind, you know how to contact me." He pushes away from the table he's leaning against and walks away, looking back at Blaine and me.

"Thank you. That was... a shitty ex from years ago. He's the last person I expected to see here." I nervously laugh as someone bumps into me, pushing me into him. I press my hands to his chest to push myself off. "Sorry, sorry. Not my fault." I look up to see he's not looking at me. Following his gaze, I see he's still tracking Xavier's movements as he heads towards the entrance. Fortunately, the spike of adrenaline from Xavier's touch is wearing off; Blaine's presence and warmth like Xanex. In its place, a desire and voracity to pull Blaine against me. I look around, and behind us, Larissa and Elliott are getting relatively close, dancing while he's talking intimately into her ear. *Be like Katie... and Larissa, apparently?*

I grab Blaine's hand and pull him further into the dark, away from the line of sight of our table. Katie is there, just in case. But I'd rather my brothers not see this if they come back downstairs. "Come on." I smile up at him as I move closer, dancing in front of him.

"What are you doing?" His lips brush my ear as he leans in, causing me to shiver at the light touch.

"We're dancing. Elliott is dancing with Lissa... so, you can dance with me." I move closer again, enough to where our bodies are pressed together. I lay one hand on his chest, moving it slightly as my other goes around his neck. I try to dance slowly to get him out of whatever shell he's hiding in. But I notice Blaine's jaw tenses and ticks as he stands perfectly still, staring at me. Staring through me. *I pushed too far; I'm such an idiot.* "Sorry, hey, I didn't mean to upset you." I pull away, shaking my head slightly, removing my hands immediately. "We can go back to the table. I just thought maybe... I don't know what I thought. I'm so sorry." I go to walk away, biting my lip, not wanting to make eye contact after being embarrassed and vulnerable.

But he grabs my wrist and pulls me back, devouring my body in my dress before he pulls me as close as we could be. Nothing between us but shared breath. I gasp at the sensation of nearly every inch of us touching, his hands around my waist. I put my hands around his neck as we find a rhythm to the music overtaking us. He brings his head down, touching my forehead to his as his hands guide my hips in perfect alignment with our bodies. I can't help but close my eyes, taking in the feel of him against me, his scent, the texture of his shirt. I lift my head back slightly as he positions one hand on the base of my neck, holding me in place as our faces touch. Opening my eyes, the darkness coats us like a damp cloth; shadows and light just barely illuminate our faces as they pass through the room. He slowly traces his nose along mine, brushing his lips to the side of mine. It would be so easy to just... kiss him right now. I lower my gaze down to his lips and back up. Just as I think I may have the courage to do it, lifting my lips to his, it's like he reads my thoughts and turns me around so my back is to his chest. He presses me against him, one hand on my hip, the other placed gently around the front of my neck as he continues to guide us to the music. Fuck, this is so much better than anything I could have realistically thought the night would have turned into.

Our bodies move in perfect sync as his hand lowers and slides to my bare skin, where the high slit in my dress hits my hip. His fingers are under my dress, moving over the junction at my thigh, pushing me against him. That simple move is enough to make me toss my head back to his chest and reach my arm around to the back of his neck, a small, breathless moan only he can hear.

It's so dark and crowded, I know no one is paying attention. Even if they were, there are too many people in a too-dark space to be able to clearly see anyone. My hips move, grinding against his front, and I can feel the hard length of him through his pants. His hand slips further in, so slowly as we dance. So, torturously slow. God, all it would take is one tiny movement and he'd be touching me. My brain turns foggy, and I know my chest must be flushed at my body's reaction to him —this sudden desire. The thought has me practically begging in my head, moving my hips in a manner to get his hand just a little closer. Just a little... *god, please, just a little closer.* I feel out of my mind, acting on sheer animalistic instinct.

He moves his lips over my ear, brushing against them, a feather-light warning nip at my lobe. "Lily... behave. I'm not going to touch your pussy for the first time in a dark club with your brothers in the next room. As much of a fucking turn-on as it is having your perfect ass hugging my cock." I've never heard him speak like that and I almost whimper; his deep voice so close to my ear it's like every cell in my body comes to life, floating just outside of my skin. "Behave." His deep rumble when he speaks is enough to make my knees weak. I'm so dizzy that I almost open my eyes to make it end. I've never really thought of voices being this sexy. But just the sound of him covers my arms in goosebumps at the sensation.

He's literally telling me to stop. But, I don't know if it's the alcohol, the music, his body and hand under my dress, but all he's doing is making me far more needy by telling me to be good. To listen to his command. I know I'm not thinking straight right now, and I can't bring myself to care or think about it too much as the music caresses us in waves. I reach a hand down, the other still behind us on the back of his neck, and quickly put it over his, pushing his fingers the couple of inches so they're touching my panties and over my clit. He sucks in a breath through his teeth. "God damn it, Lilith, what are you trying to do to me," he grinds out. But his fingers are moving just enough that it feels so fucking good and dangerous, knowing he's touching me in a group of strangers who could notice at any time. My brothers and all of our friends could see at any second. "You're a fucking siren, Lily Stemmens. A naughty girl dressed up like a good one, aren't you?"

God, yes, I'll be anything he wants me to be.

"Yes." I know he hears me even with how breathless I am as his fingers move and caress that tiny bundle of nerves under my dress, his near-demanding cock in his slacks not leaving my body. He presses down heavier, and god, it feels so amaz—.

"LILY!" *Fuck*. Immediately, we both snap out of the heated trance we're in, his hands falling from my neck and dress before we turn around to see Katie making her way closer to us. "Lily, there you are. Your brothers were looking for you; we didn't know you were still over here in the club part. We're going to call it a night soon. You ready?" Blaine stalks away, looking pissier than usual, not even saying a single word, and disappears through the crowd of people.

"Yes, yeah. Xavier showed up and was grabbing on me, and Blaine came and stopped him... oh my god, Katie." I put one hand on her shoulder and the other on my forehead as if that would make me forget what just happened. I lean in closer to her. "I got him to dance with me, Katie. I got *Blaine to dance* with me."

"I knew you both looked guilty of something." She flicks her fingers onto my reddened chest teasingly. "Fifty bucks says he's rocking a hard-on walking past your brothers." She laughs. "Okay, let's go to the girl's room since he just went out there; we'll act like that's where I found you. Lissa and Elliott said they lost you guys, so they're already out there. Anyway, it's not important, oh my god! Girl's room and then home. THEN we're talking tomorrow because

I want every goddamn detail. I am fucking living for this right now." She excitedly rambles as I follow behind in a trance. Depending on her mood, Katie sometimes throws together ridiculous outfits. And yet... it always works for her, just like the cowgirl hat. Tonight, she has a fuzzy leopard crop top, shiny red pants under over-the-knee black boots, and a gold chain around her waist. And she somehow makes it look incredible and sexy.

Katie and I returned to the table to see that Blaine was nowhere in sight, and everyone else was waiting for us. Ronan's annoyed, pointed look landing on us. "Lily! What the fuck, where did you go!"

"She was in the little girl's room, and we danced awhile. Sorry! A good song came on. We had to!"

"Whatever, alright, we're calling it. Tabs taken care of, let's go. Lil, we'll drop you off on the way home. Elliott, are you good to make sure Lissa gets home safe, man?"

"Of course, I always do, don't I?" He winks at Lissa as she rolls her eyes and looks away. I don't miss the color tinting her cheeks, though.

We all go outside, waiting for our ride-shares to get there. And as everyone else chatters and yells in the cold night, and the club music blares inside... all I can think about is the fact that Blaine fucking danced with me tonight. No, he not only danced with me but had his hands and fingers on intimate parts of me as we ground against one another. The feeling of his hand on my throat and guiding my hips as I felt his erection. He wanted me... I know he did. Someone could stiletto-stomp my big toe right now, and it still wouldn't get the smile off my face.

# 17

# LILITH

## *Before:*

The smell of fresh flowers surrounds me, and the steady thump of my mother's heart echoes under my ear. My favorite place in the world is right here, in her arms. Everything about her is soft: her dark blue sweater, her long hair, and even her skin. I fight back my smile that wants to take over my lips as she holds me to her chest, one hand slowly stroking my back and hair.

Sometimes I think she's my best friend. The other kids at school aren't very friendly, and my brothers have their own school friends and sports team friends. So, I spend my time alone or with her. I don't want to be near anyone else. I'm too big to be carried around like this, but she doesn't seem to mind, so neither do I. I don't like it when other people touch me; it makes me feel sick and has too many other feelings at once to explain. But her touch, I not only allow but deeply enjoy. It's the only time I feel safe, knowing she's here with me.

The lullaby she's humming comes to a stop as I feel her pull back to look down at me, and I can't stop my smile now. I like to fake sleep sometimes just to enjoy more of our time together.

The image of green trees and the vast open area of grass behind our house comes into view as I open my eyes to her gentle words. "Is my sweet girl awake?" I shut my eyes again quickly to play but can't stop the giggle in my chest as she tickles my ribs. "Uh-huh! That's what I thought. We have a faker on our hands." Her soft lips touch my head with a kiss.

"My beautiful, brave, sweet little ray of sunshine. Have I told you how much I love you yet today?" I pull back and shake my head, her golden eyes glowing back at me. Artemis told me I have the same eyes as her. I hope I look as pretty as she does someday. She makes 'tsking' noises, setting me down on my feet. "Hmm, well, we need to remedy that asap, don't we, my darling girl?" Holding her hands directly in front of her, only a few inches in between, she bites her bottom lip. "Does this look right? Is this how much I love you?" I shake my head, holding my lips together. "Hmm... what aboutttt this much?" She moves her hands further apart, looking down at me. I shake my head again, putting a hand over my mouth to stop the laugh that wants to come out. "What aboutttt this much!" She spreads her arms as wide as they will go, smiling. I let my laugh free and nod happily in response. "And how much does my Lily girl love her momma?" I jump back and spread my arms, twirling around to make them bigger and bigger. "Woah, that much! That's a lot of love! What if I love you that much, too!" She starts spinning with her arms wide next to me, the world a blur of green and blue as I get dizzy and fall to the ground laughing. Mom stands over me, and I can just make out her smile as the world starts to slowly right itself.

# 18

# LILITH

The room Blaine is lending me to paint in is perfect. He even had an easel and two large tables brought in for my supplies at some point. The room is entirely plain and undecorated. I don't think he used it for anything. He had one of his staff -I assume Jenny- prepare the room and tape down a thick sheet of plastic over the floor to protect against paint spills. (Which has already proven to be an excellent idea on his part.) It's a light grey room, a shiny resin coating the cement floor under the clear tarp. Wall-to-wall, full-length windows facing the mountains allow the winter evening setting sunlight to stream in. My studio was too small to comfortably paint in and simultaneously store all of my canvases and finished or half-completed paintings. Him sharing his space and this room for me to access freely is unbelievable. And incredibly generous. I can't help but wonder why he would offer.

I stand back to admire my painting and can swear an energy that feels an awful lot like my smiling mother pulls goosebumps from my skin. I can't stop the tug at my own lips just thinking she's here with me, hanging out. The painting's turning out exactly as I'd hoped it would. Inspired by my dream, I see an unclothed, exposed woman seemingly partially made of life and flowers, light itself hugging every curve of her body like water. Divine feminine. Her arms and hair float as if she were underwater as dark vines twist around her ankles and legs, pulling her into a despair of darkness and nothingness. It's haunting and painful, exactly as all my pieces are. To elicit a feeling, a response, *something* to get the viewer to stop in their tracks as it relates to their own inner shadows they bury. I suppose it's true that everyone has their own traumas. However, it's not black and white. It's a grayscale of hurt leading to a pit of nothing and yet everything. Hurts are not equal. Traumas are not equal.

Sore and a little tired, I set my brushes in the bucket of water, cleaning them, and decide to lie down on the floor on my back. I take deep, slow breaths and focus on the sensation of every inch of my body connecting to the hard floor. Of the silence of the apartment. The dimming sunlight behind my eyelids as the sun sets for the evening. The dried paint on my fingers and hands, still just slightly sticky. My feet somewhat colder than the rest of my body. I've learned that sometimes, to really ground myself, following this exercise and learning to *feel* in my body was the small reminder I needed to find gratitude for simply being... existing, and experiencing life through the eyes of a human, through my physical body. The darkness, just as the woman I am painting, is always just under the surface, waiting —just the slightest opening or opportunity to pull me under too. But the idea that I am more, that we all are, has always been helpful to me. Understanding that every emotion and every experience is why we are here in this lifetime, as terrible and heartbreaking as they may be. *I am okay. I am safe. I simply am.* For every thunderstorm cursing its lightening upon me, there is a rainbow, a golden sunset, an early morning swim in the vast calm ocean. My arms wide at my side I smile to myself, *finding the nice moments. Finding happiness.* If I can find the happy, I'll be okay.

I hear nearly silent footsteps approaching the open door before they stop what I'd assume to be five feet or so from me as a deep voice rushes over me. "I see you are making use of the room."

"It's been perfect. Thank you, again." I open my eyes to meet his stark grey ones staring at me. Not the room I've made a mess in. Not the painting. Me.

"Mmm. What are you doing on the floor?" He slightly tilts his head to the side.

I can't help but widen my smile. "Why... chasing rainbows." Blaine looks at me as if he can't figure me out, and I chuckle before pushing myself up into a sitting position and then standing. Blaine looks me over, covered in paint, and then glances at the painting behind me and to his right. I see the shift in his face as his eyes land on the woman consumed unforgivingly by darkness, and I can't read his expression. Suddenly, a bit embarrassed, I feel the need to divulge. "It's not finished yet, so I know it may not look terribly great right now..."

"It's... incredible." Oh. I feel a flush of warmth hit my cheeks and neck as I watch him study the painting. "How much?"

"I —I'm sorry?"

"I'd like to buy it; how much do you want for it?" He looks over at me, waiting.

"Blaine... I... I mean, it's not even completed. Are you sure?" I half laugh, a bit bewildered at the thought he wants to purchase a painting from me.

"More than sure. I need it in my gallery. Name your price, or I'll settle on the cost for you." *Typical entitled-asshole Blaine comment.* I look at him and step forward a couple of feet, considering.

"I have an alternative idea, something better." He narrows his eyes, waiting. "One favor. You promise me one favor at my chosen time and we're even. She's yours to do what you will with." I know Blaine's reputation enough to understand that a favor I can call in anytime from him is worth far more than his money. He recognizes this, too, as he holds his gaze upon me, unyielding.

"Deal." One simple word and yet enough to make my heart skip slightly.

"Deal," I repeat, smiling. He takes a final look at the painting, steps out of the room, and makes his way down the hall into his main kitchen area. Everything is pristine under strategic lighting after his housekeeper-chef-estate manager-whatever the hell Jenny is- has left for the day.

# 19

# BLAINE

I can hear the loud patter of Lilith's bare feet on the floor behind me as I make my way back towards the kitchen.

"What are your plans for tonight? Anything on the agenda?" She stops on the opposite side of the large white marble island, watching me. I don't need to look; I can feel her eyes on me. I practically have them memorized and seared into my brain at this point.

I do, in fact, have plans. A meeting... of sorts, if that's the appropriate term. More so, a mutual agreement for sex. I don't date in the common use and understood meaning. I make it clear from the start what I'm looking for and ensure we're on the same page to avoid headaches. One night. One hour. Nothing intimate, ever. If they're looking for aftercare, that's not me. I'm strictly looking for a release and assume if they agree, they are too. Unfortunately, it seems many women struggle with the agreement and don't actually believe me when I explain expectations. Being distant and straight to the point only makes them try harder. It's unbelievably frustrating. I can be a fucking cold prick, and they still can't get it through their heads. For that reason, I have a select few women I know I can reach out to when I want sex that I've had in my rolodex, some for years. Mostly the women I meet at Ronan's little fuckfest palace: The Red Room, in their carriage house. I'm far from a hater, though. It's worked very well for my purposes. I can say with certainty having Lilith's perfect ass in my hands and pussy under my fingers is not helping the building hunger and near-desperate need growing under my skin.

"No. No plans." *Liar.*

"How... would you feel about a scary movie night?" I pause my movements, still facing the open refrigerator. That is not what I expected her to say. I'm not sure what I expected, but it wasn't that. "We could make a night of it. Invite the guys, Katie and Larissa. Snacks, beer, scary movies in your theater?" I turn to face her. Her eyes are big, expectant, and so innocently waiting, reflecting the white light from the countertop. That little smile... fuck.

She's... she's doing it on purpose, so I say yes. Sly little siren she is. I narrow my eyes, but the side of my lips twitch upward, realizing her game. I suppose I can wait another night —I've gone this long without, what's one more night... I sigh. "Send a group text, get the guys to stop for alcohol, and we can order takeout." You'd think I'd gifted her a puppy with how her eyes light up. I'm forced to rub my chest; I'm not about to address the tightness that evoked under my skin. Whatever the fuck that was.

"Yes! Yay! Okay, eight o'clock?"

I nod and walk to the south end of the penthouse. "Goodbye, Lily." I can *feel* her eyes roll behind me and I smile as I take off my coat and toss it on the back of one of my bedroom's lounge chairs, hearing the door shut as she leaves. I press the button on the wall, settling on my lighting to a deep purple, adding to the warmth of the golden lamps as the main door auto-locks in the other room. Another press and classical music plays throughout the space quietly. I lift my wrist to check the time, a mental checklist quickly building in my mind.

## LILITH

Pick up... pick up, pick up... "Hey, Lil!" I get into my apartment and practically slam the door behind me. *Shit, oops.*

"Katie, please tell me you don't have plans tonight. Are the boys home too?"

"Uhhh... yes, they're both here. I don't think they have plans; they haven't said anything to me. Why, what's up?" I can hear the hesitance in her voice.

"I need you all to come to Blaine's at eight o'clock and bring beer and snacks." When she doesn't respond, I can practically hear her wheels turning, waiting for me to say more. "I got Blaine to host a scary movie night in his theater and promised him we'd get the whole group together. He's already ordering takeout for everyone as we speak." *Lie.*

"Babe... you could have Blaine *alone* in a dark room, with an excuse to throw yourself into his lap. Are you sure you *want* us to come?" She's smiling. I know she's smiling on the other end of this phone.

"Yes, just —please? I'll text the group. See you at eight o'clock." I hang up before she can say anything further. She always hangs up on me; it's payback. If she really didn't want to come, she'd call me right back or text me.

Why am I so nervous right now? I'm thirty-two, not twenty-two. I've known Blaine for years. This is no big deal. No. Big. Deal. Should I shower? I head toward my bathroom. No, wait, I should probably pick out an outfit first. No, wait, I should make hot tea. Wait, oh my god, I have to send the group text. My head is a whirlwind. *Breathe. What is wrong with you? Get it together, girl.* I pause to pick up my phone.

> Movie night at Blaine's! 8:00 tonight - BYOBAS

**Larissa**
> YES, I'm in! What's BYOBAS LOL

> Bring your own beer and snacks :P

**Larissa**
> *Heart and cry laughing emoji*

**Ronan**
> Sounds lame. What movie?

**Katie**
> Shut up Rone. You know you're going to come. Sounds fun babe, I'll be there!

**Elliott**
> Sounds chill, count me in. I'll bring wine.

**Artemis**
> I'm game. Ronan said he's coming too. We'll stop for beer on the way.

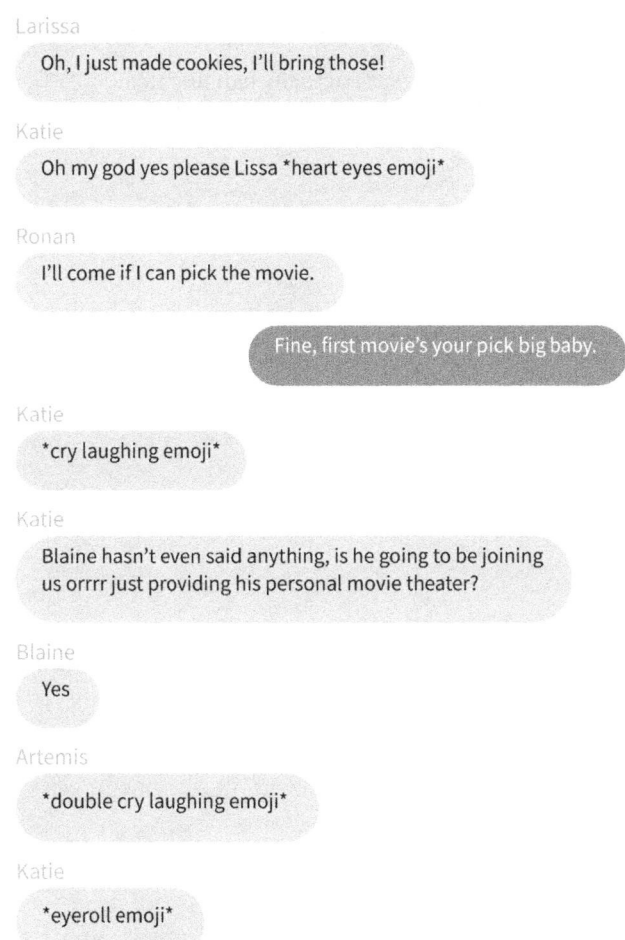

Perfect, everyone's in. I turn on my tea kettle to warm as the texts come through and go to my bathroom to turn on the shower. Now, while that's heating up, outfit. Something casual but cute enough to catch Blaine's eye. Half of my clothes are piled in my walk-in closet, and I skim my eyes over what's actually hanging first.

Keep it simple...

# 20

# Lilith

I shower and get ready. Letting my hair out of the hot rollers, I toss my hair around —looking like a bird caught mid-air, suddenly losing the ability to fly. The waves tumble down my back, and I run my fingers through them to break up the perfect curls.

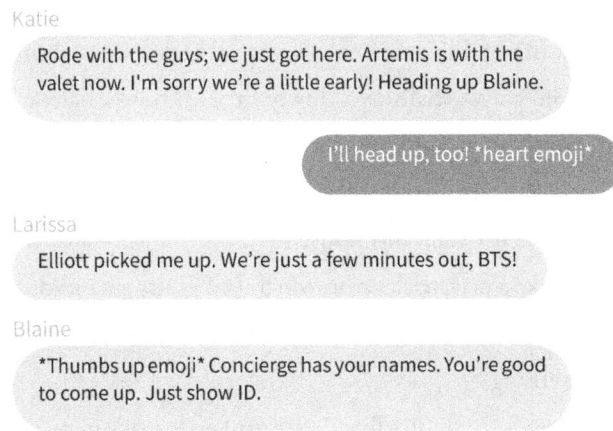

I grab my handbag and make my way down the hall towards the row of elevators, surprise hitting me when it opens to my brothers and Kat.

"LIL!" Katie gives me a big hug. "You look hot!"

"Hey, baby sister!"

"Hey, sis." Ronan and Artemis both hug me at the same time; Ronan kissing the top of my head. Thank god, no noogies.

"I'm so happy you guys came. I missed you." I reach down grabbing Ronan's hand in a gesture of appreciation and love. He looks and acts tough with his tattoos and the stupid grills he wears, but he really is a huge teddy bear. To women at least. Not so sure I'd wanna cross him as a dude. I've seen him in one fight years ago, and that was once too many. It was terrifying.

The elevator doors open to the top floor —Blaine's penthouse. The main entrance is directly ahead, double glossy black doors set against dark gray walls. —No indication of name or address. I guess if you own the building and the giant penthouse, it's a given who you are. The private hallway is lowly lit with rows of sleek black sconces emitting warmth to the otherwise cold feel of the area. Down the small hall to the right is a second single door, serving as an entrance for staff and house help. To the very left, there is what looks like a private elevator, which I'm pretty sure leads to the rooftop and the garage for his personal access, although valet also covers everything.

Artemis rings the doorbell as Katie turns and winks at me. Ronan catches it and narrows his eyes. "Hey, brother!" Artemis grabs our attention as he enters the double doors and greets Blaine pleasantly. "We brought an assortment of beer and a bottle of bourbon, I hope that works." The guys enter first, then Katie, leaving me last. When

I walk in, I can't help but notice the look Blaine gives me, setting my chest on fire. I take the opportunity to lean in for a hug like the others, and I linger just a second longer than I should, enjoying the feel of his large, warm hand on my lower back and his body against mine.

"I see you changed." As he removes his hand to grab the door, he ever so slightly brushes my ass, and my legs nearly freeze at the touch.

"I figured you wouldn't appreciate having your perfect white furniture turned into a contemporary art exhibit."

Walking into Blaine's, there is a short entryway into the large expanse of crisp, white kitchen to the right. Very sleek and modern, like what you'd expect in a California beach home overlooking L.A. The obscenely oversized center island catches your eye and draws you to it immediately, where everyone else happens to be as well. Pizza boxes sit open as everyone helps themselves. The hanging light fixtures over the countertop set off an array of shadow and light, while the pristine white marble reflects into everyone's eyes, brightening them. The effect makes Blaine's unspeakably beautiful and near angelic. Although I know between the two, Blaine is closer to being the Devil or Hades himself than an angel. But I don't believe the Devil is all bad. And I don't believe Blaine is either. He's already shown me glimpses of who he really is, buried under his hard façade. There's so much more there he doesn't show anyone.

The speaker system throughout his house plays mainstream hip-hop and dance music, the lighting all set to a beautiful purple color, outside of the kitchen itself. Past the kitchen is a darkened great room, shadowed and showing off the glittering view behind the impressive expanse of windows. In the center, is the main hall leading left or right. His bedroom is to the left hall but that's about as much as I know outside of my new painting room. Pretty sure every room would be locked anyway if I tried.

There's a knock at the door before Blaine opens it to a happy Larissa holding her cookies with an Elliott in tow. "Hi! Oh my god, I am so excited!" She sets the cookies down and starts a new round of hugs as she approaches me. "You look amazing!" She moves on to Blaine, who I feel is again by the doorway to my right. "Thanks so much for hosting tonight, Blaine; your place is incredible!"

"No problem. Hey Elliott, good to see you, man."

"You too, Blaine, looking good, man. Place is stunning as ever."

Everyone makes their way to crowd around the island, listening to music, eating and drinking, catching up. "Lily! Come here!" Katie hauls me to the hallway towards a bathroom and shuts us in. "Okay, one, you look sexy as fuck, babe. Good job on the skirt, too, easy access." She winks and smiles at me. "Actually, wait. Be right back; poor Lissa's surrounded by testosterone." She holds up her finger as she sneaks out and shuts the door. I glance in the mirror and fluff my hair; I do look pretty cute tonight, turning to check out my butt. "OKAY. Had to grab our girl first. Now... we need to get a plan. Blaine and Lil have to sit together and they need to sit in the back row of his theater room. I'm thinking I'll push the boys into the front row with me; Lissa and Ell can sit in the middle, leaving the two of you in the back?" I nod back with a half smile. "I'm so fucking happy right now, Lily. He's gonna make a move; I just know it." Katie claps her hands together. I feel like I'm in a school bathroom, during a high school dance. I mean, I am excited though. "Good? Ready?" At our nods, we head back out to the main area, the music coming to life again with the door opening.

"Girls, can I get you anything? All good?" Artemis comes up to us, smiling and charming as usual —ever the politician.

"We're good, thanks though!" We make our way back to the island.

"Girls are back. Ladies, want a shot? I'll make it taste good." Elliott asks, handsome as hell with tanned skin and dark hair perfectly combed and styled back.

"Yes, we do!" Katie pushes us towards him.

"Umm, baby, one for me!" I plead to him as he smiles knowingly. "Lightweight and whatnot," I mumble under my breath and look over in time to catch Blaine with the left side of his lips twitching. I shoot him a glare, and that just makes the other side lift, too, before looking away.

"Okay, shots and then movie time." Elliott hands out glasses to everyone at the counter, handing a half shot to me directly. "Milady." I smile with gratitude. "Okay, okay. Raise 'em! —Let's drink to life... the passing show... and to the eyes... of the *prettiest* girl you know. Cheers!" We all raise our glasses, and I notice a sly smile from Elliott to Larissa. Maybe more's happened since he took care of her on her birthday? They were sure as hell close on the dancefloor at the oxygen bar.

The music slowly drifts to an almost whisper, barely audible, as it continues to play throughout the speakers. I notice the ambient hum in place of the hip-hop is a healing frequency and bite my lip to hold in my grin. Katie gives me a look, then Larissa as she forces my brothers both through the great room and into the theater in the front row. Larissa follows suit and asks Elliott if he'd sit with her in the middle row. I guess her plan worked, leaving Bla.... *Woah.* Oh, this is so cool. Walking in, it's a massive room with an image being projected on the main wall from its source hanging in the center of the ceiling. There are three fluffy, expensive-looking beige couches, each elevated so as not to block the viewer behind or in front of it. Sconces line the walls pointing streams of light directly above and below it onto the walls, as well as matching soft light around the base of each couch and along the walkway exactly like you'd see in a real movie theater. Thick soundproofing curtains flow over the walls, a greyish beige themselves. It's so warm and inviting. Blaine is next to me and must've caught my surprise. "Do you like it?"

"Are you kidding? This is incredible…" The others take their seats, leaving Blaine and me to the back. We both sit, sadly, a safe distance away from each other.

"Ronan, you pick a movie?" He says down to my brother in the first row.

"Just sent it to you! You're all going to love it." He laughs. I look over to my left, and Blaine is looking at his phone, smirks, and half laughs.

"Yep... got it... give me a second, and I'll get the lights too." His deep voice is almost muffled by the theater, controlling everything through his phone. I settle in, grabbing a small, soft throw pillow from my right. The projector comes to life as previews play for the movie.

"RONAN! You did not. You asshole! This is supposed to be the scariest movie of our lifetime or some shit. Come on... seriously?!" Katie leans over, sitting between my brothers, smacking Ronan's shoulder as he throws his head back, laughing.

"Shhh, Katie, the movie's starting. Don't be rude to the other guests." He laughs, and I grip my pillow tighter to my chest. Fucking Ronan. I must look nervous as the lights start to dim to near darkness because Blaine reaches his hand between us, indicating I should move closer. My stupid little heart pitter-patters as I move closer to him, still holding my pillow in a death grip.

# 21

# LILITH

We barely make it twenty damn minutes into the movie before Katie screams at a jump scare. Instinctively, I grab Blaine's arm, clutching his bicep and tucking his elbow tight to my chest as I close my eyes. From below, Ronan and Artemis both start laughing hysterically, their low murmurs surely giving Kat shit in the darkness.

As I open my eyes and the scene unfolds, I become aware of how tightly I'm gripping Blaine's arm. I start to let go and pull away, but before I can, his hand shifts, settling firmly on my thigh. A soft shiver runs through me when I realize he's not moving it away. His eyes meet mine, heavily lidded with a devious smirk dancing at the corner of his mouth. Our gazes hold silently for what feels like too long, and then I realize. I nod almost unnoticeably, giving the permission I know he's waiting for. Without a word, he slips his hand a little higher... and higher, fingers warm against my skin, pulling me closer to him. He returns his attention to the screen, but his hand lingers, firmly placed near the apex of my thighs. My heart's going to beat out of my chest, whether from him or from the movie.

He slowly caresses his thumb in gentle circles against the top of my thigh, each pass sending a fresh spark of warmth through me. His hand feels incredible —strong, warm, with calluses from weight lifting that oppose my soft skin –utter masculinity. I try to keep my breathing steady as I feel the side of his palm so close to my wet panties, each touch deliberate and unhurried, until I can't take it anymore.

I wrap my hand gently over his and slide it the short distance to where I need it, as high as it will go between my legs. Forcing myself to look over at Blaine, I see a blazing heat in those illuminated eyes as he watches our hands together, and I adjust my hips slightly, rocking against him. Meeting my eyes again for several seconds, he leans closer, lips brushing against my ear in a whisper, causing chills to erupt over my body.

"Eyes on the screen or keep them closed, little siren. Break the rule, and I stop. This doesn't leave this room." I don't entirely know how he meant it, but I nod. Did he mean to look out if anyone looks at us? He wants them closed? But I lick my lips and break our gaze to look straight ahead, with a quick scan over my friends and brothers just in case. He slowly starts moving his hand, his touch hot against my sheer lace thong. I know he has to feel that I'm wet for him; they're so thin. He unhurriedly grazes his pinky against me, teasing me just to the point I nearly demand more. I briefly glance down to watch his hand moving under the opening in my skirt, building my desire. *"Good job on the skirt, too, easy access."* Katie's words echo in my mind. I couldn't help the shallow, quiet sighs I was making, wishing for more. My breathing quickens, my chest rising and falling at the chance of being caught in a most exposed, intimate act. Of doing something we both know we should most definitely not be doing.

I didn't realize I was making noise that could be drawn to us because his fingertips lift and then quietly slap down in a gentle, arousing minor punishment. I twitch but keep my eyes straight ahead, paying more attention while the movie thunders around us in a dramatic scene. I bite my bottom lip as he slides his fingers into the top seam of my thong, running his fingers through my folds, spreading my wetness to my clit. Pressing a finger on each side of that bundle of nerves, he starts moving in ways I hadn't even explored on myself. Fuck, it feels so good. I pull and bite at the corner of my bottom lip harder, to stop myself from making noise. He lowers his hand more, forcing my thighs apart wider, and I immediately feel more exposed, more at risk of being caught, and it only heightens my sense of urgency, wanting to push my body for release. He dips his fingers into my core as I move one leg slightly to give him further access. Slowly, so slowly, he pushes all the way into me, adding a second one.

His hands are so big. He feels perfect inside me, like his hands were created and molded just for my body by God herself. His fingers begin waving in such a way I nearly moan aloud as he suddenly hits a spot I didn't know could feel so good. Keeping his rhythm he firmly presses his palm on the entirety of my clit that feels so fucking good,

I can feel myself already chasing my climax, begging for it silently. Sweat starting to coat my skin. I'm so close...

In the next moment, I was there, about to go over the edge. I could feel it was a few seconds away from crashing through me, shaking against his hand. It took everything in me not to whimper or make noise, my fingers digging into the soft fabric on either side of me. Until... *no*. Artemis gets up, and within the span of a second, I know he's going to turn and look back into the theater at us, my legs spread and his best friend's fingers buried inside me. Blaine doesn't stop pushing in and out of my sex as I try and fail to fight off my orgasm. Instantaneously, Katie stands behind Artemis, grabbing his attention on his opposite side, away from us, leading him towards the exit. Blaine never stops; his tempo never faltering as I come on his fingers, squeezing him, raising a hand to cover my own mouth.

I let the pleasure flood through me, grinding on his hand. Oh my fucking god... he continues to move, still giving me the touch I need after my peak, reveling in the sensation of it all. I still my movements, staying quiet as he pulls his hand from me, bringing it to his mouth, dragging an obscene lick along the palm of his hand and up his fingers. He places them in his mouth and sucks them clean, releasing a growl deep and low enough I know only I can hear. *"Fuck"* he whispers, sucking his fingers one more time. I watch him, spent, but still so turned on, as he licks my release clean like it's the best thing he's ever tasted. He meets my eyes during his last lick and follows mine to the evident and considerable bulge of his cock straining against his pants. He knows exactly what I'm thinking and leans closer to me before I even have the chance to try. "Hands to yourself, Lilith."

Ronan gets up and exits the theater, chasing after Katie and Artemis, leaving Blaine and me alone with Larissa and Elliott. I glance down at our friends to see his arm around her, her snuggled against him. I don't know if I am just not capable of feeling shocked at the moment or if I genuinely am not surprised to see them together. But, I'll ask her for details later. I'm still processing the fact that *Blaine*... Mr. Out-of-my-league himself just finger fucked me in the same room as my best friends and both my brothers and then devoured my arousal from his hand afterward.

As the rush fades, a sudden awareness settles in. I just broke my own self-imposed dry spell. Years of dedicating myself to honoring this body, of proving to myself that I'm more than a vessel to be touched or taken, that I'm worth more than the temporary warmth of someone else's hands. And yet, I let Blaine practically own the most private, guarded part of myself — physically, yes. But not just my body. The part that's worked so hard to be untouchable.

But there's no flicker of regret, no pang of shame or self-doubt creeping in as I expected there might be. There's only a deep, liberating calm. A calm that tells me I chose this —him, this moment— for all the right reasons. I feel good, a kind of good I forgot I could feel.

For the first time I can remember, intimacy doesn't feel like something I've surrendered but something I've reclaimed. It feels like a gift I finally know how to receive, with no strings, no buried expectations, just... peace.

# 22

# BLAINE

*What the fuck am I doing.*

*What the actual literal fuck am I doing.*

The *one* person I should not be attracted to, and I can't stop myself from thinking of her.

Every damn day, she eats at my brain as I become more and more stupid, pulling at the threads of my control —each laugh, each look, pulling me in deeper— until I'm so insanely caught up in her that I *do* something stupid.

The way she tightened around my fingers during the movie, practically dripping and so soft... so easily submissive. It took everything in me to stop there. Every ounce of self-control to not throw her over my shoulder like a fucking caveman and lock her in my room to fuck her so good, so thoroughly, my name was the only one she could remember. The only *word* she could remember. And when I tasted her, I knew this would not end well. I somehow haven't touched another woman since before Larissa's birthday, and now I have zero desire to. I know exactly what I want; my cock buried inside a tall strawberry-blonde flower that I can't have. Lily fucking Stemmens.

Lilith is a puzzle and I'm not sure all of her pieces even fit. Light and shadow, all at once. What if Lilith is both the storm and night waging war and the angelic lightness she parades as a mask, consumed by both? Her smiles are hard-earned; this much is obvious to anyone who looks deep enough. The shadows in me are drawn to the shadows in her that are hiding, waiting, begging; my own barely restrained.

The darkest parts of me want to pull her down with me.

What would Hell be transformed into with a queen? I find I suddenly can't help but wonder. But the closer I get, the more her light causes my own malevolent inclinations to shift. All I've ever known is darkness, and now... now I don't know what to think.

Chasing rainbows, indeed.
How pathetic.

# 23

# BLAINE

## *Before:*

A symphony of voices and a few laughs echo after me, my feet pounding one after the other.

"He'll be fine."

"Atta boy, B!"

"Let him be. Give him a minute."

They grow distant the further I run. I just have to fucking get away. I run until my legs get heavy, and my lungs feel like they're on fire. I just have to get this energy the fuck out of me. Curses fly from my lips as I trip on a rock, face and chest hitting the cold ground first, the wind knocked out of my already struggling lungs.

I try to grasp a full breath of air, the feel of cold, wet, fallen leaves against the side of my face and under my palms.

*Fuck, fuck, fuck—*

I crawl a couple of feet away, swaying closer to a tree before bile makes its way up my throat, landing on the bark at its base. Coughing, I wipe my eyes and mouth before actually looking up. It takes a minute for the spots at the edge of my vision to clear. I have no goddamn clue where I am. Little recollection of how I even got here outside of the wave of panic and sickness pushing my feet further and harder.

I don't know how long I sit there, the images and sounds of ending a man's life haunting me. The begging, the blood, the piss, and broken skin. The insane things my father's so-called brothers spit out at a mangled and riven man.

It's long enough for my tears to eventually stop and for the all-consuming sick anxiety to give way to what can only be described as nothingness. I feel nothing. Not the air that should be cold against my exposed skin, not the pain, the regret, the self-loathing. There's just nothing.

Shouts in the dark draw my attention, and I robotically make my way, wordlessly, towards the men calling my name.

There's nothing left in me.

# 24

# Blaine

*Long hair feathered recklessly around her face, Lily lays on her back in my bed. The dark grey comforter and smooth sheets a mess around us, contrasting her glowing skin. My face is nestled between her soft, pale legs as I kiss my way slowly to the apex of her sweet thighs. She sighs and spreads wider for me like a good girl as I press the flat of my tongue over her sex, focusing my attention on her clit. God, she's so wet and warm. She tastes so fucking good; summer, honey, and feminine musk incarnate. I pull her closer to me, anchoring her in place with my hands on her hips, greedily taking every bit of her. Groaning against her and tracing my tongue over her sensitive nub, breathing her in, I slowly dip my middle fingers into her with my right hand. She meets my thrusts as I palm myself, hard and throbbing; her cries drowning out my own groans against her as I tongue her cun...*

"BLAINE!" Ronan spits out. *Fuck.* He snaps me out of my daydream as he struggles to re-rack the heavy weight of his bench press. I quickly reach down and help him, taking the weight off and back into place. "What the fuck, man? I said your name three fucking times."

"My head is elsewhere. Work, it's nothing. That's my bad." It only makes me more frustrated remembering the fact that Lily is his younger sister, as I'm imagining eating her pussy, with him four feet away. One of the only real friends I've ever had. A twisted part of me gets off on the idea that she's theirs and I'm going to ruin her, take her. I rub my hand down my face, gathering my composure. My cock is pressed hard against my pants as I turn to adjust myself so he doesn't notice. "New PR, nice work man." Ronan removes a weight on each side of the bar and paces a few times before situating himself back on the bench.

"Pay fucking attention this time?"

"Just go, dick." I glare down at him as I stand behind the bench, spotting him.

I'm obsessed.

Every day, I can't get her out of my head. I've been purposefully changing my route to the office, going to the same coffee shop I know she loves, and I hate to foolishly admit; I've had extra eyes on her occasionally, feeding me updates, on top of me watching the security cameras in our building for glimpses of her. Tren and Zachariah don't need to know why they're keeping an eye on her so long as she's safe and I get the updates. Zach needs the distraction right now, anyway. I don't know what the fuck is wrong with me.

Ronan and I leave the athletic club we're members of, stepping out in the cool air. "Later, man."

"Yeah, man, talk soon." I nod back at Ronan before pressing the auto-start to my McLaren, the engine roaring to life. I checked my watch and saw it was almost ten o'clock. Perfect timing. I get in my car, acting as a blacked-out and shadowed cave, away from prying eyes. I head back towards my place, parking closer to a small coffee shop just a few blocks away. It's a cushy little cafe and plant store on Sixteenth Street, around the corner of an office building in the Financial District. It sticks out like a sore thumb, but it seems to create heavy traffic and has a walk-up window to order for convenience. So, I can safely assume it's doing well enough profit-wise since opening. The exterior is painted white brick with large bay windows, a small patio gated in with faux tropical plants, and string lights crossing overhead. I overheard Lily speaking enthusiastically about it once and now know it's her favorite coffee stop. Since it makes me think of Lily, it's also preening itself to the top of my list of favorite stops.

Sure enough, after just a short wait, I watch Lily step out onto the walkway in front of the strip of buildings, coffee in hand, headphones in. She's certainly in her own little universe right now, I can tell. I'm in awe of her angelic presence but also feeling a surge of annoyance and possessiveness that she's not paying more attention to her surroundings. Anyone could be watching her, and she'd have no idea. I wait from my car as she makes her way closer to me, just a few buildings from the café. Every Saturday, like clockwork, Lily grabs a coffee and goes to the bookstore close by. I decide to head to the café and order a coffee to-go, waiting to 'bump into' her. It's been weeks since we've talked, and since I've seen her, I have to see her.

Again, I don't know what the hell is wrong with me. I feel like a fucking stalker watching her like this. Pathetic.

Sipping my coffee, I lean against a wall close enough so she'll see me when she comes out. I have a couple dozen emails I need to catch up on and a new proposal to review, but I can't seem to focus on business right now. The text is nothing but a blur on my screen. I hear the small chime of the bookstore door opening and see Lilith come out with a stack of four to five books. I'm not sure how someone as sexy as Lilith is simultaneously so adorable, but she manages flawlessly. I smile, pulling myself off the wall to walk towards her. She has her back turned to me; she hasn't spotted me yet. I'm just a handful of feet away as she tries to balance the stack of books and coffee in one hand, reaching into her purse for something with the other hand. Something slips, and the books all tumble. The younger man at the small patio table outside the bookstore goes to lean forward to help her before I walk up, glaring at him in a warning. He silently puts his hands up in defeat as I lean down to help her pick everything up. "Shoot!" She fumbles a little. I manage to help with two of the books before she looks up, thanking me, realizing it's me, and taking out her earbuds.

"Blaine! Jesus, hi. God. I wasn't expecting to see you. Thank you." Before she can take the two books, I keep a firm grip, smirking at her reddened cheeks as she tries to tug them out of my hand, and avoiding my eyes. The first is a cover of a woman, clearly a damsel in distress, resting woefully in the arms of a buffed-out man with long flowing hair and his shirt halfway off his chest. The second is more obviously erotica with a woman's head thrown back in pleasure, her nails scratching into the back of a blue alien-looking dude with horns, her legs wrapped around him.

"Romance fan, huh?"

I let her snatch the books out of my hold, still avoiding eye contact, which only makes me want to smile harder. "There's nothing wrong with reading romance, okay? It's perfectly fine; it's one of the highest-selling genres if you didn't know. And the stories are very poetically written."

"And the *poetic* sex scenes? What are those like?" I tease, her cheeks redder by the second as she looks around to make sure no one overhears. A genuine, full laugh escapes me as she takes a few steps away from the storefront, which visibly relieves a little of her embarrassment as she shyly smiles back.

"What are you doing here, anyway? Don't you like, work twenty-four-seven trying to take over the world or something? Where's your sidekick, Pinky?"

"Mmm. Taking a break today. It is Saturday. And even villains deserve a day of rest." *God, she's beautiful.* "My gym isn't far, and I wanted to stop for a coffee before heading back. I would ask you the same. But it's pretty clear you have a date later with your alien boyfriend and vibrator." She looks up at me, eyes wide, pure and dismayed, smacking my arm.

"Blaine! Stop saying things like that!" I didn't think her cheeks could get any more red; I was wrong. *Adorable.* As if my fingers haven't been buried inside her, her come on my tongue.

"Okay, Okay. I'll stop," I smile, keeping my eyes on her. "You want a ride? I know we're not far, but my car is right there." I nod my head back toward the street.

Just looking at her, being this close, I already feel lighter —her light.

## LILITH

I look up at Blaine, the back of my neck and cheeks still hot. I'm positive they're red, but I'll blame the cool winter air, not his presence and comments affecting me. "Sure, that'd be great. Thanks."

"This way, Sunshine." He tosses his coffee in the metal trash bin on the corner with a heavier-than-expected impact.

"Did you just throw away a full coffee?" I look back at the trash and then back to him.

"Not full. But yes, it won't fit in the cupholders; they're useless. It's a pain in the ass. Keep yours, though, if you'd like. You will likely just have to hold it. I'd offer, but my hands will be busy."

His hands will be busy... busy? Oh my god, *driving*, dumbass. *Get your head on straight, Lily.* "You spend nearly half a million on a car and can't even use the cupholders?" I can't help but laugh at the absurdity of the entire situation. Years ago, this would have been just another reason to hate him, the fact that he had so much money. But now, I know how hard he's worked to get to where he is, to own the things he has. I can't help but feel something strangely close to pride.

Peeking over at him, I see he's smug as he presses the auto-start on the all-black sports car. I don't really have a thing for cars, but I do get a feeling of... *something* walking up to his as the engine lowly roars to life. Everything about this man is overtly sexual. I've always recognized that in him as women threw themselves at his confidence and quiet, commanding presence. But now, I *feel* it deep in my stomach. Before I get to the door, Blaine steps in front of me, reaching to open it for me, taking my small stack of books and placing them on the floorboard. He offers a hand to me. "Princess…" I place my right hand in his, smiling, as I try to gracefully sit in the low car; the door gently shuts as he makes his way in front of the vehicle to the driver's door, waiting for another couple of cars to pass. Immediately upon getting in, the car is silent, muffling the sounds of the street, blanketed also by the rumble of the engine. God, it smells so good. It smells exactly like *him*. It's intoxicating: the intensely masculine, leather, and sensual, spicy amber —the scent of his expensive cologne and the essence of him. The windows are so tinted, and the interior is nearly entirely white with black here and there. It feels good, comforting almost, being tucked into such a dark, small space with seemingly secret visual access to the outside world.

Alone, but not.

The driver's door breaks the silence as he climbs in fluidly and gracefully. Blaine glances at his phone before placing it in the center, flat space between us. I can't help as my eyes glance at his screen searching for signs of *Blondie*. I know Blaine goes on dates or at least hooks up with people; look at him. I just suddenly feel something heavy on my chest to think of him with her. What does he see in her anyway? Other than being perfectly sculpted and model-esque, matching his level of confidence. Women like that are copy and paste, right? She cannot possibly be that beautiful, powerful, *and* have a personality. Right...

I put on a half-fake smile and glance at him before putting on my seatbelt, mimicking his movement. We sit silently as he puts the car in reverse, and I hold my warm paper coffee cup. Reaching behind me on the back of my seat, he turns and backs up the car slightly. He has a large screen on the console. But, god, his hand that close to me as he looks behind us? My eyes travel over his face, down his corded neck, to the small, exposed skin of his tan chest and his broad shoulders, licking my dry lips. *What is wrong with me? This should definitely not be so hot, right?* I glance back up to find his steel grey eyes on mine, heavily lidded as he wears a cocky smirk gazing down at me —arrogant ass, *ugh*. Too many seconds pass before he slowly brings his arm forward again to drive.

And, I swear it's like the echo of my mother's teasing laughter floats through my head at me.

I fight a smile and the playful urge to flip off the sky, the laughter seemingly increasing.

# 25

# BLAINE

"Thank you for staying here another night with me, I really appreciate it. I know how busy you are." Lily smiles at me from a barstool near the kitchen.

"No problem." I can tell she doesn't know how to feel about us being the only two left of our group from our weekend to Vail. Hell, I don't either. But I don't know what I'm doing half the time anymore when it comes to Lilith.

"So… any plans for the evening?" She glides off the seat and comes over to sit in the oversized chair across from me, near the stone fireplace.

"I need to catch up on a few things. Put out a couple of fires, and then we can grab food downstairs at one of the restaurants." I get up from the couch and head to the right, towards my bedroom, where my laptop is. "Seven o'clock, be ready." I quietly close the door behind me as she happily agrees in that sing-song way she does, running my hand over my face.

Lily, her brothers, her friend Kathleen, and I stayed in my private residence in the Ritz just outside of Vail for a 'fun' group weekend.

Vail easily has the best ski runs in Colorado, if not in the country, and it's less than an hour's flight, or a four to five-hour drive. So, pulling the trigger on a place here once one became available was a no-brainer. My buddy got the hookup before it was posted publicly. One hundred grand over asking, and it was mine; I didn't want to risk losing it to another strong offer. The rest of the crew had to head back to Denver for their own reasons I don't really care about. However, Artemis ran into a long-lost acquaintance in the Bachelor Lounge last night and landed on discussing the elaborate art collection he hosts in his place in New York, where he calls home now. Artemis quickly introduced Lily and pushed for them to grab a coffee so she could share more about her own artwork with him, as a potential buyer. It would be a great opportunity for her, so I agreed to stay an extra night with her so she could meet with him tomorrow morning before we head out.

I spent the next three hours sucked into work before realizing it was almost seven o'clock, and I promised Lilith I'd take her to grab dinner downstairs at one of the resort's restaurants. "Shit." I sigh. "Dawson, I have to cut our time short. I'll have my assistant schedule another appointment." I hang up before he responds. He's not even close to the top of my radar, enough to remotely worry about. *Six forty-five, okay.* I head into the large connecting bathroom on the south wall of my suite and turn on the water of the shower, allowing the steam to billow out while I pull a black button-up, black jeans, and socks from the closet, taking my watch off. I lay them on the bed, that calming music Lilith likes still playing throughout my room, and glance out at the expansion of windows along the north wall, taking notice of the snow starting to pick up. Alone with Lily, trapped in a snowstorm.

*"Why... Chasing rainbows."*

Her words continue to echo in my head. I don't know how to feel about it; her effect on me. This near obsession. Very literally, never in my life have I felt this way about another human. Much less a woman. I thought this was just a taboo, unattainable fuck I was chasing. But, now, I don't know what to think because that's not what Lily is. She's more. This certainly isn't part of my plan and is the last thing I should be doing, for many reasons. I've held onto my hurts as a reminder of what I'm working towards and who I am. Her presence is magnetic. Her light to my dark, and I find myself constantly thinking of her and wanting to kill anyone who even looks at her wrong to take away those hard-earned smiles. That is a part of the problem. I'm starting to think of her possessively. Not as my best friends' baby sister. As mine. Hell, I, better than anyone know my track record. Me fucking her, or whatever the hell this thing is, would only end in her heartbreak which she doesn't deserve. I might be a cold asshole, but I'm not that big of a dick.... right?

After showering and dressing, I head out to the main sitting room just as Lilith makes her way down the hall on the opposite side of the room. *Yeah, I'm fucked.* Lilith is one of the most stunningly beautiful women I've ever laid eyes on; her inner strength only adds to her presence, both angelic and yet a model of feminine power. Lily is probably a good five-nine, five-ten, and gracefully lean, with an ass and hips that could cause heart failure to the wrong eyes. Her hair flows to her waist, the most beautiful strawberry; like a West Coast sun setting on a honey hive, nearly perfectly matching her bright golden eyes. She offers me a shy smile as I take in the sight of the dark purple dress that hangs over her body like water, stopping to notice the small buds of her nipples beginning to war against the material from the chill in the air. "You look beautiful, Lily."

"Thank you." She replies, tucking her hair behind her right ear. "You're rather beautiful yourself."

I walk a few feet towards her, with a small huff of a laugh, extending my arm so she can grab the nook of my elbow.

"Do you have a restaurant in mind?" She gazes up at me as we make our way into the hall of the resort, softly lit with warm sconces along either wall. Even with her height and in heels, she still looks slightly up at my six-five frame.

"I did. However, a dress like this…" I scan her body. "…deserves far more. In which case, The Ellis Cellar should be more well suited." We make our way a bit further before turning left into the elevators, heading to the main level where a majority of the resort amenities are located.

As we make our way down the stone hallway, nearing the restaurant entryway, we're greeted by our host. "Mr. Vogeleir, how pleasant to see you. Table for two, sir?" I can safely assume staff are required to acquaint themselves with the owners and residents by face and name. At my nod, he escorts us to an isolated table near the wall of windows, presenting an expanse of falling snow and mountain views amongst the darkening sky.

"This is perfect, Blaine. The restaurant and view are beautiful! Thank you." She smiles brightly.

*Not as stunning as you.* "I'm glad you enjoy it." The décor is far more ornate and intricate than the other places in the resort, offering more character than the modern, sleek, dark, and steel-covered restaurants and bars. We're enveloped with warmth from the yellow and bronze floor-to-ceiling window treatments, furniture fit to satisfy the queen and intricately patterned wallpaper. "This is one of my favorite places to stop, but rarely find the opportunity to do so anymore."

"Well, I appreciate it. Thank you for sharing it with me." Lily reaches out to gently brush her thumb over my knuckles before pulling away, the small sweet gesture somehow going straight to the growing bulge in my pants. I glance over the top of my menu at her sweep of pretty bangs and soft hair over her exposed shoulders and chest, down to her taut nipples brushing against her dress. I'm hit with a wave of possessiveness at the thought of anyone looking at her body and beauty like this, other than me.

"You're scowling. What's wrong? I thought you loved it here?" She asks, her bright golden eyes searching my face.

"It's nothing. Work."

"Ookayy. Well, anyway, do you have a favorite dish here?" I clear my throat.

"Yes. I always get the lobster and wagyu steak." The chef here is phenomenal.

"Mmm. That sounds incredible. Although, the mac and cheese sounds pretty great too." She hums, completely serious, looking over the menu items.

"...Mac and cheese, Lily?" A smile twitches at the side of my mouth. "Mmm. Macaroni and cheese and cupcakes. Both duly noted." The waiter appears to my left with a greeting to take our order. "Sparkling water, a bottle of red, your choosing. Two wagyu steaks cooked medium, two lobster tails, house salad, and... an order of the macaroni and cheese, as well as whatever the best dessert is." I roughly hand the server my menu after noticing his eyes burning a hole into Lilith's dress. My jaw tensing, I glower in return directly into his eyes in a silent warning as he finally looks my way, takes the menu, and stumbles to leave. *Imbecile. Soon to be dead, imbecile.* I release an audible sigh, leaning back.

# 26

# BLAINE

Wine, dinner, and eleven hundred dollars later, I find myself escorting a giggling Lilith back to our residence. However, I can't help the smile that grips my mouth at her contagious laughter and the fact that the altitude has clearly provided her alcohol with an additional boost. It's when we're making our way toward the elevator that the power momentarily flashes and then wholly goes dark. I tense as Lily grabs tightly onto my arm, pulling at my shirt. I let my eyes adjust to the darkness as the pathetic excuse for emergency lights come to life on the expanse of walls. "B-Blaine...? What happened, wh...what do we do?" She whispers.

"The power went out most likely due to the storm; it must have turned into a full-force blizzard in order for the power to go out here. Not a big deal." I feel her start to tremble and pull her closer. "Lily?" Silence... I reach for her in the near complete darkness, pressing my hand to the side of her neck. Barely audible, she whispers.

"I'm sorry. I'm scared of the dark. I know it's stupid." I run my thumb against her jawline and grab her left hand with mine. She doesn't openly admit something like that, so I can safely assume this is serious for her.

"Lily, never let me hear you apologize for your fears again. Keep hold of my hand and follow me. Everything's fine, sunshine. I would never let anything happen to you. I've got you."

"Okay…" I barely make out her nod as I pull out my phone and turn on the light, guiding her to the stairwell.

"Good girl. Follow me. Everything's fine." I know realistically, logically, this is due to the storm. However, with as many hits and retaliations that are on my head, I can never be too confident. Anyone who ever got close enough to me would be dead before they knew what hit them, especially with a trembling and vulnerable Lily at my side.

We slowly make our way up the carpeted stairs with the guidance of my phone light and the near non-existent moonlight from the windows on each floor. I pause at the top of the stairs, silently opening the door, listening, and on alert, just in case. Her hand still in mine, we make our way down the hall back towards our place. I guide her inside with my hand on the small of her back, glancing one more time down the dark hall before stepping inside and locking both locks, placing the battery-operated alarm under the door in case of attempted break-ins. That small wedge alarm is loud enough to wake the entire fucking resort if activated, giving me enough of a warning head-start to do what I need, grabbing my gun. Simple, yet effective. Unable to be disabled or hacked into.

I guide her to the couch, my phone lighting the space before making my way through the darkness towards the fireplace. "Sit." The embers still glow slightly, so it's still hot. I know the vent is open, but I still double-check, add logs to the metal grating in the center, kindle, newspaper, and light the fire, adjusting until it grows larger. Turning back to the couch, I see Lilith watching me as she offers a soft smile but doesn't say anything. "I can't anticipate how long the power will be out. But we have a fire, snacks, water, and wine."

"So, you're saying we're set for a few days? You had me at fire and wine."

"Lily, with the way you drink at altitude, we're set for a couple of weeks." I walk towards the bedroom as she laughs and sighs. I notice she's not trembling so she must be calming down now that she's safe and warm. A bit of pride swells my chest at the thought that I was able to make her feel safe and protected.

"Where are you going?" I barely hear her over the gust of wind outside as I grab the blankets and pillows from my bed to bring into the living room by the fire.

"Well. I want to assume the fire would heat the entire place without power, but I honestly have no fucking clue. This is a first. So, I'm bringing out blankets and pillows, and I figure it'll be better to stay close to it so I can tend to it as needed. So, if you want to stay out here by the fire to stay warm, I can grab your blankets, too."

"Are you asking me to make a blanket fort and have a sleepover?"

"—No." I hear her audible sigh in response.

"You're always so grumpy. Fine. We'd be building forts if Katie and the guys were here." She murmurs quietly, awfully close to what sounds like a pout.

"Thank god they're not fucking here," I grumble to myself in return as I turn toward the other hallway to grab everything.

I don't know why hearing her calling me grumpy is slightly unsettling. She's right. I'm an asshole to everyone. The words coming from her, though, don't sit right. I want to be more for her. I'm just not sure I know how.

When I come back out of the room, Lily's got the table pushed back and is already laying down blankets on top of one another. "It would be more comfortable if you fold them in half to double the padding Lils." *Lils? Why the hell did I just call her Lils?* My mouth has never formed that word in my life. I sigh and curse under my breath at my own stupidity. At this point, I'm convinced she's breaking my brain. Maybe it's that frequency shit she listens to.

"Umm, I assumed we'd be sharing blankets, so we can just layer them. You know, share body heat and whatnot." She walks past me with her cell phone in hand for additional lighting, and I can't manage to form a response. "Changing into P.J.s, be back." *P.J.s... sharing body heat in the dark, in a snowy mountain escape...* Yeah, this is a bad idea. Fuck me. I grab the bridge of my nose, forcing myself to lay down the additional blankets and pillows before throwing them in the fire. I cannot lose my control tonight. I think briefly; maybe I should actually sleep in my room. But I want to make sure the fire stays warm all night for her. I start unbuttoning my shirt as I make my way towards my bedroom to change into sweats and a t-shirt. I feel a slight flush at our situation, which I should not. My dick is practically begging for attention. This is a terrible idea.

Shaking my head, I return to the living room to see her in an oversized, faded T-shirt. I don't know what I was expecting, I guess, but it wasn't that. But damn if she doesn't look sexy. I start to get pissed before I realize it's a C.U. tee, probably one of her brother's old shirts. She belongs in my shirt. She's mine, not theirs. I have plenty she could take. I shake my head to clear my thoughts before I rip off the one on my back, throwing it at her with a command to wear it.

I settle in next to her on the blankets, pulling one to lay loosely on top of me. "Fuck it's hot with this fire." I lay on my back and close my eyes, listening to the crackling wood, and get pulled into Lily's scent. She smells like honey mixed with vanilla, spice, and leather. *God, her perfume smells so good.* I can feel her lay down next to me and give a contented sigh that mingles with the quiet sound of the flames. After a few moments of silence, the words I've been holding onto finally escape my lips. "Can I ask you something?"

"Sure, of course."

"What's the reason you're fearful of the dark?" I can hear her breath hitch slightly. She takes a few seconds before answering me, her voice low.

"Bad things happen in the dark."

"Did something bad happen to you in the dark, though?"

"Yes." Her response is almost clipped. When she doesn't expand, I don't want to push, so I leave it alone. Hell, I get it. After several moments in silence, she whispers, "You know our parents died when we were younger?"

"Yeah." Of course, I did. Always thought it was strange as fuck three orphans just happened to live together in a dorm in college. It's statistically incredibly unlikely.

"Yeah... I always blamed myself and thought... if I was a better daughter, I could have saved them both, and mine and my brothers' lives would have been so much better. I've always carried that with me and molded stories and imagined the days that could have been. Somedays, it's all that kept me going; being able to daydream about how different it all could have been. My brothers deserve so much happiness." And, what, she doesn't? "I remember every second of the nights we were told. Our lives were over as we knew them, and our hearts broken beyond repair. Both nights haunt me. The screaming, the crying, the chaos, the numbness. The sounds of sirens and flashing lights." I watch as she huffs out a breath and smiles bitterly. "I still have nightmares. After all these years. Still have moments where I suddenly feel like I'm drowning out of nowhere. All because I hear a loud sound, someone says something innocent enough that triggers my brain, or I just let my mind wander a little too long and get caught in the old memories."

I hear the pain in her voice she keeps trapped in her throat and catch the silver pooling at the ends of her eyes. "It should have been me. I just know. Everything would have been so much better for everyone if somehow I had been the one to die instead. The months I spent thinking about that nearly did kill me. I know the thought doesn't make any sense logically, but it just feels right. Everyone I love dies or leaves me, Blaine." I fist my hand and focus on the pressure of my nails biting my skin to stay grounded to the spot and not interrupt her. I have to hear her keep going.

"When.. umm." She clears her throat slightly, jaw visibly tense. "When I was younger— before our parents died, I mean. Our father's brother. He spent a lot of time at the house. Worked a lot of late nights. "He... umm. He would—" *Our father's brother?* Their Uncle? It's such an odd phrasing; I just somehow know. I just fucking know. I tense at her reluctance, her words barely audible... tense at what the next words are she's going to say. I can feel it coming.

"Your uncle what, Lily?" I manage in an even tone. Silence. Getting a better look, it's like her eyes are almost unfocused, unseeing what's in the room in front of us anymore. "—Lily..? Hey."

She sighs and shakes her head slightly as if clearing it just as I find my hand reaching for hers. "Nothing. Never mind, it doesn't matter. Yes, bad things happen in the dark. Everything bad happens in the dark. Plus, the violence and abuse I was exposed to in the system for years after our parents died, too. There are moments and memories that are burned into my mind that would make normal people sick to their stomachs. I always wondered if the universe was punishing me. So many nights I spent trying to hide in the dark under my beds, away from it all. I just wanted to be alone. That was my dream."

*The system. Beds-plural.* Fuck, I'm so dumbfounded, I can't make any full sentences form in my brain. Much less push them through to my mouth to respond. Holy shit. That entire time she was gone, that's what the fuck was she going through? It seems we might have more in common than she could possibly realize. I always knew her brothers were hiding something about her. I felt it in my gut every time I laid eyes on her. She was the mysterious sister for so long.

But, fuck, her uncle... *Robert.* I know exactly who the fuck he is. Do her brothers know? Is that why they kept everything such a big secret when it came to her? I know exactly what she was fighting to get out. They still talk to him, though. No. There's no way. I can feel the fire building in my body at the thought of what I knew she was about to say. It makes me so fucking abhorrent I'm ready to pound the sick piece of shit until he's begging for me not to kill him. She doesn't need to finish that story. Too many thoughts race and fight each other for my attention. Fuck, I could be wrong though. That's a huge accusation on my end. The sinking feeling in my gut tells me I'm not wrong, though.

Lily's half-whimper, half-sigh breaks me out of my dark fantasy, Robert's blood on my hands. I look over, and she's lying on her back, looking up at the ceiling. "Lilith, look at me." She does. Slowly. "It may feel like these things were your fault, but there was nothing, nothing you could have done to prevent these accidents. There is zero connection between you and your parents' deaths. There is nothing you could have done to help or prevent it. And I never want to hear you say you should've been the one to die again. Ever. I don't believe in fate or a higher power, but god damn it, Lily, if I don't believe you're being protected by... I don't know, fucking something to keep you safe. You *are* the light, Lily. You are here for a reason on this earth. Every smile you share, every painting you create, you give your light to those around you. *You* deserve the world, and if something would have ever happened to you..." I Sigh. "...You've unintentionally taught me so much just by being who you are. And I know you do the same for everyone who gets to know you. You are rainbows and sunshine and puppy kisses and whatever the fuck else that makes people smile. You're perfect. Please never doubt that. You never deserved any of this shit. You're not being punished. Fuck, you might be the strongest person I know. Never doubt yourself, okay?" I don't even know how to begin to address her uncle or her growing up in the system. So, I just don't mention it. That act, too, washes shame over me that I can't do more for her. I'm not good at this shit.

"Okay..."

I grab her hand and bring it to my lips, running my other hand along her forearm. It's taking everything in me to control myself and not touch every inch of her body until she smiles again. Just allowing myself to think of her not being here makes me feel an ache I didn't think I was capable of feeling, not like this. It hit me like I was fucking speeding into a brick wall... this woman is mine. She doesn't know it, but she doesn't need to.

I think I've been pushing her away for so long now, years even. I mean, it's been well over a decade I've known this woman. Of course, I fucking noticed how beautiful she is, how could I not? She was always Ronan and Artemis' sister, though. Off-limits for a fuck. That door didn't even so much as exist. She's always been in her own little category in my mind; best friends' sister, not a friend, not a fuck. But now... it's different. I will do everything in my power to make sure she's happy, safe, and taken care of. But hell, if she doesn't deserve the world and so much better than me. Suddenly, it feels like the ground under me is turning to quicksand.

We both settle on our backs again for a long time, not speaking. I find myself just being in the moment, taking in the smell and sound of the fire, the feel of the blankets. *"Taking a mental screenshot."* I replay her words from the night on the balcony.

"Tell me a funny story or something I don't know about you, Blaine." I can feel her smile, touching every single inch of my hardened, dark heart with her sunshine. There it is. The thing I now crave so very fucking desperately.

"Mmm." I hum, considering. I run through stories and scenarios in my head and land on one that's appropriate for her ears, and audibly release a huff of a laugh. She'll like this one. "I know a story you'll enjoy. In college, when your brothers and I lived together in the house on Downing, after we left the dorms, Ronan always pulled his dumbass pranks, and I finally got him back. One time before a Halloween party we had at the house, I had paid to have all the cabinets in the kitchen and all the lights in the house rigged to an app on my phone."

"WAIT, omg! I know exactly the year and the party you're talking about! Ronan STILL brings it up anytime someone mentions ghosts! That was you?"

"Yep." I smile, smothering my laughter. "While he was the only one home, I was watching the central part of the house from the cameras. I kept making one of the cabinets slam open and close until he came out of his room and followed the noise to the kitchen. The idiot thought someone was breaking in and grabbed a piece of plastic Halloween decor before checking it out. When I saw him get to the entryway of the kitchen, I made all the cabinets open and slam at once and had all the lights in the house flash on and off." I actually have to keep myself from laughing through the story. "Imagine all six-three, tattooed, daredevil Ronan falling on his ass trying to scramble and run out of the house. I still have never told him it was me. He loves to tell the story. But I know that house was never haunted by anything other than me." The high flowing through me is an entirely new high. One I haven't felt in a very long time.

Lily laughs so hard she can barely breathe, and every dumb, annoying, grossly inaccurate retelling by Ronan makes it worth these few minutes of her happiness right now.

# 27

# LILITH

I look over at Blaine, wiping my tears from laughing so hard, and can't possibly believe that grumpy, icy Blaine would have ever pranked anyone. I sigh as my laughter starts to die down, and I notice how breathtaking his genuine smile is —dangerously charming. If he smiled more often, God help womankind. I turn onto my side towards him as he looks at me with his head turned, lying on his back. I lean closer to him, examining his chest and putting my ear to it. "Blaine, if you're in there, make your host body cough twice!"

"Lily, what the hell are you doing?" He stiffens under my touch.

I lean closer like I'm listening to his heart, laughing, feeling behind his ears and on his chest. "Oh, I'm sorry. I just assumed you must be a shapeshifter or an alien that's inhabited Blaine's body. The Blaine I know doesn't know how to laugh or smile with the permanent scowl he wears; I think his face is stuck that way by now. Just checking for an incision scar!"

"You're ridiculous." Blaine wrestles me and grabs my wrists while I fight him off, laughing.

"I know you're in there, I'll save you!" Before I realize it, Blaine has me flipped onto my back, with my arms over my head, straddling one of my thighs, pinning me in place.

"You think you're funny, do you?"

"I got you to laugh, so I'd say there's pretty strong evidence in my favor to prove that I am." I grin up at him before realizing how close he is, how hot his body feels this close, pressed to mine. My eyes dip from his to his far too-perfect lips and back up. By the low light of the fire, I can see his breathing speed up to match mine, and his pupils dilate as our bodies touch. This is the first time we've touched like this. Both very awake; alone. I can feel him growing hard against my thigh as he has me trapped, pinning my right leg down. I lean forward to break the tension and kiss him, but he slides his head slightly enough to the side that our lips don't connect. He just groans and rubs his lips against my cheek as he briefly grinds his hips against me subtly enough maybe he thought I wouldn't feel it. He looks me in the eyes again before closing his, letting go of my hands, and rolling over onto his back again, rubbing a hand down his face, sighing.

It takes me a second to process what just happened. I've heard my brothers joking about how Blaine doesn't ever kiss anyone and how he only treats sex like a business transaction, basically. Whatever the hell that even means, I don't know. I do know he's never had a girlfriend, either. If he has, it's been in secret. I just never... I guess I never thought about it until now. I can't help but feel a little sad. He refuses such sweet, beautiful pleasures. I sigh softly. I couldn't imagine being so distant from intimacy to refuse to kiss someone. He is blatantly pushing away happiness and intimacy as if he doesn't deserve it. My heart aches so profoundly at why he must treat sex in such a way. Why he must so deeply believe he's so undeserving of love and care?

It's then I realize I've been doing nearly the same, only perhaps far more drastically, for nearly four years. I've been abstinent, pushing anyone and everyone away. I thought it was to take back control of my body after years of mistreatment. But what if the truth of the matter is that I don't actually believe I am deserving of love either... the thought knocks the wind out of me enough to feel near dizzying. I also realize with a new clarity I've now technically broken that with Blaine, haven't I?

Neither one of us speaks; we just lie there for a while in silence, lost in our own minds. If he didn't have his eyes open, I'd think he was sleeping. Blaine finally moves to sit up and pull his shirt off over his head. He can't be serious. His frame is huge, and his back and biceps are so masculine and defined. His upper back is tattooed just like his chest is. "What? I can feel you looking at me." He gruffly lets out, tossing his shirt.

"What, what? I wasn't; I was just thinking."

"About?" He says tightly. *I see the grumpy asshole is back. Neat.*

"Nothing, goodnight."

"Lilith."

"Blaine."

"Lily. —Don't make me say your name a third time."

"Fine. Why are you taking your shirt off? Maybe I'd appreciate it if you'd keep your clothes on." He's still sitting upright with his back to me, his head turned to the left looking over at me.

"It's too hot." I watch as he lays back in the same position, hoping he doesn't catch my eyes tracing his body.

We both lay in the dark, silence settling between us again. I guess we're going to sleep then. Somehow, we ended up so close, though, and I can feel his body radiating heat. Even with the fire, his warmth is comforting and grounding. I close my eyes, relaxing. After several minutes, I shift, bending my knee without thinking, and it brushes against his thigh, nudging his hand. I consider, but don't want to move it, though; it feels too nice being so close like this. He makes no effort to move at all, either.

Under the blanket, his hand I've bumped slowly inches its way toward the area of my thigh above my knee. His slight graze is enough to make my breath hitch and my eyes open. He moves his finger so lightly back and forth, tracing idle circles, causing me to ache for more of his touches, more of him. It's so light, it's nearly torturous. I feel him switch to the pads of his fingers, one by one touching and feathering tiny designs so slowly that the skin on my arms and thighs pebble in response.

He keeps moving higher, the teasing sensation deliciously unhurried, each touch careful, sensual. My hips shift involuntarily, a silent plea for him to continue, but when he reaches just inches from the apex of my thighs, he pauses.

I open my legs wider in an unspoken invitation. His fingertips stay in the same place like he's not sure what to do. "Blaine..." I whisper. He's silent but hasn't taken his hand off of me. "Blaine, please..." I say again, feeling breathless, my heart rate picking up, skin flush, and needy.

"Fuck, I love hearing you beg. Please, what?" He groans.

"...Please touch me higher. Please don't stop." I whimper. He slowly starts moving again; closer, knowing exactly where I want him. He trails so lightly up and over my lower stomach until he dips just under the edge of my lace panties. I can't help the shiver that washes through me and my breathing at this point. He keeps going running his fingers along my clit and folds, to my core; I know he feels how wet I am for him. Blaine practically growls in frustration or pleasure, pulling his hand from my panties quickly, and gracefully turns onto his side to look down at me, eyes full of intensity.

"If I touch you tonight, I have two rules." He holds out his fingers to count as he says them. "This doesn't leave this room, and you keep your eyes closed." He takes his free hand this time and moves it up my thigh until he reaches into my panties from the edge along my thigh, cupping my sex. "Can you do that?"

I close my eyes, nodding and waiting. I can not only hear but feel his growl with how close he is to me and can feel his own arousal as his right thigh moves to hold mine down where he wants it. Gliding his fingers through my lower lips again, he brings them back up to my clit, circling and then placing two fingers on either side, perfectly handling my body. His hands are so warm and masculine; his touch feels like too much and too little.

I don't fight the soft sighs and whimpers that escape me. There is something erotic about being forced to keep my eyes closed. And it feels so different with it just being the two of us: no crowds, no potential audience, no friends or brothers in the same room. I desperately want to look at him. But having my eyes closed intensifies his touch as I imagine his face and his eyes tracing and trailing down my body, watching his own fingers touching me. He moves his hand lower, lining his finger to my entrance, and pushes in, both of us moaning. He pumps into me slowly a handful or two times before pulling out of me and I hear him licking and sucking on his finger. With a low groan, I hear him clean his hand again before returning it to me.

"Do you know how *fucking* good your pussy tastes?" God, his voice and words make everything so much sexier; I can't help but whimper, goosebumps like lightning over my skin. He dips into my core again and again, pushing as deep as he can with two fingers.

"Your hands are so huge; feels so good." My breath hitches as I try to speak. He pushes into me deep and hard before switching to more of a waving motion, curling his fingers. Placing his thumb against my clit, he adds pressure and friction as he moves in and out.

"Is this what you wanted? My fingers buried inside you again, fucking this pretty pussy?" His curled fingers move just right, hitting that same spot I didn't even know could feel so good. I move to meet the thrusts of his fingers, tilting my hips, adding friction, and breathing heavily.

"Oh god, yes, yes." I know he's hard; I can feel his cock in his sweatpants moving against me, adding to his own pleasure as he touches me. All I can think of is how he would feel inside me.

"You have no fucking *clue*... how badly I wish this was my cock fucking you, pushing into you. It *infuriates* me to not be able to give you what you really want. What this sweet little cunt needs. I just know you'd take every inch like a good girl, too, wouldn't you? Let me stretch you and fill you?" He growls low into my ear, and my already-closed eyes practically roll back into my head as I quiver. "Mmm... that's what I thought. I know you love when I talk about pounding your little pussy. I can feel you clamp down on my fingers, every inch of your body reacting." He whispers. "I want to feel you and watch your cunt squeeze my fingers as you come all over my hand. And when you do, I'm going lick every fucking drop off and memorize your taste so I can think of you every night when I fist my cock."

Between his words, rumbling voice, and the pounding he's giving me while rubbing hard against my clit, I'm on the edge of coming. I throw my head back, tensing. "I'm... Blaine! I'm..."

"Just like that, keep going, come all over my fingers. Focus on your body and how good it feels." I squeeze my closed eyes tighter, letting out a throaty moan as I feel my climax peak and flood through my body while he keeps pumping into me. "Good girl. That's a good fucking girl. Give it to me." He growls next to my ear so closely his breath blows into it. I can feel his cock grinding against my thigh as he keeps fingering me, getting every breath and sigh of pleasure that he can until I collapse. He slightly brushes the sides of my sensitive clit, causing me to jump. Pulling his fingers out of me, I open my eyes as he sucks them and licks them clean, moaning, "I hate that you taste this good." He takes his leg off, freeing mine, laying again on his back, leaving me to come down from my high.

For minutes, we just lay next to one another. "Lily?"

"Yes?" I breathe out. He looks over at me... and I know what he's thinking without saying it. "I know...." I whisper. He looks back up towards the ceiling and closes his eyes.

"Goodnight, sunshine".

"Goodnight." I lay there with my eyes open for a bit longer, listening for Blaine's breathing to slow back to normal. I know I'm probably about to cross some sort of a boundary with him. But he didn't include this in his rules...

I lean over and press a gentle, easy kiss to his cheek as he stiffens but doesn't open his eyes. I tuck myself under the covers, snuggling a few inches from his warmth, taking in his scent and his presence before falling into sleep.

# 28

# BLAINE

## *Before:*

All that I have left of my father is his favorite knife, and this fucked up legacy I'm trying to live up to. The person I'm trying to be for his MC. The men I can feel watching me, standing too close. Eyes too heavy.

My own eyes are squeezed shut, chin shaking as I try to just fucking get it together. To make my dad proud. To just breathe. It doesn't matter if I think I can do this or not. I have to; the option not to isn't there.

Focusing my attention on various parts of my body, I land on my hands. The left fisted, the right holding the end of his knife. Tipping my head back, I open my eyes. A concrete ceiling's the first thing I see, throat bobbing, before moving to see the rest of the room and the mess of a man in front of me.

Peeking over at Rye, his arms are crossed, and all he offers is a lifted brow. Fuck, the weight of the world is somehow on my chest right now. I give him a small nod in return and walk around the chair in the center of the room. This bloodied, half-dead mess tied to it. It's silent outside of his haggard breathing and coughing. Each step, one foot in front of the other, I use all the energy I have left to remove myself from the rest of the room, imagining nothing but blackness outside of me and him.

I twist the blade through my fingers. A skill I've managed to pick up, spending all my time holding and hating this damn thing—*step, twist, step, twist.* An almost meditative fog eventually blankets me. The air around me turns a little lighter, the rest of the room in turn darkening, and I channel the energy I know is in me to do this one goddamn thing. This won't be a replay of the first time. This is a representation of my father and his son. I will not be seen as weak.

It starts to feel like all the energy in my body makes its chaotic way to my head, static filling and surrounding every thought I have that's not *kill*. Not pushing me to do this.

A different part of my brain comes to life and takes over, a smile stretching my lips, and suddenly... *fuck,* suddenly, I can breathe and let the rest of my brain take the backseat. The rage, the hurt, and the helplessness all converge into a storm so wild I'm surprised I don't fall over from the effect. It's like I'm several shots deep in a bottle, loose and on fire.

I decide right now. This is the new me. Whatever God that just ignited my soul and kickstarted my high gets my thanks.

This man is a bad man. This man is a piece of fucking shit doing nothing but leaving a trail of harm in his wake. This new thought makes me feel almost excited. I'm really doing some good here, aren't I? Is this what I've been waiting for? This new sense of reality?

"Shit, there it is. There's the old man's kid." Holy claps his hands in the room, a huff of a laugh escaping him. He's talking about me.

"I told you, he has it in him too."

A long, warm breath leaves my nose, touching the sweat on my upper lip.

Letting the fog around me push back a little further, I stop in front of this man, kicking his boot to wake him up a little more. Tilting my head, I watch. Suddenly, it's just fucking pathetic, isn't it? I watch as my free hand snakes out and grasps the stained black roots thickly coated with blood and sweat. Pulling backward, his eyes open slightly, meeting my own. The stark contrast between the bright blue of his eyes, the black hair, and the red blood holds my attention. Each on its own, nothing. But together, powerful, speaking to a deep part of me. I find myself mesmerized, soaking it in, his wheezing the background soundtrack.

The edges of my lips tilt on their own, not reaching my eyes as I let go and stand fully, turn, and step back. I have a sense of shadows moving from my path, but I don't care about them —they are nothing to me but smoke. Stopping, I stand momentarily with my back to my prey, knife in hand, spinning it a few times, the light on the ceiling reflecting off its surface.

A soft chuckle makes its way from my lips, and I turn, world tilted, focusing my energy into this man. This new haze in my body takes over, wanting a release of this built-up rage, and my arm swings with more force than should be possible. My knife lands in the chest of this man, and I find all I can do is watch. I stand silent, watching, listening, memorizing.

I don't know how long passes. But I know the moment I need to go. When my body starts to feel like my own again, and my limbs become heavy.

Without a word, I leave.

# 29

# LILITH

"Oh my god, Lily! Wait... sorry, one sec..." I can hear her put her hand over the phone *"Lily and Blaine were stuck in the storm last night... she's fine.... well, I'm trying to find out...* sorry babe, Artemis is home and wanted to know what happened. Anyway, you're okay, right? Storm was all over the news."

"Yeah, no we're fine. I made it back home a couple of hours ago."

"Wait, what happened with Mr. New York?" She pauses.

"He apparently had to leave as soon as the snow let up and couldn't meet." I sigh softly, knowing we both are aware that's not the case. She hums.

"Fuck that guy, he sucks anyway. So... snowstorm? What happened?"

"Yeah, the power went out as we were heading back from dinner. Luckily, his place had that giant fireplace in the living room, so we were able to stay pretty warm. Had food and everything, so we were fine." I twist my hair around my finger nervously while pacing my studio. I have a great view of the mountains from my studio, everything is still bright from the snow despite the fact that the sun is nearly down. I already know Kat thinks something is going to happen between Blaine and me. Not only thinks, but she's also pushing for it. Little does she know... I'm praying she doesn't read between the lines here. I'm dying to tell someone, but I know I shouldn't tell her. I trust her not to tell my brothers, though.

".... Lily...." There it is.

"Yes?" I cringe.

"I'm going upstairs to my room and closing the door. Spill. I know there's something you're not telling me; I know you too well. I'm going to find out eventually."

"Look... If I do tell you something happened, which I'm NOT saying. You have to promise you won't tell anyone. I mean it, Katie." The squeal on the other end of the phone is enough to pull it away from my ear.

"I KNEW IT! I told you he has a thing for you! I was RIGHT! Oh my god, Lily. I'm dying, pleeasseeee tell me what happened between you two." This is an awful idea, but I literally have to tell someone. I'm so tired of keeping secrets. And Katie is my best friend; we tell each other everything.

I go on to tell her all about dinner, the snowstorm, the power going out, our talk by the fire. And eventually, end up telling her about our first sleepover and our little moment during our movie night. I can't help but clench my thighs, replaying it. "Katie, before he would touch me, he made me promise two things and one of those agreements I've already broken by telling you. This literally has to stay between us, promise me. Do NOT tell my brothers."

"I promise, I promise! You know I'd never do that, roommates or not. Oh my god, babe. I fucking knew as soon as we left to head back down the mountain. Oh my god, I'm so happy! This is perfect! So, what was the other thing he made you agree to?"

"You know how he apparently doesn't kiss anyone?"

"Yeah, I've heard the guys giving him shit about it at their last poker night. *Which I totally wasn't eavesdropping on*. Artemis claims Blaine says it gives the unwanted illusion of intimacy or false hope to his partners or some bullshit. I'm sure those are his words, though. I know he doesn't do the whole face-to-face thing when he's fucking either. WAIT, did he kiss you!"

"No, no... that's what I'm saying. Stop yelling, Artemis is going to hear you! I tried to kiss him, I really wanted to. But he turned his head away. He wouldn't do it. But that's not the thing. He made me promise... to keep my eyes closed the entire time? Just like in his theater the first time he touched me, he wouldn't let me look at him." I can feel the wheels turning and the confusion running through her head. Another day of that, and she'd be where I am now. Still confused.

"Hmm, okay. Well, first, that pisses me off he wouldn't kiss you. But... secondly, I gotta say I'm a little confused as to why he would want your eyes closed. Like, wouldn't he *want* you looking at him, consuming his soul as he got you off? Most guys love that shit. I guess he's not like most guys though, fucking weirdo. Jesus, he really does hate intimacy. Hmm. Okay... well, how do you feel though?"

"Honestly... I don't know Katie. Had he wanted to fuck me last night, I absolutely would have and not thought twice, which should be shocking in itself. I don't know. This is all too complicated. I'm exhausted. I need a hot bath or something."

"Yeah, *or something* being our keyword there. AKA: Blaine's dick. We have to get him to kiss you, though. It's my new mission in life." She gasps so loud I already know whatever is about to come out of her mouth is going to be an awful idea. "Lily! The Gala, that's it! We already know he's going to be there. We get you a bomb-ass dress so every man there drools over you. And voila!"

"What, voila, I don't follow?"

"We get him *jealous*, Lil. We already knew, *well I knew* he had some type of feelings for you even before he got all sexy on you during the movie. Now it's doubly confirmed. Men get possessive Lily, trruuust me. If other men start giving you attention, dancing with you, and buying you drinks, he's going to notice. And Mr. Cool, bored, and grumpy is going to be overtaken by big boy feelings."

"I mean... for once, you may actually have a decent plan. But Katie, even if I want to try to pursue whatever this is, I can't. He's my brothers' best friend. I don't even know what the hell I'm doing here. It would cause too much of a mess between them. I can't do that. And we don't even know if he's going to take the bait."

"Okay, well, first, I'm going to act like you didn't just imply all my ideas are terrible. Secondly, we're going shopping this Friday. Four o'clock; meet me in Cherry Creek. Shopping, pedi's, then cocktails. Byeee!"

"Katie! Wait—" She has to stop hanging up on me like that. If I was close to a pillow, I think I'd scream in it. What's worse, is I kind of want to go along with her idea. She has a point, and it really isn't her worst plan. I don't want to leave Larissa out. I pick my phone up again to send a group text.

I guess it's settled then.

Get ready to eat your heart out, Blaine.

# 30

# LILITH

## *Before:*

Tears and snot cover my face as I beg. I cry out in pain as his fist tightens in my hair, pulling my body uncomfortably further up, scrambling for purchase to find some sort of relief against the burning. God, everything burns. My skin, scalp, face, and eyes are on fire. My hand finds his knee as I clench my teeth, and suddenly, that's on fire, too.

"You have ten minutes, girl. I'm itching to punish that fucking useless, idiot of a brother of yours. You want that? That what this pathetic show is for?"

I try to shake my head and only manage to intensify the pain before letting a meek *'no'* slip past my lips. The image of Ronan comes to mind, and I know I have to keep going. I would die before letting anything happen to him or Artemis. He already struggles so much. He deserves so much more, so much better. I've spent years at this point protecting him. Protecting them both from our uncle's wrath. After what we've been through, I can't bear to imagine them suffering any other loss. And that's exactly what this would be. If Ronan and Artemis, if my family knew what my father's brother did to me, everything would fall apart. And if he follows through on his threats, which I've come too close to comfort in finding truth to his words before, Ronan will be even worse off, taking what should only be my punishment. No, I can't let that happen.

Giving him a small nod, I reposition myself and close my eyes, praying for the door to my *Other* place to let me in.

His hand loosens, the sting turning to a pulsing pain as I lean over his lap. The door finally, finally opens in my mind for me to step through to escape this nightmare.

# 31

# LILITH

"Are you excited?" I can hear Katie on the other end of the phone turn on her shower and walk away as it quiets.

"I don't know. I should be I guess, but honestly, it's been so long, it just feels like I'm already exhausted by the idea. That sounds terrible I know... he's the stepson of a receptionist on the ninth floor at my office building. I'm sure he'll be nice enough. I'm just not... excited, no." I'm more excited about the idea of Blaine.

"I understand, and it's totally valid to feel that way. Don't feel bad. You can always cancel, too; don't feel obligated. You sure as hell don't owe anyone anything. I will say, though, Lil... it's been what? Almost four years since you've gone on a date. It might be a good idea to try to get back out there. You deserve happiness, Lily. You deserve love. I... I just don't want you to hide forever. And plus... not to mention, if Blaine hears it through the peanut gallery grapevine that you went on a date, I think our plan of getting him jealous may kick in before the Gala." She laughs as she walks on the other end, her footsteps echoing.

I can't help but sigh, I knew that one was coming. Okay, well, *both* of those things. It's brought up by my friends all the time; to start dating again. They don't understand, though. How could I possibly expect them to when they haven't experienced what I have? *Story of my fucking life.*

I'm always aware of how different I am from everyone around me. Every story, every experience and traumatic event molding me into something *Other*. There's no way I could ever forget it; watching and listening to my surroundings like a half-ghost with painted-on smiles.

They mean well, and it comes from caring, so I shouldn't be upset. Things with Blaine have always felt different, though. I have no clue what we're doing, but the butterflies in my stomach certainly don't hate the idea of it progressing. "I understand where you're coming from. It's just difficult for many reasons. But hey, I need to finish getting ready. I'll text you afterward, once I'm home. Love you."

"I hope I didn't upset you, really, I didn't mean to. If you need anything at all, just call or text 'Pickles', and I'll speed my ass there, okay? Love you bunches, babe. Be safe and try to let yourself have a good time. It's just drinks, and I'm just a text away!"

"Thanks, Katie. Love you, talk soon. Bye." I hang up and sigh… yeah, I really don't feel like doing this. Mary-Ann is an older woman in my building I run into on coffee and mail runs occasionally, and she trapped me in the café in the lobby last week trying to set me up with her boyfriend's son, around my age, a few years younger. I don't typically find myself attracted to younger men, even if only a few years, so that isn't a good start. But, this is on me. I could have said no. Maybe Katie's right. If anything, it'll be practice for when I do actually start to date again. Maybe distract me from Blaine, at least for the night.

I take a final look in the mirror, checking my appearance. I do love dressing up, though. It makes me feel more powerful in an odd way. Like a costume of confidence; playing a character. At least until I get to my destination, then it all goes out the window.

I opted for a high-waisted miniskirt, a long-sleeved silk top, small black Chanel bag -courtesy of my brothers- and strappy heels. Hair curls around my face, small gold hoop earrings peeking through messy strands. I am mildly thankful that he asked to meet for drinks after Mary-Ann passed along my number. That's easier to get out of if it goes terribly.

I make my way down to the lobby and step out to see Blaine near the entrance of the building. *Of course, tonight of all nights.* He eyes me up and down as he stalks towards me. "Plans tonight?" He's just a couple of feet away from me as his scent envelopes me. There is something about the way his cologne smells, lingering with the natural scent of him that hits my stomach every time.

"Just going to grab a drink with a friend. You?" *I'd much rather be grabbing a drink with you, dumbass.*

"I see. A date then." It wasn't a question. Looking into his eyes, his face is unreadable, but there's a spark —a fire even, just for a moment before disappearing.

"Technically, yes." His eyes narrow as he takes my figure in again. Is he jealous? No, why would he be? He's Blaine. He probably goes on dates every night with supermodels.

Now I'm annoyed, I can feel it. I go to push past him tight-lipped, but he stops me.

"I'll take you. Let's go. I was just leaving." Was he? He was coming inside, not leaving.

"Umm, okay? Thank you." What the actual fuck? He's just fine with literally driving me to meet another man for drinks? For all he knows, I could be planning to go home with him. I can't believe this. God, I feel like such a fucking idiot; a little girl with a schoolgirl crush. I feel the heat and prick of tears wanting to swell.

No, I'm not letting him ruin my night. He doesn't get that privilege.

He told me to wait just inside the warm lobby while he had the valet grab his car and lifted his head in a nod to come out just as the car pulled up, the all too familiar sound of the engine washing over me. He walks around to the driver's side as the valet attendant gingerly helps me into the car and shuts the passenger door.

After asking where to drop me off, Blaine was silent and clearly didn't want conversation. Which, honestly, I didn't know if I did either. We hadn't spoken a word about what happened at the club, in his theater, or in Vail. What the fuck are we even doing? Just thinking about the heat in his eyes as he licked me from his hand makes me shiver.

I left it alone and we drove in near silence outside of the surrounding creamy instrumental music flowing through his speakers gently. Occasionally, I peeked over at him from my peripheral and noticed his knuckles were white from his grip on the steering wheel. Not going to ask, not tonight. Whatever his deal was, he could handle it. This isn't on me. He can be a big boy and sort through whatever bullshit that is.

We make our way through upper downtown before approaching a four-way corner of bars, hotels, and other sky-high buildings. I spot the place Ryan asked to meet; a large two-level bar painted a dark grey with black accenting areas, outdoor seating, and multiple fire towers illuminating the space. There's a doorman in a suit standing near the entrance watching as a couple of small groups gather on the patio under the net of black fairy lights reflecting like a grand, gothic chandelier. "Umm, that's it there; Breven Lounge," I say quietly. As Blaine pulls in front of the building, I thank him for the ride awkwardly and reach for the handle.

"Stop. Stay." He gets out of the black McLaren, all eyes on him, both men and women and makes his way to my side of the car. Opening my door, he takes my hand, helping me out before leaning into me closer, his presence enveloping me. "Lily... any man not willing to pick you up for a date with flowers, much less meet you at a bar versus taking you to a nice dinner, isn't worthy of you. Do better." He sneers. He practically slams the door, making his way back to the driver's side before his words sink in and I stand there watching as he drives off. He didn't even look back before the roar of his engine took off. I can't even think about what a mess that was right now. *"Do better."* The man's so hot and fucking cold. "Prick," I huff.

I make my way inside, showing the doorman my ID, and see the man that's surely Ryan Lanning, sitting at the bar. Certainly not terrible to look at. Black button-up, dark grey pants, nice shoes, hair combed back in place. He has a glass of dark liquid, probably whiskey, in front of him as he happens to look over to his right and spot me. He smiles and keeps his gaze on me but makes no effort to get up to greet me, so I make my way to him before claiming the open chair next to him. "Ryan?"

"Lilith, I take it?" His eyes wander down my body and my long, exposed legs like he sees through my clothes. "Great to meet, please sit." I can smell the alcohol oozing out of him; how long has he been here? Something about him makes me feel nervous and uneasy, but I brush it off as just being out with a man for the first time in, well, a long time. *Give him a chance. Just practice dating.* He is quite handsome after getting a good look at him. He has a gold chain around his neck that I spot under his button-down, a matching gold watch, attractive hands, and lush lips. Mary-Ann had told me he was handsome, but I assumed she was exaggerating. Maybe I could get back out there after all.

After a couple of drinks, his tattoos, touchy hands, and dangerous aura didn't seem so threatening. We chatted about Mary-Ann, his job, favorite bars, movies, and even shared a few laughs. I'm a bit of a lightweight; so one cocktail has me feeling pretty buzzed and happy. I excuse myself to the bathroom and smile into the mirror, now fluffing my hair, touching up my lips, and overall feeling pretty good, loose. He's certainly charming. Suddenly, I feel a pang of guilt as Blaine comes to mind, and my smile falters a little. I don't know what the hell is going on with us, but he made zero effort to speak to me after everything and still, even tonight, showed zero interest in me. No, went out of his way to prove he had zero interest in me. Katie and I were wrong. We should have honestly known better. As excited as I was at the prospect of Blaine being into me, he was still Blaine. Dating and sex famously meant nothing to him. *I* meant nothing to him. I stare at my reflection, remembering his words as he left. *"Do better."* I will do better then. I feel foolish and embarrassed for even thinking he'd be interested in me. As pissed as I was, now thinking of Blaine, I remember the hot, bad boy that sat at the bar waiting for me. Who is clearly interested in me. "You're right, Blaine, I will do better," I whisper to myself before one final hand through my hair, and I make my way back to Ryan as he casually, effortlessly smiles, waiting for me.

"You look stunning, by the way, if I haven't told you. One of my biggest weaknesses when it comes to women is high heels and long legs." He lightly strokes a warm hand over my thigh as I sit before placing it behind the back of my chair. "I ordered you another drink, hope that's not too presumptuous." He slowly drawls.

"Not at all, thank you. Cheers." I smile and can't help but scan my eyes over his big, muscled body, and exposed chest at the top of his button-up, humming happily.

"Cheers…"

# 32

# BLAINE

I slam the door to my place as I storm in, heading straight for the bar. I pour a shot of bourbon into a glass and down it, focusing on the burn as it goes down, my head bowed, arms resting on the counter. It could never happen. It's a disaster waiting to happen. *If she only knew half of who you really are, what you've done, she wouldn't so much as* look *at you again.* She deserves so much better than me, and it just pisses me off more. I could never be the type of man she deserves. The type of man she *wants.* I know enough of Lilith to safely assume exactly what she wants. She wants a knight on a white horse to come save her. To gently brush her hair and make love to her on a fucking blanket in a meadow or some shit. I'm not capable of being what she needs. I pour another shot and down it, slamming the glass with a growl hard enough that it shatters. "FUCK." I should reach out to Francesca and reschedule our meeting to tonight to clear my head of beautiful strawberry blonde sirens fucking with my head.

Something felt off about tonight. Not just seeing her sexy as hell meeting another man, the image of her sighing and begging for pleasure under another man, as much as that pissed me off enough to pass as Hades. No, it was more than that. I couldn't shake it. *"God damn it!"* I rub my hand down my face, still standing over my bar, and pinch the bridge of my nose, trying to get clarity on what the fuck I'm actually feeling.

No. Something wasn't right. Hell, maybe it was, maybe it wasn't, but I can't just sit here doing nothing. I have to go back, just a glimpse at her to make sure she's okay. See if she's smiling at him, *for him*. I knew. I *knew* this was a terrible idea and yet common sense went out the window once I touched her. Before I touched her, I was fucked, and I knew it.

I leave my coat, grabbing my spare keys since the valet has the other set, and head straight out my door to the private elevator to my right, for the garage.

I circled a few times before I was able to pull into a parking spot close enough to the bar that I could just barely make out Lilith through the windows. I knew it was her, even from this far away. And so, I sit. And wait. I needed to shake off the two shots I downed, too, now that they were starting to hit me.

Twenty minutes later, Lilith makes her way to the entrance with fuckboy in tow right behind her. I know this guy; I've seen him a couple of times, actually. He's a cokehead with mommy and anger issues when he doesn't get his little bitch-ass way. *This guy Lily, seriously?*

They say their goodbyes in front of the bar as he leans in for a hug and grabs her face for a kiss, the other on her waist slowing dipping to her ass. It takes everything in me not to get out of the car and break his fucking hands for touching her. "Don't even think of leaving with that piece of shit, Lily," I mumble to myself.

I watch as he releases her and starts to walk away, and she pulls out her phone, no doubt, to order a ride-share. Good girl. She can't know I'm here; otherwise, I'd obviously take her home.

Just when I start to loosen my grip, he turns around toward her again, saying something, grabbing her hand, and pulling her towards the side of the building. She obviously doesn't want to go, her phone still in hand, showing him her screen. Her ride must be on the way then.

He pulls her to the side of the building, where it's nearly dark, into a completely shaded alley. I'm seeing red and reaching for the handle before I realize what I'm doing.

*Dead. You're fucking dead.*

# 33

Kindly, check trigger warnings before moving into the next phase of the book if you have topics that are sensitive to you as a reader.

# 34

# LILITH

Ryan leans in to say goodbye and kisses me as I'm thanking him for the drinks. His strong hands grip my hip and neck as he forces his tongue into my mouth too harshly. Asking me to come back to his place for a nightcap, he holds me against him. Something is screaming *bad idea*. Plus, I am way too tipsy and don't plan on jumping in the sack with the first guy I go on a date with after four years, no matter how good-looking they are. "Maybe next time," I joke. "I had a fun time tonight with you, though; I'd love to get together again."

"You sure? My place has a rooftop with the best view in the city?"

I laugh to shoulder off his forwardness and pull out my phone to request a ride. "Maybe next time. Thank you again, Ryan."

He starts to walk away as I order my car. *Ten minutes away.* Damn. I look up at the sound of footsteps, to Ryan making his way back to me, trying to show me something in the storefront around the corner. "Oh, I don't... I don't know. My ride's almost here." I pull out my phone showing I have a ride coming.

"I promise it won't take long; you'll love it."

"Umm, okay, I guess?" He tugs my arm, pulling me into an alleyway, everything darkening as we move further from the city life of the street. I don't like this. Alarm bells immediately start going off, and my heart rate jumps. I already feel trapped and start to panic as he pulls me into a completely shadowed alcove in front of a store. "Wh... what did you... want to show me?" My voice barely escapes, small and uncertain.

"This." His voice drops, and before I can react, his hands grip my shoulders and push me back into the cold, hard wall of the alcove.

A sick feeling rises in my chest. No. No. *No*. His body presses against mine, forcing me back, his thigh wedged between my legs, heavy and unyielding. I try to turn my head, but he catches my face, his mouth colliding with mine in a rush of hot, whiskey-laced breath. His tongue forces its way in, rough and invasive. I'm trapped, every muscle frozen in fear.

Flashes of memories flood me —unwelcome hands gripping too hard, tears, pain, terror— the voices I've tried so hard to bury. Panic overtakes every cell in my body, clawing at me. I try to twist away, but he's too strong. I can't find the words —my voice gone, my breath stolen.

"Mmm... that mouth feels so good. You taste so good, baby. I knew you would." His voice curls around me, thick with alcohol and a sick, eager satisfaction. Before I even process what's happening, he has his hand up my skirt pulling at my panties. Still pinned in place, he drives his mouth onto mine. His other hand's in my hair, holding it so tight I can do little to persuade him. My pulse hammers; I'm losing control, slipping into a spiral of memories, the same helpless, trapped feeling. I can't speak, can't form words.

I force my hands between us, numb and trembling, finally breaking his hold just enough to turn my face away. It's like I'm underwater, thrashing for air, desperate for some way out, anything to make him stop.

"Stop. Please stop... please." I whimper, scrambling against him for freedom. He pushes against my hands, slamming his fingers into me as I cry out and tears form and fall.

"Sshhhh. Don't I feel so good inside that tight pussy. You love it." He shoves his fingers into me again and again, my numbness extending as my body shuts down to override the intrusive pain. "You don't have to put on a show like you don't want this. There's no one around to hear you. Just relax and enjoy it. Your secret's safe with me. I bet you want my cock, too, don't you? I saw the way you were looking at me tonight." He laughs, breathing heavily. "Baby just needs a real man, huh? Someone to take charge, take control, make you feel good?" He grabs my hair tighter, forcing his mouth onto me to quiet me. I struggle against him, using every single ounce of strength I have coursing through my body, shaking. Suddenly it's as if there's an extra set of hands somehow helping to push him back enough to try to yell for someone... anyone. I use the split second I'm given to scream out. "HEL..." He slams a hand over my mouth, silencing me as tears stream down my face.

"Bad idea, Lily," he hisses. I hear the clear sound of his belt being undone. He's too strong, I can't.... I use both hands and pull his other hand off to yell as loud as I can for help the second his hand is off mine. His belt is undone, and I can feel the cold metal bite my hip. He slams my head against the window so hard my vision spots, and I cry out in pain. *"Shut the fuck up.* You were all over me tonight don't act like you don't want this all of a sudden. This is exactly what you want, little sluts like you, I know it is... I'm just giving you what you want. Stop fighting, and I swear I'll make it so good for you. Just fucking relax and take it." My screams are muffled again by his hand, my head throbbing. He's about to rape me, and no one can hear my screams for help. My eyes are blurred over from tears and mascara, my face cold from them covering my cheeks.

I look towards the street as I struggle and see someone. Someone's coming. Oh my god, "PLEASE HELP." I try to get out through Ryan's hand, sobbing. But he's too strong, my attempt just comes out a muffled pathetic plea as he fights to hold me and I give ounce of strength I have to try to push him away.

Not even two seconds after I'm able to make out his face, has Blaine grabbed Ryan by the back of his shirt, throwing him into the brick wall on the other side of the alley. Ryan's pants are falling down as Blaine punches him over and over, blood covering his face as he tries pathetically to fight Blaine back. It's not even close to a fair match, the sounds of grunting and shuffling echoing. *I'm safe. I'm safe. I'm safe. Blaine is here. I'm safe.* I'm shaking so violently that I stumble as I try to shamefully pull up my panties and wipe the tears from my eyes so I can see. I know my makeup is smeared all over my cheeks. I can't speak. Can't find words. I'm frozen, trembling, watching Blaine beat Ryan's face into a bloody heap of flesh. He's going to kill him... "Blaine," I barely manage in a gross whisper. He has Ryan by the neck, slamming his head into the brick wall. "BLAINE." He turns to me, growling, looking more animalistic, more primal than human.

"WHAT."

*"You're going to kill him."*

*"Good."* he drawls out, his eyes are rage and pure fire. Ghostly obsidian darkness surrounds him in an aura that could go head-to-head with the angel of death. He turns around and punches an unconscious Ryan several more times before throwing his body down like he's a bag of trash. He turns towards me again, covered... covered in blood. Not his blood. Ryan's blood. The man that just forced himself on me and tried to rape me in the alley behind the bar where he took me on a date. "Lily, are you hurt?"

I don't... "I don't know. No. Yes. I..." He grabs me by the face, pressing his forehead to mine.

"You're safe." He wipes the tears and mascara from my face, only to replace it with the wetness of warm blood. I'm numb and shaking, but I feel him pick me up, one hand under my knees, the other around my back, cradled against him. I stare straight ahead at nothing as he places me into the passenger seat of his car. I hear and feel him get in the other side, vaguely aware of him calling someone with an address; this address, before hanging up again after those few words. We sit for several seconds before he starts to drive away. Numbness warms me like a blanket.

I can feel the rage still emanating from Blaine as we drive for several minutes through the darkened, bustling streets. "What the hell were you doing with that piece of shit, Lily? Do... do you understand he would have raped you or WORSE had I not shown up? Are you fucking kidding me?"

Just hearing the word rape and what feels like chastising is too much. I can't hold it in. I wince, bowing my head away from him, crying. "I'm sorry... I know, okay?" Doesn't he understand that I know it's my fault? That everything is my fault. I can feel him looking over at me before he abruptly pulls over, undoing my seatbelt and pulling me into his arms as much as he can from his seat.

His voice is just barely a whisper now. "Lily... I'm sorry. I'm so sorry. You're safe. I didn't mean to yell or scare you tonight. I'm just glad you're okay. None of this is your fault. None of this. You're okay." He caresses my arm and pulls back my hair as I start to sob against him on the side of the road. "You... I care about you, Lily. The idea of you hurt makes me want to vomit and destroy everything in my path. I'm taking you home. You'll never see his face again, I promise. He's already being taken care of. Let's go, okay?" He releases me and reaches over to buckle my seatbelt again before the car jumps to speed as we take off into the night.

# 35

# BLAINE

I skip valet, taking the back entrance into the garage to usher Lily privately upstairs. Pulling into one of my parking spots, I can't help but look over at her. My heart is thunderous and broken, remembering and replaying her muffled, panicked cries for help. I have to close my eyes not to be sick or rip off my steering wheel.

I get out and over to Lily's side, immediately picking her up. I know she can walk, but she clearly needs comfort. Holding her is all I can think to do. Hell, a primal part of me needs it too; needs to feel her safe in my arms. The hum of air speeding past us in the diminutive elevator is the only sound as I cradle her against my chest. The doors part, displaying her dimly lit hallway, and I carry her to her apartment door, setting her down so she can get her keys out of her purse to unlock it. I stay back as she walks in without a word, setting her things down on the counter, and sits on the couch. I don't know what to do.

There's nothing but a heavy silence in the dark space, making it feel far less warm than it is. Like the shadows mirror their master's inner turmoil.

After looking her over, I grab a glass of water and bring it over to her silently before heading to her bath and turning on the water, adding a shit ton of whatever soap is there for bubbles that'll conceal her body. I make my way back out to her as she looks up at me with the saddest eyes. No, I don't like that. "Come on, sunshine," I whisper as I grab her hand, leading her to the bathroom.

"Blaine..." I see the hesitancy in her eyes as she stops when she sees the bath.

"No, Lil, hey. I promise I won't even look at your body. This is nothing like that. Let someone take care of you. Let *me* take care of you —please." She takes a few seconds before giving me her hand again as if deciding I have her trust. My heart swells but also breaks at the realization. I help remove her clothes and jewelry, gently. Guiding her into the tub, her hand is freezing. "Let me know if it's too hot or cold." She sits and hunches over with her knees pulled up to her. My phone goes off, and I check who it's from. A coded text from Tren relaying that the piece of shit who harmed my Lily is taken care of and waiting for me in my warehouse twenty miles out of the city.

*You're dead.* The words are a nonstop cycle through my head at the very thought of him. The threat of what he was doing to her hanging in the air around me.

I respond back in a short code myself, telling him and Zach to make sure he at least stays alive until I can get my hands on him. I leave her to grab a cup from her kitchen and come back, kneeling next to her, not saying a word. She just stares at nothing, her head bowed. The light and energy normally flowing from her completely gone, lifeless. My chest tightens, and I almost panic, wondering if I'm going about this right. I don't know what the fuck I'm doing. "Hey, sweetheart, do you want me to call your brothers? Or Katie? If you'd be more comfortable—" I ask, clearing my throat.

"No! Just... no. Please. They can't know about it."

"Okay..." I release a deep breath.

I gently wash and condition her hair, using the cup to carefully rinse everything away. Not only the soap; but the entire night. Any lingering scents, touches, stains, or physical reminders of what happened. I wet a sponge she has on the tub with a chamomile honey body wash, rubbing it to foam up and release its mild aroma. I reach for her hand and quietly ask her to stand. Running the sponge over her arms, her back, chest, stomach, and legs I stop, putting the sponge in her hand and turning around. "If you want to wash... any other places. I'm not looking."

I wait until I hear her sit before using the cup to rinse her shoulders and hair once more and have her stand to dry her, grabbing a towel from a rack. Waiting in her fluffy white towel, I lead her to her bed. I go into her closet and find a stack of sleep shirts and lounge pants and help her change before lifting her covers and helping her into bed. I get her water from earlier and put it on her nightstand. "Goodnight, Lily. You're safe, and I'll have security keep extra precautions for your peace of mind. I'll check in on you tomorrow, okay? Do you want the TV on or anything?" She looks up at me a little blankly but offers me a hint of a smile. It doesn't reach her eyes. I lean down and press my lips to the top of her forehead, brushing her wet hair back. I go to turn but feel her grab my wrist, stopping me, the touch near feather-light.

"Will you... just stay a little longer, please?" She looks away before I can answer, pulling her hand away. I stand for several seconds, but it's not really a debate.

"Anything you want from me, I'll give you. You just have to say the word. I'll stay as long as you need." With that, she pushes back, to the center of the bed, opening the blanket as a silent invitation to join her. Looking down at my clothes, I note the blood and mess, not wanting to touch her with this. She must see my thoughts racing.

"I trust you if you want to take off your clothes first." I manage a nod in response, removing my clothing down to my boxers. The fact I again have her trust doesn't go unnoticed. Climbing in gently beside her, I open my arms so she can shift closer to lay against me.

"Come here, sunshine."

As I hold Lily, there's nothing but the sounds of our breathing and the faint echo of cars passing below on the street. The only thing keeping me anchored is the feel of soft skin, her back raising and falling with each breath.

# 36

# BLAINE

## *Before:*

I'm waiting for the moment when it starts to really kick in that I made it the fuck out. That this is the new beginning I've been working so hard towards. Right now, it doesn't feel like anything. I guess it's the numbness' turn for the time being. Fine.

Tossing the last few shirts and odds and ends into my duffle bag, I look around the futon and the floor, making sure I have everything. I made sure to take down the sheets I had hung for walls in Rye's living room and leave everything how it was when I got here. Like I was never here. That's the fucking goal. Forget I was ever here.

I didn't tell anyone I was leaving today. Better this way. I left Rye a note; that'll be good enough. He never wanted a teenager in his home disrupting his life.

I also got a new phone number too. I didn't leave it in the note.

I leave my key on the kitchen table and make my way to my car, tossing everything in the back seat before getting in. It's not until I'm driving down the gravel road, do I finally look back. The image of worn to hell, pastel trailers lining either side of the road, a gust of gravel dust trailing me. I just know this image, this moment right here, is going to be one I never forget.

# 37

# LILITH

Having Blaine beside me feels like a lifeline I didn't know I needed. His hand lightly brushes through my hair, the gentle pressure of his fingers along my arm grounding me. His warmth seeps into me, his scent —complex and familiar— surrounds me like a shield, holding back the cold that threatens to consume me. I press closer, my arm draped across his chest, clinging to the comfort he offers without words. Usually, I push people away, sabotaging the moments when I most need someone. But this? This is different.

I've never allowed anyone to stay at my side like this. Not before. Not when it mattered. But tonight, I needed him, and he hasn't left. It feels foreign, like standing on the edge of a precipice, unsure if I'll fall or be caught. I've always dreamed of being caught. The night that started with so much promise spiraled into something so much more painful than I could have possibly ever anticipated. And now, I'm left here —reeling and ashamed that I froze when it mattered most. I just froze. I barely fought back. The control I've fought so hard to hold onto slipped through my fingers like sand.

In an instant, I was suspended between two realities, drowning in an ocean of memories while a storm raged around me. The past and present collided, dragging me down.

"Thank you," I murmur, my voice raspy from disuse. "For everything tonight. Coming after me... staying with me. It means more than you know."

"You don't need to thank me." There's a pause, a hitch in his words. "I'd do anything for you."

I feel the hesitation in his voice, the crack that tells me he's not entirely sure of his own promise. But, honestly? I don't care. Right now, he's here when I need him most, and that's enough. More than enough. My thoughts swirl in the aftermath of what happened. I don't know what to make of our connection or the tangled feelings I have for him after the mess of this night. It's too much to consider. Not now. Not yet.

"Tonight..." I begin, my voice faltering as I search for the right words. "When— god, I'm sorry." I take a deep breath. "When he pinned me against the glass, and I couldn't move... it wasn't just the fear of him, you know? It was everything. Every buried memory I've tried so hard to forget. They all came rushing back. I felt paralyzed like I was trapped in the nightmare I've lived through a hundred times."

Blaine listens, silent but steady, his presence a balm against the storm in my chest. I draw in a shaky breath, the words tumbling out before I can stop them. "I don't know if my brothers ever told you why I was disowned, why I was actually raised apart from them?"

"No, they never have." I'm not at all surprised.

"Our mother —she had an affair. I was the result. When she told my father, she confirmed I wasn't his biological daughter, not like my brothers. His entire side of the family was told so many lies by my uncle. My father never defended us and never addressed half of the lies my uncle told. Whether it was shame or hurt, I'll never know the reasons, on either side. But they disowned me even before my mother passed. Holidays, family gatherings... I was invisible. They ignored me and shunned me. I didn't understand why I was so unworthy of love, why they looked at me like I was a stain on the family while my brothers were so prized and adored."

My chest tightens as I revisit the memories. The years of isolation, of wondering what I'd done wrong. Before I could have even known how much worse it was going to get. "But it wasn't just the indifference... it was my uncle. He hated me."

I feel Blaine tense beside me, his body going still at Robert's mention. God, just thinking his name makes me physically sick, his phantom hands on my skin.

"No one —umm, no one knows this part," I continue, my voice trembling. "Not even my brothers. But, when I was little, my father's brother would... he —fuck, I'm sorry." I take a second to blink away the tears and loosen my tensing muscles. "He —made me do certain things. And as I got older, after my mom died, it got worse. So much worse. He hurt me for years. I don't want to say it aloud, not all of it, but I can't keep it inside anymore." I can't contain the tears and ache in my voice as I try to say this out loud to someone. It feels like I'm choking on the words as they lodge themselves into my throat. I've never told anyone, and it feels like that part of my heart is fighting me to keep my mouth closed like it's our secret. If anyone knows, they'll see how used, awful, and unworthy I am. How dirty my body is. How *weak* I am.

I crack under the weight of what I'm finally admitting, the unspeakable truth I've carried alone for so long. "He threatened to kill my father and my brothers if I ever told anyone. He said I wasn't real family, that I was nothing. With everything my brothers were already going through, I stayed silent. After my father died, Robert controlled everything. I was cast aside and sent into foster care while my brothers were forced to stay with him. He took everything —my inheritance, my connection to my family, my childhood. I was erased from the family as if I had never existed. Do you know how fucking hard that was? How heartbroken and alone I felt?"

My voice quivers with the weight of it all, the years of being forgotten, alone, moving from one home to another, surrounded by violence and pain. "I lost everything. My parents, my home, my brothers. I escaped my uncle, but at what cost? I was thrown into a world that was just as cruel, if not more."

The memories flood me —the fear, the helplessness, the darkness that's followed me for so long. "Tonight wasn't just about Ryan," I whisper, tears slipping down my cheeks. "It was about every man who's ever used me, taken what wasn't theirs. Every man who pushed and begged after I said no. I learned long ago to shut down, to escape into my mind, into a world that wasn't real, but safe.

Whatever book I was reading at the time, my friends in it, everything. I ran there. I hid there. That's why I haven't been with anyone in years. I've kept myself away from that, from men. But tonight... tonight brought it all back."

I laugh, a bitter sound that's more sob than joy. "And look how it ended. The first date I've been on in years, and it turned into my worst nightmare. I don't know why I'm telling you all this, Blaine. Maybe because I feel safe with you for the first time in a long time. Maybe because I just needed to say it out loud, finally."

I can feel the phantom weight of my uncle's hands on me, the lingering scent of fear and sweat clinging to my skin. His voice echoes in my ears, his threats still lodged deep in my soul. "Thank you," I manage through the tears. "You have no idea how much I needed this. How much I needed someone to just... be here."

The smells, touches, sounds, and images of my uncle sit heavily on my chest. The storm inside me rages on, but for the first time in years, I feel a small glimmer of something. Hope, maybe?

Blaine is here. He knows the ugly truth I've kept hidden for so long, and he hasn't turned away disgusted. He's still here, holding me close, his warmth a near literal shield against the darkness that still haunts me.

## BLAINE

Every part of me is screaming to get out of this bed, to track down her uncle, and end him —slowly and violently. The urge to rip him apart with my bare hands, to break each bone, to drag my blade through his skin and carve out his twisted sins —*it's overwhelming.*

My body vibrates with the need for violence, the sickening fury roiling in my gut as I fight it down. I hold Lily tighter instead, grounding myself in the warmth of her small frame against mine. Even as my mind races with images of how he's going to pay.

Lily, nestled against me, soft and small. Her quiet strength is the only thing keeping me anchored. I've never known anyone like her. Her soft smiles, those shy, fleeting glances, the far-off look in her eyes when she's lost in thoughts, drifting to places I can't follow. For so many years, I saw her as naive, thinking she didn't understand how cruel the world really was. But now, I see that I've had it wrong this whole time.

The sweetness, the light she gives so freely? It's not ignorance —it's goddamn resilience.

Despite everything, she still looks to the future with hope. She still finds the strength to smile, to laugh. Where I've built walls of anger, where I've become the storm —*she's remained the light.*

A flood of memories wash over me, flashes of the last decade —stolen glances, how she seemed to float through life untouched by the darkness I carry. I used to think her optimism was absurd, childish even. How could anyone still see the world with hope? But now I know better. She's lived through more pain than anyone I've ever met, including myself. Yet somehow, she still looks at life with a kind of grace I'll never have.

*"Trying to find the nice moments."*

Her words echo in my mind, over and over, and I can't speak. I want to. I want to tell her everything she deserves to hear, everything I *should* say. But I don't know how to comfort her. I don't know how to be gentle, how to hold someone without breaking them. I'm the storm —anger, destruction. She's the sunlight that filters through after the rain, still standing despite everything.

Fury burns inside me, at her uncle, at every man who's ever hurt her. It's all-consuming.

"Lily," I whisper, my voice rough, heavy with everything I can't say. I want to offer her comfort, to tell her something that will take away her pain, but the words just don't come. I'm not built for tenderness, for kindness. Love —if I've ever really known it— feels like a foreign language I've forgotten how to speak. "I…"

"You don't have to say anything; that's not why I told you," she whispers against my chest, her voice soft, like she's the one comforting *me*. I'm hit with a wave of disappointment at myself. That I can't be more for her. That I can't be what she deserves.

"Lily… I don't have the right words. I'm not good at this. But I'm sorry for everything you've gone through. You've endured pain that most people could never even begin to comprehend. And I know what that does to someone. I know how it makes you feel different and isolated, even in the most ordinary moments. I can't fix that. But

I need you to know... you deserve every bit of happiness this world has to offer. Every sunset, every smile, every rainbow, every little bit of peace. You have me now. I know... we've known each other for a long time because of your brothers. But you really have me now too. For anything you could ever need, I will do whatever I can for you. Just say the word. I promise, and I don't make promises that I can't keep."

I pull her into me tightly, trying to hug the broken pieces back together. That's what I can do: physically adore and worship her. In such a short time, this delicate, sweet, unbelievably strong woman that I've known for years has become special to me. I'm not capable of love anymore if I ever truly was. But I feel something for her and know I mean it when I say I'll do anything for her. Keeping her safe is at the top of that list.

I'll be her sun. She'll never be in the dark again. Never be scared of the dark again.

She deserves the world. I'll make sure she gets it.

I need to talk to her brothers and get their side of things before I act. Whatever details they have could be useful when I finally make my move. Her uncle's days are numbered. I'll make sure of that.

But first, we pay our new friend Ryan a visit. He and I have unfinished business.

# 38

# BLAINE

I laid in bed with Lily until she was deeply asleep, the TV playing her favorite comfort show in the background quietly. All I could think about were all of the ways Ryan and her uncle will die at my hands. Two of my men picked Ryan's body up from the alley next to Breven and brought him to my warehouse, outside of the city. I left her a note letting her know I had to leave and to call or text for anything at all.

I pull up, my tires crunching over the loose gravel of the long road, the stark image of the garage doors to the warehouse fading as I kill the engine and headlights. The ground is still covered in an endless black from the night sky and lack of moonlight. I sit in my car, taking a few deep breaths before the side door opens, letting loose the faint light from inside. Tren —'Tree', stands in the stream of light, gun in hand, as he lifts his chin in acknowledgment of my late arrival. The man is huge, hence the nickname. He's an ex-Navy Seal, several inches taller than me, putting him at around six-eight, and is a fucking beast. He's always immaculately put together, never a sleek dark hair out of place. If anyone could best me, it'd be Tree.

Zachariah, also here, is close to my build and height with what can only be described as shaggy light brown hair and a charming full smile that makes me want to roll my eyes most days. He invariably wears the most hideous headbands to hold his hair back and has his nails painted, typically a variant of pink or red, I've noticed. He is also a highly skilled mercenary and hacker fucking genius. The brut and the brain; and the only men I trust with my life.

Tree and Zachariah have Ryan waiting inside for me. Hopefully, they didn't have too much fun without me. It's never as fun if they're already halfway to Hell's Gate.

I get out, the car door closing with a soft thud in the silent night as I make my way towards Tree and put on my white leather gloves. He isn't too big on speaking when it's not necessary. When he does, though, his voice is so deep even my own panties get wet. He just leads me into the warehouse, where my new friend awaits our playdate.

Inside, the warehouse is virtually empty and seemingly abandoned by design. Its center is one large room, resin coated cement flooring –easier cleanup- with an open second floor with lodging and bathing units for when needed, as well as a highly secure storage room that leads to a basement underground. There are a series of metal bars and low-hanging industrial lamps, adding a sinister feel to the dimly lit center of the lower room. Ryan mostly hangs limp, his hands bound above him, holding his body up under a metal lamp's spotlight. He's still covered in his blood from the evening's earlier events. About twenty feet from him to the right is a table with various tools and playthings for my friends who get to come visit me here. It's very exclusive; they should feel honored.

I make my way towards Ryan, nodding my head to Zachariah as he trades places with Tree, admiring his neon pink manicure, and smiling. I can't help but let out a huff. Zach goes outside as a set of eyes to stand watch just in case, with a pair of advanced night vision glasses, and Tree stands tall and quietly inside with me, half in the shadows.

I smile, what feels more like a baring of teeth, approaching Ryan as he looks over my figure and gloves, visible fear setting in as he surely realizes the underworld deity is here to make good on his sins. Staying silent, I circle, taking in his current state. "Please... I'm sorry. You have the wrong guy. Please, let me go. I won't tell anyone, just please. I swear. Whatever you want I can get for you. Anything."

I stop in front of him, sneering at his pathetic display before going to my table of toys, picking up my father's knife, and heading back in front of him. I like having a little fun and they always stay awake for my games a little longer when they're scared and pumped full of adrenaline. So, just as a cat would with its prey, I stay quiet. The only sounds in the warehouse are the sounds of the chains above Ryan clanking as he tries to move, and the barely audible drip of water somewhere to my back. I slowly drag the dull side of the blade across his stomach and chest and then press the sharp end under his chin forcing his eyes onto mine. He tries to plea and drives the tip of the blade into his skin further.

*There it is,* I grin, my lip curling upwards in sick delight at the sight of his blood starting to drip down the blade from my love tap. He deserves this.

"I'm hurt, Ryan." I bend down slightly so our eyes are level. "Just a matter of hours ago, we were so close. And now." I sigh. "Now, you act like we're not even acquaintances." I tsk my tongue at him in disappointment, digging the blade just ever so slightly deeper, feeling the pleasure in my stomach as he squirms. *Weak.* "Did I hit your head a little too hard in the alley, or are you trying to play games? If it's the latter, I promise, I play them better." His eyes suddenly widen with fear, huffing air through his nose as he tries to scramble back the best he can, chains restricting his every movement. "Ah. Now you remember me." I step back, laughing in satisfaction.

"L... look... look, I'm sorry okay. If that's what this is about, I didn't know she was your girl. She was all over me, man, I swear."

My arm is swung around, the blade slicing through his chest before I even process what I've done. "The next word that comes out of your pathetic fucking mouth better be an apology to Lily." My chest is heaving from his words. I press the knife to his throat, waiting for him, spit flying from his mouth as he huffs in air through his teeth in pain.

"—I'm sorry... Lily."

"Again," I seeth.

"I'm sorry, Lily."

"Now. Are we done lying?"

He grits his teeth as he glares at me. "Yes." This would be the part where he suddenly acts unafraid; his final stand and opportunity to not go out like the little bitch he is. Because he knows now; there will be no leaving this room. That should be apparent.

"Good. Now! —What exactly were you planning on doing with her in that alley?"

With an all-too-brave bloodied smile, he replies, "Look man, you weren't there alright. She wanted me to make a move. Just giving her what she wante..." His sentence dies as he screams in pain from my blade stabbing his thigh.

"I SAID NO MORE LIES!" I turn, pacing back and forth in front of him after spitting on his cheek. "Now... try again." After several seconds pass and he doesn't say anything, I smile and kneel before him. "Three... two... one..." I slice the sharpened blade over his other thigh, taking a long slice of skin and muscle before he starts screaming, thrashing under my touch.

"STOP! Stop, please fucking stop, please I'm sorry! PLEASE."

I stand up, hands behind my back, smiling, and tilt my head politely, waiting for him to speak. "Yes?"

"I... I... I..."

"I... I... I..." I mock him, waiting impatiently. I suddenly feel like the fucking Grinch meeting Cindy Lou and think of how much Lily would laugh at that, her adorable little smile radiating her sunshine. I bite my lip, thinking of her happiness, before remembering the piece of shit in front of me, turning to face him. I catch sight of Tree smiling to my side. He enjoys this as much as I do, the sick fuck.

"How about... I help you out?" I stick the blade back underneath his chin as he stiffens at the touch, tears, and snot covering his bloodied face. *Fucking gross.* "You thought that it was perfectly okay to trap my girl in the dark alley and...? Come on now... prize if you answer right." I smile sunnily with my upbeat tone.

"And... touch her." I freeze, my body humming in anger as I feel the fire burning behind my eyes and in my veins. I stay quiet, stretching my neck to break up the tension before redirecting my attention, my head bowed down, pacing.

"You know, a fun fact about my pretty little Lily, is that Lilies are actually her second favorite flower. Her favorite is roses. Red roses." I toss down the knife and make my way to the table, grabbing a much smaller, more precise exacta knife. "I know, I know; I could see how you'd be surprised to hear that. But I guess when it's the beautiful name you hear every day, it may lose its appeal." I shrug. "But you know. I have been secretly practicing my artistic abilities to impress her one day —she's a very talented artist— and... I could use a new canvas." I look over his body for an area that isn't yet covered in blood. *Disgusting.* "Now. I wanted to display my skill upon your cheek. But, seeing as your face is coated in mucus, blood, and pathetic tears, I guess this will have to do. Now, hold still." I hear Tree's demonic chuckle as Ryan's panic sets in again.

Closing in on his chest, I start to carve the inside petals of a rose, adding layers of petals around it, until it's a full, blooming rose, drops of blood falling down each petal, down his chest. My canvas squirms and huffs through his teeth as I work, and my hand slips from his movements.

"Now look what you've made me do." I sigh frustratedly, reaching down for my favorite knife and slicing his throat *just* enough. I'm not done playing quite yet. I stamp it through both cheeks as his mouth is open from his incessant screaming. His cries become slightly muffled and more deranged from the blade sitting through his cheeks, between his teeth. I smile and nod, going back to my portrait to finish the stem, adding thorns and leaves.

"What do you think, Tree?" I nudge my head, calling him over.

"Well done, sir. Very nice." His shadow looms over my workspace.

"You know, this would be a lovely red for Lily to paint with. Too strange to take this to her?"

"Uhh, yes. I'd advise against it. Strongly advise against it." I slowly nod and throw a charming smile over my shoulder towards him in agreement before refocusing my attention. I would never do such a depraved thing; at least... I doubt I would. But these moments give me such a high it's easy to fall into a character, my fucked up alter ego. It's what saved me all those years ago.

"Anyway. Ryan, back to you. Now... that's not all you were planning to do with my little ray of sunshine, was it? Now, remember..." I hold up my hands. "You want to be honest." My finger-wagging at him, I make my way over to my table, trading my exacta knife for a handgun. Turning around, I see Ryan spot the gun and rest his head in defeat against his right arm, still hanging above him, the knife sticking through his cheeks. We can't have that.

I shoot his knee without thinking, still wanting to play; his muffled screams spreading loudly through the warehouse, chains clanking. I stand in front of him, grabbing his throat. "Now... pay fucking attention." I force his eyes to mine, seeing all the pain and sorrow and exhaustion in them. *Good.* "What else were you planning to do with my sunshine before I found you?" I stare into his eyes, promising hellfire.

He tries to speak, his voice rough and muffled from being locked in place.

"Oh, oops." I smile and grab the handle, pulling the knife out of his cheeks and tossing it to the ground, his teeth clamped down, screaming through them. "There, there." I roll my eyes. So dramatic. "That's better. Now, I couldn't quite catch that – say again?" I tilt my head waiting.

"... I was going... to fuck her." He throws his head back, closing his eyes before I snap his throat in my hand, squeezing his airways, watching his face turn purple. Just before he loses consciousness, I let go, punching him in the face, watching as he growls in pain.

"That's right." My voice is so low and guttural, that I almost think a demon's taken over my body. I grab his throat again, holding him in place. "And when you were planning on fucking my girl, was she begging for it?" He looks up at me, silent outside of his labored breathing. "Was her pussy soaking fucking wet?" I lift the gun to his forehead. "ANSWER ME!"

"No." He chokes out.

"No... that's right. Because she didn't want it, did she? She was screaming for someone to help her, fighting to get out from under your body, mascara, and tears coating her pretty face... isn't that right, Ryan?" The image that will forever haunt me.

"Yes."

"That's right." I barely manage to whisper. "That's right." I step back, pacing, head down. All I can think of is her face. Her muffled cries, pleading for help, so terrified. Her desperate eyes clinging to me as she spotted me. I stop pacing, standing still, half in a shadow, half in the light. The image of him with his fucking sick fingers inside her, forcing her while she's crying for him to stop, smashing her head into the window to silence her. I turn my head to the right; positive I'm possessed by the devil himself with the amount of hatred and evil running fire through my veins. I could swear my shadow grows horns and smoke as I shoot the mother fucker in the other knee, in both shoulders, and in the hip. I glare at him, snarling, taking in every second of his screaming, until I find myself inches from his face, holding his chin in place to look at me as he agonizes in pain. "I'm just giving you what you want, Ryan. I know you wanted this. Don't look so upset." I deadpan.

I turn to Tree, making my way to him. "Cigarette?"

He tosses me the pack of menthols, and I pull one out with the lighter hidden inside the pack. Making my way back towards the table. I lean my weight against it, lighting my smoke, taking a deep breath savoring the harsh sensation. I zone out to near silence and darkness as Ryan's pathetic sobs reach a new level of distress and wariness. I hate cigarettes, they're fucking disgusting. Lilith would probably hate it if she knew I had a cig in my hand; give me shit for it. However, it's become a ritual over the years, since I was a teen, whenever I find I'm forced to have death on my hands. I sit on the table, finishing my cigarette in otherwise silence, thinking of Lily. She's mine. She may not know it, and I may not actually be able to have her, but she's *mine*. I pick up another knife on the table, making my way in front of Ryan, about fifteen feet away, watching his eyes begging for me to grant him death. A look I know well.

"Don't worry, Ryan. I'll find you again in Hell." Tossing him a feral possessed grin, I throw the knife, landing it through his throat, flicking my smoke into one of the small pools of red at his feet as he dies, trying to get air. I watch the ember slowly go out like the light in Ryan's eyes as the crushed tip soaks in his blood.

I look up at Tree before making my way to the bathing quarters upstairs as he nods, letting me know he has clean up handled.

Upstairs, I enter the old pink and cream-tiled bathroom. Turning on the water of the rusty shower, I stare at myself in the mirror, listening to the sounds echoing in the tight space. I'm covered in another man's blood. I tortured and killed him. Not because someone held a fucking gun to my head, forcing me. Because I *wanted* to. Because I get a sick pleasure in it. Because I wanted to punish and inflict as much fucking pain in that piece of shit as I could and be the one knowing I took the light from his eyes as his soul leaves his body.

*If she only knew half of who you really are and the things you've done, she would never look at you again.*

I bow my head, hands resting on the sink in defeat. I will never be good enough for her. She can never truly be mine. She deserves so much better than this; better than me.

I'm not a knight in shining armor, I'm the twisted fucking prince of darkness.

# 39

# LILITH

### *Before:*

The beep resounding through the air following each number I press into the phone sends chills down my spine. I'm three numbers away from the most significant moment I can recall in years, and my hands are shaking so violently I almost lose my grip on it. The voice of my mother's ghost, which still seems to haunt me, fills my head. *Breathe, my sweet girl. I'm so proud of you.* Planting my feet solidly into the broken concrete of the alleyway, I focus on slowing my breathing and remind myself it doesn't matter what happens. It doesn't matter if they want nothing to do with me. I'm a survivor and am fine on my own. I don't need anyone. The worst thing that happens is I'm still alone, and I move on permanently with zero regrets.

With one final deep, slow pull of air in and out, I press the remaining three digits, glancing around to both ends of the small alley. The line doesn't even have a chance to finish the shrill ringing sound before a deep masculine voice that somehow is so familiar picks up on the other end. "Lilith?" My breath gets trapped in my throat, and I freeze, unsure of whether I need to throw up, sob, or collapse to the ground. "Hello? Hey, are you there? Talk to me, Lily. I'm here. It's Artemis."

"Y-yeah. I uh, I umm."

"Fuck, Lily, it's really you. I can't believe it. I mean, we knew it was you, but god, hearing your voice..."

"Yeah," I huff a laugh, tears falling freely, fighting the sobs waiting to break loose. "It's really me. And, it's really you?"

"Yeah, baby sis, it's me." That does me in; the endearment is the final straw, and I can't feel my legs as I slide down against the rough brick wall behind me, scraping my hand, trying to find the air my lungs so desperately need and can't seem to fully grasp. "Hey, hey, sshhh, hey. We're here. We're coming and getting you, Lilith, literally right now. We're already in the car, you just gotta tell us where we're going to pick you up."

Sobs wrack my chest, and I fist my left hand as hard as I can to gain some semblance of control of my emotions, vision blurry from tears. I usually have such a firm grasp on my emotions that it's overwhelming in itself to not feel in control right now when I desperately need to. "S-s-sorry. I'm sorry. It's just uh, god. It's.."

"It's a lot, I know. We've got you."

Never did I think three words could have such an effect on me. *We've got you.* I squeeze my eyes shut tight and bite my lip to keep my composure.

"Can you tell me where you are?"

"Uh, yes. Yeah. I'm at the public library in Wentworth." I sniffle through the words, wiping my nose.

"That's perfect, thank you. We're on our way, Ronan and I. Okay?" I nod and then realize he can't see me. "Lily?"

"Yeah, yes. I'll be here."

"You want to stay on the phone with us while we drive?"

"Oh, um, no. Thank you, though. I'll wait inside. This isn't my phone, but just call it or text when you're close?"

"You got it... we won't let you down. We'll be there."

Saying goodbye and hanging up, I feel too many things to put a name to, and somehow, it all starts to blur into familiar numbness again.

All I can do is stare blankly at the wall opposite the one I'm sitting against. The muttering and chatter, wind, and daily noises fade to near nothing behind a bubble, muting it all. I stare, stone-faced, on the ground until the chill in the air gets to be too much, and I force myself to stand, nauseous and more than a little terrified.

The feeling of hope is just out of reach. A shadow I can't quite wrap my fingers around and hold to my chest.

I can't believe this is happening.

# 40

# BLAINE

"Hey man, what's up?"

"We need to talk." I sit in my car, caught in Saturday mountain traffic —the city's residents who didn't make the usual Friday evening rush after work, heading up now. I knew I had to play this smart after last night with Lily. It took every ounce of strength I had to calm myself and stay in bed with her instead of ripping out her uncle's heart after maybe force-feeding him Ryan's. I have to talk to Ronan and Artemis to get their point of view and see what the hell they know or don't know.

"Okay, are you breaking up with me?" Artemis, easy-going as ever, jokes on the other end.

"Trust me, now's not the time to fuck with me. It's about Lily. I'm already driving to your place; I'll be there in twenty."

"Lily... is she okay? Did something happen?" I can feel his panic in his faux calm voice.

"The details aren't mine to tell, but she's fine. I need a personal account from you and Ronan. Like I said, I'll be there soon. She's fine and at her apartment. I've got eyes on her."

"Okay. I'll grab him. We're both home." I end the call without responding and before he can say anything further. There's no way Ronan or Artemis know anything about their uncle touching Lily. Right? The thought alone makes me sick. I have to talk to them. It just doesn't make sense why they never questioned or battled him for the shit way she was tossed into the system and treated like trash her entire life. At this point, I've been up nearly all night between staying next to Lily and visiting Ryan. I may have gotten three hours of sleep.

I pull up to their estate in the long, curved drive, wrapped around a ridiculously oversized stone fountain. The exterior is white with four heinously extravagant pillars outlining the exaggerated entrance and perfectly manicured foliage framing the house, even in late Autumn. The remodeled carriage house is behind the main house, several acres away. This was their parent's home, where they all spent their younger years growing up together, long before I knew them. Before their parents both died and their uncle took Ronan and Art in, until they came of age.

Artemis opens the door, stepping out with his arms crossed and a scowl on his face. Very rarely does Artemis portray any emotion other than cool, calm, and collected. He's always easygoing and charming. Exactly as his uncle and father raised him to be, as the heir to the fortune and businesses. It was apparently always known Ronan would never be of value to their social, political, or business endeavors.

"Well?" His eyes follow me as I walk up to him and up the stone stairs to the pillared dais.

"I need to speak to you both about your uncle and Lily." I watch his expression for any lead that they may be hiding something. I've known them for years and consider them my best friends, but I don't truly trust anyone. Two things about me: I'm incapable of believing in anything one hundred percent, and I don't trust anyone. I don't notice any indication on his face that he knows what I'm hinting at. I walk past him, into the foyer, him following behind.

"Let's go to my office." He turns and then leads me down the hallway towards his home office. Ronan approaches with a slight nod in acknowledgment but otherwise says nothing as we all walk into Artemis' workspace. He sits slightly on the edge of his large wooden desk, arms still crossed as Ronan and I sit on opposite ends of the leather couch a few feet away.

"So? What the fuck's going on?" Ronan leans back, sprawling his long arm over the back of the couch, looking back and forth between Artemis and myself. Artemis just shrugs as if he's waiting too.

"This is important. I need you to walk me through why Lily had such a fucking shitty childhood and was thrown into the system.

What the fuck happened with your uncle." It wasn't a question. It was a demand.

"Why? What happened to Lily? What triggered this conversation?" Artemis asks, genuinely. His demeanor is stiff, and I don't know if it's simply because they are so protective over Lily or if it's something more complex.

"Something happened last night but it's not my place to speak on it, it's hers and only hers if she feels like telling anyone. I need to fucking know the full story, though, and then I'll tell you why I'm asking." I can feel myself tensing. I don't have the time or patience to play these games right now. Ronan looks to Artemis with a shrug and slight incline of his head in silent approval for him to speak, with their twin mind chatter.

"Look, I know you wouldn't be digging or asking if it wasn't important. We've known you for years and trust you deeply. It's just become an unspoken rule not to bring any of this up, and we don't like to talk about it for obvious reasons." He audibly sighs and hangs his head for a second before looking back up at me. "I don't know where you want me to start, so I'll just give you an overview from the beginning.

"When Ronan and I were younger, we knew Lily and our mother were treated like outcasts. It was overtly obvious. The rest of our father's side of the family practically shunned them, constantly either spoke down to them or just flat-out ignored them. They were never accepted into the family and never welcomed. At one point growing up, we found out that our mother had an affair, and that's how she got pregnant with Lilith. The family had found out, and that's why they were treated so poorly. It's fucking ridiculous and disgusting. Trust me, I know. But they're not good people, and have a superiority complex, living in an elitist, delusional world. They treated Lily like shit, never got her gifts on Holidays, never asked about her, or spoke to her. They saw her as a bastard child and nothing more. As if she wasn't the sweet, loving little girl she was. Anyway, our parents' relationship never recovered. Our mother stayed in the house, but we knew they had separate rooms and hardly spoke directly. It was clear they were staying together for us. Although, our father never particularly got close to Lily either. I think he tried. I think he just looked at Lily and was reminded of the heartbreak and what our mother had done to him. So, he kept her at arm's length.

"Our mother ended up passing away when we were eleven, and Lily was nine. That was the point where Lily really started to turn inward, stopped speaking much, kept to herself, and literally was always reading. She practically lived in the study, never brought over friends—you get the idea. Our mother's death destroyed her. It only seemed to get worse between our father and Lily without our mom around, and we were all already heartbroken. It affected her more than us though, I believe. The house staff was kind towards her, and Ronan and I tried to love her as much as we could, as much as she would let us. I know she loved us; we were all she truly had.

"Then... our father died several years later." Artemis grabs the bridge of his nose, pausing, and preparing for what he's about to say next. I can see his eyes lined with tears. The sight tenses my fists, waiting. "Our uncle was left with everything. He took the place of our father, raising Ronan and me for the time being, and handling our finances; obviously, we were too young at the time. He took me under his wing to learn the family businesses, where my father left off. Ronan... coped in his own ways as a teenager. But... Lily went to live with her biological father and his family. Or at least that's what we were told by our uncle. That was what was best for Lily and for us both. She was actually in the foster system, and we had lost all contact with her, and our uncle wouldn't tell us how to get ahold of her. I don't even know if he knew how in all honesty. It broke our hearts. We were crushed. Not only did we lose our parents, but now our baby sister too. We begged our uncle to ask her to come back home and to let us talk to her or write her letters; anything. We just wanted her back with us. We found out years later that she wasn't with her biological family at all. It was so much worse.

"Over the years, we'd try to get any information out of him on how she was doing and if we could talk to her, but nothing... he'd beat us, whip us with belts, or burn us with cigarettes, so we'd stop bringing her up. We had searched several times on social media; at least the few social sites that existed at the time, googled her, tried to find her biological father with the limited information we had at the time, and did everything we could to find her. But we always came up empty-handed. Little did we know back then, that the center she was staying in wouldn't allow computers or internet access, and they weren't allowed to have their own phones. It wasn't a home. It was a fucking prison.

"When we were eighteen, our uncle made us sign an extravagant document that included a small section mentioning that should we ever become in contact with Lilith, we could in no way support her with financials gained from our trust funds or the family businesses. We had to sign it in order to receive what was rightfully ours. And at eighteen neither of us really thought to fight it. We just knew we would need that money and felt helpless.

"A couple of years after that, Lily found me on the biggest social platform there was at the time after she had emancipated herself. Ronan and I immediately went to find her. She needed us, and it broke our hearts to see her. She looked.... just..." He releases a quick, heavy breath. "Anyway... she had debilitating night terrors and thought it was from the house. That time Rone and I left our dorm in college to come stay here for a few weeks? Yeah, that was why. She wouldn't have been able to stay long at the house with us anyway. We pulled some connections and got her an admin position at a friend's company and helped her secretly with rent and other basic things for her first apartment when she'd accept the help. She hated taking anything from us; she still does. The night terrors did mostly end up going away from what she told us; we don't talk about it anymore though. She's always felt like everything is her fault and just wants to live in the shadows. She won't accept our help unless we find a way to gift it to her because she doesn't want to be the reason we could lose everything. All that she's been through... *we've* been through, has just become an unspoken rule that we don't talk about it unless Lily were to bring it up. Which you could guess correctly that she never does. It's been so many years since we've talked about any of this, and we don't want to upset her."

"What about your uncle?" I push.

"What about him? I mean, when our parents passed, he moved in here and took over everything. He was a fucking prick to us when it came to Lily. But everything else, we were able to deal with." I just sit in silence and examine both Ronan and Artemis' faces for something... anything. I audibly sigh and place my forearms on my knees, hanging my head. "Blaine..." I take my time before looking back up at Artemis, trying to simmer my rage and the bile that wants to make its way up my throat.

"Your uncle raped Lily for years." I immediately feel Ronan pierce his fingertips into the couch and tense next to me; Artemis perfectly still, meeting my gaze.

"Lily told you this?" Artemis whispers. I can see his chest starting to rise and fall more rapidly in shallow movements, and his eyes darken, unlike anything I've seen from him.

"Yes. Last night she confirmed it. But, she had hinted at it while we were in Vail when the power went out. She confessed it all to me last night." Artemis looks like he can't wrap his head around what I'm saying, standing and walking around the desk.

"I have to talk to her... I can't believe... I.... *FUCK!*" He throws a small glass, shattering it against the wall before he bends over, placing his hands on the edge of the desk as if he's about to flip the entire thing over. I've never seen Artemis like this. I can feel his rage, shock, and disgust. The sick, dark part of me loves it; seeing even the charming white knight isn't all good. "We have to talk to Lily, Ronan."

Ronan stands next to me from the couch, almost too calmly before he goes to walk out the door, down the hallway towards the foyer. "Ronan, where the fuck are you going?" Artemis calls after him.

"To kill him." Is all he says before Artemis runs after him, down the hallway, and out the front door. I follow outside to the row of vehicles as Ronan nears the black G-Wagon.

"Ronan! Wait. We need to check on Lily and talk to her. STOP!"

"You can either get in or stay. I don't give a fuck, but I'm going to burn him alive." Artemis growls in frustration undoubtedly from not having control of the situation, but throws open the passenger door as I reach for the back passenger, getting in. As long as I get my turn to slice Lilith's name into his skin like a fucking Louis Vuitton logo, break every one of his fucking bones, and do it all over again for a week until he bleeds out —I'll be happy. I can't help the twisted sick pleasure just at the thought of watching this piece of shit beg for mercy, making my lips curl up into a smile that doesn't come close to reaching my eyes.

# 41

# BLAINE

### *Before:*

*Fuuuuckkk,* this feels good.

There's nothing.

Nothing but the darkness behind my eyelids and the rain storming down onto my skin, soaking my face and hair.

Palms to the sky and arms out, the euphoria pumping through my veins is indescribable, man.

Groans and sputtering outside of my little bubble sneak through, and my smile widens. An insane laugh leaves a throat that doesn't quite feel like my own.

I am un-fucking-touchable.

"P-please, man. Hey, just, I promise. I'll do anything you want. Just let me go." Ah, my little friend. That's right. Turning, I feel my smile transform from manic to content. "Ple—"

"Shhhhh. Shh, shh, shh." I swipe my favorite knife I threw into a tree, and crouch in front of my new pet, surveying my work.

"Anything else you got for me? Any new..." I twirl the tip of the knife in the air a few times and feel my skin prickle in excitement, the piece of shit's eyes in front of me following the movement, bracing for the next impact. "...information? Hmm?" The cool tip traces his bloodied lower lip, around his cheek and slices back down the side of his face, following his jaw. "Mmmm." I hear nothing he's saying. His screams muffled as if living behind a thick glass wall. I'm entranced by the red, dribbling down... down.. down. "Beautiful."

"You're fucked." His gritted-out words reach me, more clearly, drawing my attention to his eyes, now closed tightly.

I can't help but chuckle. "I'm not the one tied to a tree in the middle of nowhere, though, now am I?" Not today, anyway. Not yet. "Hmmm.." Looking more closely, considering, and taking in every detail, I savor it and absorb the feeling for later. I close my eyes and let the fire build in me, the energy that takes over and masks me. Amazing what a few years' difference can make.

I meet his stare, his mess of a head flopping back into the rough bark behind him, mouth open and panting. The fire, euphoria, and rage converge into something so damn powerful I nearly lose consciousness. My fingers find their way to the neck in front of me, painting a heart on the bloodied canvas, and I take a deep breath. Slowly, I watch as those same fingers surround both sides, thumb brushing gently before meeting his stare one final time. All the strength my body could muster focused on the hand around this throat, until there's nothing. No breath. No movement. No life.

"Hey, Kid." A deep voice comes up behind me. A presence I already knew to expect.

"Rye."

# 42

# BLAINE

The car launches forward as we head towards the main road, Ronan seething, white-knuckling the steering wheel. The impact of his uncontrolled driving causing the metal of my friend tucked into the waistband of my pants to bite into my lower back.

"Now, will you fucking listen to me?" Artemis sits half sideways in the front seat, looking back at me before refocusing his attention to his brother driving like he thinks we're in a level of fucking Grand Theft Auto. "Look, we have to play this smart, Ronan. If we kill him now, all we're doing is hurting Lily. You remember the wards and extensive bullshit Robert put into that document we signed. You don't think I feel sick to my fucking stomach thinking about him touching our sister! This is our chance to *help* her. We have to get Robert to propose a new, modified, and signed contract giving everything he stole back to her. Everything we both know Lily deserves. Okay?" He looks back at me knowingly. "Do whatever you need to. Just don't kill him until this is done." He pings his eyes back between the two of us before adjusting and sitting forward, darkly. "Then the piece of shit will get what's coming to him."

Robert's assistant lets us into his home without so much as a second thought despite the radiating depth and promise of pain surrounding the three of us. "He's in his study, I believe. I can let him kn—"

"No. Thank you, Samantha." Artemis steps forward first, turning the corner towards the study. I can't help but stop to get her out of here, as they head further into the hall.

"Don't you have an errand to run?" I stare down at her tiny, petite form and wide, innocent eyes in warning, sliding on my white leather gloves. She can't possibly be taller than 5'2" or so and incredibly young and beautiful. Doesn't take a genius to make a connection there, the sick fuck.

"Umm. Yes. —Yes, of course, sir." She's realizing something is off about our visit and trusts me enough -or is scared enough- apparently to follow my suggestion to leave us, turning back for her coat and purse before she races out the door. Glancing around, I notice the cameras. I called Zachariah on our way. He's already in the system and masking us.

Within a matter of seconds, I hear crashing and Robert gasping for breath as I make my way down the hall, following the pathetic cries.

"Did you touch my fucking sister! DID YOU!" Ronan has him by the neck, pinned up against the wall as the sick piece of shit scratches against Ronan's hand. He certainly isn't a small man by any means. But Ronan's making it look too easy to hold him up. Robert catches a glimpse of me, a distinctly evil smile on my face as I tilt my head, staring into his eyes before he looks back to Ronan. He opens his mouth but can't speak due to the force. Ronan drops him enough so that he loosens his grip.

"What are you talking about! Get your hands off of me, boy! What the fuck do you—"

"You have five seconds to tell the truth before you're begging for fucking mercy." Ronan slams his head back into the wall hard enough to cause Robert to grit through his teeth in pain. His eyes feigning innocence, darting around the room.

"Please, I don't know what you're talking about!" Ronan's grip tightens as he slams his head into the wall multiple times, heavy fists marking his twisted face as he lets out his anger. Something snaps in his uncle's face as he looks up harshly, letting out a half laugh, half groan at us. The demon surfacing. Unhinged; he was unhinged and undiluted rage. *There it is.*

"So, I take it the little bitch finally told you?" He sneers, staring into Ronan's eyes in challenge. My gun is in my hand, pointed at him in under two seconds, getting his attention. "You think I'm scared of you and your toy? I know all about your ties and reputation, boy. You don't know a goddamn thing about how this works if you think your pathetic display will do anything here." He tries to start laughing again before Ronan flies his fist into his quickly bloodying face repeatedly, breathing heavily. He tosses him down into the center of the large room, knocking him into a small chair sitting in front of his massive, wooden desk.

"You're dead," is all Ronan spits out before Artemis grabs his arm, stubbornly, wrestling to stop him.

"You can't kill him yet, Ronan." Robert's rough, struggled laugh crackles through the air, getting our attention.

"You won't kill me. I've given you everything! She was never your real family in the first place, you ungrateful little shits! That whore of a mother of yours—" His stream of bullshit is replaced with screaming as I blow a bullet through his fucking knee, stepping closer.

"My turn." I bend down, resting on my haunches staring at his disgusting face, screaming, gritting breath through his yellowed teeth, and holding his useless knee.

"I've been in this game longer than you've been alive, princess." He manages a bloody smile up at me, nothing but evil in his eyes. "Not sure why you're so upset, though." He drawls, drowning in a cough. "Unless you're fucking her now." He looks up at me as I stay silent, watching him, before he tips his head back, laughing. "That's it, isn't it? Let me ask you something. Is her tight little pus—" He screams in agony as I drive my knife into his thigh, twisting it, his hands reaching for me before Ronan and then Artemis hold him down. I'm leaning over him, throat in hand against the floor, seething at the way he's speaking about Lily.

"You know what I call pieces of shit like you? Pathetic, weak little bitches that prey on defenseless women and children? Forcing yourself painfully inside their bodies unwillingly? Huh?" I squeeze harder, his face a far cry from a flattering purple. "Threatening the people they love's deaths in exchange for silence?" I drag my blade, lightly slicing over his skin from his chest down to his lower stomach, panic rising in his eyes. "Forcing your worthless, tiny dick inside their bodies, traumatizing and torturing them?" My hands are shaking, aching to drive my blade into him over and over, until he goes numb from the overwhelming pain, like I know my sunshine did. I lean in, inches away from his face, resting my knife on his groin, ready to ruin him. "Dead. I call them dead." I laugh, staring into his face as I push my knife through his groin; piss and blood staining his pants as he screams and shakes against the hands holding him in place. There it is. I smile happily down at him as I pull my knife free, standing to my feet. Both Artemis and Ronan look at me in shock at what I just did; the screaming and darkness surely too much for them. Artemis looks like he's about to vomit. I can't bring myself to give a shit even remotely about their feelings. I admire my pretty white gloves, coated in his blood, stepping further back.

Artemis finally speaks, looking down at his uncle, an unreadable expression on his face. "Look at me." He continues to hold him in place as his limp, blood-covered uncle blinks the tears from his eyes, looking up at him in agony and begging. This has to be fucking with their heads, especially Art. He's always been a gentle soul. They've never experienced anything like this. To me, it just... is. "We're going to let you go today, allowing you to seek medical attention. But you're going to change the contract you have in place against Lily's well-being, removing all sectors that work against her in any way. You're reassigning the businesses and estates to the three of us: Lily, me, and Ronan. You lose everything in exchange for your life, or these visits will keep happening until you do. Until you're begging for it to stop. Yes?"

"Yes." He looks and sounds disgusting, coughing up blood as he speaks. *Repulsive. Pathetic.*

Artemis goes to release him before I put up a hand. "Wait." I smile. Quietly. Calmly. The model of placidity. "You'll have to forgive my memory, Robert. Sometimes I'm just so forgetful." I bend down between his bloody thighs. "I have a special treat, just for you. I know how much you love to inflict pain, and I thought to myself, 'Hmm.' This is perfect. I rather believe you'll enjoy it." I grab my knife, carving into his skin, his screams echoing through the room as he struggles against the arms and knees holding him in place.

I sit back to reveal my love note. 'I rape children' messily carved into his chest, blood bubbling and falling down to his sides and pooling in the indent in the center of his grotesque chest. I lightly stab the knife into his chin, silencing him and holding his fat fucking face in place. "Can't say it's my best work, Rob." I pool his blood onto the knife, swiping it across his lips for the hell of it. "There we go," I whisper before getting up and walking away towards the door, stopping at the doorframe. "Play nice, Robert. I'm having so much fun with you."

# 43

# LILITH

I stand, staring out numbly to the grey expanse of snow and sky in front of me, the burn of the hot mug in my hands nearly too painful; but I like the feel of it, holding on as long as I can before it's overwhelming. Several seconds go by before I realize I haven't blinked, my contacts drying out, blurring my vision. Not that I was even actually looking at anything.

I'm home, in my stuffy studio. There's a white layer of snow covering everything outside of my huge window, the city silent as the sun prepares to set far too early, casting its darkness before it's even five o'clock. I press my forehead to the icy glass, grazing my eyes over the mountains barely visible through the drifting snowflakes. The occasional faint orange or blue headlights down below, slowly make their way until they're out of view. The coolness of the window on my forehead starkly contrasts with the overwhelming heat of the chamomile tea in my hands.

I close my eyes, retreating inward, and am greeted by an oppressive darkness so heavy it feels like it's closing in on me. I can feel it chasing me, threatening to consume me any minute. Hunting its prey.

That's what my storm does. Every dark emotion, every debilitating, awful, painful memory, gets pushed under until the storm grows thunderous, waiting for the opportunity for lightning to strike. For the clouds to devour the sun. Some days… it wins. I feel every stir of tragedy clawing at me, digging into my skin, in every cell of my body, begging for me to give in. Just a single thought, and I'd be so easily pulled under.

I stand on the dreamlike shore, staring into the monstrous, night-dark clouds covering everything in their path, and I know… I know I won't outrun it. I can't. —So, I let it take me; every depleted inch of me. And it feels like home. Like sinking chilled arms into a well-worn coat. The comfortable and cold embrace of chaos, numbness, pain, and darkness.

Step by step into the unforgiving water, I let it sweep me into the ocean under crashing waves until I'm so far under that there's nothing but stillness. I wonder how much longer I can hold my breath until I'm drowning, clawing, and crying for the surface —for the warmth and light of the sun. Only by then, it's too far. I'm too far. No one is coming to save me. With the light drifting further and further away, it becomes easier to give in to the idea of letting go forever. How strange, the peace that comes with surrendering.

I tried so hard to outrun it.

It's a tidal wave unleashing itself. Waves of shame and guilt cause my body to crumble. I vaguely recognize the pain of hitting the hard floor as the pain pushes its way out of me. Every hidden memory my mind keeps secret from me, chasing and flooding me at once.

Suddenly, I'm drowning.

Every feeling, every memory, crashing down, reminding me of the truth I can't escape:

I will *never* win.

*Chills blanket every inch of my body, the cool air hitting my bottom and thighs. My shivers have nothing to do with the temperature of the room or the exposure of my skin.*

*Anticipating what's coming, I scramble to fist the blanket under me into my hands, stuffing enough in my mouth to bite down. Rough hands are all I feel. I try my best to relax my lower half, and my upper body is as tight as I can make it. My chin wobbles against the rough comforter, protecting my teeth, as I nod and obey his commands, so this is over sooner.*

*Hot liquid floods my eyes as I squeeze them closed as tight as I possibly can, matching the efforts of my fists and jaw. My chest feels like it's going to explode from the pressure I'm putting into the ball that is my upper body until, finally, there's nothing. Nothing but silence and cool air pebbling my exposed, abused skin.*

*I stay in the same position until the door shuts, and I can finally move my stiff fingers, wiping my tears.*

*Sliding off the bed, I collapse to the floor, entranced by the image in the mirror now opposite me: the blotchy red skin on my soaked face, the tiny colorful flowers on my jeans pushed down to my shins, and my favorite penguin stuffed animal a few feet away, carelessly on his side.*

*I'm not sure how long I sat there, but everything became numb, and I found I didn't feel much of anything as I lay down and curled up in bed that night, surrounded by my stuffed animals.*

It feels like a kind of fucked up sanctuary. A comforting chaos indeed. A deserving, safe house of chaos. Pain and loneliness finding its roof and walls holding me where I belong.

*You deserve this, you deserve this, you deserve this,* chanting in my head from whispers that don't feel entirely my own.

*Black is all I see.*

*No. Black eyes, void of any remote human-ness, bore into mine, the cold porcelain of the bathroom sink biting my thighs.*

*This isn't the first time he's cornered me, and it won't be the last. I tried fighting the first few times, only resulting in his fist around my throat until I passed out. To which I know my body was still used. The only thing worse than being cognizant while being assaulted? Being unconscious. The fear and scenarios the brain comes up with in the place of reality are somehow far worse. Either way, the images haunt me; I'd rather know they were at least real.*

*I try to close my eyes, just wanting to escape to the forest cottage I've built in my Other space. The unreachable echoes of streaming water from the river taunted me just out of reach. The pain of having my head slammed into the mirror behind me pulls me to the surface of reality, forcing my nails into my palms to distract from the pain. The only thing I see is his twisted face, sneering and reaching for my throat.*

*This boy terrifies me. There is absolutely something wrong with him. I knew the first time I met him and was forced to shake his hand, moving into this shithole of a foster home —all two boxes of belongings behind me. No, there's something evil in him. I feel it as soon as he enters a room, the way he stares at people and smiles when he's violent. Picking up his pace, I grimace in pain from him inside me, just wanting him to be done. I need to close my eyes, but he never lets me. Fuck, the pain builds, and I have to. I'm going to crawl out of my skin. I just need a couple of seconds of relief from his eyes boring into mine.*

*His laugh follows the bright burst of agony as he slams my head into the mirror again. Forcing my eyes to meet his, his excitement is palpable at my pain, sick smirk pointed. His deep chuckles blanket my skin as he comes, movements stuttering as he uses my body to ride out his pleasure. "Fuck yes. God, I needed that," he mutters more to himself than to me.*

*Shivers start to wrack my body as he pulls out and buttons his pants before turning to leave without a single other word to me. The sick part of me is relieved that the clock restarts until he finds me again. I know the next couple of days should be okay, then. Just another reason I know something is severely wrong with me.*

*Sliding down from the sink, my body aches, and my feet hit the cold tile. I try to grasp the edge to stop myself from toppling over, lightheaded from the impact on my skull. Reaching back, there's no blood, thankfully. My limbs feel like nothing but static; some chemical my body is releasing flooding my system.*

*I flush cool water on my face, legs shaking, refusing to look at myself in the mirror. I can't. All I'd see is a stained and used girl no one will ever love. Numbness takes over, and it's all I can do to just stand here staring at nothing.*

I blink, and it's gone. The darkness pulling back, retreating to the edges of my vision.

But, I know it's still there —waiting for me to give in, ready to swallow me whole again. Luring me with its song and promise of familiarity, of deserving comfortable chaos.

I'm curled into a ball on the floor, hands covering my face as I rock myself back and forth. I don't know when it happened or how I got here. Broken shards of the mug glint beside me, the tea staining the floor.

My face and eyes feel so swollen, I'm lightheaded, and my arms are numb, shaking terribly. I scream out to no one, raw and desperate, trying to clench my fists, begging; for what? I don't know. To make it go away. To please make my pain go away.

"*I'm sorry, I'm so sorry.* Everything's my fault. —I'm sorry." I sob, choking, the words spilling out of me like a broken record. I gasp for air, struggling to pull it into my lungs. It's not enough. I'm drowning in it. "It hurts. Oh god, it hurts. It hurts. Please, please, please." I miss my mom. I need her. For once, her voice isn't haunting me, when I need it the most. My head pounds, the pressure unbearable. I'm going to black out.

It registers there's a knocking and someone shouting my name... I don't know where it's coming from. The noise in my head drowns everything out. The door slams open, and then hands —strong hands— grab me, pulling me close. I force my eyes open and see my brothers crumpled on the floor with me.

Ronan holds me against his chest, panic etched into his face as he rocks me. Artemis is beside us, running his fingers through my hair, his voice soft and soothing. "You're okay, Lily. We're here. Breathe. Deep breaths. In and out. You're safe." Their voices become clearer as the pressure in my head starts to dissipate. My breathing slows, and I focus on that.

I stay cocooned in Ronan's warmth, his arms keeping me newly grounded, until I feel depleted of all my energy, the inevitable exhaustion setting in. I don't know how long passes, but eventually, he lifts me to the couch. Artemis hasn't stopped stroking my hair, pressing gentle kisses to my head. I'm so thankful for them always, but especially now.

The world moves in slow motion, and I wonder if things will get better, even though I know. I know even if they do, this will come back, chasing with teeth and claws, clamping into me and pulling me down again, exposing the scars that should be hidden, should stay hidden.

# 44

# LILITH

I wake up warm and cozy, opening my eyes to see Artemis at the foot of my couch, offering me a weak smile. "Hey, sis. Nice nap?" Confused, I look up and see my head resting on Ronan's lap as he gives me a gentle noogie before brushing my hair out of my face, smiling. I try to sit up, pushing off of him, sitting between their giant bodies. Everything comes back to me as my pounding headache sets in. I rub my eyes, moaning, mostly in embarrassment. "Lil... do you want anything? Food? Water?"

"Water, thank you." My voice comes out incredibly rough before clearing my throat. Art gets up to grab water while Ronan turns the TV down to a murmur.

"Sis... if you want to talk about anything, you know we're here for you. We would actually love it if you could feel safe enough to open up. We want to help. Blaine stopped by our place this morning and mentioned something happened last night but wouldn't tell us what. He just said it wasn't his place, and if you wanted to talk about it with us, then you would. When we walked in and saw you crying and screaming like that, I didn't know what to do. I just want to help you. Please let me help you. I love you so much, Lily. Please tell me how to help." Ronan looks down at me with such love and worry in his eyes it almost breaks my heart. They really don't know anything. I've been so worried about upsetting them... and I've done just that by keeping my secrets. Artemis sits on my other side, handing me my water, and helping me drink.

"I'm not an invalid. I can hold my own glass." They both laugh, and Art puts his hands up in surrender with a genuine smile. I sit in contemplation while I drink my water and he reaches for my hand, holding it. I get a little teary-eyed just thinking of how I got so lucky with my brothers. They're the best men I've ever known in my life. I don't know if I really deserve them. If I open up to them, what will that do to them? The last thing I want to do is to make them feel guilty or hurt. A small part of me thinks if I tell them everything, they'll see how damaged I really am and won't want me in their lives anymore. I feel tainted, guilty, and ashamed. What if—

"Sis...?" Ronan's voice snaps me out of my own mind, and I take a deep breath.

"Okay..."

If they disown me, at least it will be because I'm no longer hiding who I really am.

So, I tell them. I tell them everything —all the parts I swore I'd keep buried forever. They knew some of it already. A few of the horror stories from the homes where I was shoved from one nightmare to another. But this time, I leave nothing out. I let them see it all —the bruises, the screaming, the nights I stayed awake, trembling in the dark, praying for them to come save me. I watch their faces shift as each ugly truth lands, and for once, I don't look away.

I end, raw and exhausted, with last night and my date with Ryan and how Blaine showed up to stop him. I guess I didn't tell them everything... the fact that Blaine stayed with me, bathed me, and cared for me would be crossing an entirely different line. I'm so not ready for that. Getting through everything was easier than I expected. I think I disconnected a little in order to get through it. And, although drained, it's like a huge weight has been lifted off of my shoulders. Ronan silently kissed my forehead and told me he loved me more than anything before stepping out into the hallway with a barely constrained rage. I guess he just needed a minute alone. Artemis cried and apologized for failing me, which is ironic. And now I sit here, as he holds me, pressing kisses to the top of my head. "Are you happy here? Do you want to come live with us at the house? We can find a therapist if you don't have one, look after you, and make sure you're safe." I look up at him, a little shocked; I wasn't expecting that.

"Artie... I appreciate the offer. I don't know if I'd ever really be comfortable there. I like staying here, downtown. I like the lights, the noise, the traffic, and being able to walk everywhere. I want to stay here for now." He gives me a weak smile, nodding in understanding as Ronan comes back in, grabbing a beer from my fridge and sitting on my other side, close to me again.

"I love you so much, sis. I just don't want you to ever doubt that. You mean everything to me. To both of us. I will say, thank you so much for trusting us and telling us everything. I think we're all done with the apologies for tonight. I just love you." He grabs me in a one-armed bear hug before I push him away, softly smiling. I catch a glimpse of them sharing a glance, having a twin-talk, I call it.

"Hey, hello? What are you saying in your brain connectors there?" Looking back and forth at them, waiting, I watch Ronan lift his head for Artemis to speak. He sighs and rubs his hand down his face.

"Lily, I guess we're just curious, is all."

"Okay... about?"

"Is there something going on between you... and Blaine?" He glances quickly up to Ronan behind me and back down, meeting my wide eyes.

"What? No! ...No." He tries to smile slightly, a bit tightly and forced as Ronan gently sets his hand on my right arm to get my attention.

"That's cool if there's nothing between you. But I still have to say this, Lil. Blaine... isn't good. We love him, and he's honestly our best friend. He has been for a long fucking time, you know that. But, I don't know. I guess I just wanted you to know. You deserve better than him." He puts his hands up. "Just in case there were to ever be a crush or anything else there. He's a good-looking guy and has the whole grumpy, tough, rich, bad guy thing going. I should know. The ladies love a naughty boy." I roll my eyes before planting my face into my hands, gaining a laugh from him. "Okay. I'm done, I'm done. But, he's not good enough for you though. I'm serious, Lilith. You deserve someone... different. If you knew him like we do, you'd agree. He doesn't treat women... well. And he's been into some really shady shit, sis. Just, do us a favor and don't get close to him." He palms the back of my head, shaking me until I let go of my face groaning.

"Listen to us on this," Artemis adds.

"I don't want to talk about Blaine. Are you done being all worried or whatever?"

"For now." Ronan shrugs. "Sooo... pizza and wings, anyone? And beer, obviously. I'm literally starving."

"On it." Artemis pulls out his phone to order takeout, and Ronan turns the TV up far too loud.

"Literally? You're *literally* starving?" I roll my eyes teasing him.

"You kidding, baby sis? I've lost five pounds of muscle since I've been here. Guy's gotta eat." He shoves my shoulder, pushing me completely over into Artemis, who just glares at us both like we're children, going back to his phone.

I'm emotionally drained, but I feel so good. I feel free, in a way. And having these two dorks by my side makes me feel like I can do anything. If telling the truth felt this good... maybe, it's time I tell

Kathleen and Larissa too. A contented sigh leaves me before realizing what they just 'sat me down' to say about Blaine. They don't know him like I do if that's really how they feel. He's been nothing short of amazing to me. Right? Sure, he's a little intense. And... well, he definitely does have the whole grumpy hottie vibe going. But he *is* good. I can't tell them how I really feel. I already knew that, but now it's confirmed. But every moment with Blaine, I fall more and more for him.

# 45

# BLAINE

I'm zoned out, driving back to my place, utterly exhausted. Stoplights, cars, and buildings are a blur, nothing really keeping my attention.

*I take my headphones off, pausing the song playing way too loudly in my ears to drown out the party happening in the main room. Rye brought me to the clubhouse tonight like I'm a child and can't fucking take care of myself. Considering his idea of being a 'parent' is a closet full of ramen noodles and a box of condoms, I'd say I'm already caring for myself. It's ten at night now, party is in full swing. I get off the wooden chair in the small kitchen separated from the main room, in the back, and make my way towards the double doors.*

*Immediately walking in, there's a wooden bar to the right. Holy is playing bartender, for now; it'd seem. He inclines his head towards me in greeting as he spots me, and I return the gesture. Off to the left, there's one of the pool tables, the other at the front, which is across the large open room. Some dart boards, and a few random tables scattered throughout. Everyone is obviously toasted. "Jesus," I mumble, looking around at everyone. A good amount, if not all the motorcycle club members are here, all in their jackets representing their involvement in the well-known one percenter gang my dad was in. Some women are here, too, hanging around. One of which is being fucked in the corner to the left, against the round wooden table in the corner. Rye is here somewhere, I guess. Probably fucking some random bitch like damn near every other night. Walking over to the bar, I spot multiple mirrors coated in piles of their biggest money maker.*

*"Hey, sugar. How ya doin'?" Brandy, a member's wife pulls up next to me in a high-top against the bar, smiling. She always checks in on me when she sees me. She's nice and chill. I don't mind her as much as some of the others.*

*"Okay. I guess. Tired." I look back at the bar at the bottles of liquor lining the back wall. She gives me a sympathetic smile and rests her hand on my arm in what's supposed to be a caring gesture. I try to hide my cringe that she's touching me.*

*"Listen, kiddo—" Just as she starts to reply, three men slam through the door with a man covered in blood, barely able to walk without them holding him up. "Go on —go, baby. Get into the back. Now." I just look at her, a bit in shock and horrified at the bloodied man being thrown onto a table. "NOW, Blaine. Damn it, listen to me." I slide off of the chair and make my way towards the back room again, stopping at the door frame to watch as one of those three men punches the shit out of the guy on the table. I turn and run back into the room, back to my chair, and grab my headphones.*

I come back to the moment out of my flashback at a red light. Fuck, I can't even remember the drive here. Memories of that night.

The first time I knew, I heard a man be tortured and killed; and by the people I spent my time with. I knew what my parents had been into. I wasn't stupid, he was in a fucking MC. A bad one. But hearing and being around it happening was completely different. For hours, I sat in that room, listening to the music coming from one wall from the main room, everyone still partying like nothing had happened, and the horrendous screaming from the other wall. That was the first of many nights, many fights, and moments I'd begun being exposed to the real world. The one hidden in plain sight that no one wants to believe is real. The shadowed people. I don't feel much anymore when I replay the memories. I don't really feel anything anymore. But there was a time when I was thrown to the wolves and had to adapt; that fear ruled me until I learned to be the one in control. To control my emotions and my reactions, and numb myself to everything. I learned to hold the power.

That handful of years was all it took for my heart to blacken and harden into what it still is now. For me to learn how to fight, fuck, and finish a kill; fallen, like the rest of them. The best of them. Like my father.

The light turns green, snapping me out of the half haze I'm in. "Fuck." I sigh. I need to check in on Lily before heading home. I haven't spoken to her today— ringing overtakes my speakers as I glance down and see it's Ronan, before accepting the call. "Hey."

"Hey, man. You home?"

"In five minutes, I will be."

"Cool. Artemis and I are here at the building. We'll meet you downstairs, outside the valet drive."

"Okay? Any updates I need to know about?"

"No, man, nothing like that. We just want to talk and catch you before you head up. We'll see you soon, we're heading down."

"Okay." He hangs up, and I'm left wondering what the hell happened between this afternoon and now. It just feels off. But the entire fucking weekend has been a shitshow. I run my hand down my face in frustration, a few blocks from my building.

Pulling up, sure enough, I see the guys around the corner on a bench, waiting for me. The deep purr of my engine echoes in the space in front of the valet as I head over to them. I walk around the corner, nod my head and wait.

"Hey man, how's it going?" Artemis pats me on the shoulder as Ronan stands next to him. At least they look like shit too.

"Fine. What is this?" Artemis sighs and grips the bridge of his nose briefly before looking at his brother and back to me.

"Look. It's been a long fucking day. For all of us. I'll just get straight into it. We don't know if there's something going on between you and Lily, and frankly, we don't want to know if there is. If there's not, great, ignore what we're saying. But... if there is..." He sighs again. "Just... we think you should stay away from her." I glance at Ronan, noting his scowl and crossed arms like he's trying to read my face, anger burning through my neck and eyes at their bullshit. "We've already offered for her to move back in with us. She told us everything tonight. Like, everything."

"—You *what?*" I snarl. If she told them everything, what the fuck aren't they getting about her hating that fucking place, a fucking nightmare around every corner. I let out a small huff of a laugh, my lips curving into a grimacing smirk on one side, not moving my eyes from Artemis.

"She needs something different. Ronan and I love you like a brother. You've been our best friend for over ten fucking years. But when it comes to Lily —just think about it, man. You're both adults and obviously free to do whatever the fuck you want. But what Lily *needs*... what she really needs, you know you can't give her. She needs someone like fucking Elliott, that will love and adore and dote on her. Someone who will heal her hurts. It's what she deserves, whether she realizes it or not. You know as well as we do, that's not you, Blaine. If you sleep with her and toss her to the side like every other woman you stick your dick in, you're just going to hurt her more. And then have us to deal with. Just leave her the fuck alone. We're serious on this."

I'm seething by the time he shuts up, my chest rising and falling heavily as I try to force my lungs into submission. I don't trust myself with words right now. I stare at Artemis and then Ronan for too long to be comfortable before turning and walking away without a word. The worst fucking part is they're right. They're fucking right. I already knew this. But to have someone else, someone she loves telling me this shit...

I slam through the lobby doors to the elevator like a bull, my head buzzing from the built-up pressure. The elevator doors open, a solid mirror reflecting my image back to me as the doors close behind me and it carries me higher. I can't help but stare into the pale eyes looking back at me, worn down, and full of rage. Lily will always be mine, even if I can't actually have her. I knew. I knew deep down this day would come, and yet I fucking fell for her anyway. My eyes change from rage to pain. I've never felt this way about a woman. Hell, I've never cared for anyone this much; ever. *I fell for her...*

The doors open behind me to the looming black entrance of my penthouse and the dark hallway on either side. Breaking my gaze, I turn around and make my way inside. Jenny left hours ago, but there's a note on the island of food in the fridge. I'm so sick to my stomach that I couldn't keep anything down if I wanted to. I stop by my office bar and swipe my favorite brandy taking it back to my bedroom. The curtains are open, just enough light from the city and snow illuminating everything in front of me. I don't bother with the lights, taking off my coat, or shoes. I sit on the side of my bed facing the city and take a huge swig, staring straight ahead.

My phone vibrates in my pocket —a text from Lily.

> Lilith S.
>
> Hey Blaine... I hope you had an okay day. I just wanted to check in but also say thank you again for being so great and kind to me. It meant the world to me having you by my side... Thank you. Goodnight x

I ball the phone up in my fist, positive it's going to break, before letting it drop to the side of me on my bed. I take another swig before setting it down on my nightstand and rest my head in my hands, my elbows on my knees.

It doesn't matter how much I care about her or how much she may care about me. Her brothers are right. I'm right. She deserves better, and knowing Lily, she won't be the one to make the right decision for herself. We have to. *I have to.* I grip my fists, willing the tightness in my chest to ease before giving up and going into my office. I can't do this. I need to busy myself with work until I can't keep my fucking eyes open.

It's been two weeks since I've seen her.

Two fucking weeks an— my phone goes off, and I glance over to see it's Lily, immediately opening her text thread. To the messages she's sent that I haven't been able to respond to. I can't. If I do, that confirms everything, and she really will be out of my life. I just can't.

Lilith S.
> Hey... haven't seen you or heard from you. Are you okay?

> Umm hey?

> Seriously, Blaine. Are you okay? Do you need anything?

> I get it loud and clear Blaine. I don't know what the fuck I could have done that would justify you treating me like this. But you're an asshole. I can't believe this. I don't know why I expected better from you.

> Lily... I'm sorry. You have every fucking right in the world to be pissed at me. But It's best if we stop seeing each other and stop spending time together. You deserve better. We both know it. I can't give you what you need. I meant what I said about being there for you though. If you ever need me, I'll be there for you. I'll see you around.

> Blaine... I need you now... I don't understand...

> I'm protecting you by doing this Lily, trust me.

I set down the phone, dropping my head in my hands. "I'm so sorry, sunshine." I'm exhausted in more ways than one, and there's a pit in my chest that's never been there before, not like this. I hate that I'm hurting her. I was never going to win.

I'm not sleeping more than a few hours a night, pushing myself to work day and night, and other than the meals Jenny force-feeds me, I don't have an appetite. I'm so tired already, and I miss her. I actually *miss* her. I've never craved anyone's presence and touch like I do hers. I don't even really know when this all started to change; my feelings for her. I have Tree tracking her when needed, so I know she's safe. Their uncle is a stupid prick that will burn in Hell, but let's hope he's not so stupid as to go after Lily. I haven't heard much from Artemis and Ronan, but I trust they can handle him to get the legalities taken care of before I have a little more face-to-face time. An outlet is exactly what the fuck I need. I'm not done just yet. Especially not after this bullshit. I wonder how that portrait is healing. How he felt going to the hospital with my note carved permanently into his chest. For the first time in two weeks, I actually smile at that thought.

I want more than anything to comfort Lily and hold her. I'm fine being the villain, but not when it comes to her, it'd seem. I'd rather her be angry at me and hate me than sad, though. I can't handle the thought of her sad. Not over me. I'm not worth it. I know her brothers were right, but the darkest parts of me want her so badly I don't care if I drag her to the seventh level of Hell with me. She'd wear the crown so perfectly next to me.

A client tried to schedule a dinner meeting in San Diego for Saturday, two weeks from now; abruptly reminding me of the Gala we've all been planning to attend for months. I know she'll be there. We attend as a group annually, without fail. Just a glimpse of her is all I need... I would be lying if I said I wasn't doubting if I should attend this year. I know how much she looks forward to it, and she deserves a night to have fun without worrying over my lurking shadow. I sigh, lifting my head. "I need to fucking go home." I've spent every night behind a screen until nearly three in the morning. At this point, I can barely keep my eyes open.

# 46

# BLAINE

## *Before:*

Walking through campus, trying to find my dorm suite, I noticed a few looks from people. I guess I don't really fit in with all these preppy fucks.

The guy who self-assigned himself to help me find my way around must've given up once he realized I had no intention of talking to him or listening, really. I'm too in my head right now. Glancing around, I see that he's gone. Thank fuck.

Walking up to the large stone building, two skillfully carved wooden doors sit open, leaving the entrance to the hallway easily accessible. Adjusting the duffle on my shoulder, I make my way down the line of doors —some lay open, excited chatter streaming into the hall. A few girls pass me, cheeks red, their giggles and murmurs about my appearance floating behind me. I can't help the smirk that tilts my lips.

Room A-22 comes into view, door cracked. I tap my knuckle a few times in warning before pushing it open, letting myself in. Steps from a room to the far right catch my attention, a built dark blonde with a huge smile comes into view. Damn, dude really looks like Prince fucking Charming. "Hey, man! I'm Artemis. My brother Ronan's in the shower." Cool names.

"Blaine." I nod and shake the hand extended to me. Weird. But, okay.

"We already grabbed a couple of the rooms. But honestly, if you want a different one, just let me know. I'm not beholden to one over another." Beholden. Who the fuck is this guy?

"Uh, right. Thanks." After a quick look around, I noticed the clearly available room in the far corner to the left.

"Ronan will be out soon. I'll introduce you. You probably wanna get settled. But it's great to meet you. We can talk more later about communal living stuff between us. We have a couch, TV, and some other things we plan to move. Figured we'd check with you first. Didn't know if you had anything coming too."

"Nah, do whatever you want. I doubt I'll spend much time out here."

Prince Charming nods slowly in return, arms crossed, before offering that damn smile again. Probably picking up on the fact I'm not much for conversation right now. "Cool, man. Nice to meet you."

"You too." I step through the space towards my room, lingering on the two huge windows that overlook a line of trees and vivid green.

The room is what almost anyone would consider small. Honestly, it's fucking perfect. Tossing my bag down, I run my hand through my hair and huff out a short laugh, a smile finally really hitting. There's a bed, a small desk, and a closet with some shelves and a mirror. Best of all? A fucking door. I close it behind me, as I hear the shower shutting off in what'll be our shared bathroom. The second the lock flips vertically, it's like I take my first full breath in what feels like years.

Looking around the space, I think of a couple more items to add to my list. My bank accounts look pretty good, considering all the cash I've managed to save. One thing about shady shit and drugs through the MC? People fucking pay. And well. That's the one thing I am thankful for. That Rye had a hand in making sure I had jobs and always got my cut.

Plopping my ass down on the bare mattress, I hear the two guys —my new roommates, talking past my door. Now that I'm here, it feels different.

Now it's real.

# 47

# LILITH

I sit at my desk, absently staring at my computer screen as my phone vibrates on my desk, snapping me out of whatever trance I was in, causing me to jump. I open the text and immediately scramble up to grab my coat and purse, practically running through the lobby to the elevators.

I half jog, heading towards my apartment building before the bus stops just ahead of me, giving me time to jump on. I'm panting so hard, a little girl looks at me like I'm crazy or something before looking away, and grabbing her mom's arm. I just sigh, resting my hand on the metal rail as the bus takes off again, carrying me the next four blocks to the corner of my building. *Blaine's* building. I rush inside to the elevators, catching one just as the door is about to close —an older man wide-eyed at my rush inside. "Sorry. In a hurry."

After the man gets off, the elevator takes me up, opening to the floor that's all too familiar. There is a code box to access his penthouse. He never changed it; at least not yet. I stop, a little nervous, in front of the looming black doors before knocking lightly twice. As a part of Blaine's bullshit plan or whatever he's doing, he's prevented me from having entry to the painting room he provided me. Jenny gently and sympathetically dropped everything off a few days after we had last seen each other. I did notice the half-finished painting I promised Blaine wasn't returned. That made me feel relieved for some reason. I'm guessing my brothers had something to do with this, considering they basically told me to stay away from him the same day he started ignoring me. I don't *entirely* blame them for this, though. Blaine is a grown man and handled this fucking poorly. I'm *pissed*. I refuse to believe the last few months meant nothing to him. I just... I guess I don't know what I'm actually doing here. But his 'goodbye' text is bullshit. I'm the one that runs from everything. I'm not going to run from this.

Jenny quickly opens the door ushering me inside. "Thank you, Jenny. I got here as soon as I could. I didn't want to miss my window."

"Yes, of course, of course. He's been a real pain in my ass the last couple of weeks. Talk some sense into the dummy. He's back in his room. I didn't tell you he was home, though, got it, missy? As far as I'm concerned, you broke in. Now, he just got here not long ago. Go—go on."

Trying to keep my nerve, I march my way back to his bedroom and slam open the door, causing it to bounce off the wall even startling me, as well as Blaine. *Shit*. I almost cower and cringe just at that. He jumps up from the side of the bed, eyes wide. "Lily... fucking christ. What the hell?"

"You!"

## BLAINE

"You!" Lily, looking a little fiercer than a fluffy kitten this time, charges toward me, practically growling in anger, as I stand by my bed, shocked. She stops in front of me, banging her tiny fists on my chest, trying to shove me. She's so clumsy I don't even move more than an inch, staring down at her in both excitement that she's in front of me, touching me, and sadness at seeing her.

I grab her wrists, stopping her from her efforts as she tries to twist and free herself. She's going to hurt herself before she hurts me. Jesus, note to self: get Lily self-defense classes. This is scarily ineffective. "LILITH. Stop... please." She stops her struggle, huffing and her chest rising and falling, scowling at me. God, she's fucking adorable and so beautiful. "What are you doing here?" I ask quietly, gently.

"Are you kidding me, Blaine? Are you fucking kidding me! You basically ghosted me, and you have the nerve to ask why I would want to come see you. Especially after... what happened when I saw you last. What the hell changed?"

"Lily..." I close my eyes and slightly shake my head. "Lily, look, I'm sorry. This isn't what I want, but it's what you *need*."

"—I'm sorry, wanna say that again? Since when the hell does everyone around me get to decide what I want or need?"

"No... that's not... *fuck*. That's not what I meant. I just mean... you have to move on from whatever the fuck it is we were doing. This was doomed before it began in so many fucking ways. You and I both know what you deserve. You deserve to be treated like a queen, adored, and god damn worshipped every day. You deserve someone who knows how to be sweet and gentle and care for you. Someone that knows what to say in the moments you need it. I'm not the man that can give you everything you deserve. There's a reason I have a reputation, Lily... there are things I've done and will continue to do, that would cause you to never look at me again if you knew. I'm trying to *protect* you, Lilith. Can't you understand that? The life you deserve, the white picket fence, the knight in shining armor? That's not *me*, sunshine. It will never *be me*. When I say I'm protecting you by doing this, please just trust that I'm being truthful."

She looks up at me with so many emotions in her bright honey eyes as tears start to fall from the corners, I can barely stand it. God, I can barely control the urge to bury her against my chest. Anything to get that look off her face.

"Let go of me..." I barely hear her; her voice is so quiet. I carry her wrists down, gently letting her go.

"I'm sorry, Lily." She looks at me, searching for something in my face, waiting before she steps back.

"I guess Katie was wrong after all. I'm so stupid..." I can barely make out the words as she says them; she's so terribly quiet. I feel helpless watching her walk away, stopping at my door to turn around one last time. "I'll move out of the building Blaine... just give me a few weeks." Her head's down as she walks away. I can't find my voice. She doesn't even stop to look at me again before she's gone.

I think a person's heart can only be broken so many times before it simply becomes broken beyond repair. When I looked into her eyes, that's all I could see. Hell, when I look at me, that's all I see. I stand frozen in place, staring at the doorway, and don't stop my eyes from lining in tears. I can feel every shadow of light, hope, of my heart itself, leaving me. All I can do is pray that soon I'll be completely hollow. Whatever life she gave me is gone.

# 48

# LILITH

## Two weeks later:

After telling my brothers the details and in-betweens of my story, I decided to come clean about everything with Larissa and Katie as well. Only, they also now know everything about Blaine and me. I really needed someone to talk to about everything. And that required telling the full story, all the secret parts I had promised to keep to myself. After telling them, I felt even more guilty because they were so great and supportive. I should have never doubted that.

Katie still thinks he's full of shit and wants to parade me around to the single men tonight at the Gala in hopes of getting Blaine's attention, even if in the worst way imaginable. She claims to know how men supposedly operate, but this isn't my style. Larissa, on the other hand, is there for anything I need, ready for any rescue mission, ready to ply me with alcohol, ready for hugs, and trying to remind me of what a 'catch' I am. I can't help but sigh, loudly.

The look on Blaine's face the last time I saw him plays on repeat in my mind. Carefully blank. I kept waiting, searching for a hint of the emotion underneath I was praying he felt in return. Foolish. I'm always so damn foolish when it comes to him.

I've spent the last couple of weeks tearing apart the memory, dissecting the seconds. It finally hit me as I lay in bed, unable to sleep, that, as embarrassing as I felt my outburst was after the fact— it was because I felt safe enough to show my feelings. I felt safe and comfortable enough to know he would never hurt me. I regret raising my voice and acting out of shame and anger. But, knowing something shifted in me felt a little like hope and healing. There was never a single time, a single house I lived in, with any of the families or other kids that I would have ever even thought of speaking my truth, expressing my feelings, much less my needs or wants. The fear that smothered me for years. Phantom screams, hands, and things being thrown squeeze my chest, even still today. Still, after so long.

I push myself into the present and murmur quiet affirmations for the evening ahead.

Despite our divided beliefs regarding Blaine, the girls and I *did*, however, mutually agree on a girl's night and limo ride to the event —courtesy of my brothers, who I'm sure feel a little guilty for my foul mood. Certainly, doesn't hurt...

I step out of my closet quietly as the girls drink champagne in the kitchen, laughing. They look stunning. For a moment I simply take them in, observing their joy. They're the most beautiful, amazing, smart, and caring women I've ever met. I'm so lucky to call them my best friends. I can't bring myself to voice the words, though. I never seem to be able to.

Larissa has on a pink, sexy, and classy, long-sleeve gown. Katie has a gorgeous purple gown molding her body with a deep plunge on top and a slight billow of silk in the lower half. I'm wearing a deep red, full-length gown with delicate embroidered beads and gauze. The detail and glitter catching the light just right add another level of awe. I momentarily imagine my mother pushing for us to take pictures, and my smile widens. Artemis paid for my dress. There's no way I could afford something like this on my own. Honestly, I feel like a princess. I think he really wanted me to have a good time tonight. I clear my throat, letting my heels lightly clip the floor a little as I walk closer. They turn around, and both their jaws drop.

"Umm, good?"

"Holy fuck. You look like a goddess of Hell and flame. And I mean that in the most flattering way I could possibly word it... wow." Katie eyes me up and down before closing her mouth and wickedly smiling. A look I am all too familiar with.

"Lily, she's right. My knees want to crumble and force me to bow to you." I press my hand to my chest, laughing. I love the dramatics.

"Oh yeah. We're having a good night, ladies... raise 'em." Katie hands me a glass and smirks before toasting to the night and sisterhood as her phone goes off. "OH! Wait... party bus? I thought the guys were sending a limo?" Katie tilts her head, confused but also excited. "Oh my god, I pray to the woman upstairs, they got us a fucking party bus! Remember the last one with the vibrating saddle! LET'S GO BITCHES!"

We grab our purses and make a speedy exit to head downstairs for our awaiting chariot, our dresses floating and glittering in the dimly lit hall.

"YES!" Katie turns to look at us with a huge smile when we make it to the entrance. They got us a fucking party bus. And a nice one, too, by the looks of it. A man in a suit stands by the door, gesturing for us to enter, offering his hand.

"Ladies, welcome —watch your step, please." Katie stops in front of him before stepping up with a sweet smile on her face.

"So, can we like... hang out in this bad boy at the hotel before we go in for the event? Please?" She flutters her eyelashes at the man as he laughs, promising we surely can, as it's ours to do as we wish until nine o'clock. I follow Katie up the small stairs into the darkness that is the party bus. "Oh, my godddd!" The music is already playing, speakers pumping Ginuwine's 'Pony.' Glittering lasers are in full effect, a long row of ice along the wall to the right full of champagne, vodka, and mixers, as well as... "we have two stripper poles!! Get the fuck on here, Lilith!" Katie quickly pops a bottle of champagne from the ice bringing it directly to her lips, swinging around the first pole before passing the bottle to me.

Grabbing a bottle of vodka for herself, Katie takes a small swig of that as the bus slightly lurches forward, all of us laughing hysterically reaching for the poles. "Babes! Cheers to the fucking weekend, making memories in this sick-ass bus, and a special thanks to the men who paid for it! Ayyy!" We throw our heads back, laughing, lifting our glasses into the air in celebration. I'm genuinely happy and smiling for the first time in what feels like forever.

I'm absorbing the love and appreciation for my girls as the bus slows to a stop outside the Four Seasons.

"Nope! Don't even! Just like our dearest driver said —this thing's ours, and being on this bus with you is way more fun than what's going on up *there*." Katie reaches towards the glowing screen controlling the music, putting on 'Pony' for the third time since we've boarded. I can't even be mad or annoyed, it's literally the perfect song for this bus. Fists start banging on the side of the bus before the door opens, and Ronan steps in.

"LADIES. You all look absolutely stunning tonight. I'm told you're in need of a little... entertainment, though?" Oh god.

"Ronan! Seriously, remember your sister is on this bus and has eyes!"

"Might wanna close 'em then because it's about to get..." He playfully touches his nipples like they're hot to the touch. "...Hot in here." He grabs Katie, gently pushing her down into the seat in front of the pole closest to the door before ridiculously gyrating around it, sticking his ass in her face before climbing on top, straddling her, and grinding his hips. Katie's laughter carries over the music, grabbing his hips and moving against him like it's the best night of her life. Goddess, help me.

Artemis and Elliott step onto the bus, eyes landing on Ronan's junk in Katie's face before they both start laughing hysterically. "I should have guessed! If there's a stripper pole, Ronan's on it. Lily, angel—" Art makes his way around Ronan to me, giving me a huge hug and kiss on the cheek. "You look breathtaking in this dress." His eyes are lit with energy, and his smile charming. The guys all look fantastic, in their custom-tailored suits and fresh haircuts, Ronan showing off his tattooed chest, unbuttoning his top buttons. "Lissa, hi beautiful. You look stunning. Absolutely stunning." He reaches down to kiss her hand in affection. Art has always been charming. He knows how to work the room and make everyone fall in love with him. He's always genuine, though. He never plays games or says things he doesn't mean. It's just how he really is, naturally: a lover.

Elliott is passing out flutes of champagne for a group cheers as the lights float around the bus, shadows and colors dancing over everyone's smiling faces and clothes as the music blares through the speakers. He holds up his glass, everyone else following. "Here's to good vibes, good times, and no goodbyes. Ladies, here's to you most of all because god DAYUM!" Everyone breaks out in laughter, high on the energy, downing our drinks. 'Get Low' comes on, and Ronan goes absolutely off the rails, dancing around the pole like a fucking idiot.

Elliot grabs my hands, pulling me in for a dance as Artemis reaches for Lissa. I turn, pressing my back to his front, moving against him as the chorus comes, and we all yell, "To the windowww to the wallllll!" I lean against him, letting him touch my hips as we dance together, smiling and singing the lyrics. Katie's dress is pulled up as Ronan holds her at his waist, her legs wrapped around him, arms in the air. Larissa faces Artemis, a bottle of champagne between the two of them like a microphone. If there was ever a time when life slowed like it does in the movies, it would be now. Everything is perfect. I feel like we're going to a high school prom in our fancy clothes with this old-school playlist. I look around and take it all in, my cheeks sore from smiling to remember this exact moment. I take a mental screenshot. I lift my arms, feeling free as Elliott traces his hands down the full length of them and down the sides of my waist. For a moment, I imagine those hands are Blaine's, and chills rock my body. We dance until the song dies out, and Artemis puts his hands up, yelling for everyone to get off and head inside for the event, ushering us out as everyone tosses back their drinks. Ronan, Katie, Lissa, and Elliott make their way out of the bus laughing like fools with myself and Artie right behind them. I turn one last time to smile up at him in thanks before turning my head back around, my hair falling over my shoulder.

A figure catches my eye to the left, and I do a double take, realizing it's Blaine. I nearly trip when I step onto the pavement, trying to find oxygen. Artemis wraps his arm around me, leading me forward as everyone makes their way through the large glass doors. I can't help but turn around to look at him and make sure he's following too. He catches my eyes and offers up a small smile, his pale eyes glittering as he walks under the chandelier's golden light. Why wasn't he on the bus if he was outside? God, he looks so painfully handsome in his all-black suit. My heart stutters, and I have to swallow to keep my throat from closing, from choking on the emotion threatening me.

# 49

# BLAINE

I stay in the shadows, waiting outside the bus while everyone else climbs in. I know her brothers arranged this specifically for her and the girls. So, I don't have to ask if she's inside. I want her to be happy, and if that means distancing myself so she can enjoy herself, I'll do it. I don't give a fuck about the event; I've already donated. I don't plan on staying long. I just can't stop thinking about her. I just needed to see her, that's all. I know she's okay. But, knowing and seeing are completely different. I hear the chaos inside and can't help but smile a little. Yeah, she's having fun. Good girl. I don't want her sad over me.

Ronan and Kathleen make their way off the bus first, catching my attention, followed by Larissa and Elliott. I wait, holding my breath as the hints of a glowing maroon dress make their way into the light. Lily follows behind, her head turned back to her brother. She steps down like a goddamn queen in that dress, a huge smile on her face as she turns forward. *Fuck.* She barely looks human. My eyes pierce into her, taking in every inch as she turns her head back towards me, seeing me, surprise marking her face. I think I smiled at her, I'm not sure. Artemis wraps his arm around her, pulling her inside. She turns once again around her brother's embrace, probably making sure she saw correctly. I keep my hands in my pockets, sure to smile at her this time. She looks so damn pretty, it hurts.

I keep my expression stony as we exit the elevator, making our way out to the pool terrace into the cool winter night. The terrace has been transformed for the evening. A huge white tent covers the entire space as well as a reinforced sheet of glass covering the pool lit below. There are rows and rows of lights strung across the interior, as well as an obscene amount of fire towers heating the place more than enough to be comfortable. Nothing less for the ultra-rich, here to donate their spare pennies and dollar bills to the starving homeless children in Nepal. Looking around, there are many white cloth tables off to the right; on the East side of the terrace, one of which is ours. In the center, there's a fifteen-foot or so fire pit casting a golden hue on everything. To the left, an open lounge space and dance floor, with the DJ against the wall. Looking past the fire, I spot Lily and Katie at the long bar with a couple of men. The flames separating us with a glowing heat-induced haze. I imagine her in a crown surrounded by black obsidian walls, on a dais and throne carved of serpents. She already looks like the queen of the underworld in that dress, but imagining her on a throne full of fury sets me ablaze. I would gladly kneel before her just for the opportunity for our eyes to meet.

I want to give her space so she can have an amazing evening. I trail the guys to the left, closer to the DJ, as we sit down in a large lounge sectional. A server takes our order as Artemis looks over to me. "Hey man, about our uncle and our situation— I just wanted to let you know everything has been smooth. He's dragging his feet, but it sounds like we did a number on him when you came with us, and he's all too happy to work with us. We just need to get Lil taken care of, and then we can talk about what to do with him."

"I figured. I have eyes on her in case he does something stupid."

"Thanks, man." I look up as our server hands us our drinks and walks away. "Listen, are you good?"

"Fine." It goes without saying to drop it if we don't actively talk about an issue. I think Ronan and he speak more fluidly about shit. I don't. I take a swig of my bourbon, savoring how smoothly it goes down. Ronan follows suit, putting up his hand in greeting as two women walk towards us. One sits next to me while the other sits across, making her way between the brothers.

"Mm! Blaine— this is our friend Penny. Penny, meet Blaine." She looks up at me, smiling sweetly, waiting for me to speak. I nod my head in greeting and take another drink, crossing my ankle over my knee.

"So, how do you know these two?" She tries to make conversation as her other friend sits close to Ronan 'fixing' his collar, leaning in.

"College."

"Oh, that's cool! Did you go to a university here in Denver?" I wipe my hand down my face, taking another drink, trying to smother my annoyance and be nice enough. I could give a fuck about anything that could possibly come out of this woman's mouth.

Pretending to give a fuck isn't my forte. I'm not exhausting myself for someone I could give two shits about. Artemis picks up on my mood, leaning towards us.

"Yeah, Pen, we sure did! We all shared a house together not too far from here. We had some crazy parties in that house. There was no chance of getting our security deposit back by the time we moved out." He laughs, smiling at her. "Would you like a drink?" She nods happily, and Artemis stands, nudging his chin towards the bar for her to follow. I have no idea if he was doing that to help me or if he was pissy, but either way works in my favor.

I sigh, glancing at the bar for a glimpse of *her*. Katie's introduced her to another group of men, all too eager to meet the mystery woman in maroon, before leaving her surrounded by four predatory assholes as she heads towards Art at the bar with what's-her-face. Polly, I think.

I'm fairly certain Katie and Art are fucking at this point and have been for a while. And, if that's the case, I can't believe the fucking irony and audacity there, going after Lily's best friend but having the balls to warn me to keep away from their sister. I almost hope they are screwing. Pretty positive they have been for months. I just didn't give a shit until now. I don't see that ending well or lasting long with how opposing their personalities are if they are secretly together. She'd be a much better match with Ronan out of the two of them; they're both insane, and I guarantee she'd be down for his exclusive parties. A woman like her will get bored of Artemis eventually. He's stable, reliable, charming, and constantly in the spotlight; meaning she has to dial it back for him to avoid hurting his public image. She'll need more eventually. I notice her lean into Artemis as his hand wraps around her waist, sliding to her ass. I have to fight back a laugh at how ridiculous the timing of that is. *Of course, I'm right.* I lean back and note Ronan's eyes scowling a little too hard at the interaction himself.

Interesting. Noted.

*Are you fucking kidding me?* Another new douche is talking to Lily, touching her lower back as she throws her head back, laughing.

*What. The. Fuck.*

The guys a fucking joke; Instagram motivational speaker wanna-be. I hate social media, but Ronan sent me a screenshot of one of his recent posts at a Lambo dealership claiming, *"With dedication and consistency, you too could have your dream car. Sign up for my 8-step course here!"* The dude couldn't afford a quarter of a Lamborghini if he shared it with three friends.

"Shot?" Ronan reigns in my attention as he stands to go towards the bar. I follow. Whether the invitation was for me or a way to interrupt whatever the hell is happening between Katie and Artemis, I don't know. I don't really care. The man looks like a mafia lord's son tonight. He has a great suit that's clearly tailored to him, golden rings on half his fingers, a diamond chain, and enough of his shirt unbuttoned to show he's covered in dark tattoos. I wouldn't be surprised if he has his grill in, too, despite the fact we're at a charity event. I smile and pat him on the shoulder, following him to the bar.

After we find our place at our sponsored table for a few speeches and itinerary items, I spend the next hour seething as half the men here take their place practically in a fucking line to speak with Lily like this is an episode of the fucking Bachelorette. This is Katie's fault. I know she's behind this; Lily doesn't do this type of shit. I stand with Larissa, Elliott, and a few others near the center fire, watching Lily from afar. The mafia lord's son and prince charming disappeared with Katie upstairs. I need to call it a night and let Lily have her time, but I don't trust any of these shit stains pining for her attention. She walks away, towards the side entrance, and I lock in on her as everything fades to black.

"Hello? Blaine? Are you even listening?" I hear what's-her-face Patti huff in annoyance or disbelief as my eyes trail Lilith.

"No."

"You're a fucking asshole, wow." I don't even spare a look at her as I hear her step away, her obnoxious heels snapping to the floor. I watch as Lily makes her way across the terrace to the hotel, my feet moving behind her before I can think.

# 50

# LILITH

I make my way, smiling at friendly faces and glances toward me as I cross to the east side of the terrace, to the two open doors leading inside. I just need a minute to myself. Katie's plan is exhausting, and I don't even know where she went.

I want to go home, honestly; I'm drained. Blaine has barely even so much as looked at me. And I saw him with Penny, which makes me feel nauseous to even think about it. I think my heart would shatter if I had to watch him take her home tonight, to his bed. I pass the restrooms to my left and keep walking another twenty feet or so before turning the corner on the right, into the empty hall in search of somewhere private to breathe.

"What the hell do you think you're doing, Lilith?" I jump, turning to see Blaine scowling as he stalks towards me.

"Excuse me?"

"You're entertaining every available man in the metro area. And trust me, Lily, I know these men. They're certainly not humorous enough for you to be laughing at their so-called jokes or lines designed to get you in their bed later. What the hell's gotten into you?"

"Oh, pardon me, Blaine! Listen to yourself! You've made it perfectly clear you want nothing to do with me, and now suddenly, when you realize that other men might *actually* be interested in dating me, you're invested? So, what? You don't want me but no one else can pursue me either, is that it? That's not how it works." I can see his jaw tense at my words.

"Trust me, Lilith, those men aren't looking to *date* you. You need to pay more attention to who the hell you're throwing yourself at. Behave Lily. Consider this your warning."

"You are *insane*. Why the hell would I listen to you? Like you ever wanted anything more from me either, right? You just couldn't get that far because of my brothers. I'm sure it would have ended *so* differently otherwise. Right? I'm well aware of your so-called dating patterns. Why don't you go find your date, *Penny*. I hear she's an easy fuck." I practically spit her name at him, meeting his intense stare, and release a huff of disbelief. "I'm having a lovely evening, in fact, so if you'll excuse me, Mr. Vogeleir." I break his glare and attempt to push past him to rejoin the party before he grabs my arm, pulling me back to face him. He's silent outside of his breath and intent in his stare. God, all the power of a lightning strike in those pale eyes is being directed at me.

"Lily..." He finally drops my arm, jaw ticking, his voice so deep it sends chills through me and a hitch in my breath.

"*What.*" I snap.

"Listen to me. None of those men have your best interest in mind," he says icily. Calmly. Why am I even bothering with this; he wants nothing to do with me.

"Well, it's a good thing I'm not looking for their best interest. Maybe I'm looking to get laid." I go to forcefully turn, but he stops me, grabbing my wrist again, pulling me down the hall, practically growling. Not enough to hurt, but enough to show me he's in charge right now.

"Let go, what are you doing? *Blaine!* Ugh!"

He pulls me into a dark, empty dining hall to our right, past a couple of tables further into the room. "I warned you, Lilith.... next time you'll actually fucking listen." In the next moment, within the span of a breath, Blaine has me flipped around and bent over on a dining table, dressed in a white cloth. I go to speak and lift myself back up but am silenced by the hand on my neck gently holding me in place. He yanks my dress up, and his heavy *SLAP* of his hand hits my bottom. I can't help the sudden, surprised gasp that escapes me, my eyes wide in absolute shock he just *spanked* me. He smacks my ass three more times before he loosens his grip on my neck enough for me to turn, looking at him incredulously, advancing to smack him. He catches my wrist, and we silently wrestle as I try to free myself of his grip while he watches me with a blazing, stern look. He's not even struggling to hold me in place.

"What the Hell is wrong with you! You're such an asshole sometimes, *Psycho!*"

"Whoever you got your information from is wrong, princess. I'm an asshole *all* of the time." He leans forward. I stop moving and meet his glare, my chest heaving from my breath, before lowering my gaze from his eyes down to his full lips and back up. I drag my tongue out slightly enough to lick my lips and bite down as Blaine's gaze drops to watch. There's electricity between us we've never shared like this. I've found him attractive, *obviously*.

But this, this is new and nearly overwhelming, like I'm going to crawl out of my skin. The calm before the storm as lightning breaks through the sky in the distant dark clouds. Every part of me feels awake. Blaine softens his eyes and closes the small distance between us as I lean back against the table behind me. His left hand gently wraps around my neck as his right hand slowly makes its way up my thigh and over my hip, through the long, hidden slit in my dress. Unlike our time in the mountains and in the movie theater, there's nothing but eye contact between us now. A mere handful of inches separating us, failing miserably to hold the storm at bay. He slips his hand under my dress, through the slit, lifting it just enough to my waist so he can have access to the bare skin just above my sex. His eyes devour me as he pauses, waiting for my small nod of approval to keep going, desperation and longing in his pale gaze. I know he'd never touch me without permission, and if I truly said stop, it would immediately end. He may be a psychotic dick, but I trust him not to really hurt me, ever.

He moves his thumb under the seam of my panties to my clit, tracing a figure eight of sorts, his other hand still on my neck, gently holding me in place as I grab his wrist to steady myself. I can't help the hitch in my breath. My lips part as he then traps my sensitive nub between his thumb and curled forefinger, slowly rolling his hand. God, it feels amazing. Everything with Blaine feels more intense. My breath shakes, and I can't help but start moaning in response, my mouth slightly open as I stare up at him, fighting my eyes from rolling back in pleasure. I want to make him look at me; make him watch as he pleasures me.

"Shhh. Be quiet unless you want to get caught, princess." I press my lips together and nod slightly, following his gentle command. As he touches me, I reach for his belt and start to undo his pants.

"Stop. —What... are you doing?" He pauses his movements, waiting.

"Let me touch you. Please, Blaine," I whisper as I look up at him.

"No."

"No? Why not?"

"I've told you; you'll regret it. Especially after the last few weeks." His expression's hard and unreadable like he's about to walk away and put an end to us yet again if too many seconds were to pass.

"Yeah, you keep saying that. I think you're making excuses. Maybe you just have a small d.."

"Lily..." He interrupts. "I know what you're doing, and it's not going to work."

I keep looking up at him, softening my eyes and keeping my voice low, barely above a whisper, in the dark, silent dining hall. "If you won't fuck me, then I'll find someone who will. I'm tired of it. It's been years since I've had someone inside me. Someone pushing into me, fucking me, moaning my name. There are fifty men just outside that door that would kill to have their tongue between my thighs and have me spread open for them in their beds." Am I goading him? Absolutely.

He goes perfectly still, his expression turning to ice as his jaw very visibly tenses and ticks, staring at me with such intent and threat behind his eyes. Before I realize it, he has me flipped over onto my stomach, on top of the table, holding me down by my neck again. "If we cross this line Lily, do you know what you're asking of me? Do you know what that will mean?" He pulls my dress up and rips my red lace thong down, and smacks my ass *hard*. I can't help the small whine that escapes me from the sting this time, my now bare sex exposed, in the position he's holding me in. His fingers move to feel how wet I am, and he curses, pulling away.

"It *means*..." he leans down to my ear. "That you're mine. Do you understand that? You belong to me from this moment forward. Fuck what your brothers think. Fuck what your friends think. You're mine. Is this what you want? Say yes or tell me to stop, and I'll walk away." He practically growls the words into my ear, causing my knees to give out, my eyes rolling back.

"Yes."

Within seconds he frees his cock and enters into me in a few rough movements, a string of curses leaving his lips. A deep groan forces its way out of me from the shock of his impact as I press my hands flat to the table under me. He barely moves for several seconds, allowing my body to start to adjust to his size, to the near-foreign intrusive sensation. "Is this what you had in mind, princess? Is this what you need to behave?" He slowly, ever-so-slightly, gently rolls in and out of my heat, hitting so deep, stretching me. I can feel him reveling in the sensation of our bodies joining. He pulls almost completely out and slowly back in several times, so deeply I swear my stomach tingles, while I adjust to being so full. He's giving me time, I realize, so he doesn't hurt me.

After several slower thrusts, he pulls out again and pauses before thrusting into me from behind so hard the sound of our bodies hitting fills the dark silent room. He wraps my loose hair around his fist and pulls just enough, while still holding my neck in place with the other, fucking me. "Is it? Is this what you wanted? To be fucked where anyone could come and see you bent over a table, taking my fucking cock like the naughty siren you really are?" I open my mouth, and only a throaty, forced, uneven groan comes out as he pulls my hair, pounding into me. He pulls me straight up, still fisting my hair gently but firmly with his left hand, leaning close to my ear. "Shh... I thought I told you to be quiet unless you want to be caught. Are you trying to get caught? You want an audience? Want one of your little boyfriends out there to see you a mess, taking my come, bouncing on my dick? Huh? Wanna show them who this pussy belongs to?" *Fuck, oh my god*. I hold my moans, and all that's left is my heavy breathing through my nose. He reaches forward and presses two fingers on either side of my clit, firmly rubbing, and I feel myself clench; the sensation feels so fucking good. I can't keep quiet; I open my mouth, mindlessly moaning, not caring how loud I am.

"*Yes. Oh my god, yes.*" Blaine drops my hair and covers my mouth to silence me while pleasuring me.

"You're so fucking wet, princess. You love this, don't you?" I manage a muffled moan and nod in response. He slows his thrusts and whispers, his lips brushing my ear. "Bad girls get disciplined, though. And you didn't want to listen or behave, remember? I warned you, Lilith." He's still slowly pushing into me when he suddenly slaps my pussy so hard it's a good thing his hand is over my mouth, muffling my scream. He slaps me again, picking up his pace again, *slap...slap...slap.* The overwhelming pain and pleasure are too much, and I feel myself tightening, on edge.

"Your cunt feels so fucking good clamped down on my cock," he groans. "That's better, isn't it? What you need? Being so good for me. But let's get one thing straight. You're *my* good girl. Isn't that right? Any man even so much as looks at you, I'll carve portraits into their skin and slit their fucking throat without thinking twice, understand me?" He grits out. *Slap.* He goes back to quickly circling my clit with such a heavy hand, I'm going to come right here in this dining hall, my eyes tipping back in my head. "That's your one warning, Lily. You wanted me, you got me, and now you're *mine*. Don't so much as *think* of another man's hands on you ever again unless you want their blood on mine." I scream against his hand as the most intense orgasm I've ever felt rushes through my entire body. Blaine moans deeply behind me, and I can feel him shudder as he growls through his own release, filling me. He slows his pace as he comes inside of me, still rubbing my clit as I start to come down from my climax. Holy shit. I can barely stand. I didn't know an orgasm could feel like *that* without a vibrator. His deep voice, the way he was speaking to me, *claiming me* as his. It was all too much, and I fucking loved every second of it. I've never experienced sex like that.

Blaine slows his thrusts entirely, holding me against his chest as we both wait for our breathing to slow, coming back to reality. He keeps me against him, holding me lovingly and stroking my hair and arm, pressing his lips to my exposed skin before he slowly pulls out of me. Gently, he releases me to turn me so I'm leaning against the table again, facing him. He reaches over and picks up one of the white cloth napkins, spitting on it to wet it. He gently starts to wipe away my ruined mascara and lipstick smudges from my face where his hand was. Running his thumb across my lower lip, he looks at me with such beautiful, caring, soft eyes. When he's gentle like this, or smiling, he's almost too breathtakingly beautiful. He's perfect.

After cleaning me and readjusting his pants, he kneels down, and gently runs his hands over my shaking bare thighs under my dress, pulling my thong the rest of the way down my legs.

"What are you doing?" I roughly whisper. He helps reposition my legs, now taking my freed wet panties with him, into his hand. I watch in shock as he lifts them to his mouth, his tongue blatantly running over my arousal before balling them into his pocket.

"Worshiping what's finally mine." He presses an utterly gentle kiss to the top of my mound, running hot breath over my skin.

"Whose cunt is this, Lily?" He whispers. Pressing another kiss on my skin before giving me a long, hard lick over my sensitive clit, not breaking eye contact. I close my eyes and moan, remembering to keep my balance. "Hmm?"

"Yours." I manage. *Another half lick, half kiss.*

"Good girl, baby. Say it again." *Kiss. Lick.*

"Yours. My pussy's yours." I breathlessly manage to respond. He moans in such pleasure and gives me one final, sensual lick, stopping to dance his tongue around my bundle of nerves several times slowly.

"That's right." He straightens my dress and stands to his full height, running his hand over my shoulder, and smiling at me. He looks me over once before offering me his hand. "Let's go, sunshine. And don't worry, I won't count that as our first kiss." He winks, and I suddenly can't breathe, following him blindly.

# 51

# BLAINE

## *Before:*

Stepping into the Library, the smell of worn leather and musky staleness hit me first as I softly close the door behind me, muting the chaotic noise of the party entirely. It's shrouded in near darkness, the candelabras softly reflecting a dull, warm light across the bookcases and leather furniture in the large room, the bay of windows directly ahead painted nearly black from the night sky. Stopping at the top of the short series of steps in the space, my eyes trace the stacks and jump to the far right of the room at a slight movement. A few steps further, and the shadowed, assumedly tear-stained face of a girl greets me from around a corner.

This must be the mysterious sister. Although, she noticeably looks nothing like either Artemis or Ronan.

Seconds tick by in silence as she says nothing, and neither do I. I tilt my head slightly in curiosity, examining her. I swear I can hear her heart beating out of her chest from here. Hell, maybe that's my own. She's beautiful. Not in the way the other women are at college. No, she's beautiful in the way art is, the way blood tends to land in abstract designs. Something intrigues me about her. Her silence only encouraging that interest.

It's when I take another step forward that her wide, bright eyes track the movement. She pushes away and back as far into the corner as she can possibly be, pulling her knees tight to her chest. A sound somewhere between a hum and a growl vibrates my throat, causing her brows to pinch together as she starts to rock back and forth in narrow shifts.

Taking a step back, that tension clouding her eases enough to notice, and I realize she's behaving like a trapped animal. Something I can understand. I wonder what her claws would look like.

The sound of the door being suddenly opened causes her to jump and suck in a breath. Giggles and shouts under a layer of music stream inside the dark room.

"I knew you'd fucking be in here. Come on, man, my new friends Christina and Abby here are ready to play a little game, just the four of us. You coming?" Ronan's voice booms, both blondes visibly drunk and hanging off him. I glance back to the ball of nerves in the corner before heading back towards the door, not sure what to say. So, I say nothing. "Alright, that's my man." His hand grips my shoulder and hands me a red plastic cup, introducing me to tonight's conquests. I make sure to close the door to the library softly, my world tunneling to one thing as I follow my best friend down the extravagant cream-coated hallway, and it isn't the woman now spilling her drink on my arm.

# 52

# LILITH

As we ride back to Blaine's building, we share a comfortable silence, holding hands, and stealing glances and smiles at each other. I close my eyes, resting my head back, as the city lights travel over and past us, and listen to the soothing hum of his engine. I savor the feel of his callused yet soft, large hand in mine and let myself feel it all. I'm so content and happy I don't think I could suppress my smile if I wanted to.

"You okay?" Blaine lifts my hand and presses a kiss to the top of it, glancing at me as we stop at a red light downtown.

"Perfect." I smile over at him before looking back out to my right to the city lights and buildings drifting past as we start to move again. The sigh of happiness that escapes me is so full of light, that I'm on the cusp of bursting. *You'd like him, Mom. He's rough around the edges, but he's good. I know he is.* The sudden pain, knowing they'll never meet, is heavy but fleeting as I focus on the now.

We pull into the private entrance to the garage into one of Blaine's parking spaces as he kills the engine and comes around to help me out of the car, leading me to his own elevator. "What do you think, sunshine? Would you like to come up for a glass of wine? I may have something in mind." His devilish smile makes It incredibly hard to say no, my heart skipping a beat at how gorgeous he is when he smiles. *Why doesn't he show this side of himself to anyone?*

"Mmm... I suppose I can spare a few minutes." Feigning contemplation, I slip my hand into his as he reaches for me to step into the elevator.

I can't control myself anymore with him. Not now that I've had him. My fingers sensually play over his large hands, my other resting on his chest. He hasn't kissed me tonight, and I don't want to push him. Tonight and the last few weeks have been a dangerous game between us, and I don't want to break whatever spell is containing the magic that is this evening. He nudges me forward as the door opens, towards his towering black double doors, into his penthouse with his hand on the small of my back. We walk into the dark and quiet of the lavish space. I'm sure Jenny left long ago, but I can't say I'm sad to find it confirmed.

"Why don't you head to the sunroom, and I'll meet you there?" I don't say anything before smiling and turning to head down the hall to the right towards the sunroom on the northern side of the building. It connects to a huge, stone balcony, easily bigger than my entire studio. There's a heated pool lit with soft blue lighting, accentuating the steam slowly drifting from the water, connecting to the chill of the night past the warm sunroom. The golden string lights zig-zag back and forth, covering the entirety of the patio, with two unlit fireplaces near the outdoor seating area and the pool itself.

I stare out past the patio, into the tall buildings that surround the north and east sides of the building. It's the perfect city view at this angle. I take it all in, watching as snowflakes start to fall from the sky generously but gently as I hear ambient music starting to play throughout the house speaker system. He loves instrumental and classical music. It clashes with his mysterious and murderous mask. I hear his footsteps approaching before he stands behind me, placing a glass of white wine in my hand. "Cheers." He stands behind me in silence, one hand on my waist as we slightly start to sway to the music, enjoying the view and the moment. I'm not sure what's going through his mind, though.

He sets down his wine, grabs mine, and leaves it next to his on the long, thin white table in front of us. Both of his warm hands grab my upper arms, gently caressing me before he reaches up to brush back my hair on the right side of my neck and over my left shoulder. I focus on his hand as he continues to adorn me with loving touches, and he leans in, dragging his lips and nose against my neck and ear. I audibly sigh and visibly shiver at how nice his touch feels. How perfect he feels. How wonderful he smells.

"What do you... think of a late-night swim?" My mind is immediately flooded with images of us in the steamy water, touching.

"Okay," is all I manage my lips to get out, in my haze of him. Blaine softly chuckles and slowly unzips the back of my dress, dropping the tiny straps over each arm, allowing it to fall to the floor, an expensive puddle of red at my feet. He hums in pleasure in my ear, reaching around to cup my breasts, running his thumbs over my nipples before grazing his lips and teeth over my neck. I turn around to face him as he still holds onto me, as if scared to leave my skin bare of his fingers for a moment. Reaching up, I help take off his jacket and unbutton his shirt, as he undoes his belt and drops his pants, taking his shirt the remainder of the way off. We stand facing, taking in each other's bodies, exploring the other. He reaches down to grab his wine, nudging his head slightly, indicating for me to grab mine as he takes my other hand in his, leading me outside towards the pool and the night snowfall. We're hit with a brisk chill but I'm so entranced with the entirety of the evening, I can't find myself to fully care. We don't take many steps before we're at the edge of the pool, stepping down into the warmth. I watch as he steps into the bright blue water, pool lights reflecting the small waves. His broad shoulders and tanned, tattooed skin disappearing beneath. The lights in the water reflect into his eyes as he stares at me, into me, nearly taking my breath away with the glow. The warmth and steam of the water contrasting the snow and winter chill of the night is the perfect sensation.

"Come." He gently pulls me deeper, setting our glasses on the edge of the pool, stopping us just as the water hits just above my breasts. He presses me gently against the wall of the pool, raising my thighs for me to wrap myself around him, smiling down at me. We stare into each other's eyes in near silence, as the snow falls around us. The only sounds are the faint piano playing from his speakers and the distant city noise below. I feel like I'm in a movie. I can't stop looking at him, touching him, believing this is real. He lifts me higher, so our faces are closer, pressing his body into mine and resting his forehead on my own before gently running his nose along mine in shared caresses.

"Lily," he whispers, his breath so close. "May I kiss you?" He sounds like he's nearly trembling at the thought. *Blaine doesn't kiss anyone.*

"Yes. Yes, please kiss me." I keep my voice just as low, mimicking his own. In an instant, his hand is cupping my face, his lips pressed to my own as he has me pinned against the wall. I reach up to wrap my hand around his neck, the other on his face. Slowly, so slowly, he kisses me, deepening our touch, dipping his tongue for me to open farther, allowing his own to meet mine.

Minutes pass with our bodies pressed together, our tongues and lips slowly and tenderly dancing to a sensual rhythm that hits my stomach with enough butterflies to make me dizzy. "Blaine," I whisper, turning my face and opening my neck for his taking. His lips and tongue trail the curve of my neck to my ear, which always drives me wild with need. I rock my hips against him as I feel his length pressed to me, causing him to groan and grab my hips with both hands. He moves our bodies in time as his bare cock runs along my folds and sensitive nub. Our quiet sighs and movement of the surrounding water fill the heavy air around us.

"I'm here."

"Blaine, I want you inside of me." I breathlessly get my words out as he pauses, kissing my ear, pressing his forehead to mine, and looking into my eyes silently. Carrying us out of the water into the cold air, our wet bodies press together, and I wrap my legs around him. "I need you." He kisses me as he carries me down the hallway to his room, settling my soaking body oh so delicately onto the bed. There is nothing rushed or forceful about our joining this time. It's slow, loving —magic. It's everything we individually need; what our souls long for.

"You're perfect, Lily. You're so perfect." He lays over me, settling himself between my wet, shivering thighs as he deeply kisses me again, tracing his hand over my face and then down to my breast. I feel him line up to my entrance as he slowly pushes into me, and we both sigh at the sensation. He's filling me, inch by slow inch, and I'm convinced God herself crafted him for my body alone. Our heartbeats but mere inches apart, calling for the other in a rhythmic song. He's fully inside of me as he pauses for a moment for my body to adjust before rocking his hips slightly, entering me repeatedly, so beautifully and deeply. There is no rush in his movements, like he's savoring my body as much as I am his. I don't need to hear the words to know this is his first time making love face to face, sharing such intimacy. I can feel it in every breath, every touch, every kiss. It's why he's always had me look away or close my eyes; he needed that emotional separation. The distinction between love and sex. He reaches between us, touching me, adding another level of pleasure as we both moan and exchange breath, our mouths so close; bodies moving in time against the softness of his plush comforter.

He kisses me while touching my clit before pulling away to look me in my eyes with so much affection I force myself to fight back tears as our bodies join, and he fills me so damn deeply. Not just my body; my heart too. I can feel every crack and shattered edge of the last several weeks, healing. There are no words between us, no vulgar exchanges, no domination or submission. We both feel what we need to in the moment as it comes. I close my eyes as he nibbles and sucks on my ear, moaning. His touch, his sighs of pleasure, kisses, him deeply inside me. God, his scent. It's all perfect, and I feel my climax approaching. Different this time; slower, bigger. Whatever fortress that I built around my heart is falling in a matter of minutes. I give myself over; to the orgasm, to Blaine, to the moment. I allow myself the fulfillment. It washes through my body as he continues to push into me; I can't help the scream that finds its way out of me as I'm overcome. My body reflects the frenzy and essence of a thousand stars, consuming me, bursting free. Blaine groans and shutters as he releases inside of me, my walls fluttering around him.

Our breathing slows as every inch of our bodies that are able to touch, connect. His movements slow, but he still continues to push into me as we both settle from our high, relishing in the sensation of our joining.

"Lily..." His voice is rough as he says my name and cups my face, kissing me tenderly. All I can do is smile, receive every bit of intense emotion his eyes portray, and hold him to me, loving him the way he deserves to be loved. The way we both deserve to be loved.

"I know."

# 53

# BLAINE

Lily and I hardly escaped the bedroom over the course of the following two days. Jenny's been not-so-subtly sent home with paid leave, allowing me to claim Lilith on every fucking surface of my home. The dining room table may be my personal favorite. Seems appropriate with as many times as I've devoured her cunt this weekend. She's stayed at my place, wearing my T-shirts or far less.

I'm letting her in, and it worries me how much I care about her. How much I trust her. I worry it's all going to be taken away from me. I still don't entirely believe I am capable of love. And I am certainly not deserving of her. I know what she deserves, what she needs. I don't know if I can be that man, but I have to try. She's mine now. I don't know if she fully grasps that, seeing as we haven't spoken on it since our tryst in the dining room at the Gala on Friday. Which, God help me if the flashbacks don't kill me. If she doesn't understand yet, she will.

Her stomach rumbling snaps me out of my thoughts. "Are you hungry? I'll order us food. What do you want?" We're laying in bed, half watching a re-run of an old popular TV series she loves. Just hearing her quote the lines verbatim and the sweet sound of her laughing is enough for me.

"Yes! Cupcakes. I want cupcakes."

"Lilith..." I chide. "Fine, but what else? Pho? Mexican? You need something with sustenance." I trace my fingers over her stomach, watching her squirm.

"Mmm... maybe something else. But I doubt it's on the menu. It's more of a specialty dish." She turns over, cupping my shaft with mischievous eyes. She needs to eat first.

"No, food first, baby." I remove her hand and lean over for my phone to order us food as she sighs loudly and throws herself back down on the bed. I can't help but chuckle at her dramatics. I have our text thread pulled up, and the name at the top that reads 'Mine' pulls something near primitive from me.

"Tacos then, please."

"Good girl." I place an order for delivery and message the concierge to approve the delivery to my door. A thought crosses my mind... I set my phone down on the nightstand and turn over, facing her with a wolfish grin.

"What? What is that look for?"

"You know..." I shift further down the bed, moving and positioning her soft legs around me. "I always have been a fan of dessert before dinner though." I lean down and place a long, firm lick through her pussy, keeping eye contact. Her thighs instinctively try to clinch, and I hold them open wider. I wink at her as I throw the sheet over my head and bury my tongue into her core, lapping up her honey. "I can promise you, nothing will ever compare to the taste of you, Lily. Fucking nothing." And I mean it. To desire a woman to taste like fruit or some other bullshit is absurd. It tastes like pussy, that's the entire fucking point. I crave her.

*Mine.*

## LILITH

I walk down the sidewalk towards my office, paranoid I'm walking ridiculously. Blaine and I certainly made up for my dry spell. I stayed at his place the entire weekend, and he stayed; well... inside me. *Sorry Jenny,* I inwardly cringe. She doesn't need to know about the kitchen island, dining room table, his office desk, the shower, or the couch. Fairly certain my cheeks are bright red just replaying the images and how many times the word 'daddy' came out of my mouth at his command.

Only this morning did we have to return to real life before I made my way downstairs to my apartment to get ready for work. My body is feeling the effects, but I wouldn't change a single thing. I haven't felt this light, this happy in... I don't know if I've ever felt this happy, actually. I haven't told anyone about us yet. I haven't exactly had the time or opportunity to. But it feels weird having this huge thing and not telling Katie about it. Part of me wants to rip my phone out of my purse and scream it at her, but another part of me is scared to jinx whatever this is. He said I was his and that no man would ever touch me again. People say a lot of things in the heat of the moment, though; I don't know what we really are. Are we dating now? Am I really his, as in exclusively? Surely Blaine wouldn't use me for the weekend after everything I've shared with him, would he? I did tell him Friday I was just looking for someone to hook up with though. Which was a blatant lie to bait him. Although, I'm happy he was the one to break my bout of abstinence. I wouldn't change that. I just... I don't think I could bear it if all we get together is a weekend of affection, after all this time. Yeah, I can't tell anyone yet. Especially not my brothers. Would Katie tell my brothers? I haven't allowed myself to even consider how they'll react. I'm planning too far ahead; I don't even know what I am to Blaine yet.

And just like that... my happy mood is replaced with something much darker.

It's been two days, and I haven't heard from Blaine. I can't hide that I'm an anxious, sad mess. What is wrong with me? It's been two days.

Fuck it. I pick up my phone next to me on my couch.

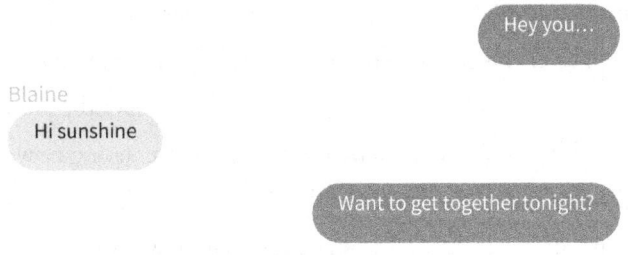

> I wish I could. I have things I have to handle and I'm playing catch up from a certain long weekend away ;) going to be a late night.

> I understand. Have a good night – good luck with work!

Why don't I feel better? I sigh. Mom would be kicking my butt moping over a man. I could go paint in the room he provided me since I have that again. But that almost feels weird now. I make my way over to my bookcase to find a new one to start. Big blue alien man it is. My book boyfriends never let me down. I mute the TV, still enjoying the background image as I snuggle up with my blanket. My phone goes off again, and I see it's Blaine.

> Friday night, let me make it up to you.

> Sounds promising… I guess I'm in. As long as you're there.

> Hmm. I was planning on just dropping you off somewhere for the evening. I guess I can stick around.

I can't help but let out a snort of laughter at that.

> You wouldn't dare!

> Wouldn't I? My schedule is rather tight darling.

> Get back to work. Wouldn't want the boss to punish you.

> Baby, I am the boss. No one punishes me but you.

Wow. Yes, he is... oh, he's giving me so many ideas.

> I guess you are in my debt seeing as you did a pretty good number on me Friday even though I listened so well.

> We have vastly varying ideas of what constitutes listening well it would seem...

> Hmm we'll discuss that one further later. Although, I do have a package for you. Mandatory that it be hand-delivered to your office by me though. Interested?

> How could I refuse when such a stunning woman is delivering it?

> Always the smooth talker. Be expecting it sometime tomorrow. Night Blaine.

> Looking forward to it... Goodnight Sunshine.

I slam my book shut and head straight for my closet in search of... *there.*

# 54

# LILITH

I walk up to Blaine's office building in a long black coat and large sunglasses, just around three o'clock, claiming I didn't feel well and needed to utilize a few hours of sick time. Walking through the revolving doors and into the bright, marble-covered lobby, my heels click as I make my way to the concierge for permission to his floor that requires badged entrance. Offering a smile and 'thank you', I enter the elevator, momentarily trying to fight back my smile and nerves. I've never done anything like this before. Walking into his private floor, I approach his assistant who leaves to let Blaine know I'm here. Looking around, it's exactly what I imagined his office space would look like. Masculine, dark greys, coppers, and touches of white.

"Mr. Vogeleir will see you now, Miss. Stemmens. This way." She leads me down the grey hall to the left into a large, glass office, with deeply frosted coloring. I almost panic, but thankfully, notice you can't see through it even remotely. I walk in to see broad shoulders straining the fabric nesting them sitting behind a massive dark desk, and grey eyes blazing as they cut straight into me.

"Thank you. See to it that my next hour is free for Miss Stemmens here."

"Yes, sir." I stare back at Blaine as his assistant closes the door behind me, and I make my way over to him, behind his desk.

He reaches for me before I can do much of anything and pulls me onto his lap, kissing me. Running his hand under my coat and onto my bare thigh, he pauses when he realizes I don't have much on underneath. "Lilith..." I stand up to remove myself from his lap and start to slowly untie and unbutton my knee-length coat. Letting it gently open, sliding down my bare shoulders and arms onto the floor, I stand before him, tossing my sunglasses onto his desk.

"Your package came unwrapped. I hope that's okay." Blaine's gaze turns scorching; that glint, purely male, as he eyes my figure. I have a black, lace bra and panty set on with matching black heels and nothing more. He starts to stand, but I push him back down into the chair, not breaking our eye contact. His look is punishing, but he wears a smirk as he grips the arms of his chair, growling deeply in his throat. "Shh... you have to stay quiet, Mr. Vogeleir. Unless you want to get caught." I drop to my knees and crawl under his massive desk, reaching for his belt. I undo his buckle and unzip his dress slacks, freeing his prominent, already stiff length, biting my lower lip at his piercing grey and green eyes. I'm under his desk far enough that I'm covered from view but still able to move freely enough, as I need. I run my hand over his shaft several times before leaning in and licking just the head of him, watching his grip tighten on the arms of his chair, restraining himself. I hum in delight as I trace my tongue over the underside of his cock, dragging my wet lips with it. I grip the base of him as I focus my attention teasingly, tracing my tongue and lips over his head in sensual, slow, torturous movements. "Mmm."

"Lily." He grits out quietly. "Get on the desk. Now."

# 55

# BLAINE

"Get on the desk. Now."

She doesn't listen; of course, she doesn't. Instead, she starts stroking my entire dick.

"Ah, ah, ah." She lowers her mouth over the head of my cock, slowly making her way further down and back up, until I'm hitting the back of her throat. She's not even half of the way down. She starts a steady rhythm sucking the life and damn-near any restraint out of me, firmly massaging the rest of me with one hand, reaching her other to gently play with my sack. Her spit drips down from my cock, onto my balls; the sensation sending chills through my spine. I can't help it, I toss my head back, closing my eyes in the overwhelming sensation. Holy fuck, she feels so good. I tangle her hair around my fist, keeping a tight hold on her as she moves up and down, gagging on my cock. Fuck me, the sound of her choking on my dick; she's going to kill me.

"Fuck, sunshine. Your mouth..." I lean my head back upright, watching her, and tense, holding her hair back to stop her as the door handle moves at the same time someone knocks and enters. Evan...

"Sorry, sir, I know your door is closed, but it's important. It's the Dannington deal." Naughty Lily continues to stroke and suck me silently from deep under my desk, despite my hand in her hair. I don't say anything right away. I stare at him, waiting for him to speak. "They're trying to pull out." If he only knew the fucking irony there. "Three-million-dollar, eight-month contract, and they're trying to back out suddenly before signing the proposal we modified to their requested standards."

"Why." I'm staring at his fucking face while Lily's under my desk, sucking me off, struggling to keep my composure. Jesus Christ. The sound of his voice drags into oblivion the closer I get to spilling down Lily's throat as she quietly bobs up and down, speeding up her hands. Fucking vixen.

"Get out."

"...Excuse me, sir?"

"Get... out..." I stare at him with nothing but threat and promise in my eyes as I pull Lily's hair hard enough that she's forced to stop pumping me. To her credit, she stays silent. Evan looks at me with anger and disbelief as he stalks towards the door. "I'll meet with you in thirty minutes on the matter. Lock the door behind you." He huffs, obviously frustrated, as he harshly closes the door.

I release Lily's hair, pulling away from the desk to see her playfully innocent eyes, blinking up at me with a grin, dark mascara lining the sides of her eyes and cheeks. So fucking filthy. I silently reach out my hand and she knows better than to disobey me again, placing hers into it as I help her to her feet. "Naughty, naughty, little kitten." I eye her beautiful body before pulling her black panties down, helping her step out of them, and unhooking her bra, freeing her small, perfect tits. I glide my hands, griping her ass, waist, and up to her nipples, lightly running my thumbs over each tip, watching as they harden from my attention. "On the desk."

Lily sits on the edge of the desk as I stand between her thighs, easing her onto her back and pushing items aside, a few papers and pens falling to the floor. I lean down over her, kissing her, moving the hand I'm not resting on, to the apex of her thighs. I can't help but release a deep rumble finding her wet and ready for me. Fuck she's so *soft*. I dip a finger into her core and start pumping, applying pressure to her clit until she starts to sigh and breathe heavily against my mouth.

I pause, righting myself and remove my finger, sucking her taste off, and lean down for a deep lick over her pussy. If I was a cat, I swear to fuck, I'd be purring. Gathering all of her dripping slick, I lean back down to kiss her, her arousal still pooled in my mouth and feel it spilling into hers. I want her to know how incredible she tastes. I move my hand to her breast, running my bare cock along her silken folds, covering myself in her wetness. Mesmerized by the image, all I can think about is taking my belt to this sweet little cunt, punishing and teasing her clit until she's swollen and red, begging to come. *Fuck.* Someday. My sunshine might not admit it, but she likes it a little rough. Greedy little cunt needs it to get off. And fuck if I'm not more than happy to give it to her. I'll give her anything. Pretty sure I'd rip out my own heart if she told me to.

As her hips start to buck under me to add friction and our sighs become fevered, I push myself into her entrance, thrusting into her as we both moan. I nearly collapse, releasing a curse as the edges of my vision turn to static. "Fuck, Lily. You feel fantastic. Every single time I enter your body, I can barely breathe; you're so perfect." I move my hips, pushing in and out of her hot body, over and over. I'm so close to going over the edge. I reach between us and start tracing her clit with a heavy hand. Her movements become frantic, her nails digging into me as I speed up my efforts, our moans filling the air around us, chasing release. I continue to fuck her on my desk, uncaring if the world hears her or hears me in the throes of passion.

They need to know she's fucking mine. Only mine.

She feels so phenomenal, I let out a loud groan as I know she's about to come, holding her breath and tightening around my cock. "I'm going to come, baby. Come for me first. Need it. Need to feel you." She shudders and cries out as her orgasm claims her, pressing her hand over her own mouth, and I release my seed into her, exploding. "Take all of me like a good girl." I continue to pump into her and touch her clit as her cunt continues to ripple around me while we share the moment of ecstasy washing over us; through us. "That's a good girl. Fucking take it all. Every drop of me inside this pussy. My pussy." Our breathing slows as I lay over her, buried inside of her, slightly moving my hips to make sure she receives every second of pleasure she can. "I'm afraid you've ruined me for all other women. There will never be a day any other name, but yours leaves my lips when fucking." I stand up, bringing her with me, staying buried inside of her, simply loving the feeling of her body connected to mine. The one touch I now crave deeply.

# 56

# LILITH

## *Before:*

I stare ahead at nothing in particular, eyes wandering and scanning the room. I've found myself back in the one place I never thought in a million years I'd be forced into again. The house we grew up in and spent our childhoods. Only the walls feel smaller, even more haunted somehow. My experience here seems to have varied vastly from my brothers'. I can't stop my mind from wondering what it was like for them, too, living in this giant house once both our mother and father died. Did they actually care that I was suddenly gone? Or had it been more of a relief somehow? It's been a whirlwind of change, and a lot was brought to light after Ronan and Artemis came to find me and brought me here.

They're in college now and don't live in the house full-time anymore, for starters. I wanted to beg and scream and collapse to my knees for them to take me anywhere but here. The words always find themselves stuck in my throat, my body frozen. If I'm too much of a burden, they'll get rid of me and then where will I be?

They have no idea I haven't slept a single night in my old room. They think it's comforting to be in my childhood bedroom. That alone tells me how different our upbringings really were before our lives went to hell in a handbasket.

No, they have no idea I've slept curled in the corner of the library in hiding, as I am now.

It's mostly quiet, sounds muffled from the party outside. My brothers are having people over to drink and hired a DJ to set up and play music for people to dance to. Ronan keeps talking about turning the carriage house into a party house someday. I almost snort at the thought. At his ability to think of such simple and fun things. The ability to just enjoy. I don't think I'll ever be able to enjoy anything again. Not fully.

Running my hands over the soft blanket covering me, I take a deep breath and start to slowly exhale, until the door opens, a dim light and music pouring into what should be near darkness. I don't want the light, but I don't want the terrors of the dark, either.

I keep any hint of a whimper in my throat, slowly moving as far as I possibly can into the hidden corner, reaching for the kitchen knife I have tucked away next to where I've been laying my head at night.

Just then, a young man around my brothers' age slowly appears, completely silent. My hand freezes in its task as I take him in, now staring at me. I refuse to take my eyes off him. No, something about him seems very different from other guys their age. Not threatening... not really. Powerful. Certainly, an aura of something I'm not sure I can put a name to. The longer he stands there, the more I feel my body start to shake, ready to pounce for the knife.

He takes a step towards me, and it's suddenly as if he's jumping on top of me, pinning me down. Any second, I know it's what's coming. Any bravata I may have tried to muster seems nonexistent, my legs scrambling under me for purchase, pushing into a ball as tight as I can, rocking back and forth. No, no, no, no. My knife, need my knife. Something, anything.

With what looks to be a curious expression, he backs away, and it's like a small weight has been immediately lifted from my chest. I try to keep my shivering and trembling under control, eyeing him and watching for any indication he might come closer again.

Suddenly the door practically slams open again, causing my already on-edge system to trigger, jumping out of my skin. The guy looks away, and then I hear my brother's voice. The relief that washes over me is enough to make the tears lining my eyes fall. Fuck, I wish they'd just leave me alone. I fight the release rushing its way to the surface, almost overwhelming me, chin trembling.

"I knew you'd fucking be in here. Come on, man, my new friends Christina and Abby here are ready to play a little game, just the four of us. You coming?" Ronan's voice practically echoes off the walls directed towards this man and I internally beg for them to just leave.

With a final glance my way, he turns and heads towards the door, voices and steps fading to nothing as the door shuts, and I can finally breathe.

Once I'm calmer, I get up to move a piece of furniture in front of the door. I make my way back to my hidden corner, a certain pair of eyes already haunting my memory. God, they were beautiful, even in the low light. He was beautiful.

It's much later in the night that I finally fall into sleep, images of him never drifting far. For the first time in a long time, I realized I felt something other than fear from a man: intrigue. The fear I have is conditioned, and it has been, time and time again. But I realized my fear wasn't for him specifically. No, it was a reaction. He was the source of a new feeling entirely.

I just wonder who he was.

# 57

# LILITH

The rest of the week has flown by reassured that Blaine and I are in a good place now. I've been looking forward to his surprise tonight since early this week too. I asked him what I should wear, and he said, "Literally anything." Which I think may have been the least helpful response he could have given me.

Although tempted to show up in a fly-fishing ensemble, I'm going with tall boots and a casual dress that I paid a repulsive amount of money for. I wear my hair down with light makeup and no lipstick for obvious reasons. I'm planning to kiss the hell out of him tonight; to kiss the haunted shadows out of his eyes.

I can't get enough of him. Even two days apart, I'm craving his presence and cuddles, amongst other things. I'm putting in my earrings as I hear his knock and the whisper of the door being opened. I smile, turning the corner. Stepping out to see him, he looks sexy as hell in all black, tanned chest peaking through his button-up, broad shoulders, and biceps clear as day through the material. There's no way this man is mine. Stopping my shameless roaming over his body, my eyes catch on what's in his hand.

"You got me flowers...?" I ask softly, surprised as I walk towards him, eyes wide. "Blaine. They're stunning, thank you." No man has ever come close to even thinking of getting me flowers. How is he so amazing? He has a bouquet of roses, lilies, and baby's breath reached out towards me, with what seems to be a cautious smile. I won't mention the adorable blush tinting his cheekbones. Although that's an image I'll never forget. I grab the flowers and lean in to kiss him in thanks. "Thank you, handsome." I pull away to grab my vase from a cabinet and fill it with water before we leave. I place them on my counter, leaning to smell them as he comes up next to me, gently moving my hair behind my shoulder and grabbing my hand.

"Ready?"

"More than ready." I grip his hand back in excitement and grab my purse from the hook by my door before we head out. "Still a secret? No hints?" He grabs my shoulder, pulling me next to him as we walk to the elevator.

"Nope. You'll have to see for yourself, sunshine."

We head down to the lobby and grab his car from valet before driving just a handful of blocks before we find a parking spot downtown. I look over at him before climbing out, and he gives me a little nudge of encouragement, signaling that we're here. I tried to imagine what we could be doing this evening and I couldn't really come up with anything solid. I thought maybe a sports game, a play, a concert, a nice dinner. Hell, I even thought maybe he'd plan our 'coming out' party to our friends, and I'd walk in to see everyone.

I can't help but chuckle to myself at that one. That would be a disastrous date.

Blaine takes my hand, leading me a couple of blocks, and I know where we are. We're right by my favorite coffee shop and local bookstore. It's not until we get closer that I read the sign in front of the bookstore, "Welcome, Lily and Blaine." I slow my steps, looking over at him in surprise and confusion. It must be evident on my face because he smiles and leads me into the store, entering behind me. It's... magical. *Oh my god.* I'm speechless and can't help but bring my hand to my face in shock as I take it all in. I can feel my eyes start to fill with tears as Blaine watches my reaction.

"Blaine..." I can barely manage that small, raspy whisper. The inside of my favorite, old, small bookstore has been transformed. There are groups and pillars of candles everywhere, dimly lighting the space, just enhancing the wonderous beauty of all the books neatly stacked along all of the walls, desks, and stairs to the open second floor above. In the center of the room, there's a table finely adorned with a candle, white tablecloth, and a basket; music playing low in the back. I can't believe he did this. And for me.

"You like it?" He cautiously asks as if I could possibly say no. I bring my hand down from my face, looking over at him to my right, and kiss him. I don't trust myself with words right now. A smile and nod are all I can manage so I don't break out in tears and ruin it. "I uhh. Well, I had my assistant help with the logistics and aesthetics. I just thought since you like this bookstore, I'd make it special and rent it for us this evening." He pulls me over to the table where the basket sits, opening it. "I had some takeout delivered so we could have dinner here." He rubs the back of his neck, not wanting to look at me. Is he nervous right now?

"Blaine. This is the most thoughtful, beautiful thing anyone has ever done for me. I don't really know what to say to express how meaningful this is to me. It's more than I ever imagined. I can't believe you did all this." I watch his face as the shadows and light from the many candles dance across his pale eyes and skin, the most beautiful smile I've ever seen crossing his face before he looks away.

"I'm glad I could make you happy then, beautiful. I wanted our first date to be something you'd remember. Here, sit." He opens the basket unpacking two warmed, wrapped plates of pasta, garlic bread, and a smaller plate of three different kinds of cheesecake. "Good, I'm glad to see it's still hot. Take your pick."

"Oh my god, it looks incredible! Are you kidding me? I'm so hungry." I think that relaxes him a little as he removes the basket and sits across from me, handing me a bundle of utensils

We finish our dinner and dessert, ending the meal with me moving to his lap, talking and laughing about our weeks and some ridiculous stories about our friends. I rest my head against him as he runs his

fingers through my hair, over my thigh, and our hands entwined in silence. "I don't know if I've ever said it out loud, but one thing I love about you is that you never try to fill the silence. Sometimes it's the most comfortable to just be in peace. I love that I can do that with you without feeling strange."

"I feel exactly the same, sweetheart." He leans over and presses a kiss to my hairline. "As much as I am thoroughly enjoying our time wrapped up together. There is another part of the evening." I look at him in a bit of shock.

"There's... more?" I search his face before he nudges me off his lap, both of us standing. He positions me in front of him as he leans forward, resting his chin on my shoulder, wrapping his arms under my breast and waist.

"There is. I almost forgot." I can feel his deep chuckle move through his body. "I had the owner set up an account for you earlier. I put a couple grand in, so you have credit to last you a little while." I push away from him incredulously, turning towards him in utter shock.

"A couple... GRAND? A couple grand Blaine! You can't... I mean... I can't. Oh my god, Blaine. I..." A genuine, full laugh and smile comes from him as he steps towards me again.

"It's nothing. I'm happy to do it, and I know you enjoy the library at your brothers' place. I figure this is a good enough start for your own collection. We can always add more money to the account later."

My words come out muffled as I hide my face in my hands at this gift. "Blaine... I can't ac.."

"Oh, but there is one stipulation." That gets my attention. I look up at him.

"Stipulation? What type of stipulation?"

"Well... I thought it might be fun if you picked out one of your favorite *poetic* books for me. And... one day, not tonight. But, one day— we're going to reenact your favorite chapter, exactly as you want it after I finish reading it." I'm pretty sure I'm glitching because I can't stop staring at him with my lips parted in shock and naughty thoughts. Finally, I snap out of it and manage a smile, biting my bottom lip.

"You know what? I may have something in mind already." I grab his hand, leading him towards a secluded corner of the store in the back, nearly dark without the light of the candles. "I once read a book where the main characters got a little naughty in the corner of a busy library where the boyfriend worked. It may not be busy. And, it may not be a library. But... I've always fantasized about trying that one day?"

"That... sunshine, can easily be made a reality." His possessive, hungry look hits me in the stomach as he drops to his knees in front of me. He runs his hands up the back of my thighs, up under my short dress, and grabs my ass, pulling down my panties. Hooking one of my legs out of the fabric as it drops to the floor around my other foot, he hums in pleasure. He moves my leg over his shoulder, kissing my inner thigh, working his way higher. "Is this..." *Kiss.*

"What you had…" *Kiss.* "In mind?" *Kiss.* "It's true that it may not be a busy library. But the owner could certainly be in for a pleasant surprise if he watches his camera footage tomorrow." He looks up at me with heavily lidded eyes and a suggestive grin, winking.

# 58

# LILITH

Last night, I let Blaine feast upon my body, pressed up against the bookshelves until I couldn't stand and was covered in a sheen of sweat. He entered me against the rows of books, again on the table, once when we got back to his house, and again twice this morning; once in bed, once in the shower. I'm not sure what's overcome us, but we can't take our hands off of each other now that we've broken through the wall he held between us for so long. It feels so fucking good to be this happy and to see him so happy.

We're sitting in the dining room, enjoying the spread of foods Jenny made for us as she vacuums in the other room. I've been putting off this conversation because I've been too scared. But, if I don't bring this up, I'm going to continue to be anxious, letting it consume me.

"Hey, umm... I want to talk to you about something. Well, a couple somethings, I guess." He looks up from the papers he has near him giving me his full attention as he reaches for his orange juice.

"Okay."

"First... I don't really know how to say this. I don't want to freak you out or feel like I'm pressuring you into anything. I'm only bringing this up so we're both on the same page, you know. It's just... I mean. What am I to you? What are we doing?" He cocks his head to the side enough to imply he wants me to keep going. "I just mean... are we dating? Exclusive? Boyfriend and girlfriend? Friends with benefits? Do we continue to see other people?" His brows furrow, and I can sense the sudden iciness in the air due to my last comment.

"What is it *you* think we're doing, Lily? What is it you want? Tell me." Oh boy, I woke the beast, okay. Breathe.

"I know that I want to be with you... exclusively. But if you don't want that, I understand. I know you don't do... the relationship thing." I can't read his expression. It's gone completely blank, again. My heart is pounding out of my stupid chest.

"Come here. Sit." He pulls away from the table, waiting for me to sit on his lap as I make my way shakily towards him. He pulls me into him, adjusting my legs so that I'm sitting in his lap, straddling him. He simply looks over my face, dragging his hands over my bare thighs and under the large shirt of his I'm wearing, to my hips. "Lily... I thought I had made myself clear on our agreement. But perhaps not, so I'll say it again." He touches my hair, tucking it behind my ear before cupping my face and bringing me in for a sensual, deep kiss, grinding himself against me, spread open for him. "Did that feel like I want anyone else? That kiss?"

"No…" I whisper. He grabs my hips and the small of my back, pushing his clothed hard length onto me.

"Does that feel like I want anyone else? Does it feel like I want to be buried inside anyone else? Fucking someone else?"

"No…" He grabs my face, meeting my sharp gaze, anger in my eyes just thinking of him with another woman. Abso-fucking-lutely not.

"Lily Stemmens. I want you. As far as I am concerned, you're mine. No man will touch this, this, or this… *ever* again. That's abundantly clear now?" He moves his hands from my ass to my chest, to the bare wetness that sits between my legs for his emphasis.

"Yes." I suddenly feel shy under his gaze.

"Good." He relaxes and smiles, bringing me in for a quick, sweet kiss on my lips, nose, and forehead. He glances over his shoulder before looking back to me, pulling down his sleep pants. Exposing himself, he pushes into my soaking entrance. We keep eye contact as he pumps into me all the way. I practically whimper, slowly riding him, grabbing the back of the chair, causing him to hit so deep inside of me. "You can call me whatever you want, sunshine; boyfriend, lover, partner —fuck," he groans. "I don't care. Tell me what you want."

"Then you're my boyfriend, and I'm your girlfriend," I whisper as he moves my hips up and down his length, gently kissing me.

"I'm yours. I've been yours for far longer than I even realized. I meant every word I said that night in the dining hall Lily. You're mine and only mine. Forever baby, it's you and me. You're my endgame now, got it?" He's mine… and I'm his. I can't help my smile as I lean in to kiss him, buried inside me. Of course, I'm his. And I fucking love being his property. I grip the back of his neck. "Hopefully, poor Jenny doesn't see us." I chuckle quietly.

"If she plans on sticking around, she better get used to it because I plan on making you scream on every surface of this house, whether she's here or not, for a long... long time." He winks before kissing me with such emphasis and emotion, that it's hard to believe Blaine had never kissed anyone, never cuddled, or shared soft touches, never made love face to face.

Until me.

# 59

# BLAINE

I don't believe in a God in the sense the rest of the Western world does; begging desperately for something more, purpose, a reason. Even when I was a child, I never believed. I think it's bullshit with the amount of evil and suffering there is in the world. I also don't believe in anything, though, at least not fully. I'm incapable of faith.

I have faith in nothing and no one.

When all you've ever known, experienced, and been exposed to is pain and darkness, how could you possibly have faith in *anything?* It doesn't exist. It's a ghost of an idea never within reach or comprehension.

Hope is for the privileged.

Those fortunate enough to live blindly with their minds and bodies intact. There's a secret society of people walking among them, with shadows on each shoulder and chaos clouding their vision.

Some people say the best thing, the right thing, is to heal. To move on. That's bullshit too. If everyone turned their cheek to the darkness that consumed the world, there would be no light. There would be no hope left for *them* either. I can promise you, the darker it is, the more demons come out to play. What's left when all the threads of a rope are pulled apart and dissected? Hundreds of pieces now become useless, weakened. My shadows are who I am.

I lay in bed, silently resting on my side, propped up on one elbow. I trace my eyes over the woman next to me and wait for the moment I wake up, and she disappears. She's darkness, too; she just doesn't know it. And yet somehow, she holds a torch warm and bright enough to keep it at bay. She is both day and night, chaos and calm.

Shadow and sunshine. My sunshine. My North Star.

She is no woman. She is a goddess, reincarnated. And she's mine.

I lean closer to kiss her temple just as she lets out the loudest snort of a breath, causing me to impulsively toss my head back, laughing because I'm immature. She jumps, looking around confused, having just been brought back to life either by my laughter or her own heinous snoring. "I'm sorry, baby, I'm sorry." I bury my face into the pillow next to her head to control my sudden giddiness and chuckles. Groaning, she lifts the covers over her face, burrowing back into the warmth, half asleep. I hum in pleasure through my smile, running my hand under the cover down her bare thigh and stomach, tracing whispering touches over her soft skin. "Morning... are you going back to sleep, sweetheart?"

A muffled hum and her snuggling her head into the pillow are the only responses I get, and I half-laugh, half-pout. Leaning in to kiss her cheek and run my hand over her body one final time, I force myself up and make my way to the shower, grabbing my phone from the nightstand. It lights up from the movement, showing a notification from Rye.

> **Rye**
> Hey kid. Lucy and me just checking in. Hope you're doing good. Love to catch up over dinner.

I run my hand down my face, set my phone on the bathroom counter, and walk into the large stone and glass box to start the shower. Rye and I aren't exactly close. I feel a tether to the man, but we've never been close. He was obviously a little younger when my parents died and had no desire to have a young teen suddenly at his doorstep. Me being there wasn't reason enough he would've stopped the parties; the drugs, sex, and fights all still in full force. It wasn't until several years ago, he met Lucy and, in a sense, settled down. Not in the American dream, white picket fence in the suburbs sense; he's still involved in nasty shit with the Club. But settled down in his age, nonetheless. I guess he got the clarity he needed with time and realized he could have and should have done better by me when my folks passed. I don't give a shit; I'm not sure it would have changed anything. I'd still be me and just as fucked up.

> Hey Rye. Doing well, man. Doing really fucking well actually. Next couple weeks are tight, you know how it is. But after, let's talk. Tell Lucy I say Hi.

Do I want to spend time with them? Not really. Knowing he is alive seems good enough. I've always had an aversion to family, touchy shit. A therapist would tell you it's because I wasn't hugged enough as a child. Hell, maybe it is.

I jump back in behind the glass, into the shower dunking my head under the hot stream. Just standing still with my head bent, I let water run over my body, soaking my hair. A million things to do cross my mind as I start a mental tally. I wish Lil was up and here with me. We both struggle with sleep, although having her next to me nearly every night has helped. It's an unspoken agreement we have to let the other rest if our sleep schedules are off. Especially since tonight is going to go a little long.

The guys are hosting a fairly large private party in their carriage house to celebrate their birthdays. No one knows Lilith and I are together. The opposite, actually; given the assumption we each agreed to follow their 'suggestion' of staying apart, tonight is going to be difficult and far more unpleasant not being able to have her next to me. We've been together nearly nonstop since I claimed her as mine. She's not ready to tell them yet, though, and honestly, I have to agree. I just don't feel like dealing with what will undoubtedly be their shitty, dramatic reaction. I know I'm not good enough for Lily. *They* know I'm not good enough for her. But I have to keep her, I have to. Their predictable response will crush her. And potentially fuck our friendship of over a decade. I'd give up the world, everything I had, anyone, just to keep her though. They don't need to know the depth of what I am feeling for her or that I am trying to be... better. For her. None of my rules apply to her. Hell, my fucking personality doesn't apply to her. I've never smiled or laughed around any other human like I do with her. A faint knock on the door distracts me from my train of thought.

"It's me. Can I open the door?"

"Yeah, of course, baby. Come in." Happiness blooms in my chest. Lily opens the door wearing a smile and one of my sweatshirts that swallows her, visibly still sleepy. And damn, if it isn't sexy as hell. Mine; all mine.

"I'm craving chocolate chip pancakes. Are you hungry?" Of course, she wants to add more sugar to an already sweet breakfast. I huff a short laugh at that.

"Definitely —definitely hungry." I trace my eyes over her body with a grin, raising a brow. She squeezes her thighs together, pulling the sweatshirt down, and glancing over her shoulder like Jenny's going to be standing there eavesdropping, ready to smack her with a ruler. Before she can respond, I stop her. "Yes. That sounds good. And omelets, though. And bacon. Just tell Jenny what you want, baby."

"She's busy cleaning, I'm just going to cook."

"...Mmm."

"What, *mmm?*"

"She won't let you lift a finger."

"What, why? It's just pancakes. It's not like I'm going to mess it up or burn the kitchen down."

"Because those are her instructions. She gets paid, quite well, mind you, to do those things. More time for you to do things like shower with the attractive male that owns the place." I see her about to talk back with a sarcastic comment and raise my eyebrow at her before she stops herself. I couldn't be more thrilled she's comfortable enough with me to show me those other little sides of her.

I lean out my hand for her to come to me. After a few hesitant first steps, she makes her way to me, biting her bottom lip slightly. I step out behind the glass wall onto the white rug and lift my clothing off of her, pulling her in.

"What do I get as my reward then?" Walking her further into the steaming shower, I point and nudge her to sit on the warm bench along the side wall close enough to the streams of water that she'll be warm.

"Well, it so happens I may have a special idea for my sunshine tonight; should everything go according to plan... still a maybe, nothing set in stone." I grab a folded white towel hidden in the built-in shelves along the far wall and toss it down in front of her, dropping to my knees. She parts her lips looking between me and the open door at the end of the room.

"The... the door's open." I pull her to the end of the bench bringing her closer to me with a devious smile. Lifting one leg, I kiss my way up her sensitive inner thigh. Slowly tracing my thumb around her clit, I suck and nip at her thigh until she's thoroughly marked by me. Leaning back to observe my work, I growl in pleasure.

I know she's excited by the idea of being caught; she doesn't have to say it. I've figured it out enough by now. I am curious if she herself has realized this though. The bedroom door should be closed, however. And Jenny, by now, has the sense not to disturb us.

"I know... better be quiet, little one." I bury myself between her soft legs and plan to do so until she comes on my face at least twice.

# 60

# LILITH

## *Before:*

"Here, wear this tonight." Ronan's jersey hits me in the chest as he tosses it at me with little warning. I open it up, his number big and bold on both sides and our last name on the back with the initial 'R' in front of it.

"Better do a smell check, Lil." Artemis winks from the doorway, sticking his head in Ronan's room for a second.

"Hey! Asshole! It's clean, alright." He looks over and makes his way the couple of feet between us, grabbing the oversized fabric and bringing it to his nose before handing it back, mumbling incoherently under his breath. Pretty sure I make out the word 'prick' somewhere in there and assume his grumbling is geared towards Art and not me. Watching the two of them interact has brought back a lot of memories, and honestly, not much has changed between them.

The guys actually invited me to come check out their space here at school and maybe come to watch the football game later tonight if I feel up to it. I've been cooped up inside their other property, where the house is, for what feels like far too long. I'm not sure why they wanted me to take time to adjust and relax, but I'm ready to start my new life.

I've had nothing but time to think about it and plan out what I want to do, starting with applying to jobs on the laptop they gave me and finding an apartment.

Their college dorm suite isn't like what I've seen in movies. It's actually pretty incredible and spacious enough for what it is. I asked why they gave up the estate to live here in what must feel like a shack to them. I guess they wanted the full college experience while they could. God, what I would have done to have a place like this to call home a couple of months ago. Just another reminder of how different we really are, and I try not to let it fester before spiraling.

They each have their own bedroom big enough for a bed and small desk and share a common area with their other roommate that they use mostly for watching TV and hanging out. It even has a small fridge and microwave which seems somehow oddly glamorous.

The shared space is surprisingly clean, and I suspect that may be Artemis' doing, considering the pile of proclaimed clean clothes on Ronan's bedroom floor and desk chair. I'm not sure of the last time I owned enough clothing to even be big enough for a pile, and I fight the jealousy that claws at me for the years I spent in Hell while they got everything they could possibly want or need, all while still having each other too. I immediately feel guilty, and a sick feeling takes over my stomach at my knee-jerk reaction. That's not fair to them, and of course, I want them to be happy and taken care of. God, what is wrong with me?

Walking back into the shared space, my eyes explore the couch, giant TV, and other little items here and there. A board covered in pictures and magazine cutouts catches my attention, and it's like I have a sudden insight into their lives. Their real lives. Images of one or both of them in most photos; hiking and nature pics, sports games, holding up small glasses of dark liquid in a dim bar. Their smiles just radiate joy, and it feels like I suddenly can't quite breathe for so many reasons. Trailing my fingers lightly over the photos, I see them dressed up in tuxes with two unbelievably gorgeous women on either side. They haven't said they're dating or have partners, so maybe they're just friends, I don't know. Silly cutouts of pictures with drawn-on mustaches and glasses make me smile; the feel of the photos smooth under my fingertips.

It's when I'm getting towards the opposite side of the large board that I lose focus on anything else and home into a photo of my brothers with the man from the library a couple of weeks ago between them. It looks like they're at a bar of some kind, maybe what I assume would be a flash from a camera, lighting up their faces in contrast to the darkness behind them.

The expression on his face is blank, almost irritated. Almost. If it weren't for the small twinkle in his eye, I'd say he hated being there. You'd miss it if you weren't really studying him, as I am now.

"Pretty fun, huh? A couple of friends put this up, and it just keeps growing." Artemis' deep voice startles me out of my thoughts, and I pull back my hand, away from the photo I didn't realize I had leaned in so close to.

"Yeah, it's amazing. I love being able to see into your lives and see what I've missed." I clear my throat lightly, offering a kind smile to my now much taller, older brother. The words just kind of spilled out of me without thinking.

"I wish we had never lost you, Lilith. But I promise you, we're here now and not going anywhere." His voice is nearly a whisper, a pained expression on his handsome face. It's enough to make me want to apologize for what I said, for putting that look on his face. To my disappointment, all I can manage is a slight nod, holding in the tears I feel warming the backs of my eyes.

He looks around a bit before pulling me against him in a tight hug. My body pulses a small wave of panic before I take a breath and force my arms around my big brother's back, resting my head on his chest.

I'm not sure honestly how long we stand there before Ronan softly interjects, but when Art pulls away, it shockingly feels like a loss of comfort.

# 61

# LILITH

I'm upstairs at my brothers' estate in what's now Katie's room. It looks mostly the same honestly, as the day she moved in. A large four-poster bed with white sheer treatments delicately hanging from the wood, an ornate gray rug, dresser, and white curtains and bedding to match. I guess, to be fair, she wasn't planning on staying nearly this long. So, it makes sense she wouldn't really decorate. Larissa, Katie, and I are getting ready in her huge bathroom suite. Memories of our drunken night in the jacuzzi tub immediately come to mind. We used *far* too many bubbles and had too much champagne, and Katie ended up slipping trying to stand up, sending soapy water over the edge and into Lissa's eyes. We woke up still sticky and covered in bruises. But I don't recall many nights we laughed so hard or had so much fun. Katie holds her hair pinned in place with a curling wand as Larissa digs through her makeup bag, and I... I realize numbly, how much I am not in the mood or looking forward to the night.

My brothers put a ton of effort into this party, though. No, not party —it's a damn theatrical event. I'm pretty sure they have fire spinners and costumed servants lined up. The theme is Black and Bubbles. Everyone is required to wear black or risk not being allowed in. Everyone, except Artemis and Ronan, of course. They will be wearing all red —good luck pulling that off. There will be masks provided to cover everyone's upper face, with a choice of devil or angel; black or white. The staff and servers are following the dress code and will be passing out flutes of champagne to guests upon entry. My brothers standing out in red will make it easier for me to avoid them tonight. I don't want to even be in the vicinity of them long enough for Blaine to even come up in conversation. I can't tell them, or anyone, including my girls. It has to stay between us, for now. I don't regret a single thing. Being with Blaine has been nothing short of amazing. He's pissy and moody sometimes, but he's also amazing. And since we've gotten so close, he's nearly a different person with me. He's being vulnerable and opening himself up, even though I know this is terrifying for him. This is all a little terrifying for me, too, though.

I don't plan on staying long. Just long enough for the people that matter to know I was present and then sneak away in an Irish goodbye. If Blaine and I could freely be together to have fun tonight, this would be different. But alas, we're supposed to be keeping our distance. I don't even realize the audible and very frustrated deep sigh that escapes me until both women look over at me, pausing.

"What?"

"You just let out the world's biggest sigh. Is everything okay?" Katie looks at me in the mirror, next to Larissa who's in the middle of us. Katie has on an incredibly sexy, black outfit. It's a tight, long-sleeve, and off-the-shoulder lingerie-type top with a high-waisted mini skirt revealing two full slits in front that are tied together with leather crisscrossing through them.

"Sorry, I didn't even realize I did it. Probably just tired; haven't been sleeping the best. All good."

"Umm, okay. I don't think I believe you right now. *But* if that's the case, we have plenty of energy drinks to perk you up a bit." She goes back to focusing on her hair, her eyes bright in the reflection.

"Is it Blaine, Lil?" *God damn it.* Larissa looks over at me with curious but sympathetic eyes. "Sorry, I don't mean to pry. I just know you were starting to have your thing, and then you know... your brothers..."

"I don't want to talk about that, honestly. I appreciate you asking, though. I know you just wanna help, Liss." I offer her a weak smile before looking down and acting like I'm digging through my own bag, too, as a distraction.

Walking out back to the carriage house, there is a long red carpet bordered by two tall walls of greenery forming a tunnel; the occasional red rose here and there, making you feel like you're traveling into a new little world. When we get to the double doors themselves to head inside, there are gentlemen waiters on either side with no shirts on but black pants and masks. People have already arrived, starting to fill the place rapidly. The guys renovated this place several years ago, I believe. It's essentially been transformed into a club for this exact reason. Ronan's always been a huge partier.

There are deep purple, velvet booths surrounding the walls, in 'C' shapes, a raised stage for the DJ, who is now playing popular hip hop EDM mixes, and space in the middle for dancing and mingling. A portion of the floor has been removed and rebuilt as clear glass on top of wavering rainbow lights, as well as lighting scattered throughout, exactly as you'd see in any huge club, plus faux fire sconces along the walls giving it a creepy vampire feel. They did a phenomenal job; I have to give it to them. I can feel my mood start to lift a little bit being in here now. I went a little simple with my outfit tonight, but I gotta say it turned out great too. Over-the-knee boots, a loose mini skirt, and a fitted top with thick 'v'-shaped straps; all black, of course. We each opted for the black masks over the white ones, as most others have as well, looking around. I don't see my brothers yet, though. I guess they plan on making an entrance.

My phone goes off just as someone brushes past me lingering their hand on my lower back and through my hair discreetly. My heart skips a beat, hoping it's Blaine, but also annoyed if it wasn't. I glance down and see it's from… Blaine. It *was* him that walked past me. He's in an all-black suit and black mask.

> **Blaine**
> You look so sexy in that fucking skirt and those thigh highs. You know that's a weakness for me. I'm fucking you later in just the boots.

I look back up, watching him walk across the open space to the bar on the left, official with two bartenders and all the alcohol anyone could need.

> Thank you *heart emoji*. I can't believe you recognized me, lol. You look amazing, that suit shows off your biceps. I like it, you're beautiful. This sucks not being able to be together! All I want to do is grab you and dance with you.

> Baby, I could pick you out of a thousand-person lineup blindfolded. Stay patient Sunshine. I have a plan ;) Try to have fun with the girls for a while. I can tell you're not feeling it. I'll text you again when it's time.

I look up at him and see his devious smile before looking back down.

We exchange another glance before I suck it up and pay better attention to Katie and Lissa to my right, talking about who knows what.

# 62

# BLAINE

I subtly keep my eyes on my girl without drawing attention from anyone in our circle. God, she looks like a naughty little black devil. I can't wait to surprise her later; I hope she enjoys my plan. Few moving parts, but I have it covered. I can't wait to be buried inside that pu—

"Hey, man! Looking fresh." Ronan comes up to me, slapping me on the back of my shoulder mid-daydream during my dick's disappearing act on his baby sister. Fucker. Knowing he doesn't want me with her makes me wanna pound into her even harder, ruin her. I mean... I do that anyway. I outwardly smirk. But the look on his face when he finds out gives me a new sick pleasure, and a twisted smile forms on my face.

"Thanks for making the dress code easy. Not too hard when ninety percent of my closet is black." Ronan somehow pulled off the red. I wouldn't be surprised if the dickheads had matching suits on. He has a deep red blazer and matching pants, a white undone button-up, and all his favorite sparkly accessories, including his gold and diamond grill hinting through smiles. It's over the top. But hey, if I had a vagina, I'd be all over the rich, tattooed bad boy too. He's never had an issue with getting women.

Sure as shit, I look up and see Art coming down the stairs from the second floor —also where I have my bag stashed for later. They have identical suits on, including their matching white masks to go with their shirts. He makes his way through the crowd, dark blonde strands gleaming, with smiles and shoulder taps until he makes it to the bar where we stand. "Place looks pretty great, huh?"

"You really didn't have to try so hard to impress me, but I appreciate the flattery boys." Artemis gives me a light shove, but Ronan turns to set his glass of whiskey down on the bar, getting our attention.

"Look, Blaine. I don't want to talk on it tonight, but I needed to put the bug in your ear man; something feels off with our uncle. I don't know what it is; maybe it's nothing, and I'm paranoid, like Art thinks. But it shouldn't fucking be taking him this long to do what he has to, you know?"

"So, what are you thinking? Why are you telling me?"

"I think we may need to bring you back with us for another quick drop-in. Nothing crazy, but enough to scare him into getting his ass in gear. You'd think having your skin carved into, knee shot out, and being on the verge of dying would be enough pressure to get the job done."

"Mmm. Can't hurt." I shrug and throw back the rest of my bourbon, setting my glass down with a heavy hand; Ronan's hand resting on my shoulder, nodding in response.

"Hey, downstairs, we have another party if you're up for it. We have a friend coming tonight, Sandra... honestly, I think you'd really hit it off. She's exactly your type. Not looking for anything serious, and loves to play and get freaky, no strings attached. I'll introduce you later when she gets here, but she's a fucking bombshell. Looks like a Victoria's Secret model and fucks like a pornstar. She'll definitely be down for the basement."

"Why don't you fuck her then?"

"Not saying I haven't in the past. But, not this time, I have other plans." Ronan looks around the room just as Artemis shifts like he's about to make his getaway to mingle. I have to smother my laugh that wants to break free.

"So, which one of you gets Katie tonight?" Artemis stays collected, just eyeing me stiffly. I meet his stare without so much as blinking or moving. I'm certainly not intimidated by Art. But Ronan looks over to Art and back to me, too shocked to wear his poker face. Even through their masks, their body language gives them away just as much.

So, my assumption was correct. Either they are actually both screwing her, or Ronan has a thing for her, but she's with Art, and there's a strain somewhere. I don't even wait for a response; I could give a fuck about what they want to say back or what's actually going on between the three of them. I just wanted to subtly let them know I see their game and silently show them how absurd and hypocritical their actions are, having the nerve to *both* fuck Lily's best friend in secrecy but to warn each of us to stay away from each other. I made my point in under ten words.

Nodding slowly with a smirk, my hands in my pockets, I keep Art's gaze as I walk past and calmly make my way through the crowd. They'll be expecting me to go straight to Lily after that as if proving a point. But that's the last thing I'm doing.

I have a Sandra of my own coming. For better, or for worse.

## LILITH

The mask makes it easier to keep a discrete eye on him, held in a web of anticipation. I can feel his eyes on me too. A predator silently watching, hunting. He mostly stays by Elliott and a few others here and there that look familiar. A few women approach him unsurprisingly, and he doesn't hardly even look at them. He's locked onto me, barely responding until they give up and walk away. Is it terrible that his being rude and dismissive of women hitting on him turns me on so much? That might be another thing that needs to be rewired in my brain.

Mean-bad. Nice-good.

I ended up having a drink and dancing with the girls for nearly a couple of hours, finding our way into a booth once it became available, and even managed to start smiling and laughing.

While chatting, my phone lights up with a text from Blaine, and I immediately open it.

> Blaine
> Wait 5-10 minutes and come upstairs to the fourth door on the left, alone.

My heart rate speeds, and I try to fight the smile that's threatening to cross my face. I continue to make casual conversation, half tuned in to what the girls are saying, keeping an eye on the time. Seven minutes in, I excuse myself nervously.

I spot my brothers, separate, but both on the right side of the large open room. Making sure they don't notice me or follow my movements as I make my way upstairs, I watch and look over the railing at the open space below. *One... Two... Three... Four...*

I skip knocking and slowly open the door into a dimly lit room, finding Blaine leaning casually against the wall to the right, smiling wickedly. "You wanted to see me, sir?" I add playfully.

His eyes glow with lightning, and he pushes off the wall towards me, grabbing my waist and locking the door behind me. One hand on my waist, the other now cupping around my ear, he kisses me gently before pulling back slightly. "God, watching you all night knowing I couldn't touch you was torture, you know that?" He bends down and kisses me with a little more force, pulling me against him, as I lean completely into his touch, whimpering. "Fuck, baby." He whispers against my lips, removing both our masks.

I lean my forehead against his, gently caressing our noses together, pressing small kisses to his lips. "Is this what you were planning? A rendezvous in a dark, secret room?" I smile, touching his chest, and leaning into him as he hums.

"Mmm. You're not too far off. Just not this particular dark and secret room." I look up at him, a little confused and intrigued. "Have you ever been to the lower level here, Lily?"

"The basement? Uh, no. I've never had a reason to. I've only ever been in the renovated carriage house a handful of times, probably. I wouldn't guess there's much down there to see. Probably storage."

"Well... not quite what you may expect then. There are special things that happen in the darkness of the basement. Things I think you might enjoy, that I would love to show you." Oh, I'm definitely curious now. What the fuck does that mean...

I nod up at him in agreement, biting my lip inward slightly.

"Mmm. I thought you'd be interested, little siren." He reaches one hand down under my skirt, pulling my panties tight, and presses against my core, rubbing the pads of his fingers into the material. Moving them all the way down my legs, he gently helps me step out of them. He brings them to his nose before balling them up into his right pocket. *Holy fuck, why was that so attractive.* He reaches down again under my skirt and lightly runs two fingers on either side of my clit slowly. "If at any point you don't feel comfortable or want to leave, I want you to tell me. If you don't feel comfortable enough or able to use your words, I want you to tap the tip of my nose twice or use the word 'redlight'. I'm only giving you options; I don't think they will be necessary by any means tonight. I just don't ever want you to do anything you don't really want to. The thought guts me. I'll always keep you safe. I have a wig for you to put on under your mask to act as a disguise for unwelcome eyes. Including, potentially, our friends. Yeah?"

"Yeah." He removes his fingers from my body, stepping back to a black bag he has on the table in the dark room. Pulling out a dark brunette wig, I twirl my hair to tuck it under the wig as he helps me put it on and adjust.

"Wow, this actually feels soft, like real hair. I've never worn a wig before."

"Good, that's what I was going for, so it'd pass as authentic." He helps me put my mask back on, over my wig, making sure that everything is in place and looks realistic before gently pressing a kiss to my lips, pulling away smiling. I can't help but release a smile of my own that stretches across my face. "Ready, baby? I figure after our little expedition, we can sneak out and head home together, yeah?" I nod eagerly, clasping my hands in front of my chest.

# 63

# Lilith

We make our way with Blaine in front of me, down the stairs, through the mostly hidden hallway, and to the top of the lower-level stairs. There isn't a normal door that opens, mystical beads, or even a theatrical velvet curtain. No, it's a short black hallway, completely unlit, that ends abruptly, opening again to the right where a large mirror sits. Our figures are hardly even visible in the near dark, looking back at us. He grabs the side of the mirror, opens it, and pulls it towards us. Here, there's a black, metal spiral staircase leading into the secrecy that's awaiting me. He squeezes my hand in reassurance and comfort as we near the bottom. I can't help but feel a little nervous. What the hell is down here, hidden behind a mirror?

Making my final step, I take in everything around me, trying to hide the positively blatant surprise that's bounding from me. The room is huge, just as large as the main club above us, and drenched in a fire-red hue. There are chandeliers glowing red covering the ceiling, victorian sconces lining the long walls, and red LED lights on the floor outlining most areas. Most areas seem lit well enough. However, engineered spots hiding in the shadows jump out as scattered depths of darkness here and there... interesting. Immediately upon walking in, there are rows and rows and racks on either side full of whips, chains, racks of skimpy lingerie and costumes, blindfolds, handcuffs... everything, including so many items I don't even have a clue what they're for. Looking past that, there are cages large enough to hold round beds, bars, and chains, and things I can't quite make out hanging from them. God, there are swings from the ceiling, several large crosses —one of which is being utilized and observed by many eyes— a small elevated stage, dance poles, mirrors lining nearly every inch, and even what's clearly a hot tub illuminated in red at the furthest corner.

My mouth must be betraying me by hanging open because Blaine leans closer kissing my hand and then my lips, getting my attention. "Okay, so far, baby?" I absently nod at him, still looking around in interest. "Come with me." He starts leading me through the various areas and people. Several of them are getting whipped, multiple threesomes, a woman getting her pussy licked, and a dildo thrust into her... I'm almost relieved I am wearing a wig and mask right now.

Blaine leads me to one of the several spots seemingly designed to serve as a shadow, a place to see but not be seen.

It's like walking through a wall of magic, and I can find my full breath again. "Umm...I... what exactly was your plan for bringing me here, Blaine? I'm not sure I'm ready for—"

He holds me against him, embracing me with his scent, his comfort, and simply *him*. "No, angel. I didn't bring you here to throw you to the wolves. I brought you here to see if we could play here. Here, specifically, in the shadowed cells. I know you are curious and excited by hypothetical exhibitionism, yeah?" I feel a little more confident and at ease with the calm way he's speaking to me, holding me, reassuring me and I smile shyly and nod weakly at him. He's not wrong, as embarrassing as it is. I'm surprised he noticed. "Mmhmm. So... my thought was that you and I could claim this area under the comfort of darkness, which would allow you to watch everyone else while you are hidden from sight. Maybe get used to the idea of being watched without being fully exposed for all to behold. This is all just an idea, baby. I never, never want to do something you don't want to or feel one hundred percent comfortable with okay? That's why I need you to be really honest with me about this. You don't feel comfortable, don't want to be here, we leave now, no questions."

"Yes. I wanna do it. I wanna try. And... if I, you know."

"If you want to stop, we stop. Period. At any point. 'Redlight,' 'stop,' or tap my nose with your sweet little finger if you can't find your words; I'll find them for you." Waiting for my final approval, he tells me to sit on the almost invisible couch behind us. I didn't even see it. I wonder what type of lighting this is to cause this odd effect. It truly feels like being blocked off and hidden, as if the darkness is swallowing any light at all.

Peeking back at me with a ridiculously sexy smile, I watch him walk away.

# 64

# LILITH

I sit on the couch, feeling the soft texture beneath my hands, and let my eyes explore what's happening around us and all the sounds of pleasure reverberating against the walls amidst the thumping, sensual music. Blaine comes back with water bottles, wet wipes, a towel, a small bottle of lube, and a Magic Wand. How does he know about all this? Does he come here a lot? Are these the women he dates? I have a feeling I wouldn't like the answers much if I were to ask him. "Come here, baby." He sits down next to me and pulls me so I'm sitting across his lap, held in his arm. He takes notice of my bunched brows. "What's wrong? Are you okay?"

"Yeah, I'm fine. I just..." I sigh and fiddle with my hands a bit in my lap before meeting his eyes again. "Do you come down here a lot? Like, do you come here and hook up with women? The women that are into all of this?" He looks at me, unblinking and unreadable, as his throat visibly bobs. That's all the confirmation I need.

"...I have. —Does that upset you to know?" We both study each other, sitting so closely I can feel his heart rate pick up.

"It does. I'm sorry. I know it's unreasonable, and I have no right to feel that way, but it does kind of hurt for some reason. I don't know why. I mean, I knew... some things... from my brothers and Katie." I grimace slightly, feeling awkward bringing it up. "But now, seeing all this, I'm realizing I might never be enough for you, Blaine. I'm sorry." I start to look away, but he traps my chin in his fingers, forcing me to look at him.

"You have the right to feel all of it, Lily. Don't ever apologize for that. If anything, it just shows me you care. Trust me, Lilith, never in my life, up to this moment, have I ever really regretted the shit I've done. If any part of me believed or knew that I'd end up on this couch with you, caring about you as much as I do, I would have done a hell of a lot differently. But I can't change that. I can't suddenly take back what I've done or the women I've been with. If I fucking could, I absolutely would, just so I wouldn't have to see you hurt because of me. You're not just enough; you're more than enough. So much more. You're the most incredible person I've ever known. You're so perfect." There's genuine intensity in his eyes as he watches me, searching my face. What he's just said... is almost enough to make me want to cry if we weren't in the middle of a fucking sex room.

"Blaine..." I almost don't even know how to respond to that with words. "I lo—" I clear my throat and stop myself from spewing the stupid *stupid* words my brain just almost dumped onto him. "You're more than enough for me, too. You always will be. I'm sorry I brought this up. I know I can trust you; I do trust you with every part of me. Just —kiss me, show me, teach me."

"Yeah? You're sure?"

"I'm positive. Please show me."

He leans his face down to mine, stroking my cheek, pressing gentle kisses to my exposed skin on my face. "Just us. No one can see us remember. Not unless we press this button over here." He shows me a bulky remote attached to a thick black wire leading somewhere. "This top button is what's on now, allowing us to be hidden. The middle button will allow for a small amount of red light to ease its way onto us, allowing us to be nearly silhouettes open to wondering eyes. And the same for the last two buttons here and here. In order from dark to light. The last button here fully brings us to the room. I won't touch unless you want me to or instruct me to. And the strips of light around the edge of the floor, there? The fact that they are lit in red means the space is occupied; no one will interrupt."

"Okay." I relax into his arms, thankful that he's explaining everything so simply and is very clear that this is for my enjoyment, no one else's. Not even his.

Well, maybe a little his.

I start to kiss him gently, sensually. Running my hand over his hard, muscled chest and arms, free to touch now that his suit coat is off somewhere. I hum in pleasure against his mouth, causing him to deepen our kiss and slowly tease the skin on my inner thigh before his fingers touch my bare softness, stroking and caressing me. "More, please," I whisper against his lips. He dips his middle finger into me, all the way, pumping in and out, thumb never leaving my clit.

"That's it, baby. Fuck you're so wet already. Does that feel good?" He continues to stroke and curl in and out of me at a perfect pace.

"Yes, yes. I wanna use the vibrator." He pauses.

"God, you are so fucking sexy." His right hand leaves my body, grabbing for the wand. "Sit up and turn around, your back to my chest. Wrap your legs on the outside of my knees —just like that. That's perfect. Good." He has me sitting on his lap, facing outward, my back to his hard chest. He uses his left hand to adjust me and push me into his body so we're perfectly conformed. The other reaches to my clit as he spreads his knees, in turn forcing mine open wide, on display. I smother my gasp as it takes a second to adjust and glance around remembering no one can see us. He presses his lips to my ear, teasing me with his tongue, trailing down my neck, biting between warm licks. He pushes his finger inside me again, pumping as he focuses on my ear, and his left hand reaches up my shirt to tease my hard nipple. I can't help but start rocking against him and sighing; it feels so good. *He* feels so good, his hard length pressed against me. "You like that? Knowing one button would light up your pussy for everyone? *My* fucking pussy. My finger sinking deep, fucking you as you cry out, and everyone watches sweet Lily come undone?"

"Yes, fuck yes." He bites down where my shoulder and neck meet, marking me before sweetly licking away the pain. I feel him reach over, grabbing the wand, the sound coming to life as he wraps around us pressing it to my front. We use the same wand nearly every time we have sex; this isn't anything new. But every time it hits my skin, the first few seconds are overwhelming, and I can't help but cry out in a moan, pressing my lips together to smother it. I feel him roll his hips under me for pleasure of his own and can't help but rock my hips against him as he holds the toy in place for me to control. "Blaine…" I close my eyes, focusing on the sensation in my body and how good it feels, bowing my head forward and bracing my hands on his thighs. I lean slightly to my left and turn my face to look back at him before resting my forehead against his cheek, overcome with the pleasure consuming my body.

"You look so beautiful. Seeing you feel this good is the sexiest fucking thing I've ever seen. I will never get over how beautiful you are. I can't believe you're mine." He presses the wand harder to my skin, the deep rumbling causing my undoing. My body shutters, trying to collapse as I moan too loudly, my climax washing through me. I yell out his name, shaking against the wand still pressed to me as I come down. He pulls it away, silencing the hum, and wraps me against his body, running his hands softly over my thighs and arms. "You did so good. You're perfect. I'm so fucking lucky. You're such a good girl for me."

He brushes the wig hair from my shoulder before telling me to move over, pressing light smacks to my bottom as I move next to him onto the couch. Keeping his hand on my thigh, he moves down onto his knees in front of me. He's pulling me to the edge, burying his tongue inside me before I can even register what he's doing, causing my thighs to jump. I watch down as he runs his tongue over my inner thighs and through my soaking wetness, taking in every drop of me, groaning like my now-soaked pussy is his last meal. God, he makes me feel so good. I've never been with a man like him. I've never felt so secure and comfortable in my own skin like this. I start rolling my hips against his face, breathing heavily. I'm positive my chest is covered in red blotches. When it starts to feel too good, I arch my back, hips tensing, and grab his hair just as he slows and pulls away. I look down at him with a 'what the fuck' expression and see his wicked grin as he stares back at me, taking one full and slow final lick. "Greedy little thing, aren't you?" I try to glare at him, but I can't even manage before my smile takes over my face, causing him to laugh.

"On the floor, sunshine. Get on your knees for me." He helps me stand before I drop to my knees in front of his looming figure.

# 65

# BLAINE

I've never in my life seen anything more beautiful than her. She's so perfect my heart nearly aches just looking at her. I knew she'd at least be intrigued coming down here. I've been keeping my eyes open, glancing for her brothers or anyone in our circle. I know they'll be down here with Katie; at least Ronan will if he's fucking her too. Artemis doesn't seem like the type open to sharing. I guess I'm more invested in their screwed-up triangle than I thought. It's just a matter of timing it right tonight, though, to avoid them.

She's on her knees below me, wig, and mask on, slipping her tongue out between her plump lips. The sight makes my cock jump in my pants. I run my hand over my hard erection, staring down at her big eyes, tipping my head. She moves her hands up my thighs to my waist, pulling my dress shirt out of my slacks. I start to unbutton it and pull it off as she undoes my belt and pants, freeing my cock.

Humming in pleasure, she doesn't waste any time gripping the base of me, swiping her hot tongue against my sensitive head. I have to stop myself from letting my head roll back at the sensation. "Yes, love. God, your mouth feels so good." All I can do is watch as she drags her tongue completely under my shaft, moving to twist around the tip, pre-cum dripping out of me, into her. I grab my hand over hers, gripping my base, and tap it onto her flat tongue, rocking against it. She moves my hand, sliding me into her mouth up and down until I hit the back of her throat, making her gag on me. I want to fist her goddamn hair so badly, but I can't because of the fucking wig. I press the palm of my hand on the back of her head, pushing into her mouth, not stopping the noises and deep moans I'm making. I don't press too hard; she hates that. But hard enough to urge her and help control her movements. She twists her hand around the base of my cock that's dripping with her spit and my pre-cum, sucking me, bobbing up and down my length, gagging. I don't even want to let myself think of her ex-boyfriends and how she got this good at sucking dick. I never want to think about another man's dick in her mouth, in her pussy again. *My* pussy. *Mine.* I can feel my body start to tense, forcing myself not to come yet. I pull away from her and smile, letting my chest rise and fall. "Not yet... I'm not done with you. Get up." She swipes the back of her hand across her mouth, running her tongue through her lips as she stands.

I grab the top of my pants, bringing them back up with my left hand when I pause, spotting them. *Fuck.* They must've come in and walked right by us when she was on her knees for me. Half worry, half twisted happiness takes over at the thought. Plus, the fact I was indeed right, just reinforces that I *do* know everything. We have her 'disguise,' but there's still a good chance they're going to recognize

Lily from her clothes, once we leave the corner of the darkness we've claimed

There, near the lifted stage, is Katie... with both brothers. As predicted. On a low bed, she lowers herself onto Art's cock, pausing and bending forward as Ronan eases a glistening finger into her ass, no doubt stretching her so they can take her at the same time. *Fuck that's hot.* They're all three incredibly blessed appearance-wise. It'd be more difficult not to get hard seeing her getting fucked in both holes by my best friends. I try not to linger my stare, to avoid alerting Lily to their presence. We're covered in darkness; they can't see us anyway.

"I want you to ride me, baby." I sit down, pulling her on top of me, her legs bent on either side of my hips. Pushing her fitted top up over her pert tits, I hold her up, teasing her nipples. I twist my tongue around one tip, feeling it get harder and tighter from my attention, and moan against her soft skin. I spend my time lightly nipping and sucking, teasing both breasts before pressing her down against me. I'm so hard for her; just the touch of her hot slick and warmth on my cock makes me drop my forehead to her neck for a second. Her hips slightly rock against me, her soaked pussy sliding easily over me. I press my jaw down tightly, growling demonically next to her ear, tonguing her earlobe. I smile as she shutters, her body shivering from my voice.

"Blaine... I want you to fuck me, please."

"Mmm. And I want you to give me another orgasm, and then you can have my cock inside you." I reach for our toy again, turning it on as she bites her lip in anticipation. I know she's ready to come again, I pulled away too quickly eating her cunt. "Grip the back of the couch behind me. Sit on me." I press the wand to her clit, and she immediately tenses, hunching forward in a near sob, grip tight on the back of the couch.

"Blaine. —Blaine, oh my god." She rocks her hips against the toy, causing it to get a little too close to my dick, and I almost explode on the spot before quickly readjusting.

"That's right, baby, I am your God."

"Oh god, yes! Yes, fuck!"

"Mmm... just like that," I praise.

"Blaine. Blaine, turn on the lights. Please." *Fuck me.* Part of me wasn't expecting her to want that tonight; not yet. She has no idea her brothers are just on the other side of the room to her right. I'm so ready to come I can't even think straight. Reaching over for the remote, the lights are dimly on us in two seconds, and I can see her so clearly in contrast to the utter darkness before, I can't wait any longer. I pull the wand away, lining myself to her entrance, and push her down, lifting my hips into her in one motion. She's fucking soaked and so pleasure swollen. Pretty sure both of our eyes roll back in our heads as we moan at the sensation. "Oh, god, yes, please. Please." She grinds against me and starts rolling her hips, still gripping the couch.

"That's a good girl. Pray for me, Lilith."

"More. Turn the lights up more." *Fuck.* I couldn't refuse her if I wanted to. I turn up the lights again, and it immediately draws attention from those around us, suddenly able to watch Lily riding my cock more clearly.

"You like that pretty little pussy on display for everyone, don't you? You want everyone to watch my cock disappear into you while you take every hard inch of me like the good fucking slut you are for me, huh?" I press the vibrator back to her, and she screams my name so loudly I'm surprised the people upstairs don't hear her. I love how loud my sweet Lily gets when I'm inside her. "Take the wand. Hold it, baby." She takes it from me, guiding it against herself as I grab her hips, lifting her up and down my shaft at a good pace. "You like that? You like people turned on watching you take me? Watching my thick cock pound into sweet Lilith? Watching you come, wishing it was them touching you, wishing it was them inside you? Hmm?"

"Blaine. Fuck, baby, yes! You feel so good." My rhythm stutters for a few seconds as I stare at her in near shock, hearing her call me baby, as I do her. That's the first time she's called me baby or anything close... fuck me if it doesn't flip something carnal inside me, and I lose any sense of fucking control. *Mine.*

"Open your eyes, sweetheart. Look in the mirror behind me and watch yourself come apart for me. See how sexy you are to me, every time I get to fuck you." She parts her lips, staring at her reflection drenched in red behind me. And with the lights on I can finally see her body in the opposing mirror in front of me; her skirt and top pushed up, riding my cock. I lift her hips and start pounding into her like a ravenous beast. "I'm going to come soon. Can you get yourself there for me?"

"Yes, baby, yes! I'm going... I'm... I'm... so close." She screams my name out so loud, I see in the reflection, her brother Artemis sit up on his elbows, spotting me. A death wish forms on his unmasked face while he's buried in Lilith's best friend. I don't even think twice before pulling the wig and mask forward, off of her, tossing them onto the floor. He already knew it was her, but I just confirmed it. At the same moment she tightens around me, making her little noises and shaking, she moans my name and curses. My eyes locked onto his, I slam her up and down my dripping cock *hard* before tossing my head back, moaning out myself as stars hit the edge of my vision. *Fuck.* I explode inside of her.

I want him to see her, to see *us*. I want him to watch their little sister getting railed hard and deep by the big bad wolf, screaming my name as I ruin her. She grinds her hips against me, still shaking in ecstasy, tossing the wand to the side in silence. "Blaine... oh my god. That was the hardest I've ever come. Wow." I guide her hips, still moving against me as we both fully start to come down from the high, still relishing in the twinges of pleasure racking our bodies.

I look back up in the mirror, taking off my own mask, meeting Artemis' stare, and smile at him, nearly baring my teeth in threat. Just as Ronan follows his brother's line of sight into the mirror, landing on me, he pauses from fucking Katie's ass. Wickedness radiates from me in unforgiving waves, while darkness rains upon us as a night shield, covering us after I press the control switch one last time.

We need to leave, but I can't bring myself to get moving when my sunshine is so soft and relaxed in my arms. Lily leans forward pressing a kiss to my lips before whispering teasingly in my ear. "Forgive me, father, for I have sinned." I can't help but deeply chuckle in return, holding her to me.

"Don't worry, baby, penance comes in many forms."

"Mmm... I guess what they say is true. The Devil himself was an Angel too."

I get her quickly cleaned up, pull her clothes back in place, and toss the mask at her to slide on before grabbing her hand and pulling her after me towards the spiral staircase, her happy chuckles chasing the wind as we go.

We get home, shower, and settle in bed together. All the while, the call, the text... it never comes. I expected one of them to blow up but maybe they're waiting until tomorrow. It is their birthday, after all.

*Happy Birthday.*

My thoughts are devilish as Lily lies snuggled against me, watching TV and giggling at something. I have no clue what, I'm not paying attention. But I can't stop my hand from brushing her hair off of her neck, behind her ear, and squeezing her tighter to me. This perfect woman is somehow mine.

## K. J. FURY

I believe this might be what happiness is.

# 66

# LILITH

Blaine and I just finished a late breakfast. I sit in the sunroom, a book resting in my lap, just thinking and appreciating the view, absently. Thinking about last night, how different and amazing my life has been with him, how beautiful he is when he's happy and vulnerable, just being himself without the façade of who the world thinks he is. I guess he is that person too. When everyone else sees and knows him as one person, does the one single person really know enough to trust that the version of him she sees is true? My heart tells me yes.

I think about what will happen when we finally tell our friends and my brothers. I'm trying to mentally prepare for the onslaught of hurtful, angry responses. I don't know why they're so against us getting close. If he was such a terrible person, they wouldn't be best friends with him for over a fucking decade. I get that they're protective and want what's best for me. But, what if that's him? Maybe they're playing catch up for all the years I wasn't there, trying to play the role of father. But they could loosen the reigns. I can't help but let out a sigh at the thought. I really don't want to be the reason that Blaine's friendship with them could be compromised. I just can't even consider the idea, the way my stomach immediately turns with guilt; which is why it stays between us.

Not to mention, I kind of knew Ronan was into some freaky shit. He's slept his way through Denver several times over and has always made a few too many jokes about his sexual habits to not hold truth to them. But my brothers literally have a sex *dungeon* in their basement? I shiver at the thought and stop my brain before it takes that hellish thought any further, rubbing my eyes. Absolutely not. Thank god Blaine and I were able to sneak out without any of them seeing us leaving the party.

I think about the fact that I've basically been living here at his place, too, after I had agreed to my brothers to move back in with them. I never wanted to. I like my apartment here, even if it's too tiny sometimes. I'm comfortable there. The only reason I agreed was because I thought Blaine and I truly wouldn't happen, and I thought space might have been the best thing for us. Not only us, but our group. In a weird way, I guess I'm thankful for Katie and her ridiculous schemes. Without her introducing me to *'every available man in the metro area',* according to Blaine, we wouldn't be together and so happy.

I release a long breath and lean my head back in the oversized chair I'm in. Whether it's relief, stress, happiness, or anxiousness crowding me, I honestly don't know; maybe all of the above.

Large, warm hands touch my shoulders, causing me to jump and peek my head back to look up at Blaine's smiling face above me.

He starts to knead his fingers and thumbs over my shoulders and neck, sending chills radiating over my body. I can't stop the pleasant, happy little sound that leaves me. "You okay?"

"Just thinking, that's all."

"Mhmm, about?"

I smile and lean forward slightly so I can turn to face him, his hands falling from my neck. "You." I can tell immediately by the grin spreading across his face where this is going to go, already.

"Well... I am very charming. And attractive. And rich. And good in bed, with a great dick. And a certain air of mystery. It's understandable. Honestly, I'm surprised you're able to get through your day and concentrate on anything else." I roll my eyes and push him back, standing to walk away.

"You're ridiculous, you know that?" I huff out an annoyed sigh. I smile but don't let him see it. He stops me, wrapping his arms around me and flushing me against his body, bending to press his cheek down to mine.

"I don't know about that —but you're all I think about. My thoughts are consumed by you. Your smile, your laugh, your soft skin, the way your hair smells, the cute little noises you make... I can't make it five minutes without dreaming of you." I melt against him turning my face to press a kiss to his cheek.

"You can be sweet when you want to be, you know."

"Just telling you the truth of the matter." Holding my face in place with one hand to kiss me, his other reaches deeply into my leggings to simply cup the warmth between my thighs. He does this all the time now. Doesn't push for more. Well, okay, that's not entirely truthful; we both know he certainly likes to play. I asked him why he always just grabs my pussy, holding it, and he said, *"Because it's mine, and I can."* I can't say I hate it; it feels intimate, like he's claiming me in some undomesticated, feral way.

"I have to go get ready, don't distract me!" He grumbles and groans under his breath but lets me go.

"What are you two doing today?"

"Girls day. We're going to get our nails and pedicures done, probably get a coffee or lunch, just catch up. It's been a while since Larissa and I have been able to hang out, just the two of us. I'm really looking forward to seeing her. I love Katie, obviously, she's my best friend. But sometimes, it's nice to be a little more chill with just Larissa and I, you know?" I have a few basic clothing items that have gotten piled up here from all my nights sleeping here with him. Jenny is incredible and launders my items just as she would Blaine's. He even moved some things around and gave me a couple of drawers and a spot in his closet for items to hang. He really is sweet. Sometimes I wonder if it's too fast for something like that. But, I remember that I've known this man for well over a decade. And, it just feels right; natural.

Going into the closet and running my hands through a few things to throw on, I land on black leggings and a long-sleeve shirt. I'll wear my pink leather jacket with it. My phone goes off, making a sound indicating my financial app received a deposit. I peek out into the room, where he sits on the end of the bed. "That's weird... will you check to see what that noise was on my phone?" I grab all my items into my arms and almost run into him on my way back into the room, him holding out my phone. "Oh, you can always look at my phone. You know that, right, baby?" I walk around him and toss everything onto the now-made bed as he comes behind me to press a kiss to my cheek and gently sets my phone beside me.

"I know, beautiful. My phone's open to you too. It's the month and day of your birthday, then 1-5-9. Want company in the shower?" *My birthday.* Not his.

"I kinda like you. I think I'll keep you." Grabbing his hand, I lead him to the bathroom. "Come on."

I wasn't planning on getting my hair wet. But that went out the window pretty quickly. With Blaine's kisses, touches, and our wet bodies connecting, it didn't take long until I was begging for him. By the time he was finished taking me against the wall, my body was flushed and my hair half damp and limp. We ended up shampooing each other's hair and he tried to get me back after I formed his into a bubble-soaked mohawk that made me almost fall down from laughing so hard. He said I'll pay for that one later, but I think my punishment won't be such a bad thing considering he could barely keep the smile off his own face. His inner child glowing.

After getting out, I go to pick up my phone. I already know I'm running late and need to text Larissa if she hasn't already texted me. Before it opens, there on my home screen is a notification I had completely forgotten about. *"Blaine!"* He walks out of the closet and looks at me with his eyebrows up. "You... do you know you accidentally sent me four hundred dollars?" I hold up my phone, walking over to him to show him.

"Mhmm," he chuckles sheepishly, disappearing back into the closet.

I follow him in, still holding my phone up for some reason. "Why... why? I don't understand..." He gently pushes my arm down and presses a kiss to my forehead, hair still wrapped in a white towel.

"I want you both to have a good day together. I figured that would be enough?" I stare at him for several moments as he goes back to looking through his clothes hung up in front of him.

"Oh, Blaine..." I whisper. "I can't accept this. It's too much." He stills, looking at me before meeting me again in a few casual strides, cupping my cheeks.

"Trust me, baby, there's no such thing as too much with you. It would be my pleasure to do this. I just want you to have a good day. It would hurt me far worse if you seriously declined. Look around; we're not exactly hurting for cash, sunshine." There's so much to unpack there...

"We're?" He faces the other way, looking back through his shirts, grabbing things from the hangers, not even looking at me.

"Mhmm." So casually, like it's not a big deal. I have to shake my head to think clearly, the towel toppling to one side before I take it off.

"Umm, okay. If, you're sure?"

"Mhmm."

"Stop saying that."

"Mmm. Mhmm." I lightly smack his arm before tucking myself against him in a hug. He immediately grips me tightly, kissing the top of my hand, and running his hand up and down my back.

"Thank you..."

"Mhmm."

*"Stop!"* We break apart, both grinning, and I smack him a little harder before running away before he can catch me.

# 67

# LILITH

Blaine let me take his Maserati, and I have to say... Lissa and I are having the best day ever. The SUV is amazing, with tinted windows, and the system in it? I can feel the bass in my chest. I think we've played the top songs from the last three decades, singing or dancing the entire way. I hope to god he doesn't have secret spy cameras in here because I think we'd both die of mortification.

Pulling away from a coffee drive-thru, I pass Lissa her iced mocha. Our oldie-but-goodie Karaoke go-to starts playing, and she turns up the dial, singing.

"I'll tell you what I want, what I really, really want." She passes the invisible microphone back to me.

*"So, tell me what you want, what you really, really want."*

"I wanna, I wanna, I wanna, I wanna!"

"I wanna really, really, really wanna zig-a-zig, ahh!" We finish off the chorus together.

We burst into giggles, going for a bit of a longer joyride than we need to before heading to the nail salon. Lissa and I would have had a great day together, no matter what. But all of this... is because of him and his generosity. And I can't even tell her about how amazing he is.

"Lil, you, okay?" She turns down the music.

"Oh, yeah! Sorry I just totally zoned out." I look over at her, nodding reassuringly. "But hey... I hate to ask this of you. But can you please not tell anyone... like... anyone —not even Katie, that Blaine gave us his car today and everything? It's complicated, and I don't want to talk about it. But just... please? Can we leave it at that?"

"Honestly, I assumed that was a given." She sympathetically smiles and laughs a little, but I see it. There's curiosity in her kind, beautiful eyes. I look away before I do something foolish, like confessing everything.

We pull into the parking lot of the salon and finish the cookies we got at the coffee shop before heading in. "Oh my *god*, this is so good." I throw my head back into the seat, sitting a little sideways towards Larissa. I'm obsessed with sweets. It's right up there with sex. And honestly, up until Blaine... I would have voted for a piece of devil's food cake over dick any day. Now, yeah, not so much. I had finished maybe three times *ever* with a partner. Now, I come at least once like eighty percent of the time. Even if I don't, I just love being intimate with him. Our hearts close together feels like home. I was recently ovulating and feeling incredibly randy; he pushed me for seven orgasms, and I was out of my head, spinning in disbelief. Granted, we use toys all the time, but still. He was rather full of himself for the next two days; the jerk. I cram the rest of the cookie in my mouth. "Ready?" I sound like a squirrel with too many acorns in its mouth, trying to chew and swallow.

Larissa and I spent the rest of the day getting an early dinner chatting after our pedicures and getting our nails done. She snaps a cute picture of our sets. I chose a bright red color, and she got a creamy light pink, which oddly kind of reflects our personalities a little too well.

Pulling up to her apartment building, I get out and hug her, happy and content after such a wonderful day. "I love you. I had so much fun today."

"You have no idea, Lil. I needed this so badly. Tell Blaine thank y— err, wait, I guess not. Umm, never mind. Whatever you see fit," she laughs. "Anyway, today was honestly perfect, thank you! Text me when you get home, safe! Bye!" I wave at her as I walk around the front of the rather maleficent-looking grill, climbing back inside.

Sighing in deep contentment, I get in, turn the music to something relaxing, and check my phone. No notifications. It's already dark by now. I mostly think I know where I'm going, to get home. But I put it in the GPS anyway to be sure.

I'm half zoned out when I glance in the rearview mirror and notice the car behind me suddenly speeding up, barreling towards me. Their lights getting brighter and brighter. "What the fuck?" I mutter. By the time they're right behind me, I try to swerve to the side of the highway so they can go around me. They mimic my actions immediately and slam into the rear end of the car, blowing the back window out on impact. I think I scream from terror, but I'm not sure. *Oh my god, what do I do!* I try to take control of the swerving vehicle, righting it. I don't know if I should pull over to the side and let them know to leave me alone; maybe they think I'm someone else. Oh, god... what if they think I'm Blaine? My heart is hammering out of my chest, I can feel it in my throat, heaving for breath. Should I slam on the gas and try to lose them? I press down as far as it will go, but they're right behind me. I grip the steering wheel in a death grip in case I need to control the car again. *Think.* You're supposed to drive to a well-lit area or to a police station if you're in danger.

Suddenly, they're swerving behind me from left to right, their headlights bouncing from each of my side mirrors. Terror has me in a full grasp as I try to fucking think clearly. Shots fire out, and I scream, ducking. My body is yelling at me to *get away, get away, get away. GO!* Adrenaline pumps through me enough to practically vibrate.

I realize there's another car zooming to their side, and gunshots fire everywhere. I'm going as fast as I can, but I can't get away. Several bullets hit the car, and I scream again as I feel the back tire behind me give out, causing me to lose control of the vehicle. The car immediately behind me slams into the rear on the driver's side, sound exploding as the tire blows. I don't even have two seconds to think before I'm screaming, the vehicle skidding to the side, and I feel myself flipping and then upside down. I impulsively squeeze my eyes shut, gripping the steering wheel, the airbag exploding painfully into my face as I hear the crunch and skid of metal over the highway, gunshots still being fired. The glass in the windows blows out, and I open my eyes as I think everything starts to stop spinning, stops flinging my body. God, everything hurts. My eyes sting from the powder the airbags release, a shrill ringing deathly loud in my ears.

The last thing I can make out is headlights in the dark skidding to a halt as black boots jump out towards me. I try to breathe, shaking, and then... there's nothing.

I drift into a sea of unconsciousness and shadow.

# 68

# LILITH

## *Before:*

The sharp scent of whiskey brings me to a half state of awareness first. Just before someone roughly pushes inside me, their weight between my thighs. Startled back to a drowsy reality, I gasp and push away in a purely instinctual response, adrenaline pumping through me. "Stop. Stop!" *Xavier?* Shoving him off me, I manage to in-turn push myself off the bed, and tumble to the floor, everything coming into a dimly lit picture. The city's lights filter through the sheer curtains, illuminating Xav's face and the rest of our bedroom.

"Jesus, Lilith, what the fuck dude, seriously?" I stumble over nonsensical syllables in response, just trying to form words as I realize it's just him, and I'm okay. I think I managed an apology, moving the mass of hair that fell in front of my face. Fuck, I can't breathe. I start to shiver, fighting back tears that are burning behind my eyes. I'm okay. It's okay.

"You act like I'm fucking raping you or something! Fucking Hell." His words echo through what feels like a fog surrounding me, limbs weak and the taste of blood somehow in my mouth. It takes me a few seconds to realize he's putting on his pants and shoes.

"I- I'm sorry," I croak out, hand over my chest. I try to calm my breathing, a new panic taking over that he's leaving me. "Where are you going?" Glancing over at the small bedside clock, it's almost three in the morning. Nearly choking on my own spit, I find the strength to crawl back up and return to the bed. "Hey—"

"Don't fucking worry about where I'm going."

"Baby, wai—"

"Nah, I'm not dealing with this shit. I had a great fucking night. You know how many women I could've hooked up with that I turned down? For what— this bullshit? Come home, and my girlfriend acts like I'm raping her? I don't deserve this shit. I already told you either way I'm getting my needs met. Tonight, it just won't be by you. Waste of my fucking time."

I scramble off the bed, trying to grab his wrist. No, he can't do this. "I'm sorry! I'm so sorry, okay? I didn't mean to upset you, Xav, I promise. Please just stay, I'll do anything you want." He pulls out of my grasp, grabbing his keys from the dresser.

He mumbles something I can't understand, broad shoulders a shadow in the space as he reaches the living room and exits our front door. "Xavier! Please!" Tears start falling down my cheeks as I call after him. "I'm sorry! Please. I'm sorry…"

The sound of the door slamming is my undoing. Sobbing, I clench my chest, letting everything out. I didn't mean to upset him. I finally got my first real boyfriend, and my past is ruining everything. Anxiety wracks me just at the thought I'm pushing him into someone else's bed. Images of him with another woman. Someone who isn't fucking broken and used. Maybe that's what he deserves.

I barely make it to the toilet before getting sick at the thought. Resting my hands on my forehead, I try to stop myself from getting sick again. But it's no use.

*"You act like I'm fucking raping you or something!"* His words replay in my head as tears stain my face on the floor of the bathroom, a conjuring of disturbing images flooding me.

I have to make this up to him. I can't keep letting my past control and ruin my life.

# 69

# BLAINE

I'm in my home office, thumb and fingers rubbing my tired eyes from staring at a computer screen for too long. I lift my wrist, leaning back in my padded leather chair, checking the time since Lil's not back and hasn't texted me. Little after six o'clock. I sigh, grabbing my phone, and get up to head towards the kitchen, wondering if I should text her. I don't want to be overbearing, though. I have a feeling her independence will always be important to her. I have come to trust her one hundred percent; that's certainly not the reason. I just want to make sure she's okay.

Jenny's taking the day off since it's Sunday. It's just me. Everything's quiet as I pad along to the kitchen and grab a beer out of the fridge, looking through the meals she has prepared for us. I twist off the cap, tossing it under the cabinet to my left, in the hidden trashcan; my attention back on the glass containers in front of me.

My phone rings— Tree's ringtone. I immediately pick it up from the center island, bringing the phone to my ear, and freeze at what I'm hearing. "Track Lily's location NOW." Gunshots and bullets hitting metal echo in the background as Tree has me on speaker in his car, the noise of him grunting and hissing through his teeth. I flash into action, grabbing my keys, out the door, and onto the elevator before I even know what's happening. *Lily's in danger.*

"What the fuck is happening! Where is she!" I'm out of the elevator, sprinting to my car.

"She... *FUCK!...*" The sound of shattering glass comes through as I start the car, the call automatically connecting to bluetooth, now blaring loudly through my speakers. "She's being trailed, they're trying to—" His growling as he's clearly trying to maneuver his gun and steer, interrupting his speech. "—Trying to force her to pull over. Track her location; we're northbound twenty-five, past Hampden... fucker!"

"En route now. Hold out, Tren." The overwhelmingly loud sound of crashing metal, as a tire clearly blows, explodes through my speakers before I hear metal skidding over pavement, glass shattering, and a thunderous sound of a vehicle crashing falls.

"*LILY.*" Tree releases a deep, horrified yell, and I swear I could hear a faint female scream of terror that he must swiftly drive by.

"No... no, no, no, no, *NO!*" I pull the throwaway phone from my glove compartment pressing '1' for Zach.

"Already on it, Blaine. Hang tight..." The location of my Maserati pings on the screen of the phone gripped tightly in my hand as I speed down the road, now getting on the highway, hitting a hundred-sixty. I know exactly where they are.

"Keep eyes on them, Zach! Hack into all street cameras and fucking doorbell cams if you have to!"

I'm gripping the steering wheel so tightly; all I can think of is how scared Lily must be or if she's been injured. I know exactly who the fuck this is. The exact reason I've had Tree's eyes on her every day.

The sound of screeching tires comes through the speakers just as the echo of a round of bullets bouncing off of metal does, more tires peeling away against the pavement. *"LILY* — They have her Blai—" His voice cuts off as something crashes into Tree's vehicle, the sound of him most likely pounding into the median stopping him short.

*"TREE!* Tree!" Nothing... silence. *"FUCK!"* My foot's all the way on the floor, passing through lanes and around the sparse cars on the road, slamming my fist down on top of the wheel. *I'm almost there, baby...* There's no way they have her, no. *No.*

"I have them, Blaine. Tracking through street cams. I got eyes. Still northbound. Black SUVs – two. No plates." I barely hear Zach. All I can do is grip my steering wheel until *there.* Mine and Tree's vehicles smashed to pieces and wrecked, Tree flipped against the median in the distance. I smash on the break to stop at my car. I have to check, I have to.

"LILY! —*LILY!"* I scramble out of the car, but there's no one. They have her. "No..." I sprint towards Tree a couple of hundred yards away, the car blazing in fire from the hood. Running up, he's bloodied and unconscious, a huge gash on his forehead dripping blood over his face and down his neck. Fuck, his shoulder is bleeding through his fabric, most likely a gunshot wound. He has his bulletproof vest on, hit just a couple of inches away. I fling the door open, unbuckle him, and pull him out, my hands under his shoulders. We have to get away from this fire before it explodes the entire fucking car. Carrying the goddamn giant, I drop him as quickly and gently as I can, pulling my phone out of my pocket. I don't know when, but I lost Zach. I look around as a car passes by, slowing to gawk over the horrific scene.

"*911, what's your emergency?*"

"Twenty-five and Downing, northbound. Two car accident. One unconscious and bleeding. Car's on fire." I hang up before she can respond, speed-dial '6' for Rye.

"Hey, kid!"

"Rye... I need you, man. It's my girl."

"Tell me what you need."

"I need a group of your men from the club, that you'd trust with Lucy's life. I'll pay well. Now, right now."

"Send me a location." This time he hangs up first. I call Zach, and he immediately picks up.

"You have a location?"

"Still on the move, trying to keep eyes on cams where I can, man. They're heading out of the metro though, still north. That's all I have right now."

"Good work. If I lose you again, call or text my main line with any updates, not this one."

"Copy." I'm standing on the side of the highway, in the chaos, trying to spot flashing lights, when I hear movement behind me. *Tree.* I rush down to his side.

"Fuck man, I'm sorry, Blaine." He's dazed and can't focus as I approach, wincing in pain. Fuck, I need to apply pressure to his shoulder. I'm not thinking clearly.

"Stop moving. An ambulance is almost here, Zach has eyes on her trail, and I have Rye sending reinforcements." Speaking of, I mentally narrow down the general areas I can guess they'll be taking her if they're still heading north, out of the city. An abandoned farm and dirt road sits about seven minutes off Highway twenty-five, just outside of the city limit. I drop a pin on my phone and send it to Rye with my free hand who immediately texts back confirming.

"Zach, you still there?"

"Here, boss."

"Sending you a pin. Call Lily's dickhead fucking brothers and fill them in. I don't have the time to deal with their shit."

"Copy."

I see flashing red and blue in the distance, glancing down at Tree again. "Go... I'm fine. Go. Get Lily." I nod in thanks and take off towards my car, fishtailing as I speed away, hands covered in his blood.

# 70

# LILITH

Oh god, my head is pounding... *everything* hurts. I open my eyes, but everything's mostly dark, and I can't make anything out clearly. Where am I? What... what happened? The phantom touch of gentle hands leaves goosebumps on my cheeks and the impression my mother's energy is somehow with me, calming me a fraction.

My hands are tied above my head, and I realize I can't move them after a couple of attempts. My... my hands are tied above my head? It all comes rushing back to me; the car accident, the gunshots, the black boots coming towards me. I blink several times and move my head a little to try to take in what's happening and where I am. My heart is immediately hammering in my chest from fear. Moving my neck hurts like a bitch and sends a sharp pain into my skull and back. I try to quiet the cry that comes from the blinding pain, but it isn't enough. A voice cuts through the night-dark room, causing my body to lock up.

"Looks like our little princess is up already. Weren't expecting you for some time. You're even prettier awake, and that says a lot." It's dark, but everything flickers to life with what's seemingly an oil lamp being lit to my left. Still blurry, but I'm starting to be able to see more clearly. I try to look around. I'm in an old bedroom, I think. It's either abandoned or a fucking crack house. Half the drywall is missing from the wall to my left. The bed I'm in —tied to, looks disgusting enough that I fight back bile in my throat. There's a small, old table at the end of the room, straight ahead. And there —the man. No, two men. One is sitting against the doorframe, the other now standing, stalking toward me like an unhinged, crazed animal.

"Hi, pretty."

"Who are you? Where am I?" I wince at the slight movement of trying to pull away from where he stands at the end of the bed. God, it fucking reeks.

"Well, I'm Hinder, and this is Beck. We're watching over you to make sure you stay nice and safe, away from all the things that go bump in the night." He laughs at his own stupid joke, and I start to think I'm right about this being a fucking crack house if he actually thinks he's funny. I just stare up at him, trying to move, but I'm in so much pain, I can't even do that. This really isn't good. Neither Blaine nor Larissa have any clue where I am, and he's probably out of his mind since I haven't come home yet. Oh my god... his car. No... wait. Surely someone had to have reported the accident, right? Maybe the police can look up his plates and get a hold of Blaine that way. At least then he'll know I'm... I'm what? Missing? The thought alone just makes me want to sob. God, his car. *No.* He's going to be so furious at me. The first time he let me use his car, and after he was so nice to Lissa and me today. I feel like fucking shit. Why is it always like this? It's always my fault when bad things happen. What are the odds any of my friends would ever be fucking kidnapped after crashing their boyfriend's way too-expensive car? This is Lily Luck. Only happens to me and is always my fucking fault. I feel sick on so many levels. I wouldn't be surprised if he's so pissed he never wants to speak to me again. All I can do is lay here in pain, and let the tears slip through the corners of my eyes in silence. My brain is so foggy I can't think straight, and I'm in so much pain. Then it hits me; what if I never get away from here? From these men? I can't breathe from the flare of panic that shoots through me.

The one called Hinder smiles and moves closer to me, sitting on the end of the bed. My eyes fling towards him as he sits and I realize he's very obviously high on something. "Don't be scared, little girl. You can trust me. We're going to have so much fun later. I've been waiting to meet you." He reaches out his hand and touches my ankle. I jerk back in response, sending my knees completely bent but also an insanely painful punch to my back. "Shhh. Shh now. You're okay." He grabs both of my ankles in a firm grip, and I'm too weak to pull out of his grasp, even remotely. He's too strong. He pushes my ankles towards me, so hard they're pressed against my butt, now slightly lifted from the bed. I want to scream from the hurt. His friend by the door frame perks up for the first time.

"What are you doing?"

"Just having a little fun with her, don't worry about it." He leans forward, holding me firmly in place, and gets close enough to my sex to take a deep breath, smelling me, moaning in pleasure. "You smell so good, pretty girl." I try to wiggle away, but it's useless, especially with how stiff and in pain I am.

"Stop. Please, *please.*" I toss my head back, crying and gritting my teeth in agony, the movement blacking the edges of my vision like I'm going to pass out, wetness slipping from the corners of my eyes. "What do you want with me? Please, get off me."

"You say that now. But soon, darlin', you're going to be begging for me, trust me." He bends down completely, pressing his nose against the apex of my thighs, running it up and down, licking my filthy leggings. "Fuck, she smells so good, Beck. I know this pussy's going to be so fucking tight and warm. I get her first."

"Get *off me!*" I use any energy I have to try to push him away from me, my gruff scream piercing through the still air. He grips both ankles in one hand, reaching up with the other smacking me hard across the face.

"Shut the fuck up. You can be stupid all you want little girl. But mark my words, we'll have you begging. You think you're the first little bitch we've had to pick up that wanted to fight?" He laughs demonically, shifting on the bed so he has my ankles gripped, knees straddling my hips, and starts pressing into me, mimicking the movement like he's fucking me as I struggle to pull away, bile rising in my throat from pain. "Trust me, angel... saying yes is going to be much more pleasant for you than fighting all of us the whole way. If you're good for me, I'll make it good for you."

"*Fuck you.*" I spit toward him; I don't even know if it hits him, my vision is so out of focus. But, I immediately regret it. He flies forward so fast, choking me into the mattress, everything starts to go black what feels like within seconds, electricity running along my neck. I feel his hand reach under me, yanking my leggings upwards, just far enough to expose my ass. I'm desperate for air, unable to stop him with my hands tied, and I know my face is red from the pressure. They're going to rape me while I'm unconscious. For a split, disgusting moment, I wonder if that's better or worse than being cognizant of whatever's coming. Younger Lily experienced both. In age, I don't know which is the greater evil. I feel him rub and grind against me, the feel of his rough jeans against my skin, as I hear the sounds of his belt buckle.

Just as everything goes nearly black, there's what sounds like a huge explosion downstairs, causing both men to jump and run into the dark hall. I gasp for breath, coughing, and the dam breaks; tears pouring from my eyes and down the sides of my face. I'm in the worst physical pain I think I've ever felt and, by far, in the worst situation I've ever found myself in. I blink thoroughly to clear my eyes of tears and try to make myself think clearly; maybe there's a way out, or somehow, I can get my hands free and maybe get out the window. I just need to focus and think, past my cries and uncontrollable shaking.

# 71

# BLAINE

Artemis and Ronan have each called me about six times in a fucking row. Understandable, but infuriating. I finally answer, so they stop. "What."

"Where the fuck is she!"

"Why don't you ask your uncle dearest?"

"Now isn't the time to fuck with us, Blaine. Lily is our sister. Where. The. Fuck. Is. She?"

"Your uncle's men have her. Wanna guess why? You can do it," I seethe.

"What the fuck are you talking about —our uncle's *'men'*. This isn't a fucking mafia movie Blaine!" I white-knuckle the steering wheel so hard I'm surprised it doesn't bend.

"—I have one of my guys tracking street and door cams to see how long we can track them and hopefully where they stop with her. We've narrowed down the areas where they could be headed and I have a team meeting us at the abandoned farm to help once we have her exact location."

"What, Rye's gang pieces of shit? This is exactly what the fuck we're talking about, Blaine!" A loud sigh. "Look... we just have to get her back and make sure she's safe. We're not doing this right now. Just fucking get her back. Zach sent us the address; we're already heading to the farm." Artemis hangs up before I can speak. They blame *me?* That's rich. My phone goes off again —Zach. I immediately accept the call.

"Got her."

"Send it to me."

"Done."

"You're getting a huge bonus, Zach." He huffs on the other end.

"Go get your girl, Blaine." He ends the call before I can even answer.

I immediately send out her now-confirmed location to Rye to pass on, and then to her brothers, flooring it and changing our meeting point. Since we're all already trailing them from Zach's handiwork, we're barely behind. I could kiss the devil himself right now for that small win in this fucked situation.

Pulling up, a few minutes out from the location Zach tracked her to, it's pitch black. The only light's that of the moon and my headlights, which I kill to avoid being spotted, along with the unnecessarily loud fucking engine opposing the quiet of the night. Turning it off, I sit, letting my eyes adjust before stepping out in the dark, cold air; the only sounds are distant cars passing along the main road now and then, and crickets in the brush. Surrounding the road, there's nothing. Nothing but overgrown grass and dead trees.

I make my way to the front of the car, lifting the hood to access a hidden button in the storage trunk. Pressing it folds out a small pin pad for a code only I know. Entering it, a compartment under the bottom of the storage space frees itself, loaded with weapons. I position a bandolier over my chest and load up with a few knives and a couple of guns, a third staying in my hand. I look over the hood that's propped up before closing it and see the outline of an SUV quickly making its way with what would appear to potentially be Ronan and Artemis not too far behind them. I stand in the middle of the road and adjust everything, waiting.

The black SUV turns off its lights and comes to a stop behind my car, five men jumping out. The driver and passenger walk over to me, both wearing all black. Once they get closer, I realize I know who they are.

"Look who we have here, boys. Haven't had the pleasure of seeing you in a while. You really grown up, kid." Jungle reaches out his hand, pulling me in enough to tap my back in greeting.

"Now's not exactly the time for a reunion." The brothers pull up behind the SUV, turn off their wagon, and rush to join us. Thankfully they don't interfere or interrupt.

Jungle is a big man. He's older than me, about fifty-five or so, and looks exactly like anyone named fucking 'Jungle' would. Tanned skin, huge salt and pepper beard, a long ponytail behind him, with hair ties incrementally placed a few inches apart and covered in shitty prison ink. Glancing back at the crew, they all have their club cuts on, waiting for instruction; the brothers now closer to me. "My team was able to trace an abduction here to this location. The door cam on a house we passed is the last thing traceable. An aerial map search reveals there are only two other houses on the road before it dead ends. One's lived in, one's abandoned. You can guess which one we're headed to. They have an estimated five hired-muscle, the sack of shit leading, and of course the girl —all at the house."

He gives me an unreadable expression before taking in the area around us and the knives strapped to my chest, nodding. "This your girl they got?"

"Yes."

"Let's go have some fun then, boys."

"Keep the old fat fuck alive. Have fun but keep him alive for me. He's done a great deal to her, and we need to repay the favor."

"Understood." He glances the brothers over from head to toe and heads back to his MC without another word. He knows as well as I do, they're a fucking liability being here. The sound of guns being passed out, boots on gravel, and insects are the only things breaking the silence. I triple-check my straps quickly and spot Ronan pulling a handgun out of the back of his jeans. Artemis catches the movement, trying to piece together what the hell is going on around him.

"I don't have a gun. Everyone has a gun."

I throw one of mine at him and watch the look in his eyes as a gun flies through the air at him, before turning to march up the dirt road. Car doors thud closed, and quiet footsteps fall behind me, I assume everyone in tow.

# 72

# BLAINE

I make my way through the dark halls slowly as the chaos echoes downstairs. Rye's team had the advantage and strategically entered and attacked Lily's capturers. There are still several gunshots being fired; I assume there are still a couple of men hiding and fighting them. That's not even close to my main concern. I bypassed the attack and immediately started searching the rooms upstairs.

It's dark as shit, and they have the upper hand, knowing the layout of the house and all its places to stay out of sight. I'm walking blind. I'm making my way to the west side of the house, where there are only three remaining doors. The first comes up on my left, already open. Swinging inside, it's a bare bathroom with a busted window, letting in a small howl from the night air. I trace my steps back silently, making my way another seven feet or so to the second door on the right. The door is opened about a foot. Gun held at arm's length, I move as a shadow would in the darkness, fury buried but waiting just under the surface for the opportunity. I watch inside the open door of the room, listening for several seconds, when I hear a faint movement in the third door down the hall on the left. To be sure, I push the door in front of me open, eyes quickly assessing the bedroom; otherwise, empty outside of a stained twin mattress on the floor and a scratchy blue blanket that looks like it could have been buried with a dead fucking dog ten years ago.

I take a couple of deep breaths, knowing the last room is where my world is, and I could be walking into a wolf's den, putting us both in danger if I don't play this right. I should wait for backup. But, I'm not going to fucking do that. I have to get to her, to see her; hold her and let her know I'm here and she's safe now.

Stepping through the doorframe, I push the already-open door the rest of the way, spotting movement to the far right. An old, dim gas lamp suddenly flares to life, faintly covering the dark room in a golden haze. *"Lily."* I move towards the crying figure on the bed and make it all of two strides before two guns are both held against my head and pointed toward Lily. "I'm here. Don't worry, baby. You're okay. Just stay calm and breathe for me." They have her hands tied above her head against an old metal bedframe, duct tape covering her mouth, and... her fucking leggings are torn down below her hips. Red starts to cloud the edges of my vision as my heart pounds through my chest, seeing her like this.

"You're far too predictable, boy." I slowly turn my head to the right, where the gun is pressed against my temple.

"Robert."

"Oh, come on, you can sound a little more excited to see me than that." He chuckles, tilting his head and surveying me. "I told you now, son. You're in over your head. I've been playing the game, leading the board, since before you were even in your momma's womb. But you had to play your dirty little games, not thinking shit through. You acted impulsively, not methodically, son. You still have a thing or two to learn from the old dogs, it seems."

The best thing I can do for Lily is buy us time until Rye's men end the shootout downstairs and head up here. It's just a matter of time, so I'm not outnumbered. If I try to save Lily now, there's a bullet that'll be in my head in under two seconds. I need to get the door into my view and out of the way. Slowly turning, I offer a smile with both hands up, the gun resting between my thumb and index finger, in the air. Out of the corner of my eye, I see a shadow just outside of their view to the left of the doorframe. My body tense and ready, I control my face and voice to reflect that of calm.

"I gotta say, Robert, I don't really give a fuck. I guess one thing I've never been good at is kissing someone's ass." In the corner of my eye, in under a second, I see the shadow raise its hands, and a bullet flies past me into the wrist of the dog pointing his gun at Lily. Another flies into his shoulder as I grip my gun, pulling the trigger into Robert's shoulder and twist his wrist, watching as his injured knees give out, landing him onto the dirty wooden floors, bleeding. Another shot to the shoulder for good measure. Jungle immediately is in the room, shooting a bullet through the chest of the man targeting Lilith as he lies on the floor covered in blood. Turning his attention to Robert, gun pointed at him, I go to Lily. A matter of seconds is all it takes for these situations to go poorly, and for a life to end; seconds.

I desperately cup her face in my hands, running my hands over her body for injuries franticly, before pulling a knife and cutting her hands free and pulling the tape as gently as I can from her soft lips. "Baby, I'm here. I'm here. You're okay. You're safe." I press my forehead into hers as sobs and cries reverberate through the room, pulling her against me and seeing she winces in pain from the movement. She's hurt. Fuck, of course, she's injured. "Shhh. Shhh, it's okay. It's okay." She clings to me desperately, shaking, while I reach down and pull her leggings back up to cover her bottom. "Where are you hurt? Did anyone touch you?"

"I'm... I'm okay. I wan —wanna go home, please take me home. Pl —please. Please." She sobs against me, hanging on for dear life, and I can feel my heart breaking in my chest at her pain. It takes everything in me not to put a bullet through Robert's disgusting fucking piece of shit rapist face. I glance up at Jungle, whose attention is still on Robert, bouncing to Lily and me occasionally.

"You're never leaving me again. We might need to take you to the hospital, baby; you were in a car accident, remember?" I can't stop touching her, fuck. She's okay. I have to keep telling myself she's here with me and okay. Ronan and Artemis rush upstairs; the fight downstairs must've been safe enough for them to come into the house. Their eyes both immediately land on Lily in my lap, Jungle pointing a gun, and then fall to their uncle on the ground bleeding. "Your brothers are here, baby. Open your eyes. I'm going to give you to them for a minute." Ronan comes charging over first before I stop his arms. "*Stop!* She's hurt. Be fucking careful."

"She's my baby sister, I would never hurt her, asshole." He reaches over and pulls her to him as she winces and cries out in pain. I rise, scowling at him and grinding my teeth to keep from knocking his teeth in for causing her any more pain. I brush her hair back behind her for a final reassurance of my presence before turning to Robert.

"Fucking pathetic old man. What exactly was your plan here, Robert? Take Lilith as leverage against her own brothers so that you could what? Huh? Get away scot-free? Keep everything in the family name? Or were you going to kill them and me too, after you killed her and run off into the sunset like a fucking piece of shit?"

"You're not as dumb as you look, kid. Your talents were wasted."

I fist my hands, the nails biting deep as I stare down at him.

"You're not going to kill me, Blaine. You know as well as I do that if you end me, you're fucking over Lily and her brothers both. The three most important people in your life. And while you might still do it for tweedle-dee and tweedle-dum, there ain't no way in hell, you're gonna risk anything that will hurt that little girl right there. Isn't that right, big shot?" He chuckles, gripping his shoulder; hands and shirt covered in crimson.

I shake my head letting out a low demonic laugh, looking back down at him with a wicked grin. The edges of reality almost blurring. "Oh. Mmm... you and I are going to have so much fun together." Picking him up under the uninjured shoulder, I toss him into the hall, watching him stumble and try to catch himself on his knees. "Go downstairs. Now." I follow him down the hall towards the staircase, looking back to Lily lying in her brother's arms.

A few steps from the base of the stairs, I kick him forward to the bottom and don't even look at him as he writhes, growling in pain. All the men are here in the living room, accounted for. I scan over everyone to make sure they're not injured and nod at each of them in thanks. There are several dead, bloody bodies scattered on top of each other in the open dining room to the left, Jungle now among his men.

"Fifty grand split to watch this piece of shit while I get my girl taken care of?"

"Absolutely."

Looking over, I watch the brothers come down, holding Lily with her eyes closed, now in Art's arms. "I'm taking her to a hospital."

"Like fucking hell you are." Artemis practically spits at me, trying to get the words out quickly.

"Look, we can fight over this later, but she needs a doctor. It's not up to you."

She starts to stir a little in his arms and can't seem to focus on anything. "Blaine?" She whispers.

"I'm here, baby, I'm here. You're okay. I'm taking you to the doctor now. I need you to just rest and relax for me." I press kisses to her wrist, gently setting her hand back in place against her. She says my name again like a prayer before her head falls, eyes closing. She's covered in blood and may have broken bones or a concussion from the accident. Hell, she could have internal bleeding, for all we know. The thought makes me sick. I failed her. The Maserati was trashed and completely flipped. I look at the brothers and gently scoop her against me, nodding at the men behind me who now have Robert zip-tied to a rickety wooden chair. "I'll be back as soon as I can. If I can't make it back tonight, you will all get paid, but is anyone available to stay longer —a day or two if necessary?" Three men nod in agreement towards me. "Extra thirty grand per day. I'll be back as soon as possible. But my girl is my priority over that disgusting piece of shit." They nod and start to disperse as I leave towards the entrance. "Oh, and one more thing, gentlemen. I left a special note on our friend's chest. Please feel free to take a peek and react accordingly. Just keep him alive for me; that's your hard line. Do not under any circumstances, cross that line. I need him. For now."

Walking out, I hear the brothers following me as I step silently along the long gravel road to our cars. I lay the passenger seat back, gently settling Lily inside and buckling her in, kissing her forehead. She's not even aware of what's going on. A part of me hopes she doesn't remember any of this. Just looking at her, I can't believe how strong she is. She's been through so much in this life that should have broken her. So many reasons to give up. This sweet, smart, beautiful, and creative woman has been dealt the worst possible fucking hand in life. And yet, she keeps going. I want to give her everything. Anything. I will give her anything she wants, to keep her smiling.

"Where are you taking her?"

"Hospital."

"Don't play dumb, prick. Which hospital?"

"Saint Larsen's." I walk around to the opposite side, about to close the door as Artemis stops.

"This is your fault. You know that, right?" Slamming the door, I drive as gently as I can, not to disturb Lily next to me. The silence is nearly overwhelming as emotion clouds my eyes, glancing at her. Grabbing the hand in her lap, I grip it tightly, bringing it to my lips, and gently caress my thumb over her dirty skin.

I know this isn't my fucking fault. I was the one that saved her. Just the idea that she might be seriously hurt with a concussion or internal bleeding, anything... makes me sick. This is her brothers' fault for not forcing their uncle into action. They had no clue what they were doing.

This is their fault.

# 73

# LILITH

Waking up, I come into my body before opening my eyes. I'm so sore; *god, what happened?* I open my eyes and... I don't know where I am. It's fuzzy but comes into focus in a few moments. Oh my god. Everything comes flooding back to me. Totaling Blaine's Maserati, being fucking kidnapped, and... him literally coming to my rescue. He saved me. He... he came after me. How?

He must've taken me to the hospital. Looking down and seeing an IV in my skin makes me immediately want to pass out again or vomit. I have to focus on something else to curb the nausea. The monitors next to my bed are beeping in a steady rhythm. Where is he? I try to sit up, but it's no use. Jesus, why am I so weak? I let my eyes close, lying down, and hear loud voices. At first, I thought someone's TV was too loud in the room next to me. But I recognize those voices... both of my brothers and Blaine. They're all here, then. I want to see him and apologize; I have to talk to him and let him know it wasn't my fault. I fail at trying to sit up without getting lightheaded and give up again, searching for the call button. Wait, why are they yelling at each other? I start to panic a little bit, in my foggy thoughts, the melody of beeping changing pace. Is this because of me? Did Blaine tell them we're together?

"Blaine, you know this is your fucking fault! Lily could fucking be dead because of you and your impulsive bullshit dramatics." Ronan's voice is clear as day, drifting into my room now.

"My...fault? You're kidding me, right? I'm the one who fucking *saved* her! I'm the one who had private security tracking her for this exact fucking reason! I'm the one that had the cameras traced to find out where the fuck they *took her!* *I'm* the one that showed up with an entire *TEAM* of men to get her back!"

"You don't fucking get it, do you! You may have saved her tonight, but THIS— everything is YOUR fault, Blaine. Why the fuck do you think Robert went ballistic and went after her? Because of your little so-called love note or whatever the fuck you called it carved into his skin and the bullets you fucking put into him!" Artemis steps in, trying to get them to quiet down. What the hell are they talking about? Fuck, am I dreaming?

Blaine lets out what sounds like a muffled, exasperated laugh. "You honestly are going to sit here and tell me you believe the bullshit that just came out of your mouth?"

"You know we're right. Just fucking own it." Ronan spits.

Just hearing the name Robert makes my stomach drop. Why are they talking about him? Why was Blaine having someone tracking me? Bullets? What the hell am I missing here? I have to be dreaming. Their voices suddenly stop and dissipate down the hall; I can't hear what they're saying anymore. I have to get up, I have to stop this.

This is my fault; I know it is now. I force myself to sit up and hold onto the sides of the bed to keep myself upright just as a short, kind-looking brunette nurse comes in.

"Woah, honey! What are you doing there." She *tsks* at me, rushing to my side. "Lay back now, that's it. What do you need, sugar?" I give up, and let my body rest back in the bed, licking my lips. "Water? You want water?"

"Blaine..." God, why is my throat so scratchy?

"Here, drink. Blaine? Who is that, honey? I can see if he's around for ya. Drink first —that's good, there ya go." I hand her back the cup, which is now empty. Apparently, she was right.

"Blaine. He's here, I just heard him. Tall, brownish hair, looks perpetually grumpy but beautiful."

"Mmm. Mhmm. Okay. Hold tight, one second." I note the hint of amusement in her voice.

I hear her steps down the hall before she stops to talk to them; I assume they're all together. "Blaine...honey? —Lily's up and asking for you." Not even four seconds later, he's there, rushing into the open door.

"Lily..." He's next to me immediately, cupping my face gently, pressing his forehead to mine, grabbing my right hand into his, and stroking his thumb over my knuckles. His face looks like it's about to crumple.

"I'm sorry, Blaine. I'm sorry."

"Sorry, baby, what? God, I'm so happy you're awake, and you're okay. I've been out of my fucking mind Lily. I couldn't think straight without you." He presses his lips to mine so gently, like he's scared to break me, still cupping one hand on my face, the other grasping my own hand. I close my eyes and just let myself be close to him; the fragrance of his faded cologne and natural scent. His warm touch and grounding presence. Tears automatically form behind my eyes and spill down my cheeks, in silence.

"Everything is a little blurry, foggy. Like my brain is trying to piece things together slowly. I feel like I'm dreaming."

"Just focus on resting. It'll come to you soon enough. Just rest. What do you need?"

"Nothing, no. Blaine, look... your car... please I'm so sorry, I never meant— I mean, I didn't think—"

"What? —What, Lily, love, why are you apologizing?"

"Blaine..." Doesn't he know already? "—I wrecked your car... I'm sorry." I feel my face crumple as I get the words out, fresh tears falling. His lips curl into a sympathetic smile as he pulls back slightly to look into my eyes properly.

"It's a fucking car, sweetheart. I could give a fuck about the car. We'll get you a new one, okay? Whatever you want. Please don't ever apologize for something like that again. None of this was your fault. None of it." He leans forward, pressing gentle kisses to my lips and cheeks, over my tears, and to the palm of my hand. As I open my eyes and pull away, I see my brothers standing in the doorway. Blaine follows my line of sight and literally growls in tired annoyance but pulls away too. "I'm right outside, okay?" I nod at him with a pathetic dizzy smile, as my arm extends until he gently sets it down onto the side of the bed.

I move my eyes between my brothers, now moving to either side of me, grabbing my hands. I land on Artemis, and he smiles weakly at me. "How do you feel, Lil?"

"Okay, I guess? I don't really know. But— hey, I heard you guys yelling at each other in the hall... what happened?" They share a twin look before he turns back to me.

"Blaine... I mean, we know you're seeing each other. We're not —we're not mad at you, Lily. We're pissed at Blaine. But let's talk about that later when you're rested and feeling better." He runs his hand over my arm and tucks hair behind my ear. My anger surges, clearing a small amount of fogginess.

"No. Stop. You can be mad or upset, both of you. But... I care about him, and he cares about me a lot. You don't get to see the side of him that I get to. I'm not going to stop being with him. He's mine, and I'm his. This isn't a fling like he's using me or something or whatever you think is happening. He's your best friend, I don't understand why you're so upset about this." Ronan paces to the end of the room and back while Art bows his head, rubbing his thumb and fingers over his eyes.

"Lily. Please, let's just talk about this later. You need rest."

"Fine. Then why were you talking about Robert?" They both stop and look at each other like they just saw a fucking ghost appear. "What's going on?"

"Lily..."

"What. Tell me, now."

"Around the time you told us about... everything, we just wanted to do what we could to reverse what had been taken from you. And, we pushed him to undo the legalities stonewalling you from your trust and everything else hindering you. But while we were there—"

"Don't." Ronan's glaring at Artemis, the two of them having a secret twin conversation.

"Don't what?" My eyes slowly move back and forth between the two of them standing over me as my brain tries to follow and keep up. "Seriously?"

I'm torn away by a shadow in the corner of my eye. Blaine's standing in the doorframe, casually leaning against it, listening. "He needed a little incentive." He's looking straight at me, walking to the foot of the bed, and I suddenly feel tiny with three giant men surrounding me. His voice drops to a decibel so low that it vibrates out of him. "When we were there, all I could think about is what a piece of shit he is and everything he did to you, how he ruined your fucking childhood, your life, everything he took from you, Lily. I got a little rough. But I'd do it all over again in a fucking heartbeat."

Oh my god... I remember now. A flash comes back to me of being in that house. A split image of Robert tied to a chair or something. This is all entirely my fault. No... "Wait— he was the one who kidnapped me? Robert did this because you all were trying to help me?" Ronan grabs my wrist, pulling my attention.

"No, sis. He's a pathetic piece of shit. It's why he does anything. This is not your fault, I already know where your mind is going,

Lil." God my head is spinning and not just physically, my disbelief palpable.

"I think I need to be alone for a while." This is too much to take in, and I'm getting lightheaded and anxious, but my body still hurts, and there's a disgusting needle stuck in my skin. "I can't... I just—"

"Sure, sis. Whatever you need. We're not going anywhere. Rest. We love you." Artemis presses his lips to my hairline, brushing my hair back; Ronan pulling my hand up to his lips. And then they're gone. Blaine pushes past Ronan and pulls the stool next to my bed closer.

"I know you need space, baby. I'll leave. I just needed another few seconds alone with you, that's all." He's rubbing my hand to the side of his face, leaning into the touch, and pressing kisses to my palm before he's pulling away again.

"Blaine... I..." How do I— how could I possibly put everything I'm feeling into words? A handful of words? "—Thank you." He gently smiles and the wind is knocked out of me. This man is so beautiful. So mine. He leans in pressing a kiss to my forehead, nose, and then a couple of gentle touches to my lips, running his finger over my jaw. He moves so slowly, savoring every second our skin connects, before pulling away. He stares into my eyes, an emotion I can't pinpoint. But there's a storm there, nonetheless. He looks like he wants to say something but stops himself, running his fingers over my hand one more time and then turning to leave, shutting the door behind him. And I'm left alone, in complete silence other than the overwhelming ringing in my ears and the beeping of the monitors now behind me.

# 74

# BLAINE

I sit at my desk in my office and read through the entire document several times before feeling I've thoroughly dissected and modified where needed. Since Artemis and Ronan have been found to be surprisingly incompetent on the matter, I had my attorney contact the brothers' attorney and got them to agree to send the original documents they were forced to sign, turning of age. Banks took over and worked his magic, sending me the updated document now sitting in my inbox. It just needs to be signed by the right hands, and Lily will have the life she was meant to.

Lily is home from the hospital. While I didn't approve, she wanted to stay at her apartment downstairs, and I can refuse her nothing at this point. All I care about is her happiness and comfort. Tree suffered a few pretty nasty injuries and needed more time to recover, although he is set to be released today if all goes according to plan. I stopped by to see him several times during my visits with Lily. It puts that strange pressure on my chest. But, this is a part of his job, and he's seen far worse, experienced far worse, assuring me he was fine, just ready to get out of the damn hospital gown. I think the nurses rather enjoyed it by the way they took extra care of him. I've never seen a medical team so dedicated to one's comfort. Tree is a beast, but he's certainly not unattractive. Women seem to love the quiet, scarred warrior persona. Ten grand says he walks out grumbling, with three numbers and a new lay.

My plan is to have a little fun with our friend Robert before he signs the item in front of me, and then I have to kill him. I told the brothers I have my notary coming to document the transaction, providing I pay the man enough, and if they want to watch it for themselves, great; if they're not fully on board with what's going to be occurring, then don't come and I'll send it to them after. They're choosing the latter, and honestly, it's unsurprising. They need me to be the villain here. They need to place the blame entirely on me to prove to Lily and point their fingers at how dangerous and terrible I am, that I really am the big bad wolf they warned her about.

I never get tired of it, though, being feared. Being feared is far more valuable than being liked. Being liked will win you favors and greased palms. Being feared, on the other hand, will get you far, far more. Fear is the driving emotion for most, and when it comes down to it, they will do anything, *give* anything, to re-obtain that false sense of security and comfort. Such a simple thing, really. If you welcome death and have no ties chaining you, in turn, there is nothing to fear. I'm untouchable in that sense; at least, I was until Lily. She's become a weakness, but I would pay ten bodyguards to guarantee her safety so she could never be used against me. She is the only person in my life that I would give up everything for without a second thought. If she were successfully used as leverage against me, I would break and bend to their damned will. The thought alone is blinding.

Looking down at the time, I hum in pleasure. "Time to play." Someone's been misbehaving and needs some obedience training. I've checked in on him and the men staying in the house to ensure they're cared for and have everything they need or want, financially or otherwise. Their loyalty here outweighs anything, any cost. And while presumably they are dedicated to me through that of Rye's instruction, they don't realistically owe me any sort of allegiance, hence the growing monetary gain.

# 75

# BLAINE

The room is a wasteland of shadows and despair, lit only by the dim glow of battery-operated lamps. I've had a few items brought over: supplies, cots, lamps, and things of the sort regarding their comfort here in this hellhole while I dealt with other things. The air hangs heavy with the acrid scent of sweat and blood.

Circling the chair containing the pathetic excuse of a man before me, my boots scuffing the cracked floorboards, I can't help but let out an exaggerated whistle. "Now, either you didn't play nice, or my friends found out about your little secret. I'm going to go out on a limb here and say it's the latter."

I glance around at the men in the dim room, standing silent, their presence a wall of judgment. "Real men don't take kindly to that behavior, Rob... Robbie? Mind if I call you Robbie? Has a nice ring to it the way it rolls off the tongue." He sits zip-tied to the same wooden chair in the center of the living room —or what's left of it. As implied, the MC had their fun but didn't go overboard, as instructed. I very much need him alive. He's covered in blood, teeth missing, fingernails removed, and bruises covering his old leather skin. His eyes trace to the man standing closest to the entrance behind me, pleading for help. "Ohh, come now, Robbie. Our friend Allen here doesn't like rapists either. He isn't coming to your rescue; no one is. And really, at this point, it's just up to you if you get to die quickly or slowly, based on participation scores."

"What do you want?" I curl my lip in disgust just at the sound of his voice: hoarse, each word a rasp of desperation.

"God, you sound dreadful. Disgusting."

"What do you want, kid?" I flip my knife in my hand smoothly through my fingers. The only sound is his raspy breathing and my rhythmic steps over the old, hollow wooden flooring as I get trapped in my mind momentarily. The images that will forever haunt me gripping me.

I lean in closer, the tip of my knife tracing a slow path down his cheek. "I want you to understand," I say, my voice low. "I want you to feel what it's like to have no power. To be at someone else's mercy. To have your worst fucking nightmare come to life. To feel every ounce of pain and terror that little girl did. *Repeatedly.* You understand me?"

Robert's mouth doesn't move. But his eyes tell me he's far from immune to my words.

Behind me, Starburst shifts, awaiting my command. We'd spoken earlier, his anger and pain mirroring mine in ways neither of us admitted.

"You'll answer my questions," I tell Robbie, standing to my full height. "And maybe -just maybe- I'll let you die with a shred of dignity. But should you fail -*dot dot dot*- you should know Robbie... some of these men here have been without the soft touch of a woman for some time. Starburst here, just spent sixty months behind the walls of a jail cell. And you know what I'm thinking? I think sometimes the best way to learn from your mistakes is by having someone repay the favor... and oh, are we just getting started." Chuckling darkly at the conjuring of images passing like phantoms over my vision, I channel enough darkness and power behind my strides as I circle that I can feel these men internally bowing to me.

If only teenage Blaine could see us now.

I spin, lowering myself, and grip his hair so hard it's going to come out in fistfuls. I bring my knife to his forehead and run it down his face, jaw, and down his neck, spit flying through his teeth as I sneer at him, watching the pretty red run free. "Why Robbie? How could you do it?" I demand. "How could you possibly look down at an innocent *child* and abuse and hurt her the way you did?" I throw his head back, tipping over the chair, the harsh sound of his skull hitting wood echoing through the otherwise mostly silent room. "What could a child have possibly done to deserve your cruelty?"

He says nothing, prone on his back and gritting his blood-stained teeth, eyes barely able to stay open. Considering my options, I hum and examine the room, eyes landing on Star.

"Friend, would you be willing to teach our Robbie here a lesson?" I lean in closer to his ear, playing into the villain role. My long-time alter ego lighting up my skin. What this crew expects from me. "I promise you can be as rough as you like." I purr. Of course, I've already had a conversation with SB to find out if he'd be interested in assisting me with my punishment, as well as a few other volunteers. He's practically giddy with excitement. I smile wickedly, step aside, and reach my flattened palm out for him to proceed. "I do hope an audience is permittable because my oh my, have we been waiting for this." I flip my knife between my fingers absently, meditatively, teeth bared.

Robert's eyes are nearly popping out of his head now, trying to survey the room. "Would anyone be so kind as to assist our friend into a more comfortable position?" Two other men step forward as I circle slowly, hands and knife behind my back patiently. When Robert sees this, he tries to struggle with the little energy he has left in his dying body. It's pathetic, really, how quickly he submits. Soon, he's face-planted with his ass up and hands tied to his thighs, holding his naked blob of a form in place. I go to kneel next to Robert's face, looking down at him. He's not even trying to play; he's given up. That's no fun. I smile demonically and lift my chin towards Star in a show of permission. The man takes a few steps forward, the sound of his belt and zipper being undone catching Robert's attention. He flops, head-turning, realization hitting. Another man is about to fuck him unwillingly, and he panics again, struggling. I smile. "There's that fire, Robbie!"

"Okay! Okay, god damn it! Her fucking whore of a mother," he growls. "Don't fucking touch me." His words come out in raspy gasps and a sick part of me has to let my laugh free at his suffering.

I toss my head back mirroring insanity, stopping and looking to the ceiling as his voice fades into the black before I realize what he said. I pause, smile dying. Remembering every single thing he did to my Lily as a sweet little child... the rage and need for vengeance makes its return full force, and the fire returns to my own eyes, centering me. I fight the high taking over, the mask of my alter ego that consumes me, to take control of this moment as myself. Not him.

"What about their mother?"

The crumpled, pathetic excuse of a man says nothing, our silence hanging in the air as I wait before kicking his already-fucked knee.

"I told you!"

"Right. Hmm, okay then. Anyone else want a go? Maybe we should make this a group effort, huh, Robbie?" I twirl, looking at everyone, pointing the end of my father's knife at each of them in a show of emphasis. A couple other men, one I've not spent much time with, bald and covered in sparse, odd tattoos, steps forward. "We have more friends for you, Robbie. Looks like our fun isn't quite over." Soon, he'll be screaming and begging for mercy as my baby Lily would have been. "I asked you a question." The now small circle of men move in closer, nearly all palming their jean-clad cocks in anticipation at the opportunity to dole such a punishment.

"—That bitch spread her legs for anyone, and for years... years, I tried to be there for her. I tried to show her what a good man I'd be for her. Even after she married my pussy of a brother." He grunts, spitting blood and catching his breath as if he's climbing a mountain.

"Keep going. I'm getting impatient with you." His face is nearly purple now, and I smile, flipping my knife. "SPEAK!"

"—Even...after she married my brother, I was... there... for her... and she still... didn't come to me. After everything I did for her. I was a good friend for so long." His words are coming out in pants, between grunts from his pain and attempts to get a full breath of air. "She... went... and had an affair. And...still... didn't come to... me."

"You expect me to believe you raped and abused my Lily, a *child*, for years because... her mommy wouldn't love you? Your obsession with a woman justifies years of tormenting her daughter? Are you fucking kidding me?" I signal one of the waiting men and he advances a few paces.

"Y... yes." His cries of pain echo through the room as Baldy kicks the shit out of him, assumedly breaking several ribs, and continues to cry out in visible pain. Any ounce of sympathy I may have momentarily felt is gone. I keep my abhorrent stare locked onto him as I play out his next several hours of life behind my eyes. "Maybe it's time for that special treat now, Robert." I smile as the steady rhythm of footsteps draws closer from behind me. "No! Please, god, no. I get it, okay... I fucked up. I'm sorry." The man now behind him pauses, looking to me for instruction. I monopolize the power in this room. I hold my finger up, walking over to Allen with my hand out. He hands me the document and a black ink pen. I make my way to Robert's side, his face covered in blood, sweat, and copious amounts of tears, his skin a deep shade of red from the weight of his restrictive position tied on the floor.

"Robbie. If you want all this to stop, you need to sign this. That's it." His pathetic face nods, blood dripping down from his facial wounds. Reaching my knife towards his right wrist, tracing my eyes over the hack job I did, I notice his groin, err —what's left of it and burst out laughing, forgetting that I stabbed him in the dick at our last little visit. Maybe I'm succumbing to delirium, but truly, how hilarious is that? I wipe a tear from my eye as my laughter dies, stifling my residual chuckles deep in my chest. I notice a couple of the men standing side-eyeing each other; they can't make sense of me, I suppose. I snip one of the ties from his hand, and he immediately lifts it, offering new movement to his bound body. I hold the pen and paper and wait as he shakily signs and initials, sealing the future for Lily and her brothers.

Just like that.

I stand, returning to Allen and thank him for his time, the clean twenty grand already given to him. Seconds pass as I simply watch and observe what a weak, pathetic piece of shit this excuse for a man is. I stop and nod at the men behind Robert, waiting patiently for their opportunity to dole out their own form of justice, indicating for them to step forward again, quiet feet carrying them forward.

"You... you! You said you'd stop this if I signed the paperwork!" His gaze darts wildly, searching for mercy where none exists.

"I lied." His cries scatter the room as his hand frantically scrambles to move his body, to grasp at anything to help him. But it's a useless, wasted effort.

"Now, what does Lily's mother have to do with you raping and abusing her as a defenseless child?" He doesn't answer and instead keeps yelling nonsense I don't care about. "My patience is running thin with you. Speak, or my knife finds its way through this hand, and I'll fucking hold you in place for every single man here to stick their dick in your dry ass until you die or pass out. It'd be a fitting fucking way to go out, wouldn't it?" His jaw tightens, muscles jumping beneath his skin as he fights through the pain. The hatred in his eyes are like daggers and only encourages me. I can't help but bare my teeth in return. "I'm going to rather enjoy the free show."

*"Fuck...you!"* I swing the knife into his hand as he screams, effectively pinning him in place.

"I tried to warn you, Robbie. Listening is a crucial skill to obtain. Now, finish."

He chokes on his response; his mouth clamped shut, a low growl rumbling from his throat, and breathing labored as his entire body visibly shakes and trembles from the pain. "I... when I looked at... Lily... all... I could see... was... HER. It killed... me. A constant...reminder... of her."

My phone vibrates and I look to see the name *"Mine"* floating on the screen. I hold my finger up to everyone, a menacing warning landing on the piss-stain on the floor.

"Hi, baby..." I answer.

*"Hi. Hey, can I stay with you at your place tonight?"* On the other end, she sounds tired. Maybe a little out of it.

"It would be my greatest pleasure. Are you feeling okay? Do you need anything? I can stop on my way home."

*"Oh no, thank you. I just... want to see you. I've been thinking about you all day and... I just really need to see you."* I smile wickedly, masculine pride filling my chest and heat taking my face, knowing the words she won't say. Knowing what she wants.

"Mmm, be there as soon as I can, sweetheart. Finishing up a menial task." My voice comes out deep and promising, shaking my head so Robbie doesn't make a peep, watching the temptation in his eyes grow by the second.

*"Okay, baby, see you soon."*

"Goodbye, sweetheart."

Humming, I tilt my head and examine Robert, weighing my options.

"I have somewhere to be, and I'm growing bored of you. The question is if I allow our friends here to finally have some play time and I come back tomorrow or if I kill you now." I hold my hand up, immediately stopping his soon-to-be pathetic response. "No... I wasn't asking. Gentlemen..." I pull my knife from his hand stamped into the floor and stop to face them before stepping out. "... consider him your personal plaything for the evening. Don't forget, he raped a child for years and ruined her life... react accordingly. I have what I need. I'll be back tomorrow with more cash for those who stay an additional night. Questions?"

I nod to the men at their silence, each of them shuffling forward to claim their piece of vengeance. As I walk toward the door, I pause, glancing back at the mess of a man.

"I'm done here," I say, my voice cold. "But your suffering? That's just beginning." My words are a promise and a curse.

I step into the night, Robert's pathetic screams now muffled through the door, heading to my car. I need to make a stop by the warehouse to shower and change out of these clothes before going home to Lil. I don't want her anywhere near this scent or the stains.

The familiar numbness takes over as the high wears off, and I leave Robbie to the fate he so richly deserves.

# 76

# LILITH

I'm lying in Blaine's huge bed, thinking about everything I have to do. At the hospital, my brothers and Blaine fought so often, and once so loudly, security had to break it up. Punches and pushes were exchanged between them, I'm positive. It's been hell since, knowing they hate each other and their friendship is effectively ruined. This was exactly what I was avoiding; what I was running from. The inevitable happened and I selfishly turned a blind eye, giving into my relationship with Blaine. The notion that I caused this breaks me. Not only do both of my brothers deserve happiness, but Blaine does too. He's wonderful and caring, and sweet, and perfect. This can't happen like this.

I know what I have to do, and occasionally, one person needs to sacrifice their own happiness for the majority. I just don't want to do this, imagining how broken Blaine will be. But, he will get over me and move on though. Things will eventually go back to how they were, without me here causing their fights.

The door opens, and Blaine comes in, his painfully beautiful smile directed towards me. He has been so happy recently, despite my brothers.

He comes in, turning on the lamp on his side of the bed and I crawl out of the covers and get on my knees on the edge of the bed into his open arms. For a moment, I let myself forget everything. I simply lavish in his scent, the warmth of him wrapping his arms around me, the feel of his lush lips pressing kisses all over me sweetly. I place a smile on my face forcing myself not to cry as I pull away enough to look into his eyes. "Hi, baby."

"Hi, beauty. You summoned me?" He starts pressing kisses to my neck, and I move, exposing myself so he has a better angle before I can't help but put my lips to his in a slow, sensual joining. He pulls my hips to his, and I can feel him hardening against my stomach.

"Blaine... I want to... well, I have an idea, a desire, I guess?" He returns to kissing and licking my neck, humming.

"Mhmm. I love your desires, tell me. Anything, it's yours."

"—I want..." I can barely say the words louder than a whisper. "I want you to fuck me like you would if it was your wedding night." He pauses and stiffens, pulling away from me to look me in my eyes. His expression is unreadable as always, but there's a great depth of emotion there, his throat bobbing in a deep swallow, grey eyes intense.

"Baby... if it was our wedding night and I knew I had you every day for the rest of our lives, I wouldn't be fucking you. I would make love to you tenderly and so thoroughly that we would feel our souls merging. Not just in this life. But in every lifetime. It wouldn't just be sex. It would be life-giving worship. Our joining on our wedding night will be an expression of just that. Nothing less." I suck in a breath, not realizing my chest had stopped moving to collect air.

"Blaine..." I can feel my eyes line silver as I blink away the blurring effect of my vision of this man before me.

"Shh, sweetheart." Blaine gathers me in his arms and gently rests me against the bed, removing my body from its clothing before removing his own. Every movement he makes is deliberate, slow, passionate, and full of aching longing. He runs his hands over nearly every inch of my exposed skin, his lips covering the remaining untouched places. He lowers himself and goes down on me for so long, my orgasm so slowly pushed to the surface. I tremble, coming against his mouth and fingers as he moans, devouring every part of me. And, he takes me: body, mind, and soul. If there was any small part of me that hadn't belonged to him, it did now. He spends hours making love to me with so much passion that I don't bother to stop the silent tears that fall from the corners of my eyes as he pushes into me, radiating so much of his affection. The first time, we climax together, looking into each other's eyes shadowed by the dimly lit room.

And just as Blaine said, a part of me feels so much at once I wonder if it is actually our souls joining or if it's simply my heart breaking. Maybe both.

It feels as though I'm entirely consumed; we both are. Encased in a glow, the likeness of a fallen star; too intensely lit to see anything outside of what is in front of me, of him. The magic and power of something... other, something spiritual and timeless, cradling and keeping us like this.

We spend hours making love into the night, repeatedly, as if a spell had been cast upon us.

And though we both feel it, neither of us actually says the words 'I love you'.

Waking up, Blaine is gone, and there's a note next to my pillow with a bouquet of roses on my nightstand.

*Sunshine,*
*Thank you for the small peek into our future.*
*I checked the mental screenshot, and it's stunning.*
*Be back late this afternoon, my love.*

Immediately, my heart hammers in my chest, my stomach twisting in anxiety at the day ahead I have planned. I can't cry. No, not now. I squeeze my eyes shut, forcing down the lump in my throat and loosening the tightness and pain in my chest before making myself stand.

My bag is already packed, sitting in my living room at my apartment downstairs, as well as my boarding pass and burner phone. I can't have him or my brothers trying to find me. After hearing more about Blaine apparently having a hacker genius friend, I decided it would be best to just leave my phone for now. I wrote down all the numbers I could possibly need, just in case. I stop at the doorway, turning to take in the room: the crumpled sheets of our final entanglement, the note I left him, along with my phone next to it, and return to take a single rose with me. "Goodbye, Blaine. I love you." I whisper the words, heart breaking.

# 77

# LILITH

Stepping off the plane, there's not even a gate leading into the airport. No train, no shuttle. It's such a small airport, there is quite literally a metal set of stairs elevated to the plane door that leads to an open, covered area with the option of a single rotating outdoor bag carousel or straight out to arrivals. As much as I love living in a big city, this has a curious charm to it that I've never experienced. The skies overhead are incredibly cloudy and look like rain could fall at any second. It's always sunny in Denver. We actually get more sunny days than The Sunshine State; a lot of people don't realize it's far from a frozen arctic tundra. This blanket of smothering grey reflects my inner turmoil, though. It's fitting. I took a couple of anxiety pills when I boarded the plane, my body going numb from panic. I feel better now, but it doesn't stop the overwhelming sadness clawing at me, breaking my heart. The people around me, the chatter and movement, feel miles away. Almost like I'm a ghost, watching from the other side of some kind of unseen wall. Disconnected from what should feel real, as if my hands would simply float through anything I touched.

Part of me wonders if I should just call him now and turn back around to go home. But I know I need to stay away and let everyone get back into a normal, comfortable routine. It's been chaos for those around me. The guys threatened Robert and risked losing *everything*. Blaine's car was totaled. Their long-standing friendship is effectively ruined because we started dating. And, of course, the kidnapping.

I slip my duffle bag over my shoulder and make my way down the stairs out to arrivals. It's nearly dead. There are three cars sitting on the shoulder waiting; none of them my ride. I reached out to someone I lived with in foster care. We had a lot in common and we were able to build a friendship of sorts, I guess you could say. There was a point, I think all we had were each other. When your real life is a living Hell, it's comforting to envision everything as a magical cinema. We'd pretend we were sisters sometimes, like everything was normal, and we'd be adopted together to go live with an obnoxiously rich royal family in a different country.

We kept in touch over the years here and there, but nothing consistent. However, I knew if the day came when I really needed her, she'd be there, and vice versa without questions. Turns out, she ended up with her now fiancé in northern California, about three to four hours north of San Francisco, in a quiet little beach town. And honestly, I don't think I could have chosen a better place. She warned me it was chilly and rainy. There's always been an alluring but haunting and terrible comfort from a rainy, dark beach. All too fitting. So much potential for sun yet the storms rule all. I can't help but sigh deeply at the thought.

I take a final look around and glance behind me towards the tiny airport just as a blue Toyota pulls around a corner to the left, and a petite brunette waves happily through her window. As terrible and confused as I feel, that small action lit a flame of comfort deep in me. Like, suddenly everything might be okay again eventually.

"Lilith! Oh my god!" She gets out and runs to me, wrapping me in a big hug, her head barely coming to my shoulder, and it makes me smile. She looks exactly like I remember her, only slightly aged, as we all have. Taking my bag off my shoulder, she urges me towards her car, like there's a line of people waiting behind her instead of a taxi cabber asleep at the wheel.

"It's uh, it's good to see you, Kell. Thank you so much for doing this." I climb into the passenger seat and almost get stuck before I can manage to move the seat back.

"Oops! Sorry. Steven always drives; that's normally my spot —a little tight for you, I guess." She laughs as she pulls out from the airport's loading lane. "So, uh, how was the flight?"

"Not bad, thank you. How have you been?"

"Great! Steven and I just opened a café in town! Well, it's been going for a while, but it's better than we could have dreamed. We even have a little greenhouse —well, half greenhouse, half storage shed, I guess. But we grow all the vegetables and lettuce and stuff we use on the menu. It's not huge by any means, but it's been so great. I can't wait for you to see it! The café, greenhouse, and our little place we're renting are all next to each other. In town, it's pretty hilly. There are some steep areas, which makes parking interesting. But, anyway, yeah —the greenhouse is directly behind the café, and then just up at the top of the hill is where our place is, you'll see." She looks over, smiling at me. It feels nice to see her like this. She's doing so well for herself. God, does she deserve happiness. Our stories may be different, but she's suffered severely in life. I can think of few who'd remain so loving through so much pain.

"That's amazing, Kell; I'm so happy for you, truly. I can't wait to see it. I'm always happy to help out around the café or greenhouse, too, since you're letting me crash with you and stuff. If it would be helpful, my hands are your hands."

"Let's just get you settled in first! Whenever you're ready to talk about why you're here, I'm all ears. But, if you need this time to yourself, then use it for you, not to help us around the café. We got a good handle on it." I smile weakly at her, nodding before looking out the expanse of the front window. This feels like we're in the Pacific Northwest far more than the stereotypical California beauty. The whole daydreamy 'vampires live here' vibe going.

She was right; we're pulling into the small town center about forty or fifty minutes after leaving the inland airport, and it's stunning. The main streets are at the base of the hills on the right, and directly across the highway sits the ocean to my left. The hills gradually increase and roll across the picturesque view, houses scattered and covering the tree-covered, elevated land. "Wow…"

"It has its charm, huh?"

"I'd say... jesus Kell, this is breathtaking. I wasn't expecting this."

"Well, I'm glad you like it. We're almost to the house, and I'll point out the café at the bottom, but don't worry, I won't tug you down today." We pull further into the main strip, small traffic lights lining the road. Looking to the left, the ocean and sand are so close. To the right, little shops, candy stores, a hardwood store, a small movie theater, antique stores, boutiques, and other various restaurants line the road. In a way, it reminds me of the ski towns in Colorado. A lot of them are just like this in the summer; they just don't see a lot of action in the off-season.

Slowing to a stop, Kell switches on the ticking turn signal to the right and slows to a near stop to point out the café on the corner. It's exactly what I would expect from her, and it's amazing. It almost looks like an old house with the windows in front and the porch that's attached to it. She has it painted white with a seafoam greenish blue on the shutters and chairs to match the open porch. There are large clear plastic rolls tied up on each side; I guess that must be for when it's too cold and rainy. Probably functions as a makeshift sunroom to protect against the rain. There are several vibrant plants and string bulb lights flowing across the length of the porch, too. Kell rolls down the window and a little bell chimes out as someone steps through with a tray of coffee and a bag of food. "Ah, never mind. Sorry. That's Sheila. I was gonna say hello. But I'll wait. But yep —that's the café..." She pulls up a little further, pointing. "...That's our little makeshift greenhouse..." We keep going up the hill, pulling into a gravel driveway. "...And this is the duplex we're renting until we can buy. We have room, though; I'll make sure you're comfortable, don't worry." I smile silently, looking around before pulling at the handle to get out. "Oh, and Steven isn't home; he's down at the café for now working. You'll meet him later. He's a gem. You'll love him. He's safe." The two words I didn't realize I needed to hear. *"He's safe."*

Turning, the view from up here is even more beautiful, the vast ocean expanding to the end of the earth. I follow her inside and she gives me a quick tour. The space is small but cozy and they have a second bedroom with a twin bed that they've been using mostly for storage space. It'll be nice to have a space to myself.

She takes care of me like a mother hen trying to feed me and give me things before I politely tell her I need a shower so I can get some alone time. I'm starting to feel sick again, wondering how Blaine must be feeling. Surely, he's found my note by now. I get in the shower, and when the tears start, I don't stop them this time. I let myself feel everything and slide to the bottom of the shower, crying under the hot stream. The truth is, I don't want this. I want him. I want my life with him. But I keep telling myself this is the right thing to do so everything can fall back into place the way it was just a few months ago. The fact that he put so much affection into me just last night and his note... *"Thank you for the small peek into our future."* It's too hard. I break, quietly sobbing under the weight of the guilt. I fucking miss him so much already; I hate that I caused so much damage, and I never even told him how I really feel. He's the best thing that's ever happened to me. I'm not sure how I'll survive this.

# 78

# BLAINE

## *Before:*

There's a spot of gold in my peripheral that I can't seem to shake.

The sister with a mass of strawberry, glowing hair haloing her head like the innocent little thing she is. *Lilith*.

What the fuck is this guy talking about? The monotonous buzz of Ben's voice carries on somewhere nearby —all my effort going towards trying not to look in her direction. I can't help it. She's been coming around more lately, and something about her intrigues me. I'm assuming it's the half-ass, bullshit lie they're all keeping about where the fuck she went the last however many years. Suddenly, back in the picture. Interesting.

The thing is, when you've already experienced more life in your early twenties than most people ever will by the time they've hit their deathbed, everything starts getting a little more and more dull. It's the same shit, same people with different faces, same story, same goals, same fears, all predictable bullshit. What makes it even more hilarious is that everyone I meet thinks they're the most interesting person to walk the earth. I can't help but nearly laugh out loud at the thought. Stay silent long enough, and the impulse most people feel to fill it evolves into self-absorbed, narcissistic word vomit. So, when something is a variant of the mold, it catches my attention.

The sudden feminine laugh that rings in the air over the loud music feels like fingers massaging my brain in the best way and pulls my attention back to the golden corner.

Looking over, Lilith's head is tossed back in a laugh, a smile overtaking her entire being with that glow. I realize, fuck... this is the first time I can recall seeing her smile. A genuine smile, I mean. Not the fake, forced smiles she parades around in. I feel my own lips lift in response as if it's contagious and I need a hazmat.

"She's having fun, huh? It's good to see her enjoying herself." Artemis comes up next to me out of nowhere. Or hell, maybe he's been there, and I just didn't notice. Ben appears to have left, too. I hum noncommittally, taking a swig of my beer as a chorus of cheers sound in the next room from the football game on TV. "Thanks for keeping your eye on Lilith. It means a lot to know you have her back, too, man."

I can't help but pinch my brows together at that. I couldn't care less about her or her safety. But, sure, I guess.

Her eyes find their way to me, her laugh settling and fading as the conversation she's in steals her attention again. Something pinches in my chest, clenching my jaw until I feel it in my brain, and I'm left wondering if I'm the reason the smile disappeared from her face.

# 79

# BLAINE

Today has been a fucking headache. But due to my efforts *and none of their own,* the guys now possess all the items they need to proceed with obtaining Lily's inheritance and their uncle got what must have been his worst nightmare come to life. He was passed around all night with dicks in every hole, bleeding and raw by the time they finished with him.

Carving out his tongue and his stomach and then slitting his throat gave me a sick amount of pleasure. What a useless piece of shit. I may be going to Hell, but really, I'm doing the lord's work. Let's hope she's forgiving.

I'm heading home now and decided to call Lily and see if she wants to go out for a nice dinner. It may have been a long day, but this is going to be a big day for her in beautiful ways once I fill her in. I can't wait to see her eyes light up. I smile, biting my bottom lip as the line starts to ring through the speakers in my car. It quickly goes straight to voicemail. My brow furrows, wondering if she has her phone off or if the battery died. That's not like her. I could always stop by her favorite bakery on the way home and grab some cupcakes for her, I guess.

The memory of when we first started spending time together, her giving me a back rub on the couch, and the first time we ever really touched and fell asleep together comes to me. I remember it vividly. God, she's adorable. And fucking sexy and amazing. Just thinking about her lifts whatever weight is on my shoulders off, knowing I get to see her soon. Get to go home to her. She just makes everything okay, everything better. When she asked me last night to fuck her like it was our wedding night, my heart stopped. I've been wanting to tell her how I feel for so long, but with everything going on with her brothers and then all the bullshit with Robert, it just wasn't ever the right time. What if she's feeling the same way? I really want to plan an extraordinary evening to express to her how much I'm in love with her.

In love… me. I can't help but huff in disbelief a little at the idea, but it's true. I suppose I didn't quite know what the feeling was at first. I think I spent so long keeping my emotions and reactions in line that I forgot what caring for someone like this feels like. I hadn't loved anyone following my parents' death as a teen. I undoubtedly could spend the rest of my life with her by my side.

My phone rings, snapping me out of my thoughts, expecting to see her name. *Ugh.* Ronan. I sigh, leaning back.

"Yeah."

"You heard from Lily today?"

"Not since this morning… why?"

"I have a weird feeling, and she hasn't answered her phone all day. It's been off, just going straight to voicemail." Panic surges through my chest, that something might be wrong.

"I'm close to the building. Let me check her place and see if she's home. She could just be painting or something..."

"We both know that's not what's happening. She never turns her phone off or lets it die. Just check and call me back or text me so I know she's safe." He ends the call, and I speed up, running yellow lights to pull into the garage.

I make my way to her place first and end up banging on the door after no response. *No... no. Something's wrong.*

I fish my phone out of my pocket calling her again, going straight to voicemail. "FUCK." I race back to the elevator calling several times in a row, rushing into my place. It's quiet and dark... I know no one is here. I would feel her presence immediately if she was home. "No... no, no, no, no, no." *This isn't happening.*

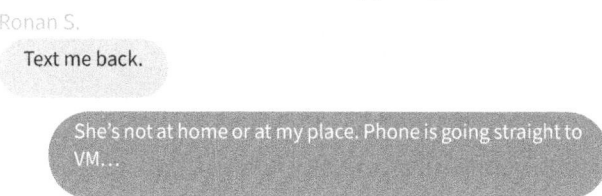

I race through the house just in case, and it's as empty as I thought it was. But, something catches my attention on the bed. Lily's phone. Why the fuck is her phone here, turned off. I run over, and there's a folded note under her phone. *Oh god, Lily. No, baby. What did you do...* I feel sick as I frantically unfold the letter.

*Blaine,*

*Baby, I'm so sorry I had to do this. I can imagine how scared and angry you must be at me for leaving. I promise you I am safe. I'm going to stay with a friend. You don't know them; no one does. No one knows where I am going, not even the girls or my brothers. I knew I couldn't tell anyone.*

*My heart is broken knowing I have to leave you, and even now, I can't stop crying. I don't even know if I'll actually be able to do this, do what's best for everyone. Not with how much I care about you. You mean everything to me, Blaine. Everything. You've become my world.*

I'm going to throw the fuck up, *leave me?* My hands are shaking so badly just trying to finish this letter.

*Last night was the most beautiful, most perfect way I could have spent it with you. I will remember every moment of it for the rest of my life. You're the most incredible man I have ever met, Blaine. But... sometimes, we have to sacrifice our own happiness for a larger purpose and for those around us to be happy. Everything the last several weeks has been because of me, whether I was aware of it or not.*

My phone is vibrating, Ronan's name playing on a loop in the hazy distance as I focus on reading every word.

*I cannot be the reason you lose your best friends. The same goes for my brothers. You are their best friend, Blaine. They love you. The thought of being the reason your friendship is over is too much. Plus, all of the chaos with Robert and the kidnapping and wrecking your car. My brothers stand to lose* everything *because of me. Because they're fighting Robert for* me. *Blaine... I'm so sorry. But, people are hurting because of me.*

*You all need time without me there ruining everything. I need you all to focus on getting back into your normal, happy, and comfortable routines. Work on rebuilding your relationship with Rone and Art, please. I left my phone so no one could track me from my location or get ahold of me. I have a throw-away phone and everyone's numbers, though.*

*I can't be the reason for everyone's suffering and chaos. It's best if I remove myself from the picture. I care about you so much, Blaine, and I didn't want this to be goodbye. But I don't trust myself to know what's best for everyone around us versus my selfishness to want to be with you.*

*- Lilith*

The letter is wadded into a ball in my fist pounding onto the floor before I realize what I'm doing. I'm on my knees on the floor of my bedroom, Lily's goodbye in my hands, and my heart is so broken I swear I can feel it shattering. She's running from her own happiness, and I feel so fucking helpless.

I make myself get up, my phone still ringing on a fucking loop. I wipe the tears from my face, the pressure too much in my head, and take a picture of the crumpled letter so Artemis and Ronan can know this is their fault. Lily left me because of them. She literally ran away due to their actions, because of their bullshit.

I send the picture and go look at myself in the bathroom mirror, staring back into my own pale eyes, ghostly contrasting against the red in them, my hair a fucking wreck. I will find her. I can't just let her go like this, there's no way in fucking hell. I told her she was mine and meant it. She's not getting away from me.

*Control yourself, Blaine; you look pathetic. Think.*

I grab my phone and ignore the incessant onslaught of Ronan's calls, dialing the only man I trust to help me find my girl.

"Yooo."

"I need your help finding Lily."

"Are you fucking with me? We *just* got her back. Please tell me she's okay..."

"She ran. I'll meet you at your place in fifteen minutes."

"Hey man, I mean, I kind of have compan—"

"I'd finish quickly then." I grit out.

"Yeah, alright." He hangs up, loudly sighing before the call drops.

# 80

# BLAINE

Stepping into Zach's apartment feels unexpected —an oasis bathed in warmth, neutrals, crisp whites, and touches of gold. The calm creates a space that feels as soothing to my nervous system as it is stunning. The delicate scent of a luxury hotel hangs throughout the space as I try to focus and take it in.

I follow him back to his office and fill him in on what's going on, somehow simultaneously demanding and begging for his help tracking her down. I can take it from there.

"Okay, jesus christ." He runs a red manicured hand over his face and mouth, his entire large figure sighing. "Well, she left her phone, so we can't track her location that way. We can try to find her travel plans and run a recognition to see if we have any matches on her name for bus, train, airline tickets, or rental cars out of Denver." He faces his wall of monitors and starts keying in information, various pages, and records floating on his screens. "Hmmm... you're positive she left Denver? Someone in town didn't come and pick her up?"

"I'll call my in-house security and have them play back footage of her leaving today." Zach nods and turns back to his screen. I'm kicking myself for thinking she'd be okay without security trailing her any longer. I should have known better; I do know better. I just never expected this of all things.

"Hold up, B. We got something..." His fingers click away as he scrolls through a few pages. "Yep, she flew out of DIA early this afternoon... to... Fractions Airport? I've never heard of it. Let me see..." I repeat the name in my head searching for something, anything. "She's headed for north cali. Fractions, CA... little north of San Fran, inland." I stand behind him, memorizing the screen, searching for even a clip of her name, wracking my brain for anything, any snippet of information she may have shared about northern California and who she knows there. She said she was safe and going to stay with a friend.

"What else can you get on her? Where did she go? Did she take a ride-share or transport after the airport?"

"Let me do some recon, one sec... —no receipt I can track for transport leaving the airport. Let me tap into the grid, run a scan for facial recognition, and see if she's been spotted outside of the airport. One sec." Zach's a black hat, able to hack his way into government access archives. Specifically, the program that utilizes facial recognition scanners in cameras across the country and can pinpoint the locations of anyone who shows enough of their face to be noticed by the system. The government can provide a false sense of security in your identity being safe, but there is no such thing with the US government. In this case and many others, it's very beneficial for us. "—There she is." I lean in, and immediately, my stomach twists, seeing her hugging another woman and getting into a little Toyota.

"Who's the friend she's with? Can we get a name?"

"I can do a scan, but too much of her face is hidden by her ballcap from airport cams —damn it..."

"What? What the fuck do you mean 'damn it'?" He sighs and turns to face me in his chair.

"There's no plate on cam for her car. Means her trail is cold for now. This is as far as we get until she uses a credit card or she moves, and the system can ping her face, putting her on the grid for us."

"What about the car, even if you don't have plates?"

"Best I can do is run a log of all the matching makes and models, etc., that fit the description in the surrounding areas." I grumble but tell him to do it anyway. "You want my advice, man?"

"I don't particularly care." He bunches his big lips and tilts his head like he's thinking. A god-awful tropical print headband holding his shaggy hair back. "Yeah, I'm gonna give it to you anyway. You're not exactly great with people."

"Oh, fuck off, Zach."

"Yeahhhh, there's the charm. Look B, the only thing I will say is that I think maybe this is something your girl needs to work through on her own and come back on her own terms ya know? You playing the white knight is sexy as fuck, going to rescue her and all. But, maybe... I don't know, maybe this time, just give her a little space so she can come to you." He throws his hands up at my glaring, silent response. "That's it. And I promise... I will keep digging for images of her, work on the car log, and keep running scans for pings of her using credit. But hey... at least we got this far. I doubt she stayed in Fractions, but what we were able to get should make you feel better. *And* she was with another chick leaving the airport, so it wasn't like she left 'cause you suck at laying the pipe, and she got a new man to dick her down."

"Jesus fucking christ. You're lucky you're cute." The eyelashes sitting south of the atrocious headband batting at me is the last thing I see before burying my head in my hands. "Fuck..." I sigh, the waves of nausea that come and go by the second, a sucker-punch to the stomach again.

Lily is gone.

She *left* me.

# 81

# LILITH

I couldn't sleep. Most of the night, I lay in bed caught between tears and numbness, unable to escape the thoughts scraping their nails into my skull. Sometime after three-thirty, I must have drifted off, only to wake again at six. Dragging myself to the bathroom, I made the minimal effort to just look presentable enough to watch the sunrise from the beach.

This early, no one is out; the area feels entirely deserted. The only sounds are the crashing waves against cold sand. The world is a canvas of black and grey, shadows devouring anything in its path, with the ocean looming ahead, vast and untamed. It feels an awful lot like a vengeful goddess claiming what's hers, a siren's call for me to join.

I settle on the sand, resting my arms on my knees, staring at the water without focus. The waves somehow serve as a reminder, a whispered, undeniable truth that there is a much larger story at play. We are nothing more than grains of sand in the ocean of the universe.

The damp, heavy cold bites through the too-thin coat I wore, seeping into my skin. But I welcome the sensation —the chill wrapping around me, turning my skin numb. I want to be entirely numb.

Growing up, my parents never so much as held hands. They slept in separate bedrooms. And, in fact, never truly spent much time together. Something that I've realized over the years is that I've never had an example of what a healthy relationship should be. Something so common, so very ordinary, was a foreign concept to me. My parents' relationship certainly wasn't healthy. It's a stretch to even call it a relationship. The homes I was forced to live in as a teenager assuredly never had relationships that held anything outside of abuse and violence. My brothers have never had serious relationships I could learn to mimic. So, I was left with ghostly images and memories of being shunned, hit, told how worthless I was, and what a burden I was to everyone around me. Outside of movies, I had no idea what a normal relationship should be. And if it's replicated in film, is it really normal? My own dating history reads like a catalog of the city's finest dumpsters. A reflection of the stories I knew, a comforting, cataclysmic cycle.

But, when I'm with Blaine, it's like everything is okay. When he holds my hand, it feels like he's holding my entire body in a womb of safeness, my spirit relaxing at simply being near his. He is comfort. He is safe. Nothing matters when he's by my side. I could die and finally know what a healthy, loving relationship is firsthand. And whatever fairytale white knight anyone thinks I need is bullshit.

What I found was a dark knight. The anti-hero willing to burn everything and everyone in the way of our happiness and my safety. And damn, if that doesn't sound far more appealing than a hero who will never quite put me first.

I don't know what I'm doing.

Watching the sunrise, it's as if life herself has come to greet me. The world wakes, and everything is slowly blanketed in the golden light of her grace, even the waves calming at her touch. As runners make their way to the beach, I sit watching the waves, thinking, and letting my mind run wild.

# 82

# BLAINE

A matter of minutes.
In a matter of minutes, my life felt as if it were over. That's all it took.

I have no idea if Lily is safe. I have no idea who she is with or where she is staying exactly. She ran from me, from her brothers. Because she felt it was her fault. My rage at Ronan and Artemis is consuming me, reaching a near level of insanity, friendship be damned. It's been three fucking goddamned days since she left, and I'm barely functioning, just waiting. Waiting for either Lily to call and change her mind or for Zach to find a better lead so I can go get her. Fuck his useless advice.

They say to find peace in being alone and happiness in yourself. Easy for them to say when they have someone there behind them to hold them up when it all becomes too much, too great to bear alone. Because they're not alone, not truly. Not like me.

The support behind me stand as ghosts, an idea of something that should be real enough to touch but is nothing but invisible static and anarchic torturous whispers.

"Love ain't real, kid. Hate to be the one to break it to you. Everyone on the damn planet thinks being in love is the end all be all, right? Let me tell you something. Love isn't what everyone thinks it is. It will never look the way you think it will and will always disappoint you. What is real? Living your fucking life. And by your own rules. Look at me and your father. At least we're living. You know how many people, those soccer moms and those dads that go spend fifty hours a week at a fucking job in a cubicle they hate enough to wanna kill themselves? They spend their lives wishing they played the board different.

"They regret everything, don't think I'm lying kid. The screaming baby keepin' 'em up at night, the fucking boss breathing down his neck every day, the wife that gets fucked once a month in missionary. They hate it all. So, no kid. Love sure ain't real. Like I said, it will never look the way you want it to. Live how you wanna. Our motto? Sex, drugs, and rock n' roll baby. Never let ya down, I can promise you that. Fuck who you want, when you want. Experience life through the lenses only drugs can give you, and live it the fuck up, no regrets. And listen when I tell ya, so-called love and sex ain't got nothing to do with one another. Keep 'em separate, and you'll always be better off, got it?"

"But my parents loved each other. They were in love."

Rye looks at me, standing behind the green felt pool table. The low-hanging stained glass light reflects off of his eyes as he just stands there looking at me, looking into me. Like he doesn't know how to respond. After pausing and staring at me for too long, the corner of his lips slowly creeps upwards, and he just places the chalk square over *the tip of his pool stick. "You're right, kid. You're right." I spent days thinking about his response. Maybe they never were in love.*

It's abundantly clear to me now that the story Rye fed me was a lie. It was a pathetic, twisted tale he told himself to justify his sins, mistakes, and unmitigated loneliness, a lie to make him feel better about his own poor decisions in life. I believed it for too long.

Love is real.

And her name is Lilith.

My salvation.

# 83

# LILITH

**Three Weeks Later**

Turns out I'm not a very good waitress.

I offered to help out at the café this morning when I was reading in the corner and noticed how slammed they suddenly got. It would seem it takes a required skillset that involves not being a depressing clutz. Customers don't like tears in their coffee or their muffins on the floor. Okay, maybe that's an exaggeration. But, not by much. I've been pushed out of their shop and now I'm not sure what to do with myself. But on a positive note, one very sweet old lady handed me a fifty-cent tip. So that means I now have $14.77 left to my name and have to start relying on my credit cards. I knew that was going to happen, though; I was planning for it.

Zipping up my coat and putting my hood on, I step down from the café porch and make my way through the intersection and over to the beach. Every day I've been here has been an episode of

Groundhog Day, an exact repeat. I eat, go to the café, check in with Steven to make sure he doesn't need help in the greenhouse, walk around town, go to the beach to read, stop by the café again, eat dinner, die of sadness missing Blaine, and eventually pass out due to exhaustion.

It's colder today, the ocean carrying in a brisk breeze and I would bet all of my fourteen seventy-seven that it's about to start pouring. But that means that there is not a single person on the beach. Good. I like to cry in peace and solitude, and every moment my mind is free, I seem to cry. Whether it's about Blaine or the unforgiving memories that have haunted my mind as long as I can remember. Either way, I'm drowning.

I plop down in the cool sand right along the line where the wet sand meets the dry sand, the waves crashing dangerously close to my feet. I dig my fingers through the loose sand, looking for shells or rocks to throw into the water. I feel like I'm being pulled apart by invisible forces, and I'm not sure how many pieces I even have left before I'm left invisible myself. What's worse? Every day the thought to fuck everyone and go win Blaine back overwhelms me. When I said he had become my everything, I meant it. I love him; I've never been more sure of that.

For the first time in my life, I understood what 'home' really meant. What it *felt* like. I've never had a place that felt like home to me, even in my studio, living alone. It was just —lonely. But I know now... my home is in his arms. My home is when he's next to me, when he says my name, when he pulls me closer to him in the middle of the night, when he... loves me. I wonder if everyone has settled with my absence and how they're doing. I think Blaine would be the only person I could worry might struggle. But that's assuming his feelings for me were as strong as mine towards him. He had gone his entire life before me, not truly dating or being close to anyone. Will he move on to someone new? Someone who isn't his best friends' sister? God, will he sleep with someone else trying to forget me? Out of anger? The thought makes me want to vomit and scream, throwing fistfuls of sand into the ocean. He could, though, and I'd have to be okay with it. I did this; I left him. I hurt him. He has every reason to hate me now, every reason to move on like my brothers wanted.

I didn't realize I was crying until a gust of wind chilled my wet cheeks. I've experienced heartbreak more times than most other humans will ever experience. And yet, this... this is far beyond so many moments of pain, etching deep into my bones and into my soul. A curse engraved into every cell and inch of soft tissue comprising my existence as something real and tangible.

*"Baby... if it was our wedding night... I would make love to you so tenderly and so thoroughly we could feel our souls merging. Not just in this life. But in every lifetime."*

Blaine's words from our last night together echo through my head and a dark, shadowed part of me is pushing and pushing for me to be selfish. To be so selfish and worry about mine and Blaine's happiness and tell every person around us that doesn't approve to get on board or fuck off.

I had programmed all the numbers I wrote down into my block of a phone on my second day here. I pull the phone out of my pocket and scroll through the contacts, finding comfort in just knowing they're there in front of me. All it would take is just a press of a button and his voice would be there taking me home. My thumb hovers over the button, shaking. Just the thought of his voice on the other end breaks me, and I drop the phone, letting my sobs shake me, my face hot from the effort and pressure. "I can't do it, baby... I can't, I can't... I need you. I need you so bad. I love you so much. It hurts... I'm so sorry." I cry until my face is coated and freezing, and getting air is a chore. I don't know who I'm talking to: God, spirit, the ocean, the wind, myself? When I stop, I look out into the ocean and realize how alone I am without him. How broken I really am, always have been. "I have to go home. I can't be without you." The words come out barely audible over the waves and gusts of wind blowing my braid and pulling loose stands of hair out. "I can't do this." *Why* am I doing this? Punishing myself by taking away the first thing that's made me feel happy and whole since my parents died? "I have to go home." The thought is so sudden, it's blinding and overwhelming —and home and comfort. It's everything.

There is a nice restaurant in the northern part of town that I have wanted to go to since I walked past it one day. It has two levels, and it's entirely made of wood and glass, offering stunning views of the water.

I went home after my breakdown on the beach and showered and changed into the 'nice' outfit I had brought, which was jeans and a black sweater. I'm planning on going home. I feel foolish for even leaving in the first place now, honestly, after my realization. Like a light finally came on. I have been sabotaging not only my happiness but Blaine's happiness, too, which is not fair to him. Before I leave, though, I wanted a dinner here, alone.

The restaurant is dimly lit, with candles on each table and wall-to-wall views of the sun setting over the ocean, and seems to be mostly couples dining with the exception of a couple of small families. I take a drink of my red wine, noting how sparkly my bracelet and ring are reflecting the low lighting around me. It's beautiful and such a simple thing. I don't know why, but I feel the need to take a mental screenshot. Not only of my shimmering jewelry and glass of deep red wine against the stark white tablecloth, but the entire moment. The ocean, the entirety of my time here lumped together in a fleeting moment, the slow music playing through the speakers, and honestly, the sadness my heart has held for the last three weeks here. I close my eyes and my conversation with Blaine at Larissa's birthday comes to mind immediately. How he made me feel before I really knew him, and the fire in his eyes as he listened to me. Really listened; really saw me.

*"Feeling it, all of it..."*

I think of the warnings my brothers gave us, and now, it just unleashes a buried fury. I am a grown woman and can make my own decisions. They were preventing *my* happiness, *our* happiness. Even after —no— *especially* after hearing that he apparently gotten too rough with Robert in vengeance for me. I love him. Good, evil. Black, white. There's no such thing.

There's only grey. And even if there wasn't, it wouldn't matter. I want him and every shadow that follows.

# 84

# BLAINE

"I got her." My heart stops as I take in the words.

"—You found Lily? Where? Where is she?" I put him on speakerphone and urgently go to grab the bag I've had packed for weeks, knowing this moment would come. It had to come.

"Greenwood Village, almost an hour north of Fractions airport, on the coast." I'm already scrambling to search for a flight out immediately. "She finally used her card at the same time she passed a security cam on the north end of town tonight around ten, alone leaving a restaurant." Why the fuck is she alone at ten o'clock, is no one looking after her?

"Bag's packed, looking for a flight out now… thanks, Zachariah."

"—I'm sorry, did Blaine Vogeleir just say THANK YO—"

"Goodbye, dickhead." I hang up, keying in today's date… "Come on… come on." Yes, oh god, yes. You're kidding me. There's a non-stop flight that leaves in a little less than two hours for that rinky-dink fucking town. It's cutting it, but I can make it. I pick up my phone and call the valet downstairs. "I need a driver to take me to DIA, I'll be down in under five."

"Yes, sir. Very well." I hang up at his confirmation and have to stop myself from feeling anxious. This is it. The moment I've been fucking living for, for the last three weeks. I throw Lily's phone, a phone charger, and the book she had picked out for me to read into the bag before grabbing a coat and heading for the front door.

It's nearly three thirty in the morning, after the time change, as I drive from Fractions to Greenwood Village. I reserved a car online and was able to access it through an online check-in and verification process granting me a code to the key box outside of the office. The road is completely barren outside of the light from my own headlights, the car silent. I'm exhausted. Not from this evening or traveling, although it didn't help. But no, I haven't slept more than four or five hours a night since she's been vacant from her side of our bed. I haven't been eating other than the easy meals Jenny prepared for me that were easy to stomach without wanting to vomit. I've barely been showering or brushing my teeth, not nearly as productive at the office, and I'm not blind. I can see my reflection; I look like shit. I just want her back and in my arms.

It's hitting me now, though, that I can't anticipate what her reaction will be when I find her. Will she be happy to see me? Or am I hurting her more by coming here against her will? I just... fuck. Am I doing the right thing here? I can't even fucking *think* straight anymore without her. I didn't tell anyone other than Zach I was coming here to find her or that we had located her whereabouts. When she's back home in my arms, in our bed, where she's supposed to be, she can tell whoever she wants.

Pulling into the town, it's deathly quiet, and everything is completely dark. I'd bet everything here closes by ten. There are streetlamps lining the main road where the businesses line the town, coated in a layer of fog. I drive through the entire thing in a matter of minutes. But I pass the restaurant that Lil was spotted on camera walking out of. I can't help but imagine her being here and how she felt being alone. Hell, how she's felt, most likely being alone here most of the time. As much as my heart has broken, it tears me apart to think of her being sad here with no one by her side, without *me* by her side... all the same people she ran away from. I pull over on the side of the road and wonder if I should try to find a vacancy or find a parking lot and sleep for a few hours before the sun comes up and then I can start trying to spot her. If she's using her card now, Zach will keep me updated on any further locations I need to follow. If I know her, she probably wanted to use her cash first and ran low. I'll get to her; I have no doubt. It's what happens then that's now worrying me. I pull up a map on my phone and search for lodging, but only a couple of options show up. In this town, they've surely got a room for a few hours. "Pines Lodge... sounds promising enough." I just realized maybe Lily is going to want to stay longer, just us. The thought hadn't crossed my mind until now; I just assumed we'd go back home. But, if we're going to stay, I don't want her sleeping in a shitty motel. I take a look at the second option on the map... "Golden Inn," I mumble; this one appears to be far less than what she deserves. Pines it is. I follow the map and luckily, it's only a handful of blocks or so away.

The old woman at the desk checked me in, shocked to see a visitor at this hour, to be sure. Turns out they had several vacancies, to no one's surprise. Walking into my room, it has a red-wood chic meets murder in the cabin vibe. I pull off my boots and coat collapsing in under five minutes, thoughts of seeing Lily and her smile dancing through my mind.

# 85

# BLAINE

The sound of a vacuum banging into a wall jerks me awake. Looking around, I immediately remember where I am, searching for my phone. Nine twenty-two in the morning. I think I slept through the night. Five hours of uninterrupted sleep feels like a miracle at this point. It's like my brain is already relaxing, knowing she's near me, somewhere. I jump up and head to the bathroom to make myself presentable enough. In the shower, every thought I have is excitement and anxiety about seeing Lily. For the first time since she's left, I'm actually hard as a rock, not succumbed with sadness, missing her. I feel hopeful. I stroke myself a few times under the hot stream of water but stop myself from going any further. The most important thing to me right now is getting out the door and seeing where she is. This town has a population of less than three thousand people. I know her well enough to find her. I'm liking my odds.

Finishing up, I towel off my hair and throw on my black jeans, T-shirt, and boots I brought with me. Everything else goes back in the bag. I make my way out into the light rain already coming down to the rental BMW in front of my door. I text Zach to see where we stand this morning.

> Updates?

Zachariah's Headband
> Nothing yet. I'm on it though boss.

Hoping for something but expecting nothing. I just plan on driving through town and seeing if there are other stores or stops that Lily would visit and starting there. She's most likely going to be spending her time in town or on the beach itself. She might be enjoying the small-town charm. But not enough to want to spend her time locked in a shanty in the woods. I turn left, heading out to the main road, and drive slow enough to look into each place through the raindrops on my windshield. There are a couple of shops and a bookstore I plan on stopping by. But knowing her, without a reason to wake up for work, she probably just recently woke up and wanted a coffee. So, I need to find—*there*. I almost laugh to myself as I spot it.

A block up, a small white and blue-green café sits on the corner with a cutesy sign out front. It screams Hallmark movie and I know the romantic in her would love this place. It is rather charming. I pull off to the side of the road, into an opening in front of the line of shops across the street. Just as I grab my phone about to open the handle… I freeze. No… it can't be this easy. Are my eyes fucking with me? My heart is beating out of my damn chest. I watch the woman with her hood raised for a couple of seconds, and she pauses, turning towards the ocean as if she's deciding which way she wants to go. She turns her head just enough that I can finally see her face behind her hood, and if my heart hadn't stopped before, it just skipped about three beats seeing her face. I push the handle, climbing out in an anxiety-riddled haze. She's going down to the beach. I... don't know what to do.

My mouth is suddenly so dry. I can't fuck this up.

The rain is coming down lightly, but enough to be wet. I'm surprised she's going to the beach on a rainy day like this instead of going to the café or bookstore. My legs are moving before I realize I'm following her silently, trying to change my breathing rhythm back to normal. We're the only two out near the water, the waves crashing in front of her. She just stops.... and stands there watching the water. Her hood is up, so she can't see me.

She has no idea... I'm right here, right behind her.

# 86

## BLAINE

"Lilith..." My voice comes out far too rough and unstable. But her silhouette stills completely, knowing my voice. She turns, pulling off her hood, her eyes connecting up to mine. Her mouth moves like she's saying my name, but nothing comes out that I can hear. I take a cautious step forward; I feel like she could bolt at any second. But it's like it hits her a few seconds too late that it's me in front of her, and her entire face crumples. She nearly collapses into the sand, almost immediately sobbing. "Baby, no, please don't cry. Please." One hand covers her face, the other in a fist in the sand beside her. I kneel down and try to pull her to me; I have to touch her. It only makes her cry harder.

"B—Blai—Blaine... I'm s—sorry. I'm sor—sorry." Her words are interrupted by tiny gasps for breath and cries, trying to pull herself lower into the ground as if she instinctually wants to hide.

"Shhh... I'm here. Shhh. Come here, please I'm begging you, Lily, please come here." I hear how disgustingly desperate I sound, but I don't care. I lift her chin up to look at me, and the moment her wet, sad eyes meet mine, I know I'm crying too, pulling her into me so tightly I wouldn't be shocked if she couldn't breathe. I'm on my knees, rocking her against my body in my lap. I don't have enough hands to touch her with. I keep my face pressed to hers, cradling the back of her head, the other arm wrapped tightly around her waist. "Lily..." Her name tumbles from my lips on repeat like a long-lost vow, a prayer finally being answered. My salvation wrapped in skin and bone.

Several minutes pass as we just hold each other, crying and not saying anything. The rain is coming down harder, but I don't think she cares, and I know I sure as hell don't. It's the only sound: the rain hitting our clothes and the mass of water in front of me, acting as the near cinematic backdrop, framing and proving love's existence.

She's here. I have her and she's in my arms, safe. I love her so much I don't want to ever let her go. I want this moment forever. The feel of her warmth under my hands, her scent in my nose. Once her sniffling and crying come to a stop, she starts shivering and I don't know if it's because she's cold or if she's overwhelmed. It's probably both. I loosen my hand behind her head, brushing her hair back and off of her shoulder, running my nose along her cheek. She returns the movement until our lips are hovering so close, we're sharing breath. I nearly shake with restraint, but I move to tentatively press my lips to hers. She kisses me back without hesitation, relief flooding through me instantaneously. I'm pulling her in tight to my chest, pressing more kisses to her wet lips before we're both breathing heavily, and I can feel her heart beating just as fast as mine. I pull back and force her eyes to mine, stunned at how beautiful she is. "...Blaine. I'm so sorry. I shouldn't have ever left... can —can..."

"Can what Lily? Say whatever you need to. Anything. Say anything. Need to hear that voice of yours."

"Can you ever forgive me?" Her lips tremble, and her wide eyes spill tears from the corners softly as she stares at me, waiting. She thinks I'm upset at her, angry at her. I cup the side of her face as she leans into my touch, closing her eyes for a moment before looking back up to meet my gaze. Her eyes are so golden even in the rain—the only spot of color I see.

"Baby..." I pull back to look at her and take her in. I have to tell her how I feel about her. I can't let her get away again. "I don't know what THIS is anymore without you." I pound my fist into my chest, over my heart. Silent tears escape me as every emotion I've had buried for a lifetime comes to the surface, releasing like a tsunami. "I feel it fucking crumbling every second you're away. Every pathetic fucking piece I'm left trying to put together like a puzzle of agony, hope, images of your smile, nightmares of your pain, and my own fucking desperation. I'm going insane without you. I'm breaking. Every day, I feel a new piece crumble, and I don't trust myself with what I'll do when the last piece falls. —If I lost you, I'd burn the world to the fucking ground and not think twice. When you hurt, I hurt. When you bleed, I bleed. When you die... I'm coming with you to our next life together because the thought of one more fucking miserable goddamn second without you is too much to even think about."

She looks up at me with shock, mouth open, her eyes flooding with tears, mirroring my own.

"Blaine... you are my entire heart. You are my *home*. You... when I lay next to you, in your arms, and I feel your heart against my own... so close, shadows and seas of stars and sun, separated and held only by skin. I know that you are my forever. And I don't think this is our first lifetime together, either. What I feel for you is so much deeper. It's a hundred lifetimes of us. A movie on repeat in every cell of who I am. My heart knows your heart. You are my home... I... I love you." Her voice drops to a whisper, her hands on my chest. "I love you, Blaine. I'm so insanely in love with every part of you that it terrifies me to think that one day, I won't have this anymore. That I don't deserve you, and it'll be ripped away. That I ripped it away. I want all of you forever. End game, right?"

My chest freezes, and my hearing slows for a second, my brain trying to replay what she just said to me... she loves me... "Lily, I love you. I love you so goddamn much it hurts.... please come home with me. Please. We'll figure it all out, okay."

Tears running down her pinkened cheeks, she nods up at me, cupping my face. "Please, I want to go home. I was..." She lets out a soft huff of a laugh. "...I was planning on leaving, actually. I realized my mistake yesterday. Like, really realized it. But I wanted to see you in person before saying anything. I didn't know how you'd react. Or, if you'd even respond or answer." The downpour has us both drenched, her hair starting to flatten around her face, wet with tears and rain. I pull her in for the most intimate, loving, and profound kiss we've shared. Her body presses into mine, and as her hips adjust against me, I can feel my length pressing against her. I move my hand to her hip and press her hard to my body, her legs on either side of me until our breath and movements become frantic, and it's clear she needs me as badly as I need her. I'll take her back to the lodge, and —god, I'd enter her right here on this beach if she'd let me, meddling eyes be damned. Let them watch; see, she's mine.

"Let's go. My rental car's around the corner." I stand up, still holding her, not giving a fuck what anyone thinks.

"No."

# 87

# BLAINE

"No...?" My steps falter in the wet sand, concern masking my face.

"I have a better idea..." She points down the street. "My friends own that café and the shed behind it." I close my eyes, pressing my forehead to hers, and laugh at the fact I was able to pinpoint exactly where she'd be, and the fact that this is her friend's shop is utterly hilarious. "There's a place in the back I think would be perfect. I need you so badly, I can't wait." I groan, trailing my head against the junction of her neck and shoulder before gently setting her down to stand.

She stands to stare up at me, grabbing my hand with so much emotion in her angelic golden eyes, my own heart is on the verge of exploding. "Thank you... for coming here. For coming for me."

"Lily, I will always come for you. You will never be alone again. In fact, you'll be lucky if you're ever out of my sight again without a fucking GPS tracker." She lets out a full laugh and it's like the rain is gone, nothing but sunshine beaming ahead of me. A golden, radiant, beautiful glow from the woman in front of me. Mine. "Lead the way, sunshine."

She pulls me across the street to a tiny shack behind the café, uphill slightly. The front is converted into a typical greenhouse, and the second half is wooden, mostly used for storage, it would seem. There are bails of hay stacked and overflowing into a puddle on the floor. "Why is there a layer of hay on the floor? This is really where you wanna do this, baby?" I look around, more than a little bewildered.

"Oh! There's a tiny little goat that makes his way around town, and Kell says he finds his way here now and then, so they wanna keep him warm. He was here once, and he was the cutest, Blaine! Someone put a hankerch—" I smile at how adorable she is and interrupt her story with a kiss, pulling her to me. I don't want to hear about a goat though, not right now.

"God, I've missed you so fucking much." It's painful how much I've missed her smiles and her adorable laugh. She bites her lip and removes my coat, running her hands over my chest and pushing my shirt up for me to take off.

"I missed you, too." She leans into me with her face up, waiting as I grab her waist and press my lips to hers, my tongue sliding across her soft mouth, urging her to let me in, to take her, claim her again. Our tongues dance in a comforting, familiar rhythm as our caresses intensify and I remove her coat and lay her down in the hay over both of our jackets. I realized in the moment that this is what she wants. What she needs. To make love with her white knight rescuer in a shack, on a bed of hay on the coastal line, as rain falls and echoes against the tin roof above us. I'm honored to be the one to be here and make this a reality.

Pushing up her shirt, I press kisses to her neck, slowly making my way down her chest and navel. I lean back and toss her boots to the side, ripping off her wet jeans. She's beautiful. My goddess lays before me, and all I can do is admire this image of her. I hold her knees to the side, gazing down at the dip in her waist and the curve of her hips. The red thong she has on and lacey little top under her shirt, now bunched above her breasts. "Perfection..."

"What are you doing?" She bites her lip, moving to rest on her elbows behind her, her hair following in a trail, gathering pieces of hay.

"Taking a mental screenshot." I wink at her, and the smile she gives me lights her entire face, setting my heart on fire. I lower myself between her legs, kissing and tonguing my way to the apex of her thighs as her tiny moans of anticipation leave her. I press a hot kiss against the fabric of her panties, and she stops me before I can move them to the side.

"Blaine... wait —I, I mean, I haven't... I haven't exactly been shaving." I start to laugh until I realize she's being genuine and is truly feeling insecure. About... body hair. Doesn't she realize how much I crave her? I lower my mouth, sliding the fabric to the side, and trace the flat of my tongue across her pussy. Not breaking eye contact, her mouth parts as she watches. I pull the small knife out of my pocket and cut the tiny fabric in my way causing her to gasp as the material falls, giving me full access without having to leave my face too far from her. I run my tongue over her sex, kissing and licking, groaning at the taste of her finally on me again after far too long. Never again.

"God, baby. I want you to come all over my fucking face. I need it." I focus my attention on her clit, press into her wet core, and back up, sucking on her as she tries to muffle her moans and sighs. Soft thighs close against my face. Heaven. This is fucking heaven. I push my fingers in her entrance, bending them and waving them in and out of her, doubling my efforts on her clit until she's tense and shaking, on the edge, not breathing. "Come on my mouth. Come." My eyes roll back in my head, moaning against her as I feel the ripple of her body around my fingers. Jesus fuck. This; I need this.

I keep going until she collapses and brings her hands to her face shakily. I run a couple of final drags across her folds before raising myself and resting between her thighs. "Keep the hair. It's sexy as hell." She chuckles, high on endorphins hiding behind her hands. Moving them with a smile, I lean in to kiss her. Reaching down, I hastily undo my pants, exposing myself, to which she hums in pleasure. I press my weight on my arm, cupping her face, and press my cock against her sensitive nub, our mouths deeply melting into one another. "I need to feel you, Lily. I need to feel you from the inside. Please." She reaches down and lines me up to her entrance, and as I make my way inside her heat, I have to stop and bite down on my knuckle. "Fuck, Lily. God, I forgot how exquisite your pussy feels around me." She squirms, hips lifting, and I press myself fully inside of her soaking, soft core. Both of us moan at the sensation, our mouths next to each other, sharing breath as I push in and out. I'm on the verge of releasing any second, focusing on not coming, to draw this moment out. I lean back onto my haunches, tilting her hips forward and just slightly to the left, causing her to immediately throw her head back as I hit that deep spot inside her. She moves her hand to quickly rub against her clit, and I smack it away before I even realize I did it.

"Mine. My pussy." I take over her efforts as she quickly starts to work towards a second climax. "Say it, Lilith. I need to hear you say you belong to me."

"I'm y-yours. Every part of me belongs to you," she manages to get out. Fuck, I needed those words, that validation.

My eyes roll back in my head at the erotic image of her like this. I don't think I'll ever wipe my memory of this moment as she tenses before she cries out, her cunt wavering around me. I let myself succumb to the sensation and release myself inside her, still pumping into her and rubbing her clit. I keep coming for several more seconds, finally slowing my movements before nearly collapsing on top of her heavily rising chest.

"Oh my god, Blaine... that was incredible." She reaches her hands on either side of my head nestled against her throat, pulling me closer and kissing me, our wet bodies still moving against each other. I press each of her knees further to the side, pushing as deep into her as I can, grinding slightly with my cock still buried in her warmth.

"I never want to leave your body. I want my cock buried in you forever." I pull away from her and kneel back, raising her hips with me so they're elevated from her laying body, and grind my still-hard cock inside her just slightly enough, pushing for every second of pleasure. The movement's near overwhelming around my sensitive head. We stay just like this for several seconds before I finally pull out of her slowly, watching as my own wet and glistening sex reappears from her body. I keep her hips tilted upward, though, until she goes to wiggle away. I stop her, holding her in place.

"Blaine, " she says, resting on her elbows, laughing. The sound music to my ears. "—what are you doing down there?"

I look up at her with a wicked smile before running my fingers through her folds and into her pussy. Some of my release is leaking out of her, and I gather it with my fingers, pushing it back inside her. She's so fucking wet and pleasure swollen. "Keeping my come where it belongs."

Her little mouth stays parted as she watches me re-fill her before bending down to kiss her with a distraction as I hold my seed inside her with my palm cupping her. "I love you, Blaine. Do you know how good it feels to finally say those words?"

"Baby, you have no idea how long I've struggled with not telling you how crazy I am about you. I love you, Lilith, so much." My head is still so close to her, our noses are touching.

"I'm calling in the favor you owe me..."

"Mmm, and what is that?" I ask, running a gentle hand over her arm. That's right, the long-owed favor.

"Take me home." I don't even fight the grin that takes over my face or the relief that washes upward through my body.

# RUIN & REDEMPTION

"To our home, sweetheart."

# 88

# BLAINE

**Three Months Later:**

Lilith and I are taking a break from everything and have been traveling across Europe for the last week and a half. We've been in Iceland for a couple of days now, which has always been a dream of hers. She's always longed to experience the Northern Lights in person. We've rented a glass igloo in a resort allowing a full view of the lights at our leisure in the warmth of our bed, privately. The space itself is larger than I would have originally anticipated. However, I did my research before settling on this location for my specific needs. I want to make this a trip that she will never forget. One of a thousand mental screenshots. A romance book come to life, just for her. I would go to the ends of the earth to keep her smiling and laughing, to keep her happy. Everything ebbs and flows, much temporary in life. Emotion is certainly one of those things. But Lily and I... she is my forever.

My beauty is at the spa getting her nails done and a pedicure. She thinks I'm working to fix an urgent work crisis. I would never lie to her, but this is the one time I will make the exception. I walk into our igloo, and it's exactly as I envisioned it. I've been in communication with a local event planner for some time now to set up the space for our night together. There are murmurs from the locals that the lights are anticipated to be incredibly bright for several hours this evening, unlike the last two nights. If there is a God, she's on my side. The room has a bed in the center, against the one wall that is private; the bathroom and closet also located here. The normal side table and chairs have been replaced, and around the glass space are hundreds of white candles, several of them staggering over scattered tables of varying heights. Rose petals sit in piles around them, and a trail of them in the snow leads from our door to the private gated entrance hidden by a row of trees about twenty feet away or so. It's perfect. I just hope she likes it. This could be the best or worst night of my life.

# 89

# LILITH

After Blaine came to me in California, we stayed in Greenwood Village for another night before getting home. As terrible as it makes me, I waited almost a full day before contacting my brothers or our friends to let them know I was home and safe. I just knew it would be exhausting and I was still enjoying my time with my love. That day, we went down to my apartment and loaded up several boxes worth of things to unpack at Blaine's. Just the essentials. He asked me to move in with him on our way back to Colorado and it wasn't difficult to readily agree. I love the man. Even though he's still a pain in the ass and grumpy occasionally. That's a part of his charm, though, to me. I love him as he is, every version, every part.

So now, we've been officially living together for a few months in his penthouse. He arranged for movers to do the work for us, and they even packed everything and brought it up for me. I hate to admit it, but most of those boxes are still sitting untouched in one of his empty rooms. We'll get to it at some point.

Katie and Larissa were thrilled for me when I told them, and we had a celebratory dinner and bottle of champagne, compliments of Blaine, of course. He loves treating me to things like that. Katie still gives herself all the credit as if our love story were crafted at her hands. And my brothers, since I left, realized they were wrong. Or at least that's what they're telling me. They seem to be getting back to an okay place with Blaine. At the very least, they're all being cordial when in the same room while I am around. Honestly at this point, thank God for Larissa and Elliott being around to be the much-needed padding in the group during this odd adjustment period. My brothers weren't happy when I told them we moved in together. But they're being supportive of any decisions I make for myself, and that includes Blaine, after our very long talk.

About three days after coming back to Denver, I casually mentioned needing to find a new job ASAP, and the man practically told me to stop working and do whatever I wanted. I'm not kidding. If I remember correctly, his exact words were, *"Baby, you could sit around eating cupcakes all day, not lifting a finger, and I would be happy because you're happy. You wanna be a rich housewife who goes to Pilates and watches TV dramas? Go for it. Wanna come to the office and hang out with me? God, please do. Hell, baby, you could spend all day dancing around to music and bugging Jenny, and I'd be thrilled. Well, I'd be a little jealous I wasn't there. But I want you to do anything, everything. Don't worry about the money you think you need. We're rich, love. Do what makes your heart full. Don't waste your life at a job you hate that steals your soul."* And after everything the guys went through, my inheritance is scheduled to be deposited in another six weeks. I told him I would like to take a break from working and focus on myself and painting. And I have been, with his absolute full and loving support. He seems to enjoy coming home every day with me there. I do tend to wait around like an eager puppy though.

The perk of knowing rich people is that they know other rich people who love to buy art. I've already had three commissioned pieces for way too much money, and I'm starting to think maybe this could be a permanent change if I really want it to be. I understand just how rare and how privileged that is for me to have their help landing buyers. I'm very aware. But I'm mindful of this and thank the universe every day for the support in making my dreams come true, returning the favor and karma to others where I can.

In a way, even though I regretted running away for so long, it's led to such drastic, unbelievably beautiful transitions in my life. I have to be thankful for that. Sometimes I just wait for the other shoe to drop, or to wake up and have Blaine no longer want me. Every previous situation in my life has taught me that is what to expect. But I try to tell myself this time is different. And it does feel different, as long as I stay grounded.

After my pedicure and sitting in their massage chair, I feel so relaxed I could fall asleep right now while getting my nails done. Blaine told me he was working on some business stuff. But I think he just needed some time to himself alone and sent me off to the spa in the resort we're at. I can't help but smile and roll my eyes. He thinks I don't know when he's trying to lie. This is the first time I've felt it from him and I'm positive I'm right on this. He just didn't want to hurt my feelings. The man couldn't lie to me. He's such a dork. I love him so much it almost hurts.

I sit in silence as the nail technician finishes up my final nail, wiping the alcohol to finalize the gel polish over my acrylics. I went with a classic almond and vibrant apple red. Smiling at her in thanks, I admire them and give her Blaine's black card to pay, before changing back into my boots.

# 90

# LILITH

Walking through the resort path it's a bit dark since the sun has now set. The only major source of light is that of the moon reflecting across the vast blanket of snow covering everything for miles in a winter wonderland. The lamps lining the open, covered walkway provide enough light to see where I am going clearly, and the light from the various igloos facing opposite directions emits through the night. It feels like I'm walking through a giant snow globe, only there's no snow falling. Which is great for us because we've been waiting for the northern lights to make their appearance. Maybe tonight will be the night.

I approach the small, wooden gate that leads to our private igloo; a large number eleven distinguishing ours from any others. It clicks shut softly behind me, and I make my way to the door, stopping shy of about ten feet. I bend down and realize there are rose petals that've fallen over the path. I look around for rose bushes, but I don't see any. Wouldn't they be out of season? I pick up a handful of them to show Blaine, opening the door smiling. I don't get two feet inside before I am frozen and drop them all.

My mouth parts in awe as I take in the sight of our room before my hand covers it instinctually. I don't know where to look first. Every foot of our room has been transformed into a scene out of a romantic movie. There are glowing candles surrounding the entire room, rose petals around the candles grouped together staged at various heights, and a heart formed on the bed. Beautiful, lovely music plays lightly in the background only amplifying the energy coating every inch of my buzzing skin. The silver wetness lining my eyes falls down my face, and I realize I'm crying. Blaine comes out from a shadow that was concealing him in the corner, a single rose in his hand. He... looks so beautiful in an all-black suit. Suddenly the room isn't the most stunning thing in my view. I look at him, lowering my hand to my heart, crying, and then look back up, taking in the room. "Blaine.... you did this? For me?" He walks towards me with a mix of concern, wonder, and love. Nodding, he comes to me, grabbing my hand and placing it on his chest over his heart.

"Look up, baby." It takes me a moment to register what he means, and I slowly trail my eyes up to the sky beyond our glass walls. I gasp at the sight, my free hand going back to my mouth in awe. The northern lights are so bright, dancing across the sky in perfect rhythm to a song we can't hear; puppets of the universe. My tears won't stop at how beautiful this moment is. I can't help but wipe them away, taking in the view. Lines of vibrant green move like water against a sky full of so many glowing white stars. It's beautiful. Sniffling, I look over at Blaine, who's watching me, and smile at him. I don't trust my voice, but I have to say something.

"This is so beautiful, Blaine. I can't believe you did this for me. It's perfect. You're perfect. Thank you so much, baby." I wipe my cheeks and lean in for a gentle kiss before he drops my hand, and my attention turns back to the natural masterpiece above us. In a moment, in a matter of seconds, we're reminded of how vast the universe is and how incredibly small we really are. "Blaine—" I smile, turning to look at him, my eyes falling down to where he now kneels before me. I stare at him with wide eyes.

He takes my hand in his, looking up at me with such fiercely loving pale eyes, that I could swear the sky's dancing lights were reflecting through them, the candlelight dancing across his skin in-time.

"Lily..." My hand is brought to his lips as he kisses my fingers before lowering it. "I've known for so long that I love you. Before you came into my life, I wasn't really living. I was existing and honestly, I don't think I had ever felt love, even as a child, as I feel it with you.

"I didn't think I was even capable of love. For years, I never allowed myself to even think about it.

"My heart wasn't fully beating without yours next to it. My entire life, I knew there was something missing. Something that I was waiting for. I thought it was the death of my parents, the void nothing could fill. But I now know... I was always waiting for you. I don't believe in much, Lily; if anything. But I believe in you. I believe in us. I know I don't always know the right thing to say or how to be the best man for you. But please give me a chance, Lily. I would go to the ends of the earth for you. I know… I know that every fucked-up thing that's ever happened to me, to both of us, every terrible and stupid decision I've ever made, every night we spent apart with a broken, lonely heart… it all led me here, to you. Led me home. And it was all worth it. I would endure every fucking minute of this life a thousand times if I knew it was going to lead me to you. Even if all I had was this very moment to cling to memory, it would be worth it. But Lily… Lily, I can't live without you…. I'll wait if I have to. Weeks, months, years if it takes you that long. I love you so much it hurts. I can't imagine my life without you by my side ever again. I… Lily —will you… marry me?"

I drop to my knees with him, grabbing his face as tears fall freely over my cheeks, nodding. "Yes. Yes, Blaine, yes." His shaking hands pull me into a kiss —the corners of his eyes glimmering, betraying his composed facade— as our hands grasp at each other. I pull away to toss my head back in a surprised, unguarded, happy laugh. "YES!" He pulls out a small, red velvet ring box from his pocket, opening it for me, and I gasp at the sheer size.

"I know it's a bit much." He laughs, wiping the shimmering tear tracks from the side of his face. "It just still didn't seem like enough to show you how much you mean to me." He reaches for my hand, placing the ring at the end of my finger, shaking with a final look at me as if I would turn away. I bite my lip, smiling and wiping away the stupid tears that won't stop. He slips it on fully, both of us smiling like love-sick idiots.

"Baby, I love you so much. I can't imagine my life without you either. I never want to again. You're the best thing that has ever happened to me. I've always felt, throughout the years, that I was waiting for something too. Like maybe I was chasing something. I could never know what the feeling was. And when you say you were waiting for me... Blaine, I feel the exact same way. I think maybe we've always been connected. We just both finally pulled the string hard enough to lead us here, to be together. And whoever you got your information from is wrong. You always say the right thing, and you do know exactly how to be the best man for me. You've been doing it for months. I love you so much. I can't wait to be with you forever."

We both stand and look in each other's eyes. His lips press to mine in a tender, loving, and deep kiss before picking me up like a bride and tossing me onto the bed, the petals flying up around me. I fling my head back, laughing, and watch my sexy future husband climb onto the bed with me, taking off his jacket. "So, baby," he says, unbuttoning his shirt and waggling his eyebrows. "I know we've made love like it was our wedding night. But what about if we make love like it's our engagement night?" Our smiles and laughter become too big for the room and we collapse next to each other, gazing into the other's eyes, appreciating the view. The only one that matters.

And we do just what he said... we make love like it's our engagement night, *which turns out to be a lot like our "wedding night"*. Blaine now stares into my eyes, on top of me, and nestled between my thighs, moving in and out of my body slowly. The candles have mostly burned down, the Northern Lights faded slightly, and our bodies and sheets are drenched in sweat from our constant efforts throughout the night. As he begins to shutter against me in his climax, I whisper directly into his ear. *"I love you so much."*

Our sweat-sheened bodies touch every inch we can be connected, our hearts close as shadows of candlelight move over our skin, and lights dance above us in a night full of stars.

I know, in his arms, I've finally found *home*.

Forever.

# LILITH

The gentle rocking and faint sounds of the ocean bring me back to consciousness. I open my eyes and I'm greeted with crisp white sheets and a view directly off the yacht, straight to the rocky coastal cliffs we're anchored close enough by. The morning glow as the sun rises paints everything in a beautiful pink halo. I can't help but smile and lean in closer to the strong, tanned arm wrapped around me. Blaine deeply and roughly hums a bit as he wakes and pulls me tight to his chest, kissing me on the neck and ear.

"Good morning, birthday girl." He purrs the words into my ear, and his voice goes straight to my stomach.

"Good morning, baby." I lean my neck giving him better access, humming in happiness. He reaches his hand under the sheet and tosses it over both of our heads, causing me to laugh. He holds the sheet in place by bending and raising his knee and using an arm to curl it around his head.

"I've heard there are rumors that birthday girls turning thirty-three get three wishes for good luck. You wouldn't know anything about this, would you, sweetheart?" His left hand wraps around my hip and reaches lower and lower. The pads of his fingers trace between my thighs, slowly touching me. "Hmm?" I can't decide if I want to close my eyes to the sensation or keep them open to watch as he touches me.

"—Y-yes. Three wishes. I think I've heard of that."

"And what are your wishes for this birthday?" He whispers into my ear.

"Well..." I bite my lip. "I think my first wish involves your very talented tongue on a certain area of my body that I know for a fact you seem to enjoy." He nips at my ear, chuckling in a low groan.

"Your wish is my command. And such a hardship for a male. Think of your remaining two." And before I can feel the lack of his hands from my body as he moves further down on the bed, his lips and tongue are taking over his efforts. Think... think, okay, I can do that. I gasp and try to clamp my thighs shut as he sucks on that little bundle of nerves, his fingers rubbing the outside legs of my clit hidden beneath the surface.

*"Blaine!"* I gasp. He only moans as I toss my head back into the pillow. One hand finds his hair, and I wrap my fingers through it while the other grips the side of the bed for something to hold on to. I cry out, intuitively grinding against his face as he goes down on me, my body hot and tense as my climax takes hold of my body. I scream out my fiancé's name, shuddering against his continuous efforts, not stopping. He's still going as I start to come down from the high until I grab his hair, pulling him away. His strong body crawls over mine on the bed and throws the sheet off of us finally, as I'm now covered in a sheen of sweat. He looks down at me with an arrogant, masculine smile, and I want to roll my eyes. He must see it on my face because he laughs and bends down, kissing me, and settles his hips between my legs, lining himself up to my now-soaking entrance, teasing me with his movements, not going any further.

"You know, pretty one, I'm positive you screamed my name so loudly that the fish now know who I am. They probably think I'm their king."

"Shut up! Stop teasing. It's my birthday, and you have to be nice to me." I laugh, rolling my eyes.

"I'm not sure if the ones at the bottom of the ocean quite heard you, though... we better try again. Louder this time, love." He pushes into me, and we both moan at the sensation.

"I love how big you are. The feeling of you filling me." He groans at my words and thrusts into me, kissing my neck and ear while his other hand rests on my lower stomach, his thumb rubbing my clit. It doesn't take long before he's pounding into me, our sighs and whimpers filling the room. He pauses to reach over the side of the bed and turns on the toy we used last night with a wicked smile. Moving slightly, he holds it against my sensitive sex, the sensation causing me to cry out and tense. Within seconds, I'm coming undone, yelling his name, and coming so hard my entire body shutters, hands grasping for anything to hold me in place. Blaine loses it and growls like a beast, releasing himself inside my body as we both finish together before he collapses on top of me, panting.

"Holy shit," he laughs. "Happy birthday."

We quickly rinse off and make our way up the small spiral stairs to the main deck, where the rest of our party awaits us for brunch. Ronan and Artemis are scowling, looking pissy as fuck as we walk over to the round table. Immediately I realize they must've heard us. My cheeks stain pink, and I want to hide at the thought. We're all adults, though, and Blaine and I are engaged. What did they think we do, play checkers every night? More like hide-the-sausage. I smirk at my own stupid, stupid joke. Katie and Larissa immediately make their way out of the booth, smiling, Katie winking at me. Yeah, they heard.

"Happy birthday!" Larissa yells.

"Happy birthday indeed..." Katie says playfully as they come to bring me in for a group hug. Looking around, I smile at my brothers and Elliott, who control their expressions enough to smile and greet me with hugs and 'happy birthdays' of their own. We all make our way back into the half-circle booth as our chief stewardess brings out champagne and orange juice to get us started, taking special requests.

Blaine took me —well, took all of us for a three-night stay on a super yacht in the Mediterranean for my birthday celebration. When the man said we weren't hurting for cash, he certainly wasn't lying. We're currently sitting in front of the Amalfi Coast in Italy. It's the most beautiful place I've ever seen, next to the Northern Lights in Iceland, for obvious reasons. The coastal hills are painted in stunning, colorful homes along the rough cliffs lining the ocean. The water is so blue, and the tops of the small hills are dressed in flourishing green. It looks like a literal postcard. I lean into Blaine at my side and take in the view and the moment as our friends' voices fade into the distance. I glance up to look at him, and when our eyes meet, it's like the world stops, and it's just us. He smiles gently, brushing the wind-blown hair behind my shoulder, and tucks it behind my ear. "I love you." He leans down and presses a gentle kiss to my lips before responding.

"I love you too, sunshine." Someone coughs a few times before I realize they're trying to get our attention. I turn around to the group and Katie smiles brightly.

The stew brings out our plates and several other dishes of fruit and muffins as Katie asks, "What are the plans for tonight? Are we staying on the boat, or do you want to hit the town and find a bar to celebrate?"

"I think I want it to just be us tonight. Tomorrow night, we can venture out, all of us." Everyone eating nods and hums in approval.

Ronan jumps in, holding his fork out after taking a huge bite of his eggs. "You know what I'm thinking.... we gotta play with the jets, and that monster slide today! The weather's perfect!" He shovels in another two huge bites and chugs his mimosa before climbing out of the seat and hopping around the back of the booth. "You know where to find me!" He races off, and just like that, it's silent.

"Umm. Alright then... anyway?" Katie says. And I can't help but start laughing, everyone else following.

We all finish eating and change into our suits, joining Ronan. The crew inflates a giant slide that goes all the way from the main deck to the ocean before bringing out two jet skis and a monstrous blow-up raft. We spend all afternoon playing. Even Blaine and Ronan are racing on the jet skis which makes my heart full to see them getting along again after all this time. Blaine flips his in a U-turn, Ronan just around the corner behind him before Ronan passes him and skids to a halt sideways, throwing water over him. I watch as Blaine curses, but they both laugh and smile freely and set up for another round, Elliott yelling for his turn. Children. They're all children. I laugh and jump down the inflated slide into the warm blue water, the girls at the bottom waiting. This has to be the best day we've all had together in a long, *long* time. Splashing in and making my way back up to the surface, the boys come back, racing over and slow when they get closer, jumping in the water with us. "Must be hard to swim with that giant rock on your finger, huh, sis?" Ronan throws his head back laughing as he moves to float on his back, Artemis coming down the slide next. I hold it up on display, the sun shining off of it.

"Careful not to look directly at it. It's been known to cause temporary blindness." I laugh at Blaine's response, and he just winks at me, hair wet, tendrils curling and hanging over his forehead. I bite my lip, looking at how unbelievably sexy he is, and he raises his eyebrow, swimming over to me with a knowing, predatory look on his face as I turn to out-swim him in spectacular failure.

# BLAINE

Lily wanted to have a private celebration for her birthday, with just her brothers and closest friends on the yacht for the evening. The chief stew did a fantastic job with décor and an easy all-white and gold theme on the main deck. There are streamers, masks, feather boas, and a ton of other secondary décor items contributing to the ambiance. She's having such a great night; it feels good to see her so happy. Not to mention, Ronan and I at least seem to have silently gotten on steadier ground. I'm not sure exactly where Artemis and I stand, still. He'll come around when he realizes he's wrong and I'm right.

The music is playing, a few disco lights and rainbow lasers shining over our makeshift dancefloor. Artemis and Katie are dancing, Elliott and Larissa, and I pull Lil against my chest as Ronan leaves her to start doing a terrible job twerking, getting a few laughs. I pull my phone out of my pocket and take a picture of him. He looks ridiculous. He has streamers cut and tied around his head like a sweatband hanging off to one side, tall white tube socks, a feather boa, and golden sunglasses that light up with the word "PARTY" scanning across.

Lil grabs my hand, and I twirl her a couple of times before she swings into my chest and I hold her close as she sways her hips against me. I nip at her ear playfully, getting a full, happy laugh from her. Smacking her butt lightly in a silent encouragement for her to have fun with her friends, I go sit on the open, rounded booth. After a few minutes, though, she spots me and comes sauntering over with a smile that makes me hum with excitement. She sits down on my lap, her knees on either side of me, and puts her hands on my chest. I grab one and press kisses to her palm, moving up her wrist and forearm as she watches, not breaking eye contact. "Are you having a good time, my love?"

"Yes..." She nods wistfully. "It's been so long since we've had a night like this together, all of us. It feels so good. Thank you for this." She tilts her head in that shy, graceful way, portraying her emotion in her eyes.

"It's my pleasure. But yeah. You're right, though... it feels good. I've missed this too, more than I realized."

"I know, baby. It's going to be okay. I saw you and Ronan today in the water, and I'd say that's a pretty good step in the right direction." She smiles encouragingly.

"How did I get so lucky?" I pull her in closer by her hips, pressing my lips to hers. Lightly at first, gentle. But as always, the world fades to gray, and all that's left are her lips and her body on mine. The kiss growing deeper and more sensual by the second, I pull her in tight to my thickening cock pressing against her through the thin fabric of my pants. Her white dress is pushed up around her hips as she straddles me, and she runs her hand through my hair, gripping my neck as she starts to just barely rock her hips and softly moan. "Let's go. Now." She nods, and I stand before she can get off of me, wrapping her legs around my waist and carrying her away.

"Be back in five. Just need to grab my phone!" She's a terrible liar, and I smirk. I carry her down the spiral steps to our floor and the remaining ten feet to our door, pressing her up against it, continuing our now near-frantic kiss. Practically tumbling into our room, I toss her onto the bed as she giggles and turns onto her stomach, lifting her dress and wiggling her ass teasingly. I growl, kneeling behind her and pull her hips up so she's on her knees and rip down her panties. Lowering my pants, I pull out my cock and push into her, eyes closed. Grabbing her by the hips, I watch myself enter her over and over, moaning before picking up my pace and slamming into her madly and desperately. There's nothing romantic about this moment; I just need her, and now. Need to feel her around me and remind her she's mine.

"Baby, I'm going to come. I'm sor—" Before I can apologize, she encourages me and pushes back into me, fucking me back with verbal affirmations and whimpers, hands planted against the base of the headboard. I come with a shudder and lean forward against her before pulling out and rolling her over. I drop to my knees, pulling her down so her legs rest on my shoulders, and focus my attention on the bundle of nerves at the apex of her thighs, pushing my fingers into her body that's leaking my release. Fucking filthy.

I press my lips around her clit and vibrate my lips and tongue, causing her to tense, and I can feel her about to go over the edge. I curve my fingers slightly and hit the textured patch of skin inside of her, causing her to ripple around my fingers, crying out. I've always considered myself to be a good fuck; good in bed. Never had any complaints about that. But, just another beautiful thing about growing with my girl is that I know her body like the back of my hand now, able to make her come quickly and many times over.

We lay in bed, entangled in each other's arms momentarily before Lily pulls away, saying we should probably get back to the party. I inwardly grumble, trying to bury the urge to tie her to the bed. I have other plans for the two of us for the evening. That would transition quite well, having her tied up already. But I can refuse her nothing. Changing and cleaning up, we make our way out of the room and head to the right, towards the slender stairs that lead to the main deck above.

"Oh! Katie still has our phone charger. I'm going to go grab it from her room while I'm thinking about it." She kisses my cheek and heads past me in the opposite direction towards Katie and Larissa's room. There were only two rooms with queen-sized beds. The other two rooms hold bunks of sorts built into the wall. They're spacious and luxurious enough. But it was obvious that Lily and I would be taking the suite. The guys, being gentlemen, all agreed Katie and Larissa should get the other room, leaving Art and Rone to share and Elliott to the remaining bunk room to himself.

Hitting the top of the stairs leading onto the deck, I look around, noticing that only Larissa and Elliott remain. It hits me instantaneously that that means the guys and Katie are together. Most likely, having snuck off after Lily and I did, thinking we wouldn't actually return. *Oh god.* Katie's room. *Fuck.* I race down the stairs and into the short hall to find Lily with a stunned, shocked look on her face, leaning against the wall. Yeah, there goes the rest of our sexy weekend. Fucking assholes couldn't keep their dicks in their pants for one goddamn weekend, even for their sister's birthday.

I walk over to her, and all she can do is put her hand to her forehead, the other silently pointing to Katie's door. "Baby, come here. Come here." I grab her hand and lead her into our room, shutting the door.

"No, Blaine... Katie." She huffs. "She's hooking up with my brothers! Plural, not even singular! *BOTH* of my *brothers* Blaine! I heard them! Oh god... I'm— I—" She paces, anger coming off of her in waves as she cups her face, laughing in disbelief. I grimace slightly, not entirely sure what to do, so I let her work through her initial emotions. "Are you fucking kidding me? After everything, *everything* they did to stop us from dating, holding this over your fucking head like you're some bad guy. And here THEY are doing basically the same thing!" She growls in annoyance, looking at me. "Why aren't you more shocked or upset about this?" *Fuck.*

I run my hand down my face, knowing I have to be honest. I thought I was protecting her by not telling her. I didn't think this would still be going on by now, honestly, either. Assumed it'd blow over. Looking into her eyes as she studies me, I see the moment she realizes I already knew. My heart shatters, and I feel my stomach drop, riddled with guilt, mad and disappointed at myself for letting this moment happen. "Lily... I'm so sorry."

"You knew." Not a question; she already knows the answer. "You fucking knew and didn't tell me." I have nothing to say. Everything she's feeling towards me is valid. I fucked up. I slightly nod my head, standing and stepping towards her. Her eyes line with silver, and it's like someone stabbed me in the heart at the hurt I caused. I told myself I'd never lie to her. And yet... by not telling her, I did exactly that. "I can't believe you kept this from me, especially after everything." She shakes her head as a tear slides down her cheek. "So, what? Everyone on this trip has been fucking lying to me. Do Larissa and Elliott know, too? I'm just the stupid one everyone's keeping secrets from, right?"

"No, Lily. No. I'm so sorry. I— I thought I was protecting you," I plead. "I have no idea if Larissa or Elliott know. Baby— please. I'm so sorry." She sinks onto the bed, shaking into her hands, and I don't know if it's from anger, tears, or anxiety. I take my chances sitting next to her and wrap her in my arms to comfort her. I lift her onto my lap and hold her, whispering apologies several times and pressing kisses to her head. I don't know if she'll ever be able to understand how deeply I fucking regret this.

She's silent for several minutes, sorting out her thoughts before she finally pulls away from me slightly. "Look, I'm not going to ruin our weekend. You paid and planned so much for this trip. I trust you with *everything*, Blaine. But this... makes me doubt that." My chest tightens at her words, tears fighting to make their way free. "But... let's just put our fight on hold until we get home. I can't handle all of this at once and my anger towards my brothers and Katie is so huge I can't even think straight. I need you by my side right now. You're my best friend, Blaine." Her face crumples and any effort I had to hold back my tears fails.

"I'm so fucking sorry, baby. I'm so sorry." I thumb the streams cascading down her cheeks, desperate for any inclination towards my touch. She nods and stands, walking to the small closet.

"I just want to go to bed for now. I need to think and calm down and figure out how I want to even handle this." She grabs a set of silk pajamas and disappears into the bathroom. The shower turns on a few seconds later, and I'm left alone, a rock in my stomach, hoping she'll forgive me for betraying her trust. This isn't just her brothers and Katie's fault. This is my fault. I'm the one person she gives her whole heart to, all her trust, and I fucked up. I hurt her just as much as they did.

Lily stirs against me, waking me up. I know we were both up into the late hours of the night. I couldn't sleep until she did. I wrap my arm tighter around her as she nestles into my touch and grab her hand against my chest, kissing her hairline. I don't say anything just yet though. She wraps her arm around my waist and tucks her leg in between mine, sighing heavily. "Hi."

I stroke her back in comfort and affirmation of my love. "Hi, sweetheart... how are you feeling?" I manage to ask.

"I'm still pissed. At all of you. But I already know you and I will get past this. You'd never do something to intentionally hurt me. We're both still learning the dynamics of a healthy relationship. We can talk about it more when we're home." She sighs against my chest.

"I love you so much, Lily."

"I know you do. Every day, I know you do. I love you, too. It just hurts right now." I pour affection into my touches and brush her hair over her shoulder, stroking her bare skin to offer a small source of comfort.

"What do you plan to do today?"

"Honestly... I don't even want to look at any of them. Larissa and Elliott can stay with us, though, if they weren't keeping this from me, too." I'm not sure entirely what she means but I don't press her on it.

"I'm here in whatever way you need me."

After getting dressed, Lily stops me and reaches for me with a kiss, and my chest swells just at that small act.

Reaching the top sundeck where the larger rectangular table is, everyone else is there eating breakfast, and there's tension almost immediately. Something feels off. Lily and I sit down quietly while

Katie and Elliott offer their *good mornings,* followed by the others. Artemis watches Lily, everyone eyeing each other as she focuses on grabbing food onto her plate, not responding. I lean back in my chair, scowling at nothing in particular, ready for anything. I brush her hair behind her back, silently reassuring her that I'm there to support whatever she chooses to handle this in her own way.

Katie speaks first, looking between Lily and me across from her and both brothers. "So, any plans for the day?"

"Yep." Lily continues eating her pancakes without another word, and Larissa and Elliott shift in their seats, looking at each other uncomfortably, surely waiting for whatever tension is building to snap.

She finishes her meal and pours a cup of orange juice before finally leaning back and staring harshly at her friend and brothers across from her. "So, Katie. I went to your room last night to get our phone charger back." She purrs menacingly. Fuck, it goes straight to my dick. I've never heard her speak with that voice. "When were you planning on telling me you were *fucking* my brothers?" Everyone at the table stills, barely so much as a breath taken.

"I..." Katie looks from Lily to both brothers helplessly, fear written on her face. I refocus my anger towards Artemis and Ronan, waiting. I can't help the slight wicked smirk that crosses my face, though, at their poorly hidden panic. As guilty and bad as I feel for my sunshine. I also feel a twisted happiness that their little triangle is being exploded.

"Lily..." They both stumble, adjusting in their seats.

"NO. What the Hell! *BOTH* of my brothers, Katie? *My brothers!* And you two! My best fucking friend? Are you fucking kidding me? You could have had any man you wanted, and you just had to fuck my brothers, though, right?" Her fingers tighten on the sides of her chair as Artemis steps in.

"Lily... look, I'm sorry." She huffs out a breath of air in disbelief at Art's words. "But... we care about her. A lot..."

"I'm sorry... we? What the hell does that even mean?" She snaps.

"It means we both *are*... and have been, dating her for.... some time now," Ronan says, what looks like sadness in his eyes at his sister.

Katie says in a whisper, "It's true, Lily... I am so sorry this happened. This is not how we wanted to tell you... especially not on your birthday trip —but I care about them too. So much."

"Look, Lil, it's not a big deal. Nothing's really changed." Ronan says.

"Nothing... nothing's changed? Oh, fuck off! Are you kidding me, after everything you've put Blaine through? Put *both* of us through for being together! You completely disowned him as your best friend! But this..." She laughs, waving her hands. *"This* is perfectly okay, though, right? Because it's you? —Sorry to burst your bubble Kat, but something tells me this little fuckfest won't be ending in an engagement, let alone two engagements." She spits at Katie in disgust.

"That's *enough*, Lily! Enough!" Artemis says firmly, putting his hand up before slamming it on the table, causing Larissa to jump and the utensils to shake.

I think the fuck not. I lean forward, arm around Lily's chair, rage radiating off of me at that bullshit.

"I wouldn't speak to my fiancé like that again if I were you. Brother or not," I say calmly, words coated in ice.

"Fuck you, Artemis! Fuck all of you. Don't talk to me. Get off the fucking boat. I don't want to even look at you. I can't believe your hypocrisy."

"Lily, wait, please. *Please!*" Katie begs.

"DON'T talk to me." I get up after Lily stands, pushing her chair back, my glare piercing at the brothers with a small smirk on the edges of my lips.

Lily stops and looks at Elliott and Larissa, sitting next to each other. "Did you two know?"

They both shake their heads. "We, uhh, found out like you did late last night, so Larissa bunked with me in my room since hers was... occupied." He grimaces, just saying it, nervously pushing his hand through his dark hair.

"You can both stay then." Lily walks towards the stairs without another word.

"Lily, come on! This is a bit much. We're just supposed to leave? We don't have anywhere to go. You can't be serious?" Ronan yells after her.

"Do you know how problematic it will be to find a hotel here for the night?" Artemis scoffs.

I turn one last time, before following Lily. "That's not her problem, and I really don't give a fuck. I'll arrange for the deckhands to give you a ride to shore in thirty minutes. I'd start packing."

I follow Lily down the stairs silently until we get back to our room and I click the door shut and lock it behind us. "Sunshine?" She just looks up at me, silver lining her eyes and nothing but heaviness in her heart. I want nothing, nothing more than to just make her smile again. I pick her up and pull her onto my lap, rocking us both and brushing her hair behind her back, pressing kisses to her forehead. "I'm here, sunshine. I'm here. I'm not going anywhere. I've got you." I will always have her.

# About the Author

K.J. Fury is a romance author making her debut with the rapidly rising "dark-ish" romance 'Ruin & Redemption'; the first in an expected series.

She has devoted her time to writing as a way to heal and discretely share the unique and heartbreaking experiences that have haunted her through life.

In each of her novels there is guaranteed to be at least one truth of herself and personal experience behind one or more of the main characters. Telling her story behind a mask and entourage of fictional characters is a way for her to work further towards healing her inner child, inner teenager, and the divine feminine everywhere.

Behind every novel, every word, Fury puts healing energy into its essence.

To her fans, she offers: "Thank you for supporting me in finally finding happiness through passion."

Made in the USA
Monee, IL
20 November 2024